MONTEREY SHORTS 2
MORE ON THE LINE

Stories by Fiction Writers of the Monterey Peninsula

Monterey Shorts 2 is published by:
FWOMP Publishing
www.fwomp.com
For more information write to:
Fiction Writers of the Monterey Peninsula
22597 Black Mountain Rd.
Salinas, CA 93908

Copyright by Fiction Writers of the Monterey Peninsula

Library of Congress Cataloguing-in-Publication
Monterey Shorts 2 / FWOMP — 1st Edition

ISBN 0-9760096-0-9

Acknowledgements

Before we get into the heavy-duty thank yous, we need to give ourselves—the writers—a little pat on the back for making this second anthology a reality. We'd also like to thank our friends and families for being so supportive over the past several years, during which time we breathed life into *Monterey Shorts* and *Monterey Shorts 2*.

Although Fiction Writers of the Monterey Peninsula (FWOMP) has been active for over five years now, and its members are undeniably the driving force behind its publishing successes, there are other behind-the-scenes individuals who deserve much thanks for their past and continued support of this unique critiquing and writing group.

Many thanks to Dan Koffman of the Art With A Smile gallery who designed the magnificent cover art for *Monterey Shorts* and *Monterey Shorts 2*. His vibrant color combinations, historical themes, and clothesline humor are the perfect match for what lay behind the books' covers.

To master editor and layout perfectionist Chris Kemp for his dedication and the hours upon hours of work it's taken to get this book ready for press, we heave tons of that "special kinda lovin'" your way (whether you like it or not).

Thanks to the independent bookstores and retailers in the Monterey Peninsula area (Thunderbird, Bookworks, Bay Books, BookHaven, and the Phoenix in Big Sur) for supporting us so prominently.

To Dawn Cope for her keen proofreading eyes.

To our printer, McNaughton and Gunn in Saline, Michigan.

To Shadee, Sergeant-at-Arms for the FWOMP meetings, we send out this little doggy bone.

If we've forgotten a "thank you," please excuse us. We've been busy sharpening our minds and our prose, and it's quite possible we've overlooked someone. If so, the groveling and begging for forgiveness will commence shortly.

MONTEREY SHORTS 2
MORE ON THE LINE

Foreword

by Joyce Krieg

Monterey stopped being a stink, a grating noise, a quality of light, and all that other bohemian Steinbeck jazz a long time ago, yet it remains a magnet for dreamers, tale-spinners and creators of magic.

One such group of latter day literary souls is Fiction Writers of the Monterey Peninsula, otherwise known as FWOMP—according to legend, the sound an unsolicited manuscript makes when it sails over the transom and lands with a plop on the floor of some Big Time New York editor's office. Savvy to the ways of the publishing world, the hardy band of FWOMPers knew that finding a traditional market for short fiction with a strong regional flavor would earn them nothing but a big "fergedaboutit." So in the spirit of "let's put on a show," they went out and did it anyway and in 2002 published a collection of short stories set on the Central Coast with the tongue-planted-firmly-in-cheek title of *Monterey Shorts*. This "little book that could" became a local publishing phenomenon, going into a second printing and earning rave reviews.

Now they're back with—you guessed it—*Monterey Shorts 2*, still more tales of romance, intrigue, suspense, history, and the supernatural, all staged in and around the Monterey Peninsula.

If you're visiting our beautiful section of California for a weekend, a week, or longer, *Monterey Shorts 2* is the perfect beach book. What better souvenir to bring back to Silicon Valley, Fresno, L.A., or points beyond than a book of stories reflective of your too-soon-it's-over vacation. C'mon, you don't really need another T-shirt or refrigerator magnet, do you? You say you're a Monterey local? Well, what are you waiting for? Obviously, you must see what's inside *Monterey Shorts 2*. Hint: this book of regional short stories is the perfect touch of gracious hospitality to add to the nightstand of a guestroom, guest cottage or guest wing. And if you're one of those locals who really does have an entire guest wing—hey, you know who you are—well, you really do need a copy for every nightstand in every room, don't you think?

Inside *Monterey Shorts 2* you'll meet the first woman lighthouse keeper at Pt. Pinos and sample secret spices in Carmel Valley. A down-and-out writer in Pacific Grove finds his literary creation coming to life, and a legendary gold mine in Big Sur dooms a pair of Jack London-esque lovers. You'll find yourself shouting, "Viva Johann Sebastian," along with Zoltan at the Carmel Bach Festival. A local vampire has an intriguing encounter at the Carmel bloodbank. You'll time travel back to the Swingin' Sixties to visit the Monterey International Pop Music Festival, while a time machine disgorges a most interesting passenger for two Salinas girls. A Carmel Valley woman learns that the sea does, indeed, give up her dead . . . just to name a few of the delights awaiting the reader.

So what is it about this chunk of rock jutting out into the Pacific that continues to draw woo-woo creative types who just can't stop writing and sharing their stories, no matter what the odds? Sure, you've got the greats of yesterday, Stevenson and Steinbeck, Robinson Jeffers and Henry Miller. But just look at who's calling the Monterey region their home today: Pulitzer Prize-winner Jane Smiley, the demon dog of crime fiction James Ellroy, hot new mystery writer Helen Knode, beloved children's author Beverly Cleary, *Beaches* author Iris Rainer Dart, chronicler of the Asian-American experience Belle Yang, plus dozens more screenwriters, playwrights, lyricists, journalists, literary and genre fiction authors – and the ten souls who make up Fiction Writers of the Monterey Peninsula.

Perhaps beyond all the touristy tackiness and the new money glitz and glam, a bit of that bohemian spirit lives on in the crisp ocean breezes, the soft rattle of the pines, the low moan of the foghorns, and that "quality of light" at sunrise and sunset.

So toss another log on the fire, pour yourself a glass of local wine (or AA-approved equivalent), cozy yourself into the easy chair, whether in a rustic guest cottage or Pebble Beach mansion, and dive into *Monterey Shorts 2*. Enjoy!

Joyce Krieg lives in Pacific Grove, California and is the award-winning author of the 2002 St. Martin's Press "Best First Traditional Mystery" contest for her Shauna J. Bogart Talk Radio Novel, Murder Off Mike. Slip Cue, *a continuation of the series, was recently released and a third novel is coming soon.*

Lore, Legend, and Life on the Monterey Peninsula
by Chris Kemp

*T*ime to begin their second journey. And the Fiction Writers of the Monterey Peninsula knew it. It wasn't a conscious decision, really; but the birthing process never is.

"I'm going to share the lore of this county," ventured some, "and contribute my own in the process."

"I'd like to add a legend or two," stated others, "to a land that is rather legendary."

"I wish to portray daily life," declared the remainder, "where the ordinary is often extraordinary."

So together they came. From the storybook village of Carmel-by-the-Sea. And Pacific Grove's blanketed quiet. From the fog-shrouded forests of Pebble Beach. And the rolling open wideness of Carmel Valley. Past hillside homes sunsplashed in the reflection of the Monterey Bay. On dusty roads leading from Salinas, John Steinbeck's hometown. Their destination: a weathered oak table deep in the recesses of an antiquarian bookseller, hidden behind towering bookcases, the air suffused with the pungency of aged bindings.

There, in a rarefied atmosphere charged with creative compulsion, they composed and talked and argued, and engaged in collective dreaming. Then they revised and pondered and argued some more—perhaps a lot more. The result?

You're holding it in your hands, a labor of love over a year-and-a-half in the making. Forged in the fire of (painfully) honest mutual criticism and—more importantly— steeped in the myth, mystery and magic of the Monterey area, this volume is full of remarkable characters moving across a remarkable landscape, sometimes spilling into each others' stories. It's a book that transports you to Monterey County's storied past and brings you back to its colorful present, often in a matter of pages.

Lore, Legend, and Life on the Monterey Peninsula

And readers of the first *Monterey Shorts*, take note. Some familiar faces await you between these covers.

So, please. Take a seat. The ride's about to begin and there are stops of interest for everyone. The sensibilities of these writers have been shaped by a place that is world-renowned for its surface beauty and tranquility—and given true distinction by what lies beneath.

They just had to share.

— Chris Kemp
Pacific Grove, California
January 2005

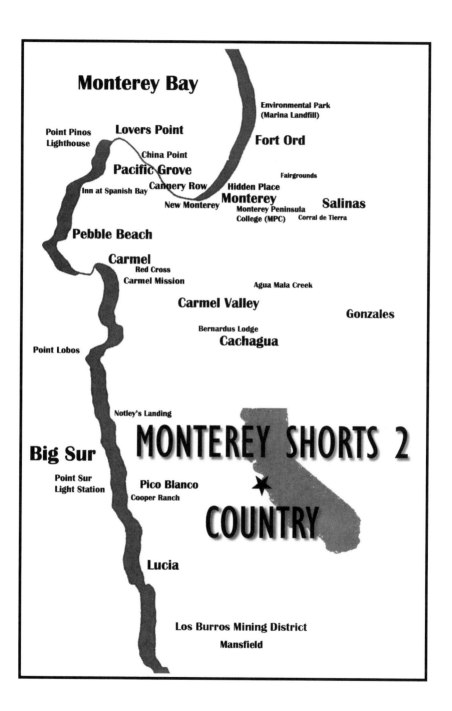

Monterey Bay

Environmental Park
(Marina Landfill)

Point Pinos
Lighthouse

Lovers Point

Fort Ord

China Point

Pacific Grove

Fairgrounds

Inn at Spanish Bay

Cannery Row

Hidden Place

New Monterey

Monterey

Monterey Peninsula
College (MPC)

Salinas

Corral de Tierra

Pebble Beach

Carmel

Red Cross

Carmel Mission

Agua Mala Creek

Carmel Valley

Gonzales

Bernardus Lodge

Cachagua

Point Lobos

Notley's Landing

MONTEREY SHORTS 2

Big Sur

Point Sur
Light Station

Pico Blanco

Cooper Ranch

COUNTRY

Lucia

Los Burros Mining District

Mansfield

by Lele Dahle

Monkeys Mourn Through the Night

Miss Misty Broebard of Maryland's Smith Island passed away on February 20th. On that evening, there could be heard commotion in the home many locals call "The Monkey House", as Miss Broebard's three little monkeys howled piteously for hours. Neighbors knocked repeatedly at her door to rouse her but there was no response, so they sent for Parson Newhouse who entered and found her deceased in her bed. The monkeys were at her bedside crying.

Miss Broebard was born in Denver, Colorado in 1863, and lived much of her life in Monterey, California before settling on Smith Island. Her monkeys were consigned to the care of the First Methodist Church in Tylerton.

This article was taken from *The Chesapeake Bay Monitor*, February 27, 1938.

My Story
by Misty Broebard

Note from Mrs. Pauline Morgan

I assisted Misty Broebard in transcribing this story. The manner of her speech has been left undisturbed, so the reader may experience her natural and earnest voice.

January 18, 1883

The Monkey House Inn

My mother was a prostitute. I never knew my mother, but have a picture of her, standing in front of a brothel posing with four other soiled doves. You might imagine they would be scantily clothed and painted, but they look like normal respectable ladies, except for those forlorn expressions etched upon their faces. A year after the photograph was made, I was a two-month old baby and my mother was dead from her own hand. I was fortunate to be adopted out immediately after her simple burial outside of town; just a crude wood cross marking the grave with words scrawled, "Dearly Departed Grace". My entire inheritance consisted of that picture, and my unruly, carrot orange hair.

Randall Broebard, a miner who'd been working his way through the Colorado, adopted me. He was 30; his new bride but just turned seventeen. She'd been picked out by him in Denver at a bordello where for three years already she had been plying her trade. She was comely, and suitable enough for marriage to a miner. Women were scarce there in the Colorado and in all of the West then, so ladies of ill-repute were often the only choice for a man who wished to wed.

My adopted father had put himself together a whole family inside of a few short days. I did not learn until nearly fifteen years of age that my new mother was a half-breed Choctaw Indian, her mother being full-blood. She had been growing up amongst her mother's kin in Oklahoma until her father, whose family hailed from up north in Chippewa and Sioux land, stole her away to go live with his own. My new mother was only eleven years old at the time and couldn't endure the cruel treatment inflicted there. By thirteen, she had fled, and then only could support herself by prostitution.

How can I describe my mother? She was something you wanted to possess, and I can understand why my father took her to marry even whilst her being tarnished. My mother had smooth, light golden skin, and wide-set-apart brown eyes. She was sweetly childlike; we were more as sisters living together than a mother and daughter. I was obliged by my father to the watching over of her from a young age, as he lived so often away, and knew she wasn't dutiful, as he taught me to be.

My father was getting rich. He had a talent for mining, and in eighteen hundred and seventy-two, when I was nine, we were gone off to California by way of the newly completed railroad. Before we moved permanent there, we stayed at makeshift houses in harsh, dusty mining towns. I don't have many happy recollections of those days, because we were shunned by most townsfolk. Sadly, a soiled dove cannot ever escape her past. For this my mother came to be possessed by melancholy.

We moved to Monterey, to an area east of town called "The Mesa". Father, who'd always had the desire of becoming a cattle rancher, home-

steaded down in the big green valley across the mountains from the coastal town of Monterey, but he made our family home in Monterey proper, where my mother and I were left most of the time by ourselves. My father built us a big adobe house that was surrounded by fragrant pine woods, with ocean views peeking through the trees. We had a caretaker who lived in a cottage on our property and managed caring of the horses and grounds. His wife helped with chores when needed. Charles was a solitary sort, and I almost never saw him.

By the time I had grown to thirteen, my mother was back to prostitution. This didn't surprise me, for the only friendships she'd ever made in town were with parlor house girls. My mother had a powerful habit for opium and spirits, and needed more money and excitement than my father would provide her. I did my best to conceal her activity from him; I believe he never came to knowledge of her misconduct, as he was away so much of the time down at the homestead and preoccupied with his accounts when he came back to Monterey.

Soon before I turned fifteen, my mother left our home forever, leaving me alone with my father, who by that time was coming up to Monterey only once a month for but a few short days. My mother confessed to me she was a half-breed Choctaw, and told many sad, sorrowful tales about her childhood. Then she was gone off to seek her mother's ancestors, to atone for bad deeds lying heavy upon her.

I cannot place blame for the lot bestowed upon me, as it was bearable enough. I stayed alone and when I became so hungry for company, feasted on childhood memories, those rich Choctaw tales passed on to me by my mother. When Father came on his once-a-month visits, we were like two ghostly creatures who barely spoke. It seemed he was mourning the loss of his wife by retreating into silence. I took long walks through the pine woods and down along the ocean shore with its white sand beaches.

After a time, I came to missing my mother so much. I wandered endlessly trying to find her, venturing even to the sorry streets of the brothels, and all the way down to China Point, where Chinese fishermen lived in their small wood huts built upon rocks against the tide, and you could often see the colorful sails of ships offshore come all the way from the Orient. Eventually I did give up searching, as it looked like she was gone for good.

One stormy evening in December, I heard a loud rapping outside. I had returned earlier from a walk and was stoking the fireplace, for a storm had begun to blow something fierce through the woodlands. I was eighteen. Upon opening the door, I saw before me a Chinaman. They were quite a presence in Monterey at the time. He was soaking wet and shivering, and jabbered at me in bad English, which I did not comprehend. I made ready to shut the door in his face when he yelled at me, "No!" Then he ran off, and I stood in the entry staring into darkness, with rain pelting my face. He came back a few moments later dragging along a frail, tiny young woman. He pushed the thing at me, yelling, "You take!" Then he ran away.

When he let go of her, she fell at my feet. As I looked down, she moaned. A more pitiful sight I have never witnessed in my life. I didn't even make out then that she was Chinese, because her eyes looked like two black holes. I should not have done what I did then. I took her inside. She protested, but weakly. I made a bed with blankets in our large pantry, as it had a door which locked from the outside only. I laid her down on the makeshift bed, placed more blankets atop, locked her in and then went off to my sleep. I feared to see her dead by morning.

By dawn's light, I had courage enough to open the pantry. The girl was tangled in the blankets. She looked up and cringed, and I could see her even more weak, so I heated some broth, and then put the cup to her lips. She drank a bit, then lay down again and closed her weary eyes. I raised the cup for her to sip several times over the course of morning. By evening she was managing to eat some porridge, and then I led her to bathe in a tub I'd prepared, as she smelled unpleasant. When I pulled her dirty garments off, what a sight was before me! There were horrible red welts across her back. And ugly jagged scars everyplace on her body, even the tender areas. The sight brought me to tears. After the bathing, I dressed her in a nice gown that had belonged to my mother, put her in the room across from mine, and locked my door.

I never stopped being uneasy at having her company. It was for my loneliness that I wouldn't face that she did not belong in our home. But as the days passed I studied her with curiosity. She was crude, like an animal. When I brought food, she tore it with her fingers, and quickly swallowed huge mouthfuls. She spoke not one mere word. On occasions when Mrs. Pierce, Charles's wife, came in the house to clean, I locked the girl up in the pantry. This went on for nearly a month.

From the time we moved to Monterey, I have loved the ocean. Sometimes, when winter storms blew the wind just right, I could hear the sounds of waves crashing mightily against rough rocks, as if just outside. I awoke one morning hearing the wild sea, and determined I would go to watch. I fed the girl, locked her in the pantry in case Charles or Mrs.

Pierce came along, wrapped my woolen cape around me and headed out. Upon returning in the early afternoon, I was astonished to see my father's rig in front of the house. The horses had been stabled, so I knew he'd probably been home for some time already. My heart began to beating hard, and I could hardly breathe. In my fascination over that pathetic girl, I had forgotten completely about my father's monthly visit.

I took a deep breath, and went inside. Already my mind was working out a plan to sneak the Chinese girl out if he hadn't discovered her. Before the front door closed behind me, I heard screaming. I ran toward the frightful sound, and saw my father in her room. He was sprawled across the bed and she was wildly chopping at him with an axe, the small one that always sat beside the kindling box by the fireplace. I stared, unable to move in my shock. The last thing I remembered was her coming after me wearing an expression of madness. Something struck my head, and I fell to darkness.

I awoke. Three days later, I am told. I looked over to see a nurse sitting by my bed, and couldn't recognize her or my surroundings. I bolted up and then started to wail for Jimmy. The nurse grabbed me and tried to lay me back down. "Miss Broebard, you must calm yourself!" Then she called to somebody, and a gaunt, bearded man came in the room. "Charles, send for the doctor. Hurry! Tell him Miss Broebard has woken up."

"Where's Jimmy!" I remember screaming, although I was weak, so likely not clear understood. "Where are my children? Jimmy!" I was calling for my husband, and wondering where my three children were, my youngest, Jonathan, being but nine months old. The nurse humored me.

"The doctor is coming soon, he will explain everything. You've had a terrible accident, Miss Broebard, and hurt your head." I lay back down and waited for the doctor. But this was only the beginning of a nightmare that would drag me into deep despair. For I was not myself when I awoke. I wasn't Misty. It is hard to explain, and very difficult for me to describe, as I am even now emotional about it. When I woke from a coma on that day, somebody else had taken refuge inside my body. Later I would remember everything that had transpired during this period, just as if I had lived it myself.

When I wakened from the coma, I knew this to be the truth of my life. I lived in Canberra, Australia, and had a husband and three beautiful young children, my eldest were identical twin girls. I was Martha Bain, daughter of Carol and Bertrand Livingston, living and breathing in the year nineteen hundred and sixty-two.

When the doctor came, he ministered medication. Then he took my hand. "Misty, I must tell you something."

I looked to him, puzzled. "I'm not Misty. There must be a mistake . . ."

Everything seemed terribly wrong.

"Misty, your father has passed on. When you've had a chance to recover, we will talk about it. For now, just rest." The medication took its effect and I drifted into unconsciousness.

I woke again some hours later in darkness. The nurse had left my bedroom, but the door was half open and I could see light radiating through the house. Then I had the worst shock. I experienced a sudden awareness of my body. It was not my body. My body—Martha Bain's body—was big-boned and muscular. These foreign fingers felt tiny and delicate. I brought them across my stomach, down to my thighs, and felt barely any flesh. I touched my head. Below the bandaging was coarse, orange hair; my own being fine and blond. I cried out then in terror, so frightened that I attempted to flee. The nurse came and held my arms down. Then she curled up next to me on the bed and held me like a newborn. I will always be grateful for that, it being the only familiar thing I could relate to in this strange world; the comfort and calming one human can have upon another. I fell asleep in her arms.

I came in and out of paralyzing panic those following days. The doctor told me amnesia is not uncommon with head wounds and I must have patience, for my memory would eventually return. I kept insisting I was not who everyone thought I should be. At the time I was so disturbed at being trapped inside this unknown world within someone else's body that I failed to recognize that time had become twisted as well. It would be yet another horror to bear.

The caretakers, Charles and his wife, asked to speak with me in confidence. Charles said some harsh things. He told me if I continued with my mad ranting about being Martha Bain, I would surely be committed to an insane asylum, and lose everything my late father Randall Broebard worked so hard for, that was to be my legacy.

I became afeard for my precious life. I was coming around to see that there was something seriously amiss with my brain, but still I prayed for this to be a kind of dreamy state I would eventually awaken from, and then be back to sunny Canberra with Jimmy and my babies. I beseeched Charles and his gentle wife to help me. They told me particulars about the life of Misty Broebard, and how I should act at being her. Hearing this kind of talk revolted me. Misty Broebard, I learned, was a lonely, frail young woman. I despised her life. I longed for the bright skies of my Australia, the lovely azure ocean; for blue-eyed Jimmy and the happy bustle of family. I worried constantly about how they would be getting along without me, especially little Jonathan, who I was still feeding to my breast.

So my play-acting began. I pretended to have my memory back, and with the help of Charles and his wife, I managed. Lawyers and accountants came by the house. They told me I was now a woman of means, as my father had left me all he possessed. I signed the documents, "Misty Broebard". This task of deciphering would have been difficult for Misty, as she possessed poor reading and writing skills. Yet Martha Bain had no trouble at all understanding what was put before her. Finally the lawyers, accountants, nurse and doctor went away.

After I was alone again, I believed I was Martha for a period of a few weeks. My mind could not conceive of living eighty-one years in the past. Mrs. Pierce patiently assured me over and again it was in fact the year eighteen hundred and eighty-one. It made me so angry I wanted to scream at her, "No, you are wrong, it is nineteen sixty-two!" And I was really Martha Bain, that she and her husband Charles were naught but an apparition dreamt up by my injured brain. But I couldn't explain away how I could be inhabiting a stranger's body, in this foreign land living far in the past, so stayed silent for fear of being declared mad. My days were spent locked in the house, staring out the windows to fog-shrouded pines, worrying for Jimmy and the children.

Then strange things began to happening with my mind. Like a tiny tear in a blouse that might expose the skin to cold, so did little rips within my consciousness begin to allow Misty in. They were mere whispers of memory at first, and then rushes of Misty would fill the space where Martha's possession had been, and force more and more of Martha out. Eventually Misty had her proper place back, and Martha was dissolved to nothingness. Yet afterwards I could still recall the tiniest detail of what Martha had thought, pondered and anguished about in those weeks. How I reveled in her memories; images of her children and Jimmy.

With the transition back to myself complete, I was left with new pain I had never known. It felt worse even than when my mother abandoned me to seek her Choctaw ancestors. I pined so for Martha. The loss of her left me despairing with such sorrow, for I realized my own wretched life held little value compared to the richness of hers.

I began my walks again, down through town and along the sandy seashore, all the way to China Point. I was filled with barren loneliness, and so missed my mother that I renewed searching for her. Everywhere I looked, and became sick by yearning. I couldn't tolerate to eat, and grew thin and taken bad. I wouldn't allow thoughts of my father, except to pretend he was still there at his homestead, alive and happy.

One day I arrived down at those China Point shanties. It was a dreary morning, with fog hugging the ground. You could smell the place long before you arrived to there. It had an intense odor of fish, which was always laying about drying, and smelled also of the strong spices Orientals used in their cooking. I looked past a row of houses and spotted an old Chinese white-bearded man sitting outside with a monkey, which clung to him around his neck and chattered loudly. Once in awhile it would leap down, scurry about his feet, and then leap back upwards. He was laughing, obviously enjoying his little monkey's company. I suddenly wanted to possess it. I reasoned to myself, I am now a woman of means, and could have whatever I wished.

I approached the old man and told him I desired to purchase his monkey. He eyed me scornfully, but I thought he comprehended my request. He must have gazed at my poor clothing. I took no care then with my appearance; my simple calico dress was threadbare, it was in fact a handout from Mrs. Pierce. I reached into my satchel and pulled out coins which I thrust at him. "I want to buy the monkey!" Surely I did not impress him, as I possessed only two dollars. "I'll come back with more! I will give you one hundred dollars!"

"Hunra dalla?" He was shaking his head now.

"I'll be back in three hours with one hundred dollars. Meet me here in three hours." I held three fingers up. As fast as my legs would bear, I ran back home. I went to my father's safe, took out two hundred dollars, and then raced back to China Point, stuffed the whole two hundred dollars into the old man's hands, and snatched that monkey. As I ran off, the monkey struggled and cried, but I held it tight until I was back home.

It didn't take very long for the little monkey girl to figure out she had come upon something good. I went out and bought the finest fruits for her, figs, apricots, and juicy oranges. She became a spoiled, willful thing, but I didn't care; I was giddy with happiness. As I could not have known what name she had, I voiced out many to her. When I said, "Cherie," she got excited, so I think she must have had a one similar. My monkey became Cherie, and she helped to lessen the emptiness of my solitary life.

I must bring back the subject of the Chinese girl who killed my father and nearly myself. For those weeks after his death, Martha was in command of my body and mind, as I already told in that strange tale. It was discovered during the reading of the will several days after my father's death that I was his natural born daughter, and he knew my true mother Grace for a long while before she killed herself. Martha, who witnessed the event of the will-reading, had no emotions attached to the subject, but I, upon piecing together her thoughts and memories, became quite agitated by this discovery.

I pondered the mystery of Randall Broebard being in fact my genuine father. I was left to wondering if he ever had cared about me; maybe he actually resented and hated me for my whole life, as I became such a burden for him after my natural mother was gone. I never understood how my mother could dare to kill herself with a tiny baby lying beside her. There seemed to be no answers that would comfort me, no end to the sorrow I faced daily. Keeping little Cherie happy was my only comfort.

As time passed, I came around to feeling more like normal again. There was some unease about my days, as letters and documents were still being delivered concerning my late father's estate. I couldn't face to look at them, so laid them away with all his other papers. I began to entertain thoughts about the Chinese girl I carelessly let into our home to bludgeon to death my father. In my house, the subject of Father's murder was hidden in silence.

One day I went to Charles and inquired as to who the Chinese girl might've been, and whether she'd been caught and punished for her crime. Charles replied, "The sing-song girl? Yes, she was captured as she ran through town with blood all upon her, still clutching the axe. But she passed on in jail two days after, by cutting her wrists with a shard of sea shell, and bleeding to death."

I was shocked, but my curiosity whetted. "What is a sing-song girl?" I asked. Actually, the name sounded like something nice. Charles said she somehow escaped from slavery in San Francisco. That a sing-song girl is a lowly kind of Chinese whore who is kept tied up in a tiny cage and forced to please any man who comes for her, willing to pass a few pennies to her owner. I told Charles that even I knew slavery was abolished, as everybody did, it was two years after my birth this was done by our President Abraham Lincoln. So how could there still be slaves in San Francisco? Charles did not have an answer to my question, he had only heard of such girls, he said, and had never ventured to the areas of San Francisco where they were kept. After that he would talk no more.

I thought long about that Chinese girl. Why had she killed my father? What horrible torturer had caused the scars over her body? Why had she been delivered to our home? Did my mother or father have knowledge of her? I pondered all of this only a few short months after my father's death. Then another set of troubles arose, which forced my mind off such questions.

A lawman arrived at my door one chilly spring morning. I showed him to my parlor after locking Cherie away, as she was causing such a ruckus at seeing him. He brought bad news. The foreman at my father's homestead had been killed, and the gang that stabbed him to death also stole many cows and horses. Father's house had been ransacked, and now sat in a state of disrepair. The vaqueros who worked there were gone away into the mountains, and the sheriff implored me to go down immediately and make things straight, for all belonged to me now.

I was but just turned nineteen and had no experience that could have prepared me to handle this new misfortune. I knew nothing even of where my father's homestead was located. The sheriff offered to send his trusted friend Mr. Morgan to accompany me, which I was grateful for.

We departed past midday, and spent the first night at a hotel in Salinas. My expectation was that Father had himself a nice big house like the one he built for my mother and me. We pulled up to a simple, two-storied wood house with a small porch, up a pretty canyon with big oaks, sycamores, and a good view of the long valley.

Mr. Morgan gestured for me to go inside. I suddenly froze with fear and did not want to leave the coach. But he stepped down and put his hand out for me to hold, so I put my feet onto land that now belonged to nobody but me. How strange a feeling this was. As I walked slowly up to the house, I could see the front door partly hanging off its hinges. I paused in the doorway and stared inside. The floorboards were hacked to pieces, so you could see raw dirt underneath. Crimson stains spattered the whitewashed walls. Then I saw there something not of this world. A powerful fright clutched me, and I fainted.

Mr. Morgan took me back to my home. I was ill for the whole trip back. Before he left me, I did have sense enough to ask him to tell the sheriff I would be sending my man Charles down to the homestead to put things right.

I shiver at thinking this. When I went into my father's house on that day, I saw the ghost-figure of the Chinese sing-song girl. It is for the image of her that I fainted. She stared to me in the most imploring way, and upon her expression was mournful sadness. She outstretched her arms, and blood flowed freely from the cut wrists, staining her white dress and spattering the mangled floor.

Recollections of my life before we arrived to Monterey were of moving through ramshackle mining settlements in Colorado, Arizona and Nevada, living in poor shacks surrounded by squalor, dust and mud, with my father working night and day so hard. When Father was absent, my mother would go in the evenings to hurdy-gurdy houses and saloons. I spent those times alone trying to entertain myself, wanting not to wonder of safe, cared-for children with mothers who weren't gone off drinking whisky to all hours of the night.

Lazy Creek, Arizona was the last rough place we lived before going to California. My father came upon a very rich gold strike in the hills there. I made friends with a Lazy Creek girl a few years older than me named

Molly. Her father, like mine, was working hard at mining and saving up so they could go further west to put down roots. Molly told that her mother, father, a brother and sister had come all the way from Ireland, across the big ocean, but their poor mum had perished on the ship.

This Molly girl spoke with a brogue so heavy I could hardly understand her. Oh, but what kind of wild tales she told! She told of Banshees, spirit creatures who foretell the death of a person. Before her mother died of fever, Molly said that a Banshee commenced to wailing, a most pitiful sound, and the ones who heard became frightened because they knew someone was about to die, and didn't wish themselves that fate. Molly herself heard the moaning and became sad when she saw her mum was close to death and knew that Banshee was calling after her soul.

Molly said I must surely be descendent of Irish, for the sight of my bright-hued coppery hair, and freckles everywhere upon my body. I sometimes wondered if those Banshees had come a wailing to me when I was a baby of two months, before my natural mother killed herself in the same manner of the sing-song girl, by letting blood flow from her severed wrists. When wind did blow fierce through the Arizona mountains, I could hear moaning inside, and imagined it must have sounded just like that when I was a little babe and Banshees came a calling.

After I returned from the visit to Father's ransacked home, I was possessed with such a feeling of helplessness and fright that I went near out of my mind. I became so brainsick that poor Cherie took to hiding in closets, pantry, anyplace to avoid me. The sing-song girl ghost was all about the house; in the shadows I imagined I saw her, so left lanterns burning in every room throughout the night. I got down on my knees to examine the floor for spilt blood, for I could hear the faint swishing of her skirts as she wandered room to room. Those were my darkest days ever. I had sent Charles and his wife to the homestead, so was all alone except for little Cherie, who didn't want me anymore. I thought about delivering her back to the old Chinaman, because the monkey girl wasn't eating or drinking, and would perish unless I did something to intervene.

I trudged out one morning; Cherie would need to go back to the old man at China Point. I arrived to there by noon, Cherie tied up with a rope that I attached around my waist so she couldn't get far away. A day such as this would've charmed anything alive. The ocean was bright and sparkling, with white-as-snow waves breaking to the shore and two big Chinese sailing ships looking grand on the horizon. The cloudless sky was a deep blue, and the warm air smelled of wildflowers and pine even through the odor of drying fish. It was summer of the year eighteen hundred and eighty-two.

I walked down the narrow streets looking for Cherie's former master. Chinese people who saw me stared like I was an intruder. I could not find him anywhere. Cherie was lying against my bosom with her little head resting on my shoulder, too weak to even be interested in where she was. Finally I had no choice but to make the trip back home.

I tried to lighten my heart as I walked, by reciting inside my head that good Choctaw story, "Tale of the Wind Horse".

Wind Horse was a pony who no one would harm, for he was so very gentle. If ever an Indian was hurt and needed a pony to ride upon, Wind Horse would carry him on his back, and also take care of him. This fast-as-the-wind pony lived in those times past when night and day had not yet made out which would come before the other.

One day, Wind Horse was feeling good from being free . . . I was so lost inside the story, that when I heard voices calling, "Miss! Miss!" I didn't look straight away. A coach was halted nearby with two nice dressed women inside waving for me to come over. It was so unexpected that at first I didn't know what to do, but finally went to see what they wanted. One of them asked to see my monkey. I said Cherie wasn't feeling well, so couldn't be disturbed. They inquired if I was going to Monterey. I replied yes, I was on the way back to my home. I did accept when offered a ride, but only because I worried for little Cherie.

On the trip, the two ladies asked if I had given myself to God. I became confused, wondering which god. I couldn't imagine they were referring to Choctaw, or any Indian gods, so likely meant the son-of-god, Jesus. I told them I knew of this Jesus, but not much. Oh, they said, I must learn more, they were staying at the Methodist Pacific Grove Retreat where there was to be a group ministering of God's Perfect Love on the morrow. They wished to invite me to come and share gospel stories of Jesus Christ with them, and would call for me in their coach.

When I got inside my house, I began to weeping. It was more for relief I did this than anything else. I hoped I would have courage enough to tell at God's Perfect Love ministering about the dead sing-song girl who was now haunting me day and night. There might be a prayer they could give to make her go away and back to the world of spirits where she rightfully belonged.

Cherie was listless and sad. I mixed honey in water and forced spoonful after spoonful into her mouth, and cooed her as a mother might. By evening she was beginning to revive, and I was feeling better also. I wrapped the little girl in a blanket and laid her close by me to sleep. In the morning she was back to her happy chattering, and went off to ransack the kitchen for food. When the ladies came a calling for me, I left Cherie free in the house to roam and make whatever merry ruckus she wished.

We drove through gates that separated the Methodist Pacific Grove Retreat from Monterey. It was not far beyond where the Chinese had built their village, but I had never walked to there before. A tent was set up beside a rocky outcropping near the shoreline called, "Lovers of Jesus Point". It reminded me of the traveling circus I had seen as a child, where a monkey dressed in a tiny tuxedo collected our coins at the tent's entrance.

Many people were arriving as we were. Once everyone assembled in the tent, the preachment started. The minister talked long about God's love, and then said he would hear testimonials from members of the flock. People went to the pulpit and told tales that weren't familiar. I was sitting in between the two ladies who brought me, one of them named Mrs. Thrush. The minister directed Mrs. Thrush to come up and tell a story. She pulled me from my chair and dragged me along with her to the front. I didn't want to go, but all eyes were watching and I couldn't cause a scene by prying myself from her grasp.

The minister asked what inspiration she had to share. She told the flock she had met me just yesterday, and I was expressing the desire to be closer to God's grace. This was true; all the previous night I had been wishing for some kind of miracle to happen on this day. The words, "God's grace", sounded lovely, and I felt the bountiful God Jesus swelling within me. In front of everyone I began to crying.

Then the minister turned to me with kindly eyes, and asked, "Will you share a story with us?" I looked out to all of the faces, staring curiously. The only story I could think of right then was the sad but beautiful Choctaw tale.

"... Wind Horse was feeling good from being free, when he heard the crying of someone needing help. Off he galloped to the edge of a forest where an Indian boy had been caught in a big bear trap. The boy's foot was cut all the way off, and he could not walk. The Wind Horse went over to the child, and bent down to let him up on his back. This boy could hardly believe that such a horse would bestow upon him this gift. All his life he had lived alone with no one wanting him, he didn't even have a name. The boy rode the wind on the Wind Horse, and he felt like he was whole again."

Suddenly, a man from the audience stood up and shouted, "What is this?" I stopped speaking. The room was quiet for a goodly while. Then the minister spoke, still in his kind manner.

"I have never heard this gospel of Our Lord Jesus Christ. Where does it come from?"

"Oh." I answered, "It is a Choctaw gospel, which was told to me by my mother, who is herself a half-breed Choctaw."

The minister said, "But we are only entertaining stories about Jesus Christ here." Then he motioned another person to come up and tell a tale. Mrs. Thrush grabbed my arm and pulled me back to my seat. I stayed with my head bowed, hardly even daring to breathe until there came a lunchtime break. Tables were set up with food, and people went over to partake of eating. Mrs. Thrush and her friend walked quickly away from me without saying one word. I stood up to take my leave when a man stepped in front of me. He was tall and heavy, and blocked my going. I looked up to him, and then he spoke. "Hello, Little Red."

I politely said, "Hello," but his expression scared me, and I had the urge to run away from him.

He said, "I come from Choctaw country—out there in Mississipa and Oklahomie. Hey Little Red, do ye know what we do there to dirty Indian squaws like yer ma?"

He put his hand on my shoulder and gripped it tightly. "We cut their teats off, is what we do. And their privates, too. And when we see a Choctaw bitch with child, we take a knife and cut the bastard out. Yeah, that's exactly what we do, Miss Red, exactly what we do."

I tore myself from his grip. Tears stung my eyes as I ran. I didn't stop until I was out of the gates that read, "Pacific Grove Retreat", then fell to the ground and tried to catch air into my burning lungs.

Wind Horse knew the boy's wounded leg could not ever be fixed or healed. He was taking that boy to the Indian Hunting Ground. At this place, all were made whole again, and had no more fears or needs.

That night in sleep, dreaming came upon me. I awoke wet with my sweat, possessing clarity to recall all I'd dreamt. *I was in one of those shanty towns of my childhood, maybe Arizona, as the earth was powdery and red. Around me were canyons rising up to high, majestic plateaus. I was upon a bluff, looking down at the town below. There was my mother! I grew excited to see her; I knew of the quest to seek her Choctaw ancestors, and thought how lucky I was to find her. She wore a gown of gold, decorated with seashells and painted-on turtles. Her golden brown hair was flowing free across her shoulders, and there were blue turtle designs on her cheeks. Colorful glass beads hung around her neck. Tears of gladness welled in my eyes.*

My mother was walking toward a tiny church with a cross on its steeple. The cross looked strange until I realized it was hanging upside down. I wanted to run to her, but couldn't lift my feet from the dusty red earth. When my mother got close to the entrance, she did something strange. She got down and began to crawl like an animal. I sensed danger, so started to cry out. I was rooted to the ground as a tree, and couldn't go to her.

Suddenly, I was in the church. This is not exactly right. I was still on the mountain. But Martha was there in the church. I was viewing her for the first time, and saw she was beautiful; tall and proud, and her soft blond hair looked as a halo. Then, to my surprise, I could now see through Martha's eyes, and perceive her thoughts as well as my own. She was at the pulpit, where a minister would stand.

The door slowly opened and my mother crawled in. Now she was stripped naked, and both of her breasts had been cut off. The only thing adorning her were the painted blue turtles on her cheeks. Martha ran down the aisle and knelt down by my mother. When Martha pulled her body up, I could see that my mother's womb had been cut into. Martha held her close, and whispered over and again, "I love you Mamma, I love you Mamma." I felt the jagged breathing, just as if she were in my own embrace. My beloved mother took her last breath, and then sank limp into our arms.

It was yet before dawn, and lanterns were blazing throughout the house. I went from room to room and extinguished them all. A newly kindled anger burned inside of me, brilliant as a hundred candles. I would not be afraid anymore. I went back to bed and lay awake listening to the quiet sobbing of that poor sing-song girl as she wandered from room to room. I gently implored her to go to the Hunting Ground where she could be freed from sorrow and whole again. By the time the sun arose she was departed upon her journey.

About a week after the sing-song girl had taken her leave, Charles returned, accompanied by that kindly Mr. Morgan. I was crying so much, for I had not yet mourned my father and the terrible manner of his death. It was only when I went to finally sorting through his papers, seeing the neat, orderly handwriting, that I remembered the faraway expression which had been always upon him, and my heart began to breaking.

Charles asked me if he and Mrs. Pierce could stay permanent down in the valley and run my homestead there. Mr. Morgan said he knew of a caretaker replacement. He told me I might not want this servant-man, for he was Chinese, since my father had been killed by that China-girl. But Mr. Morgan told me this man called Lo could speak good English, was a hard worker, and would work for little pay.

The horses and laying-hens were poorly kept since Charles and his wife had gone, as I was barely even of a mind to care for myself and little Cherie. I needed help. I told Mr. Morgan I harbored no ill for Chinese people, to bring this Lo man along, and I would consider him.

When Lo was presented to me, he kept his face down, staring at the ground while telling me he would be honored to be in my service. Then

Mr. Morgan spoke to him and he raised up his head. One of his eyes looked straight to Mr. Morgan, but the other wandered around like it didn't know where to go, then settled upwards, gazing at the ceiling. He was big, too big to be a Chinaman, I thought. His eyes didn't slant enough, and his color wasn't exactly like all the China-people I had seen. I imagined then that he might be a half-breed, just as my mother, and probably had never fit well with either side of his family. I saw suffering shining outwards from his good eye, but kindness there as well. I put my hand out for him to take, for he would be welcome at my home.

The first thing Lo asked about was my garden. I told him nobody had ever put in a garden before. Lo said he would make me a garden of vegetables, and surround the outside of my house with bright colored flowers to attract hummingbirds and butterflies. And in the back where the ground sloped upwards to the pine forest would be a perfect place for a pond, so I could watch big fat yellow carps swimming about. It would be a place where frogs would want to come and make music throughout the evening. I told Lo I should be proud to have a pond like that.

From that summer, and on into winter, I felt better than I had in so long. Mr. Morgan called upon me regular, and his wife Pauline took to visiting also. When I told Pauline I wished to make an account of those strange happenings with Martha, she encouraged me, even though I possess poor skills at writing. Lo kept himself busy each day with the vegetable garden and all manner of growing things. He gathered stones from the hills and created a beautiful pond, then planted water lilies for frogs to hop upon.

Winter is well upon us now, and I can hear the wild surf within our first storm come down from the cold north. I've been told it is summer in Australia, and did inquire about a place called Canberra. No one seems to have heard of it. But this is not a serious matter to me, as I realize it may not yet exist. I am going anyway. I have booked passage to visit Australia.

Inside of my heart is a yearning to see that special cast of blue to the sky. I long to feel the warmth there that seeps all inside, making you glad to be alive. I pine so for the blond haired twins, baby Jonathan, and handsome blue-eyed Jimmy, but they must remain only a bright spot in my memory. Beauty and sorrow shall lay together forever within my soul.

Misty Broebard

January 15, 2005

From Gail Christenson, gailchris@redman.com
To Martha Bain, mbain@marsurf.net
At The Monkey House Inn on Smith Island, Maryland

Dear Mrs. Bain,

You don't know me, but I'm begging you, please take the time to read my letter, as I believe it concerns you in the most personal and profound way. This is perhaps a lonely old widow's last sojourn. I lost my husband a year ago after 57 years of matrimony, and this discovery has kept me from feeling that my own life has lost its moorings.

Back in 1970 or thereabouts, I bid $100 for an intriguing little portrait at La Porte's auction house in Monterey. I was high bidder and took the painting home that day. It hung in the hallway of my Pebble Beach, California home for over thirty years until recently, when I elected to do remodeling. My decorator suggested I change the heavy, ornate gold and black frame to favor my new, lighter décor.

When frame was separated from painting, lying inside was a beautifully bound, handwritten little book that appears to be the partial biography of a young lady named Misty Broebard who lived back in the late 1800's.

First let me describe the subject of the painting. It is a portrait, presumably of Misty, wearing a full-length green cape. She is standing on a bluff overlooking the ocean, her back to the viewer, with head cocked sideways so you can see her profile. Peeking timidly over her shoulder is the face of a tiny monkey. When you read Misty's story, you will see why I was compelled to hire a private detective to find out if there could even be a grain of validation to her account. Please forgive me if I have invaded your privacy, for it was not my intention.

This is what my detective found. You lived in Canberra, Australia before immigrating to the Chesapeake Bay area, where you and your husband currently own a bed-and-breakfast on Smith Island, called The Monkey House Inn. In the off-season, your husband works as a crabber, as do most families there on the island. Your son Jonathan was just a baby in 1962, and your two older children are identical twin girls. Your husband James is known affectionately as Jimmy.

I carefully copied every word of Misty's story and have included it here. I've also photographed the painting which I've added as an attachment. I want you to have the handwritten original, and I also wish to pass the painting along, as I believe both are legitimately yours.

I would so love to have the opportunity to deliver them personally, and meet and talk with you about this extraordinary discovery.

Very Truly Yours,
Gail Christensen

January 16, 2005

From Martha Bain, mbain@marsurf.net

Dear Gail,

Where do I begin? I made breakfast for Jimmy before he left, and then crawled back into bed with coffee and my laptop computer, to browse the Internet, and check e-mail. As I'm writing you now, my hands are shaking so badly that I keep missing the keys, and my eyes are blurry from emotional tears. I opened your e-mail, was mildly curious about it, so did a quick visual scan of the contents. When I landed upon the name, "Misty Broebard", my heart leapt from my chest.

I know the Misty of your painting. She is the same Misty Broebard who settled here on Smith Island in 1919, in the very house where I now sit. Jimmy, the kids and I, through an odd happenstance, ended up on the island while on a visit to the U.S. back in the mid-seventies. We were immediately attracted to the dilapidated old wreck of a house perched on the waters edge, and couldn't resist buying, especially as it was selling so cheap. It had been dubbed "The Monkey House", for Miss Broebard kept several monkeys. Misty was a colorful local character; those monkeys wreaked havoc, I have heard. There are some photos of her in our Smith Island museum, one of which I had blown up and framed, that is now hanging in our entry.

I can't even begin to articulate how it feels to read a strange accounting of one's life written more than half a century before being born. Even were this some kind of hoax, it had to have been perpetrated more than 30 years ago, since you've been in possession of the painting that long. I see no way this can be a hoax. But it is a haunting mystery.

Misty passed on in 1938, the very same year as my birth (I'm going to scan and include her obituary). She did make it to Australia. In our museum is a grainy photo of her smiling, with waves cresting in the background, and a small rowboat lying alongside in the sand. The handwritten caption reads, "Jervis Bay, Australia". As a child I spent summers frolicking in the waves on Jervis Bay, which is why I chose that particular image to hang in our entry. Oh, God, now I'm really crying.

So many times I've stared out to the expanse of ocean and sky that envelop this home and wondered if Misty also felt breathless inside its incomparable beauty and solitude. You can gaze out from the living room and feel you are living on a boat, for the house was built atop a jutting rock with water surrounding it on three sides.

During summer tourist months we have the B & B open, and in winter Jimmy works with Jonathan (who is married to a local girl on the island) at his crabbing business. The twins are living not far away on Chesapeake Bay. Our B & B is closed until late spring, but you are welcome anytime. I'll be going upstairs shortly to make up your room. Gail, you've given me a treasure beyond anything I could've ever imagined. Please do come soon.

"Winter is well upon us now, and I can hear the wild surf within our first storm come down from the cold north." Bring a good warm coat.

Martha

The Monkey House Inn

Donya's Spices
by Shaheen Schmidt

Delicious aromas seeped out of Donya's kitchen and drifted over to Betty's yard. Donya's neighbor detected them right away, and popped her head over the redwood fence that bordered their properties. Betty had lived next door to Donya's river rock cottage for five of her fifty years, and had not yet gotten tired of the enticing smells that came her Iranian neighbor's window. In fact, finding out what brewed next door was one of the most exciting events of her day.

Betty saw that Donya was in her backyard picking fresh mint and parsley from her small raised-bed herb garden. "Another warm day, huh, Donya?" she called out. "Whatchya cooking, dolmeh or saffron rice?"

"I have lots more recipes than that," Donya answered, as she continued to pick. "Today it's eggplant stew with chicken."

Betty pulled her stringy gray hair out of her face. "Yum! I'm sure it's great!"

Donya looked up, holding a bunch of greens with both of her hands. Round rosy cheeks set off her big almond eyes, all of it framed by dark brown hair graying at the sides. She shone with a bright aura, health owed to age-old remedies formulated from her organically-grown herbs, spices, and other special ingredients.

Donya brought the greens up to her face and inhaled their scent deeply; her eyelids relaxed shut. "I'll bring you a small dish to taste, Betty," she said as she exhaled, then placed the greens in a wooden bowl on the ground next to her, picked it up and walked slowly back to her old, thickly carved wooden door.

From behind she heard Betty's excited voice. "Maybe it'll help me get rid of this headache, too."

Donya loved the sunny mornings in her Carmel Valley house. When July's warm air flowed across her skin, it reminded her of growing up in Iran. "Now that's how a summer should be," she murmured to herself. Indeed, her mildly arthritic hands felt much better since she had moved from San Francisco to live closer to her only son, Raha, an architect who had designed her two-bedroom cottage. He lived with his American wife, Stella, and four-year-old daughter, Christine, in Skyline Forest overlooking the Monterey Peninsula.

At 60, Donya managed well on her own; she actually preferred it that way. Her days were filled with gardening and the preparation of her tasty concoctions. There was grocery shopping, too, though the sterile, cold American supermarkets held no appeal for her. There, everyone pushed a cart around in silence, secluded in their private bubble of thoughts, rarely interacting with others. They would move from the vegetable section filled with anemic tomatoes, green oranges, and neon apples, to the processed meat and dairy aisles, to the dry goods section, finally paying quietly without negotiating prices and leaving no more satisfied than they had come.

It was quite different on Tuesdays when Donya would drive her red Volvo to Alvarado Street in Monterey for the Farmers' Market, which always buzzed with music and activity. People crowded the street carrying baskets full of flowers and vegetables, and the smell of barbecue and Indian cuisine tickled the noses of hungry walkers.

The Farmers' Market was Donya's favorite place for socializing and interacting with others. She would drag her pull cart behind her slowly, carefully inspecting the goods at each stand, searching for the sweetest melons and peaches; doing the same for purple basil and tarteezak (summer savory). Her eyes would grow large with excitement when she found rare items like fat, juicy pomegranates, sweet green and purple figs, or skinny Japanese eggplants and okra.

Donya smiled at her recollections as she opened her pantry door. The aromas of different powders in small bottles and containers met her. Each of them—which she would often greet by name—was capable of eliciting a unique memory, some garnished with a touch of melancholy, like the rice spice made of cumin, cinnamon, cardamom, and dried rose petals. It brought her back to the dimly-lit bazaar where her father, a great healer and herbalist, had worked.

She recalled the plethora of herbs and spices sitting on the shelves behind him in his tiny shop, big jars of dried roots, plant parts and seeds. Each herb was considered sacred; a precious yet powerful gift from the gods, not to be wasted.

Patients came from far and wide to seek out her father's cures, and they even visited him at his house. Donya remembered coming home from school and having to squeeze past a line of people in the front yard just to get into her own living room. As payment, people might bring a big piece of cheese wrapped in paper or a bag of eggs. Some came with nothing at all. It was a tradition Donya carried on herself, cooking healing meals to share, along with her knowledge, among friends who brought their own small gifts as repayment, although she never asked for anything.

Back in the present, she found herself reaching for the ground saffron powder. The jewel of a spice rested in the bottom of a little airtight glass jar. "Hello, saffron," she said cheerily, and turned back toward her kitchen.

The gentle sounds of her cooking greeted her. The stew simmered slowly on the stove. She lifted the lid and the hot mist of tomatoes softening in chicken broth swirled up and around her. She added a pinch of saffron, which lent a highlight of gold to the red broth and perfumed the air with its unique aroma. A dash of tan cumin and another of orange turmeric soon joined the festive brew.

Donya rinsed mint, parsley, green onions, and red radishes in the sink. These would be placed in a heaping dish at the table during the meal, a tradition. Iranians ate fresh greens with each bite of food. "A refreshing taste that is great for helping your digestion," she would tell guests.

She lifted the lid off the rice pot and poured a teaspoon of liquefied saffron over the top of basmati rice, their sweet smells knitting together to make her mouth water. After several more minutes, she picked up the phone and dialed Betty's number.

Her neighbor answered on the first ring.

"Hi, Betty. My stew is ready."

"I'll be right there," Betty said as fast as she could.

"The door is open—hello?" Donya waited a second before hanging up, but knew her neighbor was already on her way. Sure enough, the door opened moments later, and Betty's lanky figure entered, plate and fork in hand.

"Wow! It smells heavenly in here, as always." Her guest walked straight to the stove, then—suddenly, as if she'd forgotten something—stopped and turned to face Donya.

"Can I do anything to help?" Betty said, tightly holding her plate.

"Why don't you serve yourself? I'll go get the dry tea herbs for your headache. I made the mixture you asked for this morning."

"Okay," Betty replied, heading back to the pots. First she put three big spoonfuls of rice on her plate, then she dipped the ladle into the stew pot, heaping pieces of chicken and eggplant over the steamy rice, covering it all with the reddish-gold broth.

"Last time, I made the headache tea exactly the way you told me to," Betty said. "It really worked, but Al complained about the smell when I brewed it." She dipped another scoop of stew out of the pot and poured it onto her plate. "This is his night out with the boys. He usually eats with them."

"Now listen, Betty," Donya said, noticing that her neighbor's plate was afloat with the ingredients of the meal, "I didn't make soup! You're supposed to put the rice on one side and the stew on the other. Now you've gone and made a mess out of it."

"I'm sure it will still taste heavenly," Betty said, watching Donya place a small brown jar containing a mixture of dried plant leaves on the table. "Oh, I almost forgot about the tahdeeg!" Betty yelped, holding up a big spoon, obviously ready to dig up the bottom of the rice pot.

"Don't you use that metal spoon! You'll scratch my pot!" Donya got up to rescue her utensil from Betty, taking a wooden spoon off a rack above the stove and digging out a piece of golden crusted rice for her friend.

"Here's your boat to float on top of my stew," Donya said, putting the piece on Betty's plate.

"Can I serve you some?" Betty asked, her eyes locked on her own plate.

"No, I'll serve myself, thanks. You go sit down. Stay and have dinner with me if you don't have to go right home." Donya took out a brown clay plate for herself.

"You've made so much food for one person," Betty said as she took a seat at the table.

"Yeah, my son was supposed to come and visit with his daughter. I haven't seen little Christy for over a month now." She carefully placed some rice on her plate.

"Well, they're missing a great feast, but I feel lucky to be here," Betty replied. "Can I have a spoon?"

"Here," Donya said, passing it to her guest. "It breaks my heart that Christy's growing up on macaroni and cheese with soda pop or some other fast food. When my son was two years old, he ate gourmet hot meals every day." Donya exhaled and shook her head slightly.

"Yeah, my grandson won't even taste my lamb chops." Betty blew on a steamy spoonful of chicken and rice before taking a bite.

"I wouldn't either," Donya laughed and Betty started to laugh as well, bits of rice flying out of her mouth.

"Next time Raha comes over I'll surprise him with one of his favorite dishes."

"What if you-know-who comes with him?" Betty whispered through a mouthful of food. "Would she eat that, too?"

"If Stella doesn't like it, she can have some canned food instead."

"What? Cat food!?" Betty's eyes grew wide.

"I think you need some herbs just for those ears of yours . . . I said *canned* food . . ." She set free a loud chuckle, and the sound of both women's laughter passed through the kitchen window, flew upward and spread over the nearby oak trees.

A couple of weeks later, little Christy and her father came over for a short visit.

"Ooh, my sweet flower, my Bouboula," Donya greeted her granddaughter. Her smile covered her whole face as she squeezed the little body in her arms and kissed her on the cheeks.

"Ouch, that hurt. Let me go," the girl giggled, pushing her blonde locks out of her soft face and squirming out of Grandma's arms.

"I brought her lunch," Raha said. "All you have to do is warm it up, Mom. She won't eat anything else." He put a closed plastic container on the counter. "I'll have lunch at the meeting today." The light from the kitchen window made his red eyes and the bags beneath them obvious.

Donya stared at the container. "What is . . . that?"

"My mommy bought it for me." Christy started to bounce on one leg.

"It's left over from last night," Raha said, looking at the pot on the stove and inhaling deeply. "Khoresht Sabzee? My favorite. It smells delicious!"

"I'll save it for your dinner, dear," Donya blurted. Each time she saw him, a bit more white was woven through his dark hair.

"Great," Raha said, looking at his watch. "I'll be back around five. Pack it to go; we've got to get on the road as soon as I get back."

Raha kissed his mother and daughter and rushed out the door.

"So, what do ya wanna do today, my love?" Donya placed her hand over her heart and bent over the bright-eyed face. Two big blue circles stared up at her.

"I brought movies to watch." Christy pointed at a florescent orange backpack on the floor.

"Nah, let's go outside. It's too nice to sit in front of the TV. Let's check out the garden. I'll tell you about the fairies who live there."

"Fairies! Cool, let's go." She wrapped her little fingers around her grandma's hand.

Out back they spent almost an hour looking through tomato plants and strawberries. They searched for fallen seed pods from eucalyptus trees and, under the oaks, little Chinese hats that had separated from their acorns. They collected blue jay feathers and wrote a letter on eucalyptus bark, placing it in a hole in a big oak tree trunk, the mail box for fairies. Then Donya helped Christy plant a few big kidney bean seeds in the ground, and right after that they encircled them with a barrier made of tiny twigs and sticks. They wet down the adobe patio so they could inhale the clean, damp soil and moist brick, and even talked to Betty over the fence. When it got too hot, they headed inside for some cool watermelon juice.

Christy picked up a half-full glass from the kitchen table and took a sip, which left a smudge of red on her upper lip. "Hey, Grandma, are you a witch?"

"A witch?!" Donya stopped searching in the pantry and turned around. "Why do you say that?"

"My mommy thinks you are. You've got so many bottles in there with dried frog legs, and . . . and blood in them . . . and some are stinky. Do you make potions out of them?" Christy held onto her glass tightly.

"Oh, my Bouboula," Donya laughed gently, "these are just dried plants and roots." Her round belly shook like jelly as she laughed. "You're so funny."

Christy took another sip. "Well, whattchya do with 'em?"

"Some are like salt and pepper, but with different—better—flavors. I add them to my cooking. It makes things taste good. And some, I make teas with when I have a tummyache."

Donya closed the door, walked to the table, and softly kissed Christy on her forehead. "If I'm a witch, I'm a darn good one." *Maybe someday I'll give your mommy a magic potion to open her congested mind and heart,* she thought, feeling her face flush and imagining smoke rings coming out her ears.

Later, against her better judgment, Donya warmed up the two slices of cold cheese pizza that "Mommy" had placed inside the container. They looked like pieces of crusty bread with white plastic glue stuck to them. For herself, she served a plate of hot rice and dark green herbal stew with small pieces of beef on the side.

"Granny? Why d'ya eat rabbit food all the time, with lots of wegetabols?"

"Because rabbits are playful, happy, and healthy," Donya laughed. "Just like me. Besides, it's the fairies who tell me what to put in my pot for cooking."

"Really? Mmmm . . . can I try a piece?"

As Christy leaned forward, Donya told her how the meat, beans, fresh parsley, and chives ended up together. By the time she was through explaining, Christy had eaten a decent portion of rice with juicy stew. One-and-a-half slices of pizza remained untouched.

"Grandma, are you coming for my birthday party next month?"

"I wouldn't miss it for anything. Can I invite some fairies to come, too?"

"Nah, they might scare Mommy."

"Okay, but I'll have them make you something special."

"Oh, yeah? Awesome!"

The rest of the day went smoothly. While the ceiling fan cooled the air, they closed the curtains and put some blankets and pillows on the thick Persian carpet in the living room and took a nap. Then Betty came over for a cup of tea and some sweet date halva. Raha arrived on time, surprised to see his daughter had tried some different food for a change.

"Just use your imagination," Donya told him, and gave him a hug and kisses on both cheeks, handing him a bag stuffed with containers full of "rabbit food". As she watched them drive away, she blotted a tear.

A month later, on a Saturday morning, after preparing lentil rice with chunks of chicken and tiny slices of fried onion, Donya took Christy's gift off the shelf. It was in a wooden box decorated with fresh shiny rose leaves arranged in the shape of a "C" on both sides, topped with a cluster of star jasmine flowers. After putting on her orange and yellow velvet dress, Donya painted her lips bright red—which matched her nail polish—and placed a milky magnolia flower in her hair, tucking the stem behind her ear where it cast a faint but sweet fragrance. Then she took a bundle of pink roses mixed with rosemary branches and snapdragons in a glass vase for the hosts. After packing her car with her big straw bag decorated in colorful ribbons, she put her dish of rice next to it. With her dancing tape slipped into the cassette player, Donya drove away to celebrate her granddaughter's fifth birthday.

A beautiful vista opened up in front of her as she drove along Carmel Valley Road toward Monterey. Some horses and cattle grazed on green pastures; others relaxed under shade trees. She passed a covey of quail as the hills of Garland Ranch rose up on her left; wild turkeys meandered through the bushes. The small vineyards and apple farms she passed recalled to her the abundance of life in this part of the country. The green of the land reminded her of childhood summer vacations when her family would leave the crowded city of Tehran and head north for the beautiful forests and beach houses off the Caspian Sea.

Before Donya knew it, she had left the windy road to join Highway 1 north, finally turning onto Highway 68 and passing through the tall pines of Skyline Forest until she arrived at Raha's house.

After Donya rang the doorbell, a wrinkled, mahogany-haired woman in her sixties opened the door. She held a glass of white wine in her free hand, little finger up.

"Hello, hello," Donya grinned broadly and shuffled inside. The woman, who wore heavy purple eye shadow, gave her the once-over from head to toe and smirked. Donya considered how the cast of the woman's hair came quite close to the color of a newly ripened eggplant, and thought how it might serve as a good example of such to her cooking class.

Donya stood in the hallway scanning the crowd that had gathered in the living room. Thirty or so adults stood around, most with beer bottles in their hands, the rest holding wine or martini glasses. The big flat screen plasma TV, on the wall in the middle of living room, showed a commercial, but with the sound off. She saw no indication that this was the birthday party of a five-year-old, until she noticed a pile of neatly-wrapped gifts on a small table in the corner.

She squeezed in between two older couples at the food table. They were engaged in a heated discussion about politics, hardly pausing while they double-dipped their chips in the salsa dish. Donya put her ceramic bowl down next to the vegetable tray and took the cover off. The food was still warm, and the steam carried the aroma into the room, a contrast to the cold-wrapped turkey sandwiches and, of course, slices of cheese pizza, Christy's favorite plastic glue bread.

Still carrying her big bag, Donya looked for Raha or Christy or maybe even Christy's mother. She started back in the direction of the living room, noticing that the two couples had halted their conversation and were examining the contents of the rice dish.

In the living room, she saw a man in his forties attempting to clean spilled red wine off the white carpet with a wet napkin, while a woman with shoulder-length bleached-blonde hair that exposed brassy roots and frizzy cotton-candy ends stood waiting to sit down. She held a paper plate with two celery sticks and one carrot. Out of the corner of her eye, she watched a long-haired gray cat lying on the only available chair. The animal paid little mind, stretching itself and rolling over before it started to purr.

Finally, Raha and Stella appeared, talking to another couple. Raha spotted Donya, and came over.

"Hi, Mom, when did you get here?" he asked, then gave her a kiss on each cheek. Donya noted he looked quite handsome in his light blue Calvin Klein cotton shirt and navy blue slacks. Then she reached out to hug Stella. Her daughter-in-law leaned over stiffly and gave Donya a light touch and a quick hug in return. To Donya, her energy felt as impenetrable as a cement wall, and she soon disappeared among a group of guests that had just walked in.

"Where is my Bouboula?" Donya asked Raha. "Where is my princess?" She handed her son the flowers.

"She is in her room watching a video with two other friends."

"Why isn't she out here? She's the life of the party today."

Donya started to walk toward her granddaughter's room, but Christy ran out first. "Grandma, you came!" she shouted. Donya opened her arms and gave her a big hug, kissing her little head all over and planting a big juicy one on each cheek.

"Of course I came, Sweet Apple. I wouldn't have missed your party if a hundred trolls were trying to keep me away." She reached into her handbag and pulled out a crown made of jasmine branches and red rose buds. Donya placed it on Christy's head.

"Here! This is from me to my girl."

Christy walked to the middle of the living room with her special crown. Everyone's head turned. "Oohs" and "Ahhs" filled the room. Even the cat looked up.

"Wow, I'm the queen of the forest!" Christy said proudly, and gently lifted her hand, touching the tips of the leaves.

"It's beautiful," the eggplant lady told Donya. "Where on earth did you buy that, hon?" She exhaled cigarette smoke through her frosted pink lips, making a minimal effort to blow it toward an open window.

"I bought it from my garden!" Donya answered smartly, waving her hand back and forth in front of her face in a futile effort to clear the billow of smoke. She reached back into her bag and pulled the wooden box out. "And this is from the fairies, my darling Christy."

"Oh, yeah?" Christy squealed. "Can I open it now?"

Stella's voice cut in sharply, her pale skin suddenly flushed. "No! Put it next to the other gifts on the table! I'll announce when it's time to open gifts later." She pointed with one long skinny finger at the mound of colorfully wrapped gifts in the corner. With her bobbed blonde hair sitting helmet-like on her head, Donya imagined her daughter-in-law in a soldiers' uniform with a Hitler-like mustache over her injected upper lip, raising her arm, giving orders.

If you get any stiffer and drier, you might break like a twig, woman.

"You're from *I-ran*, right?" the eggplant lady asked, leaning over. Her breath stunk of tar and her lipstick had bled to the tiny lines around her lips. "Where do you find flowers or trees to make that sort of thing? It's all desert, over there, isn't it? You must have suffered some culture shock when you came here!"

Donya moved her head a few feet to the right to avoid the fetid breath. "My dear lady, of course I was shocked. I was shocked to find that the average American's understanding of geography and world culture is absolutely atrocious!"

"Oh, no . . . not me," the eggplant lady insisted. "I've seen *Lawrence of Arabia* and I absolutely loved it." She took a sip of her wine and gazed off into space. "I think of that great picture, and I dream of sand dunes, camels and palm trees, and women all covered up, working in their kitchens, making couscous and lamb."

A drop of the woman's saliva landed on Donya's cheek, who politely wiped it off with a handkerchief. "Honey, you've been living the wrong dream for too long," she told her. "It's time to wake up and smell the spices." She laughed and stepped up to the stereo, switched it on, popped in her dancing tape, and turned up the volume.

"This is my little princess' party," Donya announced loudly. "Let's all honor her by having some fun."

The sound of the tombak drum and string instruments filled the room. Donya lifted her hands and started snapping her fingers, while rolling her shoulders and moving her hips to the rhythm. Soon Christy joined her, jumping up and down, trying to imitate her. Two little boys came out of the TV room and joined them, laughing and giggling. Raha peeked through the kitchen door, smiled, and then walked into the living room, turned off the TV and started snapping his fingers and dancing, too. The music seemed to refresh his forgotten native soul, taking him back to the festive good old days of his childhood in Iran.

Donya took the eggplant lady's arms and pulled her gently into the circle, showing her the moves. Soon half of the guests were swaying to the beat. The cat woke up, jumped out of the chair, and headed for the safety of the backyard. The bleached-blonde wasted no time claiming the vacated space. She parted her mouth in satisfaction as she sunk into the comfortable seat.

Still, Donya couldn't help but notice Stella standing in the kitchen doorway holding a plate of poorly combined foods that, when eaten together, would likely bring her discomfort later. Donya squared her shoulders and walked resolutely toward her daughter-in-law.

"This is a nice party," Donya said politely, but frowned at the fish and watermelon on Stella's plate.

"It seems like you found the need to spice it up!" Stella replied. She took a sip from her glass of cold milk, avoiding eye contact.

"Well, you had the perfect guests for it, honey. They were like fresh ingredients ready to be flavored." She tried to prepare for her next line. "I wonder," she hesitated, "how does it taste—I mean, fish with watermelon and milk?"

"Great. Maybe you need to add it to your volumes of recipes." Stella chewed on a piece of white fish.

"Maybe, but in my country we take care how we mix foods together. Those are all cool-natured foods, and too many of them could upset your stomach." In her most unimposing fashion, Donya suggested, "I would add something with a little warm nature, to balance it out."

"This fish was pretty damn hot when it came out of the oven a minute ago," Stella laughed.

"Well, you know what I mean. Do call me if it bothers you tonight. I've got a good remedy for it."

"In our house, Donya, this is the way we eat." Stella leaned over and filled up her plate with more fish and watermelon, garnished with a sarcastic smile. "Would you mind bringing me some more milk from the kitchen?"

Donya stared at her son's wife in wonder. She took a deep breath, and stood up almost as high as Stella's chin. Keeping her voice even, she said, "It seems like you're really enjoying your meal, honey. I'll get you whatever you'd like." She took the empty glass and walked to the kitchen. As she filled it, she felt Stella's eyes burning on her back.

"Cheers," Donya said when she returned, handing Stella the milk and rejoining the party.

By the end of the next hour, most of the partygoers had turned their attention to Donya, asking her about recipes and Persian music. Some talked to Christy about her crown and her visits to grandma's garden. It wasn't long, though, before Stella's voice interrupted again.

"Time to open your gifts, dear."

The beautiful wrapping paper was quickly ripped off the gifts and tossed into the waste basket. Christy opened each prize and found: three sets of blonde Barbie dolls in bikinis, exactly alike; a bunch of stuffed animals; a few plastic make-up sets; and a Britney Spears CD.

Then Christy came to the wooden box. She sniffed the strand of jasmine on top and sighed with pleasure. Carefully she opened it and pulled out a rag doll in a dress made of blue and green hummingbirds' feathers carefully fitted to create a solid, velvety effect. A lei of tiny white and blue flowers encircled its collar. Little gold and silver painted seeds were arranged into tear drop shapes from the doll's waist to its neck. Two cinnamon sticks, the doll's arms, showed through puffy cheesecloth sleeves.

The stuffed cloth face was immaculately painted with the tiniest of brushes—even each eyelash showed. And green moss curls fell to its shoulders from underneath a crown made of a eucalyptus seed pod, painted frosted orange.

"Fairies really made this?" Christy gasped, eyes open in wonder—as were Stella's. Even the bleached-blonde, cat's hair clinging to the back of her skirt, left her hard-won seat to take a closer look.

Eventually the party came to an end and it was time to say good-bye. Christy had already fallen asleep next to the fairy doll. Donya kissed the child and made several circular motions with her closed hands—each filled with a pinch of salt—over the head of her treasure, a ritual intended to protect the child from jealousy or negativity. Donya then murmured a few words of prayer before pursing her lips and blowing outward into the air, several times in succession while turning in a circle, in order to spread goodwill. Then she quietly left the girl's room to gather her dishes.

The eggplant lady stepped in front of Donya.

"I would like to know more about I-ran. Where should I start?"

"Maybe by finding it on the map, and then try to pronounce it right—it's Iran, not I-ran. By the way, Iranians speak Farsi, not Arabic. That's a good first step."

"Okay, okay. I'll remember. Do you think you could teach me how to use the spices in that rice you brought?"

"Sure, come over my house sometime and we'll cook together."

It was after nine at night when Donya got home. The summer air was cooling off and the orange light of dusk was fading into the oak trees. She planned a return call to Betty in the morning, as her neighbor had left a phone message asking how the party had gone. As Donya was putting her magnolia flower in a glass of water, the phone rang.

"Hello, Mom?" Raha's voice was low, almost a whisper.

"Oh, hi, dear, what did I forget this time?"

"No, it's not that. Stella has been throwing up. She's got a very bad stomach ache."

"Oh, my." She stopped herself before she made any further comments.

"She looks pale, Mom. She told me what she ate. I can't believe she knew it was the combination of foods that made her ill."

Donya asked a bunch of questions, like how many times had she thrown up, and her current temperature. After Raha answered, she instructed him as follows: "Make her a very strong mint tea and boil some hard sugar crystal in it. I'd suggest another mix, but I know she won't drink the purple flower tea. I think mint should do the trick."

"You're probably right, Mom. About the purple tea, I mean. She hates anything too herbal."

"You need to bring her blood sugar up, too, to cancel out the cooling effect of the fish and watermelon."

She continued advising him for a few more minutes and asked him to call her if anything changed. "If she doesn't want to take the mint tea and she gets worse, you may have to take her to the hospital, but I doubt it will come to that."

Donya heard nothing more that night, but the next morning the phone rang.

"Hello Donya." Stella's voice sounded a little icy.

Still alive, I see.

"Hi, Stella, how are you feeling this morning?"

"I drank some of that disgusting purple tea last night."

Donya waited in silence.

"Your son mentioned it first, but then suggested a mint tea instead," Stella added.

Donya still didn't say a word.

"It kinda worked," Stella added, sounding surprised. "It took away some of my nausea, but I had an uneasy night's sleep."

Donya exhaled and dropped her shoulders. "I'm glad you decided to try the disgusting tea, honey."

"Well, anyway, Christy got a lot of gifts, but her favorite was the one the so-called 'fairies' made for her. I gotta go now. So, thanks anyway."

Though Donya felt Stella's energy pulling back before she hung up, she put down the phone and looked outside through the trees, wondering if the magic of fairies or the magic of spices did really melt a piece of her heart. The thought brightened her spirit more than she would have expected.

She headed to her pantry to make some more remedies.

Donya's Spices

Charlotte's Light

by Ken Jones

"Destiny is not a matter of chance, it is a matter of choice."
— William Jennings Bryan

*T*he clock on the mantelpiece struck two. Charlotte rose, pinned back errant strands of her blond hair and took a deep breath; it was time to see to the light.

She climbed the narrow spiraling stairs, following the steps her husband Charles had taken each night for the past nine months, ever since that February evening in 1855 when the light had come to life. Almost unconsciously, she went through the motions of inspecting the light, then signed the log again where five days earlier her husband had last penned his signature.

A fire struggled in the fireplace as she returned to the small bedroom. Rain splashed against the windows and a gusting northwest wind rattled the doors and whined around the tower in a macabre echo of her husband's breathing. She wrung a towel over the basin on the bed table, folded it and placed it gently back on his forehead. His eyes, half open, shifted as he moaned and worked his tongue across fever-split lips. It had been four days since they'd brought him home.

Charlotte had grown accustomed to the moods of the night in the small white house in the woods above the rocky central California coast, just west of the Port of Monterey. Their range of tempers had become part of the new rhythm of her life. This November night, however, she felt as if a shroud had been thrown over the Point Pinos Lighthouse, one that threatened to suffocate her.

Her oldest child, Chad, came silently into the room and stood beside her. The boy had matured beyond his eleven years. Since the family had moved to this isolated place, he had readily assumed responsibility for his younger brothers, William, now five, and Tom, now almost two.

"Is Pa going to be all right?"

Charlotte hugged her son to her. I hope so, dear. He's always been a fighter."

"He looks awful sick."

Charlotte squeezed the boy closer. "Would you like to sit here with me a while?"

A child's sobbing came from the room at the other end of the short hallway. "I'd better go," Chad said. "Tom's scared of the storm."

Charlotte regarded her husband and thought it ironic that he had been in a sickbed the first time she'd seen his face.

"You're late again, Miss Wade!" The shrill voice of the head nurse echoed as young Charlotte hurried through the door of the Regimental Hospital in Raleigh, North Carolina.

"Sorry, ma'am," Charlotte called over her shoulder, as she rounded the corner on her way to the wards, tying her volunteer's jumper behind her.

When she reached the ward, a round, ruddy-cheeked woman, seated behind a wooden desk as if impersonating a prison guard, pointed with her pencil to a patient partially hidden behind a rolling screen. "See to the new one," the nurse said, without looking up. "Then fill the water bottles and gather the dirty linens. Report to me when you're done."

Charlotte peered around the screen and felt her heart skip as her eyes met those of the man in the bed. Her hands involuntarily rose to tuck her stubborn hair back behind her cap and then dropped to smooth the front of her jumper.

"Well, good morning, Miss. You startled me." He looked at her with deep blue eyes, his angular features accentuated by the morning light from his bedside window. Charlotte supposed him to be older than she, twenty-four or -five, perhaps. The man smiled, then laughed. *Perfect teeth*, she thought. "Are you quite all right, Miss?" he asked, his gentle laugh and lilting English accent adding to Charlotte's sudden emotional disarray.

She folded her arms and squeezed herself tightly. "I'm fine, thank you," she managed to say. "Why do you ask?"

"Oh, it's nothing, really. It's just the odd hat you're wearing. I don't think I've see one quite like it."

Charlotte grabbed her cap and found that she'd pinned it on backwards in her early morning rush. She stepped behind the screen and righted it, emerging once again the picture of a composed volunteer . . . outwardly, at any rate.

"I'm Sergeant Layton," the man said, "but please call me Charles."

"How do you do . . . sergeant?"

"Better now," he answered, smiling still. "Do you have a name?"

She willed herself to maintain a degree of professional bearing. "I'm Charlotte Wade . . . I help out on the ward."

"Pleased to meet you Miss Wade. I'll rest easier knowing you're here."

It was then that Charlotte noticed the splint and heavy bandages on the man's right leg. Her face must have reflected her apprehension, because the sergeant quickly added, "Tangled with Indians down in Florida, I'm afraid. It looks worse than it is. The doctors have assured me that I'll keep it."

The ward nurse's voice bellowed suddenly behind her and Charlotte jumped. "If you're finished here, Miss Wade, we have patients who are dying of thirst. If they don't suffocate under their dirty bedclothes first, that is."

⬟

A log popped in the fireplace, scattering small embers across the hearth and breaking the spell of Charlotte's reminiscence, though a vague excitement lingered briefly. She rose, dropped another log into the fire and walked to the window.

Dark clouds hurried past the silhouetted pines. Sheets of rain driving through the light's beam sparkled like crystals, reminding her of the sea-spray that had swept over the deck of the ship that brought them to Monterey. As she sat down again, her thoughts turned to the chilly January morning in 1847 when their ship had dropped anchor in Monterey Bay after nearly six months sailing around Cape Horn from New York.

⬟

The deckhand took three-year-old Chad from his father's arms and handed him down to his mother waiting in the longboat below. Charles followed, and they cast off toward the shore on the strong oar-strokes of the boatmen. Soon the Layton family stood amid the confusion of the busy Port of Monterey. Wagons and horses crisscrossed the open space that swept up from the beach to gradually form a broad street lined with adobe and wooden buildings of various shapes and sizes. People rushed by on the boardwalk. The air sang with shouts and the sounds of iron-banded wheels on rough earth.

Charlotte's impression of the city was one of total disorder. Charles had been besotted with the idea of starting a new life in the West. Charlotte, though, had regretted the decision as soon as their ship left New York Harbor. She'd managed to hang on to her sanity throughout the journey despite the tedium, sickness, and appalling food. She'd vowed not to burden Charles with her misgivings, but nothing she'd seen of Monterey so far served to alter her conviction that the move had been a terrible mistake.

The family took refuge on the steps of a building near the water. When Charles let go of Chad's hand to brush the dust from his pants, the boy darted off the boardwalk into the path of a wagon loaded with lumber and barrels. The driver shouted and the lead horse reared, wild-eyed, kicking the air with its forelegs. Chad stood frozen as the giant animal loomed before him. Charlotte screamed and a man wearing a fine suit and tall silk hat grabbed the bridle of the lead horse and turned it away from the boy. When the team had steadied, he admonished the driver and then joined the family who stood now on the boardwalk with their son wrapped in their arms. "Drivers forget they're not in open country," the man said, straightening his hat.

"I want to thank you, sir," Charles said, then introduced himself, explaining that they had just that morning arrived in town.

"Allow me to welcome you to Monterey," the man said, tipping his hat to Charlotte. "I'm Isaac Wall, Collector of the port."

"A pleasure, sir," Charles said. "This is my wife, Charlotte, and my son, Charles Junior."

The sound of hammering and sawing arose from the building behind them, blending with the commotion of the street, making conversation difficult. "I'm afraid we're somewhat muddled by all the activity," Charles shouted over the din.

"Sergeant Layton," a voice called out. They turned to see a man pushing a handcart loaded with trunks. "Your luggage, sir."

"Sergeant?" Isaac Wall asked. He pointed toward an unfinished construction site on a hilltop in the distance. "Are you here to help finish the fort?"

"No, sir," Charles replied. "Discharged . . . malaria."

"Ah . . . have you rooms?"

"None yet, sir."

"Follow us, will you Tom?" Isaac Wall called to the man with the cart, who nodded and leaned into his load to follow.

As they walked to the hotel, Charles remarked on the amount of new construction. Isaac Wall appeared eager to elaborate.

"Mark my words, Sergeant Layton, Monterey is the future of California. With statehood, which is just around the corner, this port will be the hub of the West. We've got the Mexican War, if you can call it that, all but won." As they neared the hotel he added, "Why, this town will double in size in the next six months, and keep right on doubling."

After a few days in the hotel, the Laytons found small but adequate lodgings, only just affordable given their savings. Charles had become a passable carpenter during his years with the artillery, and so found regular work.

The adobe and dirt frontier world of Monterey represented a drastic departure from Charlotte's comparatively genteel life in the East. She missed her mother, the warmth of friends, and a few nice things. Charles' work, however, provided for only the essentials. With the birth of a second son, William, a year after their coming to California, there never seemed to be money to put aside. But in 1849—two years after the Laytons' arrival in Monterey—the discovery of gold to the north promised to provide the perfect solution. In the fall of that year, with Isaac Wall's promise to watch after Charlotte and the boys, Charles traveled to the gold fields. As a military man accustomed to a degree of order and discipline, the pandemonium of the mining camps proved insufferable. After six months of frustration and depression, it became apparent that he was singularly unsuited to prospecting and Charles returned to Monterey no richer.

If gold hadn't been the answer for Charles, it had been less so for the Port of Monterey. Isaac Wall's predictions of growth and prominence proved woefully overestimated. San Francisco, with its convenient rivers and ready access to the fields, reaped the bumper crop of gold-driven expansion and prosperity. Enthusiasm for Monterey's future began to flag.

A gust of wind batted a tree branch against the house, again pulling Charlotte back from her musings. The reality of the sickbed and her husband's labored breathing rocked her as rudely as if the branch had hit her instead.

What would become of her family if Charles died? She had made friends in the community and she'd even come to cope with the isolated life they lived. Still, the thought of being alone and without means in such a place frightened her to her core.

Charles coughed violently. Pain, muted only slightly by delirium, rolled across his face and for a moment his eyes cleared and fixed on hers. Again, he ran his tongue over dry lips but no words came. Charlotte tried to read his eyes. What did they convey? Fear? Apology? Or was it simply regret?

She dipped her hand into the basin and let the water drip from her fingers onto his lips. His breathing steadied and Charlotte's thoughts once again escaped into the past, to a foggy August morning in 1853 and a tiny three-room apartment on Alvarado Street in Monterey.

A third son, Tom, now two years old, had been born in the spring of '51, a year after Charles' return from the gold fields. He had awakened in the wee hours and had at last fallen asleep again. Chad and Willy played in the parlor by the fire with strict orders for silence. In the kitchen, Charles and Charlotte talked quietly over coffee when a knock on the front door startled them. Charlotte ran to the door.

"Oh, good morning, Mr. Wall," she whispered, retreating to allow him to enter.

"I hope it's not too early to call," Isaac said, slipping off his coat and hanging it on a peg near the door.

"No. We've just gotten Tom back to sleep, though, so please keep your voice down."

Charlotte led the way into the small kitchen. Charles stood and the two men shook hands while Charlotte poured the coffee. Isaac sat at the table and wrapped his fingers around the steaming mug.

"What brings you by so early?" Charles asked.

"I haven't been sleeping well, Charles," Isaac said, taking a careful sip. "I'm taking losses and I've got a problem with Washington. Coffee's delicious, Ms. Layton."

"Problems with Congress?" Charles asked.

Isaac nodded. "They're pressing to finish construction of the lighthouses on the coast, and . . . well, there are problems."

Isaac took another sip of coffee, then wiped his mustache. "You know they've been building one at Point Pinos. Well, it's finished . . . all except for the lens, which is coming all the way from Paris, *France* of all places. Lord knows when it will get here. It could be years."

"They can't blame you for that," Charles said.

Isaac shook his head. "Pinos is only one of my problems. I'm responsible for all the lights in California, and Washington's put such goddamn tight deadlines on everything, excuse me ma'am. On top of it all, I got word yesterday that the ship carrying the supplies and building materials to finish the houses up north ran aground and sank, for Christ's sake.

Pardon me again, Mrs. Layton. Is there any more coffee?"

Isaac sighed and waited for his cup to be refilled before continuing. "Point Pinos is so remote I'm afraid it will be burned down or carted away if I don't keep a guard out there."

Tom shuffled into the kitchen rubbing his eyes. "What does all this have to do with us?" Charlotte asked, picking up the sleepy boy.

"Here's what I have in mind, Charles. I've got to travel north and see to those other lighthouses. I want you to stay out at Point Pinos. You all can live in the house until that lens gets here and we light the damn thing."

"And then what?" Charlotte asked bluntly. "What are we to do then?"

Isaac continued in a calmer tone. "I hear tell some of the east coast lighthouses are run pretty poorly; mostly by drunks and ne'er-do-wells. Washington's pressing for the best people to run the new ones out here. I've always trusted you, Charles, and I'd like to give you the job. It would be your new home, if you want it."

Charlotte spoke up, "With all due respect, Mr. Wall, we don't have two extra nickels to rub together. How are we expected to pay for a move like that, let alone the rent on a real house?"

Isaac shifted in his chair to face Charlotte. "I'll take care of getting you out there, and there won't be any rent; it comes with the job." Turning back to Charles, he said, "The principal keeper's pay is seven hundred a year."

Charles sat back in amazement. "I don't know the first thing about running a lighthouse."

"Nothing to it, Charles. Just stay sober and keep a schedule. Shouldn't be a problem for a man like you. Besides, it could be a while before it actually *is* a lighthouse. Will you do it?"

Charlotte was about to say that even though the offer was generous, she and Charles would have to discuss such a big decision. But before she could speak, her husband jumped up and grabbed Isaac's hand. "Of course we'll do it, Isaac! How can I ever thank you enough?"

The clock over the fireplace struck three times. Charles' breaths were even now, each ending with a soft sigh. Charlotte refreshed the cloth on his forehead and sprinkled a few more drops of water onto his parched lips. She stretched and walked to the window. The rain had subsided but the wind still whipped the trees and buffeted the house. Backlit by a full moon, thin high clouds raced by like legions of ghosts.

"Damn you, Isaac Wall," she heard herself say.

"No," she sighed, "I take that back. This is my fault." A chill ran through her and she lifted her shawl from the bed. "I should have stopped you,

Charles," she whispered. She pulled the shawl tightly about her and looked out into the night.

Isaac had sent three men and a wagon to help the Laytons make the move to Point Pinos. Charlotte, with Tom on her lap, sat between her husband and the driver as the latter snapped the reins and the wagon began to make its way along Alvarado Street. Chad and Willy waved cheerily from the back.

The road passed through pine forests and along rocky outcroppings as it wound its way generally westward. The wagon creaked and moaned as it rolled over tree roots, rocks and dried ridges caused by the passing of even heaver construction wagons during the building of the lighthouse. The riders lurched and bounced as the axles jarred over the rough terrain. Charlotte gave up trying to keep her hair in place; it took most of her strength to simply hang on to Tom. After nearly an hour of slow, grinding progress, she squeezed Charles' arm. "Do you think we could stop?"

"Pull up a minute," Charles said.

Charles hopped down and helped his wife and son to the ground. Charlotte stood stiffly, rubbing the small of her back, and contemplated the surrounding forest. The boys scrambled over the side of the wagon. The horses snorted and pawed. One shook its head, rattling the harness chains, and then emptied its bladder noisily onto the rocky ground.

"Chad, you watch your brothers and stay close to the wagon, do you hear me?"

"Yes ma'am," Chad said.

A relative silence fell over the trail. The wind breathed through the trees, jays complained from somewhere above them, and the distant roar of the surf seemed to come from all directions at once. Charlotte felt the heavy, pine-scented air press inward around her. "We're so far from everything, Charles. When you said it was three miles, I never dreamed it would take this long."

Charles looked quizzically at the driver, who was checking the team. "How much longer do you think?"

The driver looked back down the road they'd traveled, then turned and gazed ahead. "I'd say another hour-and-a-half, if we keep moving. Maybe two."

"My Lord, Charles," Charlotte said, climbing back into the wagon, "what have we agreed to do?"

After two more grueling hours they emerged from the pine forest and stopped at the edge of a clearing. At its center stood a boxy, whitewashed structure surrounded by stumps and lumber scraps, and dwarfed by the dense pine woodland around it.

"So vulnerable," Charlotte whispered.

"What, dear?"

"Nothing, Charles."

The simple lines, the pitched roof, the ordered arrangement of windows and doors all reminded her of her east coast homeland. But the little white house seemed totally alien to its surroundings. A thick tower topped with an empty metal framework protruded from the center of the roof, adding a surreal touch to the scene before her. As the wagon rolled on toward her new home, she regarded the open iron skeleton sitting gracelessly on top of the little house and shuddered.

The men took the crates and boxes down from the wagon, and Charlotte and the boys climbed up the four narrow steps that led to the front door. She opened it and stepped into a shallow foyer. The cold, stale air inside smelled of varnish and dust. A circular staircase faced the front door and wound its way steeply to the second floor. Chad started up it with Willy close behind. "Be careful boys," Charlotte cautioned. She picked up Tom and entered the room to her left. Two windows let light into the small space. She could see a fireplace built into the east wall and a small hallway to the south. The floorboards creaked under foot as she walked through the tiny room and down the short hallway behind the stairwell. A nearly identical space met her on the west side of the house. The room had no fireplace, but an iron stove, flanked by low cupboards, stood against the west wall. As cramped as their apartment in Monterey had been, Charlotte wondered if their few pieces of furniture could find space here.

She climbed the narrow stairs and found the boys in one of the upper rooms, looking out the window at the dunes.

"Will this be our room?" Chad asked excitedly.

"We'll see, dear."

The upstairs rooms were identical to those below except that only one window provided light to each, and only one of the rooms had a fireplace.

Charles' footsteps echoed on the wooden stairs. He joined his family at the window and gave his wife a hug. "We can make a good home here," he whispered. She said nothing, but squeezed Charles' arm and pulled his embrace tighter around her.

After the helpers had started back to Monterey, Charlotte finally managed to get the stubborn new stove to breathe properly and prepared a simple supper. When they'd eaten, Charles put the boys to bed. Charlotte cleaned up and organized her new kitchen, then joined her husband upstairs.

Throughout the evening, the wind continued to gust outside and Charlotte became increasingly on edge. Once Charles and the boys had fallen asleep, she rose, descended the narrow circular staircase and pulled a chair closer to the fireplace. The evening's fire had reduced to glowing coals, but a few small branches tossed on top gave it new life. The light from the small flames began to animate the room around her.

She carefully set an oil lamp on the corner of her writing table and sat, looking into the fire, recalling the words her mother had whispered at the train station when they left North Carolina for New York where they would board the ship to Monterey. "God go with you, dear," her mother had said. "He will protect you even at the other end of the world." Sitting by the meager fire, Charlotte felt very much as if she were indeed at the other end of the world.

She had written to her mother often during the five years since they'd landed in California. Though months would pass before a reply could be expected, writing to her mother comforted her. She pulled a sheet of paper from the drawer and dipped her quill.

> *My Dearest Mother,*
> *Charles, the boys and I are in our new home tonight, but I surely do not feel at home. As inadequate as our rooms in Monterey were for our growing family, there were, at most every hour, people around. This tiny house, which will be a lighthouse someday they say, stands alone between an impenetrable pine forest where bears and wild cats roam, and a rocky shoreline where the ocean pounds relentlessly. There are no other families nearby, nor even so much as an encampment of other human beings. I have yet been here a day, but I have never felt so alone. The house whines and rattles, and the ironwork on the roof moans in the wind, which I pray will abate soon. Though this hideous metal framework will someday enclose a light, its gaping ribs now impart to me the strongest impression of a cage. Charles seems happy here and the boys, of course, see this as a grand adventure, which I suppose it is, really, except that I do not know if this feeling of profound isolation will ever leave me.*

Charlotte put down the quill and pulled her robe tightly around her. Outside, the wind had calmed and a full moon cast its soft white light over the dunes.

Charlotte became aware of her reflection in the window, and of the slow, dull ticking of the clock. She added another log against the chill and poked the fire back to life. Charles rested quietly, though his brow remained dry and hot. The storm had passed and the sounds inside the little bedroom seemed exaggerated in the absence of the screaming wind and rain. Charles' wet breaths, the snapping of the fire, the creak of the wooden chair as she sat again by the bedside . . . all seemed vivid and discrete to Charlotte. She tucked the blanket around Charles and felt a slight tremor run through him.

How had it come to this?

Their lives had settled considerably since their move to Point Pinos. Thanks to Isaac, their financial worries had been eased and, once the children came to appreciate the dangers of life in such a primitive place, she had worried less over their safety and fallen into a routine of work. She had even come to look forward to her weekly journey into town for supplies. She began, in fact, to anticipate the time alone to enjoy the beauty and tranquility of the trip.

In late January of 1855, two years after they had come to live at Point Pinos, the long awaited lens arrived. Dozens of wooden crates were delivered and arranged on the ground in front of the house. One by one they were opened and their delicate contents carried to the lantern room where they were painstakingly assembled into an immense, faceted vessel that would encase and amplify the flame. Glaziers fitted the outer windows to the tower and wagonloads of whale oil were unloaded into the basement cistern.

A new routine had to be learned. Charles followed the workers diligently, absorbing the sense and the practice of operating this thing called a lighthouse. Charlotte kept the children from being trampled by teams and workmen or injured by the tools and equipment strewn about the area.

On the first night of February, Isaac Wall led a group of men to the house and made a small but significant ceremony of the Point Pinos light's first official night of operation. The piston mechanism that lifted the oil to the lantern room stuck, giving everyone a moment of unease, but a little grease and a nudge solved the problem and the oil-fed lamp leapt to life. Charles adjusted the flame, positioned it carefully within the lens and made the first official entry in the logbook.

To Charlotte, the new tasks of operating the light were at first an unwelcome interruption to established routine. Gradually though, as she helped Charles manage, each step became something of a ritual. She began to sense a new order and importance to her life, and the feeling grew stronger as friends and strangers she encountered in town would comment on the value of the light.

Even the children expressed a sense of ownership by willingly accepting the chores related to the light. Chad and William often competed for the most prestigious tasks, such as greasing the piston or helping with the whale oil deliveries.

The lighthouse had given their life purpose and direction. Now Charlotte faced the possibility that it all might come to an end. A wave of hopelessness coursed over her as she recalled the events that had brought her husband to what seemed certain to be his deathbed.

On a peaceful early November evening, the light had been lit, the children had been put to bed and Charlotte and Charles sat in front of the small fireplace when they heard the sound of hooves scuffing to a stop outside, followed by a quick knock at the door. John Keating, the Sheriff of Monterey, stood outside and Charles invited the wiry man with the busy white mustache into the warmth of the parlor. The sheriff removed his hat and nodded to Charlotte.

"I'm sorry to have to bring this awful news," the sheriff said, working the brim of his hat around and around in nervous hands. "Isaac Wall's been shot. He was ambushed about a half-day out of Gonzales. He's dead, Charles."

Charles recoiled at the news. He paced the small room and finally came to face the sheriff. "Why would anyone . . . do they know who did it?"

"They say it was Garcia and his people."

Charlotte drew a breath and held it. She knew that name. Anastacio Garcia was a notorious bandit with a violent reputation; a man feared by many.

"Do you think it was Garcia?" Charles asked.

"We're checking," the sheriff continued. "Once we're sure, and find out where he is, we'll go after him. I don't want a big show, just a few fellows. Will you ride with us, Charles?"

Charlotte watched emotion twitch across her husband's face. She knew the answer she wanted to hear, but she couldn't bring herself to interrupt, not with the blood so high in the room.

"Of course I'll ride with you, John. I can be ready in a minute."

"It won't be for a few days, Charles," the sheriff said.

"But the bastard could be in Mexico by then!"

"Charles, *please*," Charlotte said, laying a hand on his arm. "The boys and I need you here."

Her touch caused him to pause.

"My gut says he's not running, Charles. I've sent a man to watch his place up the Salinas River; I'd like to surprise him there." The sheriff put his hat on and tipped it to Charlotte. Then, looking back at Charles, "I'll understand if you decide to stay put."

"I owe everything to Isaac, Sheriff, but . . . I have to think of my wife and the boys."

Charlotte slowly exhaled but feared that wasn't the end of it. She'd heard his words, but the look on her husband's face told a different story.

When they were alone again, Charlotte voiced her fears. "Please don't go, Charles. Leave it to others. Stay."

"I said I wasn't going," Charles said angrily.

"I heard what you said, but I can see the truth in your face."

Charles looked away from his wife. "Isaac's gone." He sat heavily on the sofa. "Isaac's gone. My Lord."

"We *do* owe Isaac, Charles, and we have a good life here now because of him. But I won't let you risk your life!" She had nearly shouted. Charles looked up at her and she could see that he was being pulled in opposite directions. "You're not a gunfighter Charles, let the others go."

"How can I just sit here when Isaac's killer rides free?" The passion in his eyes frightened her. "I have to go," he went on. "There's simply nothing else to do . . . we owe Isaac everything we have, Charlotte. And besides, there'll be other men there. Sheriff Keating knows what he's doing. I'll be fine."

Charlotte turned away and stared into the fire. For two months she'd become increasingly certain that she was again with child. But she'd been wrong before and so hadn't told Charles of her suspicion. Would telling him now change his mind? "You owe your children a father, Charles," she whispered, "and not just the boys." She turned to face her husband and put her hands to her stomach. "I'm begging you not to do this."

Charles' eyes moved to his wife's hands. "What are you saying?"

"I'm pregnant, Charles. I'm almost certain of it."

"*Almost* certain?"

"It's been nearly two months since my last time."

He rose from the sofa. "That's happened before," he said softly. He came to her and put an arm around her shoulders. He put his hand over hers and pressed them to her belly. "I'll be fine," he whispered.

Charlotte wept as he moved her to the sofa and they sat opposite the warmth of the fireplace. He stroked her hair as she continued to cry. "Don't worry, dear," he said. "I'll be fine."

Four days later Sheriff Keating came with the news that Garcia was at his place some twelve miles up the Salinas River. Charlotte wept in the kitchen as the two men stood in the parlor and arranged to ride the next day. On the morning of November 15, 1855, just after midnight, Charles, Sheriff Keating, and seven other men rode away as the children slept and Charlotte prayed.

She'd lain awake until the dawn's light began to bring out detail in the room around her, then rose, dressed and made coffee in the quiet kitchen. She didn't tell the children where their father had gone when they joined her later in the morning.

An hour past sunrise, she climbed to the lantern room and extinguished the lamp, trimmed the wick, cleaned the chimney, and made her log entry. She threw herself into the work of the house. By dusk, she had nearly succeeded in driving her fears out of her mind. She'd lit the light and stood on the lantern room balcony when she spotted a lone rider come out of the trees and race across the dunes. At first glance she'd thought it might be Charles, and her spirits soared. As the rider approached, however, she could see that it was not. She didn't recognize the man who pulled his foaming mount to a stop at the front door of the lighthouse.

Charlotte hurried down the stairs, her heart racing, but as she reached for the front door latch a strange numbness enveloped her.

She met the rider at the threshold. "He's dead, isn't he," she said flatly.

"No ma'am, he ain't dead. He's shot, but it ain't serious. They got him in town; the doc's been with him."

She ran for her coat, shouting back to the man at the door. "If you'll saddle the bay, I'll be ready in a minute. *Chad!*"

"No need, ma'am," the rider said. "They'll be bringing him home; probably on their way now. Sheriff wanted me to come tell you . . . before."

Charlotte had no sense of how long she'd sat looking out at the dunes before she heard the sound of a wagon and several horsemen in the pitch-black yard. She stood in a daze as they carried Charles past her into the house, each man taking great care not to meet her eyes.

Sheriff Keating took Charlotte aside, his face a map of sadness. "It went bad, Mrs. Layton. I lost two men today, but I think we've saved your Charles. The doc says he should pull through—if he got all the lead out. He thinks he did."

Charlotte could find no words.

"C'mon boys," the sheriff called, "let's leave these people be."

She went to Charles and found him sitting up in the bed, his left shoulder heavily bandaged, a look of utter contrition on his face. "I'm sorry," he said. His voice sounded strong and he looked as if he might have simply fallen off the porch. She knelt beside the bed and took up his good hand, kissing his fingers.

"He got away," Charles sighed. "Slipped into the underbrush and we couldn't flush him. He won't get far, though."

The boys came into the room and surrounded their father, peering skeptically at his bandages, their eyes full of unspoken questions. That evening, they all ate supper in the small bedroom; a time filled with warmth and love. Charlotte thanked God for sparing her husband.

The next morning, however, Charles had awakened with a fever that grew quickly. The doctor had been called back, more medicine had been given, but by the second day it became clear that infection was ravaging Charles' body.

Chad's touch awakened her. The boy had been drawn into the room by the new aspect of his father's breathing. Charlotte looked at her husband's face, blanched and burning, eyes fully open, but unseeing. His chest rose and fell with gasps separated by gradually lengthening pauses. She held his hand tightly in hers and Chad stood behind her. William trudged in from the hall and the boys watched over their mother's shoulder. The interval between gasps extended, finally into one long rest that went on without interruption.

Charlotte and the boys remained near the bed until the sky began to brighten and Tom began to stir in the other room. She sent them to get dressed and to play outside until she called them in for breakfast.

Charlotte sat alone. She felt her stomach, certain now that a new life had started there. Should she have told Charles she was positive beyond doubt about the baby? Would that have kept him home? Questions too painful to consider. She wept uncontrollably.

When she'd spent herself in tears, she changed into a clean dress and tied up her hair. She stripped her husband's body and washed it, covering it with a fresh sheet. When this was done, she climbed to the lantern room and extinguished the light. All she wanted to do was crawl into herself and hold tightly to her memories of Charles and the life they'd come to love. But she knew that would have to wait.

After she'd fixed the boys' breakfast, Charlotte tried to organize her thoughts. Where would she go? How would she manage with the children? Too many questions. She poured a mug of coffee and walked out onto the north yard to look at the ocean and let her mind stretch out to sea in search of answers.

She stood lost in her thoughts, watching the surf pile towers of white foam against the rocks, and didn't hear the rider approach the house. Sheriff Keating walked up behind her, his horse's reins in one hand and his hat in the other.

"Your boy told me Charles passed this morning," he said gently.

Charlotte turned to face him. "He went peacefully, I suppose."

"I can't tell you how sorry I am about all this, Mrs. Layton."

"There's nothing you could have done. Isaac had such a pull over Charles."

The sheriff nodded.

"Charles did what he had to do, Sheriff. Now I need to figure out what I have to do."

The sheriff studied the brim of his hat for a moment, then looked up. "I wouldn't do anything just yet, Mrs. Layton," he said. "Mr. Wall's assistant, a man by the name of Johnson, has taken over at the port and my guess is he's not going to appoint a new keeper right away. He has his hands full at the moment."

Charlotte looked skeptically at the sheriff. "The children and I can stay for the time being then?"

"That'd be my guess. I'd stay put here until you hear from Johnson."

He put his hat carefully back on his head and mounted his horse. "Is there anything I can do to help out here, ma'am . . . with Charles?"

"I'd like to bury him here, Sheriff, if you don't think there would be a problem with me doing so. Could you possibly find a few men to help me?"

"No doubt, ma'am," the sheriff said, touching the brim of his hat. He turned his horse and rode off toward Monterey.

The first wagon arrived at ten o'clock the next morning. By noon, most of the population of Monterey had gathered around the lighthouse. The women brought food and the men unloaded tables and benches for eating. There was music and a quiet ceremony during which the minister read comforting passages from the Bible and spoke of Charles' strength and Charlotte's need for everyone's support. By five o'clock that evening, Charles had been put to rest in proper fashion beside a stand of pines on the lighthouse grounds.

As people began to start back to Monterey, a thin gentleman in a dark suit approached Charlotte as she sat on a rock watching the water.

"Mrs. Layton?"

Charlotte looked up.

"I'm C. R. Johnson. I've taken over the Port Collector's position."

"Yes, Mr. Johnson," Charlotte said. "I've heard your name. Please, sit."

Johnson looked at the rock but did not sit. "Your husband was very highly thought of in town, Mrs. Layton."

"Thank you, sir."

"His untimely death has put you in a bad situation."

"Yes, sir . . . it has."

"Would you object, Mrs. Layton, to staying on here until I can secure a suitable replacement for your husband?"

"Of course I'll stay," she said. "But I have a question, a rather indelicate one I know, but would I be paid? I have three children to care for, and there are accounts in town."

Johnson's eyes narrowed. He'd been so concerned about the affairs of the port that he hadn't completely thought out this matter of the lighthouse. He pushed his glasses up on his bony nose and thought about her question. He decided that he would probably be criticized more for leaving the lighthouse vacant or poorly attended than for agreeing to pay a woman to do the job temporarily.

"Of course, Mrs. Layton," he said finally. "Payments will continue on the same basis as that arranged for your husband until he can be properly replaced."

The days passed, and Charlotte and the boys slipped into yet another routine. Chad readily took to keeping the grounds, tending the horse, helping his mother fill the whale-oil reservoir and keeping his brothers out of trouble. Charlotte kept her grief and her fears at bay through an effort of will and hard work.

One evening, as she climbed into the lantern room, Charlotte became aware of a sense of anticipation. Reflecting a moment, she realized that, as the days had passed, she'd found it increasingly hard to wait for the sun to set. She looked forward to seeing the flame come to life, to feeling the thrill as the beam stretched away from the house.

This evening, a mist hung in the air and a halo of light surrounded her as the flame grew and steadied. She let it envelop her; it was as if, for a moment, she herself produced the light.

She descended the steps and paused at the boys' room; her earlier fears now gone, replaced by resolve. Since they'd arrived in Monterey, Isaac Wall—even in his death—had directed her life's path. But no longer. She needed the light now as much as it needed her and she wasn't going to give it up without a fight.

After securing the light the next morning, Charlotte hooked the bay up to the wagon and she and the boys made the journey into Monterey to see Mr. Johnson. When they arrived, she left the wagon by the dry goods store and gave Chad a list to be filled. "Watch your brothers," she told the boy. She found Johnson in the Custom House, pouring over Isaac's ledgers.

Charlotte's Light

Her long, sure steps resounded on the wooden planks as she crossed the expanse of floor. Despite Charlotte's noisy arrival, Johnson didn't look up. Clerks and others in the room paused in mid-conversation to watch the straight-backed blond woman, travel coat billowing behind her, breeze into the room to stand in front of the new Collector's desk.

"Mrs. Layton," Johnson said slowly, finally lifting his eyes from the book of numbers. "How nice to see you again."

Charlotte looked down at Johnson's pale skin, thin smile and small dark eyes. The pained expression on his face contradicted his genial words. "I've come to talk to you about the lighthouse," she said. "Have you located a replacement?"

Johnson put his glasses down and rubbed the bridge of his nose. "As a matter of fact, Mrs. Layton, I have not. Won't you sit down?" He motioned to a hard-backed wooden chair beside his desk.

"No thank you," Charlotte replied. "I have a proposition for you, Mr. Johnson."

The large room stood silent. Johnson's chair creaked loudly as he leaned back into it. "A proposition?"

"Yes sir, I propose to apply for the position. Charles and I ran the house together these past months, and I've been doing it alone since . . . since his death."

Johnson looked away and drummed his fingers on the open ledger for a long moment. Finally, he turned back to Charlotte. "I naturally assumed, Mrs. Layton, that you and the children would want to be moving on."

"We have nowhere to go, sir. And I submit to you that Mr. Wall intended us to stay."

"I can't speak to Mr. Wall's intentions, Mrs. Layton," Johnson said, puffing to his official posture. "But surely he meant for your *husband* to keep the light. It's a terrible responsibility for a woman to undertake, after all. A lighthouse is a very important thing, ma'am, and as far as I know, there are no women in that position."

Charlotte took a slow deep breath. Calmly, she said: "Mr. Johnson, sir, may I submit to you that I take the responsibility of the operation of the lighthouse every bit as fully as my husband did. And as for my being capable . . . I believe the facts speak for themselves."

Johnson's eyes grew large. He leaned forward slightly and dipped his chin to look at Charlotte over the rims of his glasses, as if he'd never had a woman speak to him so forcefully. "There's no cause to be upset, Mrs. Layton," he said. He rose and made a project of wiping his glasses with a handkerchief and replacing them on his hawk-like nose.

"I'll say no more on the matter. For the time being, you will continue to operate the light, and I will continue to seek a suitable replacement. Is that clear, Mrs. Layton?"

Charlotte lifted her chin slightly and said, "We will indeed speak of it again. Good day, sir." She turned and strode out of the building without a backward look.

Johnson sat heavily. He much preferred dealing with numbers.

As Charlotte walked back to the dry goods store she noticed a small knot of women walking toward her. Henrietta Abbott, a woman Charlotte knew as a force to be reckoned with, led the group.

"Good morning, Charlotte," Henrietta said. "We're all just so very sorry about Charles. Are you all right, way out there?"

"Thank you," Charlotte said. "The boys and I are fine. It's harder of course, without Charles, but we're managing."

"I saw you coming out of the Custom House," Henrietta said, and waited for Charlotte to fill in the details. Far be it from her, Henrietta thought, to pry.

Charlotte was hesitant to air her problems. Finally, looking into the anxious faces of the other women, she said, "I've been to speak with Mr. Johnson about my staying on at the lighthouse."

The news seemed to energize the women.

Henrietta said, "That's exactly what we were wanting to talk to you about. We want you to stay."

Charlotte looked into their smiling faces. "He told me it was out of the question." Gasps of disbelief came from the other ladies. "But he did say I could stay on until he finds a replacement."

"We'll just see about that!" Henrietta blurted.

"We should start a petition," said a voice from the back of the group. The others quickly embraced the idea, and looked expectantly at Henrietta.

Henrietta beamed, "That's *exactly* what we'll do." She gave Charlotte a quick hug and said, "Don't worry about a thing, dear. We'll show Mr. Johnson what the town wants."

Charlotte climbed onto the wagon and took up the reins. As she whistled to the bay to giddy-up, she glanced at the sun and decided they had plenty of time to make it back to the Point before the light would be needed.

A week passed, and then another. The work of the house—and the house itself—became part of Charlotte. With this feeling of oneness came a heightened dread that she and the children could be uprooted; that they might lose their home any day—a fear made double because Charlotte's pregnancy could no longer be denied. The uncertainty over her future, and that of her children, grew unbearable and she decided to go to Mr. Johnson again, this time to resolve the issue once and for all.

That night, sleep eluded her—partly due to her impending confrontation with Johnson, and partly because the wind, which had come up shortly after sunset, now howled through the trees and around the lantern room. She got up, slipped her shawl around her and climbed up to the light where she found the flame struggling and in danger of going out. She went quickly to awaken Chad and sent him to the basement to check the cistern and piston. Returning to the lantern room, she adjusted the flame as best she could. She looked out on the moonless night and knew that with the sea roughed by the wind, passage would be treacherous even with the light. Without it, there could easily be a wreck.

Chad ran to the top of the stairs. "There's a break in the line," he said breathlessly. "The piston's all the way down and there's oil all over the floor."

Charlotte removed the lid of the small can of oil kept in the lantern room and dipped a ladle, which she emptied into the oil reservoir. The wick sucked hungrily and the flame recovered.

"Stay here, Chad. When the flame starts to dip, do as you saw me do. But be careful not to get the ladle too close to the flame."

Chad's eyes went wide with fear and excitement. "Yes ma'am," he said. "I'll be careful. What are you going to do?"

Charlotte wished she knew. "I'm going to the basement. I'll call if I need help."

Charlotte scurried down the steps. Chad had lit the lamp on the wall near the door. In its unsteady light, Charlotte saw that a section of the line that carried the oil to the lamp had split.

She climbed up to the main floor and called to her son. Chad bounded down the stairs. "Is the reservoir full now?" she asked.

"Yes ma'am."

"Go and find a piece of oilcloth in the shed and bring it to me in the basement."

She fetched a hank of heavy twine from the kitchen and hurried back down the stairs. Chad joined her there with the oilcloth. "Cut the cloth into strips, Chad," she ordered, "I'll be right back." She climbed again to the lantern room and refilled the reservoir. Again she looked out into the night and this time she saw a ship's lamps, blinking as if riding a heavy swell.

Returning to the basement, Charlotte wrapped the strips of oilcloth around the split then wound and tied it tightly with twine. Together she and Chad worked the pulleys to draw up the heavy piston and pumped the column full. Oil and sweat covered them both as Charlotte released the piston. She inspected the repair and, while it still seeped some, it held.

They passed the night watching the flame and rechecking the piston. When the eastern horizon at last began to brighten, Charlotte let herself relax. She hugged her son and sent him back to bed.

Charlotte and the boys arrived in Monterey shortly after noon the next day. After arranging for more permanent repairs to the light, she left the boys with the women at the church and approached the Custom House just as Mr. Johnson came onto the boardwalk. She stopped him outside the building.

"Mr. Johnson," she called, drawing herself up to her full five-foot-five height, "I would speak to you, sir, about the lighthouse."

"I'm sorry, Mrs. Layton," Johnson said. "I've had a miserable morning dealing with irate merchants and I'm late for an important meeting. I can't speak to you now." He moved to walk around her, but she stepped to the side to block him.

"This matter must be resolved, Mr. Johnson," Charlotte said forcefully. "I will not give up the lighthouse."

Johnson stared at Charlotte. "You will not, you say?"

"That is correct, sir."

"I don't have time to discuss this. Now, please step aside, ma'am, and allow me to pass."

Charlotte noticed that a group of men standing nearby on the boardwalk had stopped their conversation and were watching. Johnson, noticing her attention drawn to something behind him, looked in the men's direction. They were burly and weathered, their heavy woolen clothing contrasting starkly with Johnson's tailored attire. The tallest, a man with leathery skin and an unruly beard, removed his cap and held it in front of him as he approached.

"Excuse me, ma'am," he said, then turned his attention to Johnson. "C.R., I couldn't help hearing that you were discussing the lighthouse."

Johnson's face lost its color and he swallowed. "Captain Wagner. Is there a problem?"

"On the contrary, C.R. It was a black night last night; heavy wind and swell. If it hadn't been for the Pinos light, we'd have found the rocks for sure. I've been up and down the eastern seaboard more times than I can count and I'll tell you this—if those eastern lights were as steady as Point Pinos, lives would be saved, sir."

The other men nodded in agreement. With great effort, Charlotte kept a smile from her face. The captain looked at Charlotte. "Am I to understand, ma'am, that you are the keeper of Point Pinos?"

Charlotte's legs began to shake beneath her skirts and she felt an urge to shout. "Yes, sir," she said, looking at Johnson, who seemed to be shrinking. "Indeed I am."

Johnson cleared his throat noisily. "Captain Wagner . . ." he paused and rubbed his chin. "This is Charlotte Layton. She is the . . . ah, temporary keeper of Point Pinos."

The captain leaned forward and held out his hand to Charlotte. "James Wagner, ma'am, captain of the *Harristown*. It's a pleasure to meet you. Thank you for your good work."

Charlotte shook the callused hand. "You're welcome, sir," she answered, no longer concealing her smile.

"I'd strongly recommend that you make her permanent," the captain said, lightly tapping Johnson's chest with a weathered index finger.

To Charlotte, it seemed as if Johnson swelled briefly, then deflated. "Well, I . . . I mean . . . it's great a responsibility and I . . . we . . . the port . . ."

"Nonsense, C.R.," the captain interrupted. "You'd be a fool to get rid of a good lighthouse keeper."

Johnson's face had taken on the color of the dusty boardwalk and his left eyelid had begun to blink involuntarily. Before he could form a reply, the seamen tipped their caps to Charlotte and continued down the walkway.

Charlotte placed her hands on her hips and, still smiling, faced Johnson squarely. "Well?" she asked. Without a word, he brushed roughly past her and strode toward the hotel where he hoped to salvage his delayed lunch.

Seated at his usual corner table, Johnson ordered a steak and a beer. The words of a veteran captain regarding the operation of the port carried weight, and Johnson felt that weight now.

His food arrived and he'd just picked up his silverware when a shadow fell across his table. He looked up to see the substantial figure of Henrietta Abbott looming over him. She held in her hands a large envelope, which she placed flamboyantly in the center of his table. She folded her arms and smiled down at him.

"And what is this?" he asked wearily, shaking out his napkin and placing it over his lap.

"It's what the people of Monterey want," she said. "It's a petition to keep Charlotte Layton on at the lighthouse. Nearly everyone in town has signed it. You can see for yourself."

Johnson sighed, slid the papers from the envelope and spread them on the table. As he did so, he noticed a man he knew to be with the *Monterey Sentinel* seated across the room, writing feverishly in a notebook. Johnson read quickly through the petition. ". . . family relying on her . . . husband's appointment a reward for long and faithful service to his country . . . fully capable and worthy . . ." He fanned through the pages of signatures and sighed again. He glanced back to the reporter who sat, pencil poised, eyes fixed upon him.

"I'll take this under advisement," he said, smiling weakly up at Henrietta.

"As well you should, sir," Henrietta replied. She wheeled and left the dining room, giving an almost imperceptible nod to the reporter as she passed.

Johnson looked down at his cooling steak and headless beer and found he had no appetite left at all.

Near the middle of December 1855, Charlotte watched a buggy approach the lighthouse along the edge of the pine trees that skirted the dunes. When it drew closer she saw that it was C. R. Johnson himself who held the reins.

She invited him into her parlor and gestured for him to sit on the sofa. She pulled the wooden rocker from near the hearth and sat facing him. The boys rushed into the room but stopped short when they saw Johnson. Tom and William ran up the stairs on their mother's orders. Chad moved out of the doorway, but stayed close to listen.

An awkward silence filled the parlor. Johnson fidgeted on the sofa and at several points appeared ready to speak but did not. Finally Charlotte could stand it no longer. "Why have you come?"

Johnson started at the sound of Charlotte's voice, and cleared his throat. "I assume it is still your desire to stay on here at the lighthouse, Mrs. Layton. Am I correct?"

Charlotte nodded; Johnson returned the nod.

"Then I should say that action has been taken to allow that to happen."

Charlotte's heart raced. She willed her hands to stay still in her lap and her breathing to remain slow. "This is indeed good news, Mr. Johnson. What made you change your mind?"

"I still think it a great risk, but . . ." he paused to clean his glasses with his handkerchief. "But several conditions favor your staying." He drew an envelope from his coat pocket and passed it to Charlotte. "A petition was circulated by the women in town. There is strong support for you on the part of the townspeople. You have many friends here, Mrs. Layton."

Charlotte read the petition and glanced through the pages of signatures. Henrietta was indeed a force to be reckoned with, she thought, as a smile began to turn the corner of her mouth.

Johnson cleared his throat a second time. "The other voice of support has come from the sea captains themselves."

"Captain Wagner?" Charlotte asked.

"Not *just* Captain Wagner, Mrs. Layton. Not a day passes but what at least one captain stands before my desk with an account of how this light has saved their vessel and crew. If I were to believe them all, our entire merchant and military fleets would be piled against the rocks were it not for you."

Charlotte laughed out loud. "Oh, I beg your pardon, sir," she said. But she continued to giggle, from sheer relief and because of the look on Johnson's face

Johnson stood. "The official recommendation is on its way to Washington." He walked to the door and opened it. "There is one other thing."

"Yes?"

"I've also recommended that your income be raised to a thousand a year."

Charlotte's hands came to her face. "A thousand?"

"You'll need the money," Johnson said, his eyes dropping to the fullness beneath her apron. "There'll soon be another mouth to feed, and prices are always going up."

"Why, Mr. Johnson," Charlotte said. "You have a heart after all, sir."

Though she had thought the man incapable of the expression, there was no mistaking it—C.R. Johnson smiled.

After supper that evening, Charlotte and the boys sat on a pine log in the yard and watched dusk creep over the point. In the still evening air, the colors deepened and the sea birds slowly made their way toward their nightspots.

"Ma?" Chad said, looking strangely at his mother. "You've been awful quiet. I thought you'd be happy with what Mr. Johnson said."

She looked at her oldest son and briefly saw her husband's face. "Oh, I *am* happy, dear. As a matter of fact, I can't remember when I've felt so at peace."

William stopped tossing small stones and leaned into his mother's side. "I miss Pa."

The sunset was electrifying the western horizon and spreading quickly across the sky to the east. Charlotte looked up into the darkening sky. "We all do, Willy," she said. Then she suddenly gasped and jumped up. "Oh, my Lord," she cried as she ran inside.

"What's wrong, Mom?" Chad called out, following his mother up the steps into the kitchen. William and Tom stood behind their brother; small frowns on their faces.

Charlotte leaned over the outer railing of the lantern room and called down to the boys on the stoop below. "Nothing's wrong children," she laughed. "I almost forgot to light my light!"

Author's Note:

The main characters and the circumstances depicted herein are based on historical fact. Charles Layton did indeed come with his family to Monterey in 1847. The then Superintendent of Lights for California and Collector for the Port of Monterey, Isaac Wall, appointed him the first Principal Keeper of the Point Pinos Lighthouse in 1854. That Charles Layton died in November 1855, several days after suffering a gunshot wound sustained while attempting to apprehend Isaac Wall's alleged murderer, is well documented.

For the purposes of this work of fiction, some details have been created to help put a human face on the events that led to Charlotte Layton becoming the first woman lighthouse keeper on the West Coast. One fact seems undisputed, however. In the words of a Proclamation issued in 2001, Charlotte Layton maintained the Point Pinos Lighthouse from November 1855 until the year 1860, "... honorably and to the general satisfaction of all."

My sincere thanks go to the Monterey Public Library—specifically Archivist Dennis Copeland, to the Colton Hall Museum, to the Pacific Grove Heritage Society, to the docents at the Point Pinos Light and to Jerry McCaffery for his wonderfully written and beautifully illustrated history of the Point Pinos Light, Lighthouse, *published in 2001.*

Charlotte's Light

Gods and Ghosts
by Chris Kemp

*"*uicide is the coward's way out."

Another lie, the writer thought as he looked out his second story Pacific Grove window. *Nothing easy about it at all.*

Down toward Lovers Point the sparkling blue of the Monterey Bay twinkled through a porous barricade of bushy trees. Sun-splashed tile roofs and stucco eaves poked through squatter, fuller greenery in the foreground. The scene struck the writer as illusory—a painting or a diorama perhaps—beautiful enough to lift his spirits, if he would have had spirits to lift.

Little matter. After days of contemplation, the writer had come upon a suicide strategy with which he could "live".

It had not been easy.

Pistol shot to the head? A slight misaim guaranteed catastrophic pain.

Leap from a tall building? The thought of hurtling face first into concrete liquefied his legs.

Turning on the ignition and letting the engine run? The writer had a carport, not a garage.

As for slitting his wrists . . . the discipline required bewildered him. And who wanted to sit in tepid water as one's life seeped out?

A drug overdose, however . . . that was something else. Riding out on a magic carpet of pills—that might work. The writer supposed a vomit-choked finale was a bad end, but at least the prospects of under dosage seemed slim.

The Jim Beam chaser would be for show.

Gods and Ghosts

He shambled past boxes and broken furniture to his bedroom, making his way through his apartment's desolate, dusty living room. The damp Peninsula chill seeped through his threadbare pajamas, and he considered flicking on the thermostat, but he'd forgotten what day the utility company's pink notice had come and didn't want to be disappointed.

Stepping calf deep into a mound of dirty clothes wafting male stench, he fell onto his misshapen mattress. The throbbing resonance of his doomed life echoed through his head: episodic misfortune with a consistency of design, possessing its own perverse aesthetic.

Oblivion, my destination.

He turned on his side, reaching out to caress the orange pill bottle on his TV tray nightstand, instead knocking it over. *Damned tremors!*

The container snakerattled under his bed. He mustered an effort to raise himself, but an invisible force pushed down on his chest. The writer didn't resist. *Why fight it?* He lay back on his rag pile bed, head deep in the bag of crumbling foam he called his pillow. Moments passed, and it occurred to him that he was being pulled down, quicksand-like, into a pool of Spanish moss. The sensation gradually changed to that of something being pulled *out* of him. Painful. Akin to a body part rupturing.

Afterward, came the dark.

The writer awoke in dusky light. *I must have slept the entire day.* With disaffected curiosity, he watched the walls flicker and dance with spectral illumination.

Am I dreaming?

A stirring in the corner. *Someone's in the room.*

Tympani of pain drummed in his temples, expunging the tincture of vitality he had left, yet an obligation to confront the Uninvited nudged him. He collected himself into a raised position and saw, in the watery light of a solitary candle, a woman's strange yet familiar figure.

She stared back at him from the front edge of his weathered ottoman; sleek and young, tense and vigilant, a bird poised to fly. Inky bangs framed glowing opalescent features. The liquid darkness of her eyes pierced him; the small mouth set tightly, one small but full lip against the other, a roundish aspect disguised her cheekbones. This last lent her face a doll-like quality, a quality currently occluded—unfortunately, the writer thought—by iron-jawed determination.

"How did you get in?" he asked. It felt as if sand had been poured down his throat.

"Your front door was open," she replied in a contralto frayed with agitation.

"Ah, the open door," the writer responded ruefully, "a Pacific Grove tradition." He struggled to sit, and noted a black canvas bag in her lap. It bore an abstract symbol, a hieroglyph he'd seen somewhere before. *Where?*

Indeed, the effluvia of the recognizable emanated from the woman but remained penumbral. "Are you a social worker?" he inquired, but knew the answer before her sharp laugh of denial. The jewelry, the finely manicured nails, and the ankle-length flowered skirt exhibited too much flair.

But that was not how he knew.

"You look worse than I expected!" she asserted, somewhat cheekily, the writer thought.

He cleared his throat. "Since you're here, I could use some Jim Beam, but I'll settle for wine."

The visitor emitted a barely audible growl. She scanned the corners of the room, looked up at the ceiling. "This place reeks. A real dump."

"Do I know you?" Her aspect pleased him, not necessarily viscerally, but in a more abstract way—for a stranger she seemed . . . conceptually sound.

"You don't recognize me." The flat statement implied he was deficient. "Should I?"

She walked to the foot of the bed, stalked by her own fluttering shadow. The writer eased back into his pillow, fighting waves of nausea.

She crossed her arms, shook her head. "This is a drag. Are you telling me you don't recognize your so-called 'favorite' character?"

Understanding crackled through the writer. His leg twitched. He knew.

"Ariel?"

She pursed her lips in a mockery of a smile. "Duh."

What does one make of an individual who claims to be a fictional character released into the world of her author? The writer truculently denied the possibility. In quick succession he considered the figure a lunatic, an obsessive reader, a ghost, a hallucination.

He chose the latter, and hesitated not one second telling it so.

"You're not real," he said. "You're a movie projecting against a screen in my own theatre of dementia. I suppose it was bound to happen."

The figure eyed the puddle on the carpet and then she—it—exhaled in exasperation. "You really know how to make someone feel wanted."

"What did you expect?" the writer asked, dismayed at how easy it was to converse with the illusion. "And why are you here?"

"An irresistible urge pulled me here. I've felt it for weeks. You think *you're* going crazy . . . I can't help but feel—know—you created me."

"Yes, well, humph!" The writer snorted, pinching the end of his nose. "How did you find me?"

"Your, ugh . . . place drew me like a magnet. Plus this isn't my first time in Pacific Grove, thanks to you. You *do* remember, don't you?"

Yes, the writer recalled vaguely, there *was* a story . . .

He pondered how he had not recognized the figure more immediately. The way she looked, the way she moved . . .

"I was thinking maybe I can talk you out of what you're going to do," she added.

The writer took a moment to consider this before speaking. "If not a delusion, you certainly are deluded," he remonstrated, attaching a round of sandpapery retching onto the end of the statement. "I'm sunk. Nothing's going to change that. It's the one thing I'm sure of."

"Fine then, believe what you want. All I know is if you go, I go. And don't ask me how I know, I just do. I'd prefer for that not to happen." She left the room.

The writer wiped his soiled mouth with the back of his sleeve. How to assess the situation? He'd written a few stories with Ariel in them, but only one had seen the light of day in a small print run. Additional shadings of her appearance, speech and mannerism had never made it onto the page, yet here they were, displayed before him, including a stubborn streak he'd only begun to formulate for her. Could an imaginative figment appear so complete? Or might *only* an imaginative figment appear so complete?

The visitor re-appeared with a glass of water, taking care not to step into the pond of evacuation next to the bed.

"Take these," she said, extending the glass and handing him a couple of aspirins. "You need to get it together."

The writer palmed the medicine. Unsure of what was happening, he figured to play along a little longer. The little orange cylinder under the bed wasn't going anywhere.

When he first lost his job, the writer and his wife had charged forward with great optimism, rationalizing the setback as an "at last" opportunity to spend more time writing fiction. He did, and got better at it; but the advantages paled in comparison to good paying work. As the job market imploded and his age became a factor, he found it increasingly difficult to make ends meet. It became impossible to deny that his life was lining up and pointing to an inexorable, dreadful end. When his wife left, it figured.

The creativity leached out of him. The dream ended and his continuing, but largely unseen cast of characters evaporated into oblivion when it did.

Except for this alleged "Ariel". He looked skeptically at the presence as he touched the bitter-tasting aspirin to his tongue, and raised the glass to his mouth carelessly, spilling some of the cold liquid across his front. She lightly stepped forward to grab the glass out of his hand, then backed up as if he were radioactive.

"When did you shower last?" she frowned.

"Seems a small concern compared to the life and death issues of which we've been speaking."

"Yeah? Well, it's a start."

He took a plastic ashtray from the nightstand and tossed it at her. It bounced off of her chest and she cried out, a small sound, more of shock than of pain. She wasted no time tossing the remaining water in his face.

"Testing your corporeality," he said, wiping the liquid out of his eyes.

"Do what you want, I'm still drawing you a bath." She walked away.

"Alcohol first?" he called out feebly, but no answer came, save the rumble of the pipes and the resonant drum of water against tub. Deep, hollow sounds of friction signaled that she was scrubbing its buildup of gray green residue.

"Ugh," he heard through the wall.

Would Ariel clean a tub? He hadn't thought about her with that kind of detail. Every fact he had created for her life would fit on a sheet of paper, maybe two: second oldest girl in a mystical family—with no supernatural powers of her own; mother a strong-willed practitioner of the mystic arts; empowered siblings that were troublesome and troublemaking; covering up for her relatives all the time, lest the household be found out. It seemed so superficial compared to the entity busying itself in the bathroom.

My mind's filling in the blanks.

She was back, holding a wet towel. Dark patches showed on her skirt and sleeves, which were dusted with a powdery trail of cleanser.

"If I catch something from that . . . that . . . culture in there . . ." she admonished with a melodramatic touch that tired the writer.

"You can't get sick if you're not real," he taunted, realizing how acclimated to isolation he had become. "Despite your wild claim, I am not God. Why, I've got much more in common with a ghost, don't you think?" He held out two spidery arms.

She plopped the towel atop the mess on the floor and maneuvered under his outstretched arms, pulling him up from under the armpits. She demonstrated surprising strength for someone so slim, but then these days he added up to little more than a husk. He yowled when halfway to standing and made an attempt to step forward under his own power. Ariel refused to release him completely, marching him to the tub with one hand on his shoulder and the other on the small of his back.

Steam billowed out of the cramped, mildewed bathroom, the antiseptic tartness in the air nipping at his nose. He stepped inside reluctantly and contemplated the rapidly filling tub.

"I'll take it from here," the writer advised.

"No, you won't. Here." She held out a thimble-sized glass receptacle of dark green fluid and unscrewed the cap with her thumb and forefinger.

"What's that?" The writer asked skeptically.

"A little something from my purse. Tana leaf extract. For your nasty breath."

He downed it, if for no other reason than to quell her harping, but it burned his raw gums. He flung the container down, bouncing it off worn linoleum. "You're trying to poison me!"

"I'm not, and if I were, that would be a problem for you because . . .?"

She had him there. Without speaking she gave him a slight push in the direction of the tub and began stripping the rank bedclothes off of him.

"You certainly have a mind of your own," he said.

"I shouldn't be touching you without rubber gloves," came the retort.

"Risk is relative for a figment of the imagination."

She threatened to "lobster him"—to drop him into the steaming water—so he held his tongue and eased himself in. Soon she was scrubbing him, hard enough that he feared his skin might shred.

He did his best not to feel humiliated. Though the rubbing and the soapy lather marginally invigorated him, he couldn't shake the image of lying in a convalescent home or hospice center. The residents there likely craved death, too.

"Turn over on your stomach," Ariel directed. The writer obeyed. The rough washcloth moved in long vertical strokes up and down his spine.

"Is there anything I can say or do that will convince you to not snuff it?" she asked. "I could appeal to your fatherly pride. I turned out pretty good, didn't I? I deserve a chance."

"Can't fight the inevitable," he snorted. "Besides, there's no cause and effect here."

"That's what you think." She wrung out the cloth. "See if you can handle drying yourself, okay?" The droplets hit the base of his spine like molten bullets followed by the balled up washcloth, which sat like a lump of clay between his shoulder blades.

But he obliged her request—more a command, really—and felt no shame at his shriveled nakedness when she reappeared holding underwear, a cotton sweat suit, tennis shoes and socks. "One good thing about someone who wears the same clothes over and over," she quipped, "there's always plenty of clean ones. Here."

He made no move to accept the offering. "Are you leaving now?"

"No way. We've just started. Next step, wholesome nourishment."

He groaned.

"Put 'em on!" she yelled, thrusting the garments toward him. He took them without further protest, remaining resolute that he would play along only for a while. He dressed, finding that the sweats swam over him, so he used the excess of one sleeve to wipe the steamy bathroom mirror in order to get a better look at himself.

He certainly looked ready for death. His lazy eye floated like a zombie's. A stringy tangle encroached upon his skull. The week-old growth on his face looked diseased. Creases of loose, slightly yellowed flesh hung off his cheeks as if tempting him to tear them away.

"Looking good," Ariel carped from the doorway. She had put on his black Alan Ginsburg sweatshirt with "Don't Hide the Madness" scripted across the back.

He pushed past her into the bedroom, now filled with the smoky odor of extinguished candle, and stared at the bed, semi-visible in the bathroom's residue of light. "Looking for these?" he heard from behind. He turned. With an elfin grin she held up his pills as if they were a prize catch. The sliver of heart he had left fell to the floor like a leaden weight.

"I–I need them to sleep."

"Then you'll get one at bedtime. Let's go," she said, slipping the pills into her skirt pocket. She pulled out a white knit cap and matching muffler from her bag. "You going to be warm enough?" she asked.

The writer sat down on the foot of the bed. Rage kindled within him, but without sufficient fuel, died quickly. "You aren't going to throw those away are you?"

"If I do, I lose my leverage and you'll *never* do what I say. You've got to keep an eye on me now, right?"

The writer weathered a round of phlegm-filled coughs.

"I'll take that as a 'yes'." She pulled the cap down over her head and wrapped the muffler around her long, graceful neck.

"Where are we going?" he asked.

"Stop whining. You'll find out when we get there. It'll give you something to look forward to. Take it from me, nothing fights the feeling of impending doom like a change of routine. C'mon, let's go."

They navigated down two flights of stairs to the tree-shrouded breezeway that ran between the twin buildings of the writer's apartment complex, ivy sloping gently upward on the right. He recalled how his wife and he had considered their move from their plush condo a temporary downsize, necessary only until finances got better.

That was twelve years ago.

The path opened up onto Lighthouse Avenue. Ariel took a left turn toward town, escorting the writer by the arm to ensure his steps fell in with hers. Though a wide street, this section—between Seventeen Mile Drive and the small downtown district—filled easily with a darkness that overmatched its widely spaced streetlights and dim window squares. This was partly the result of thick juniper-cushioned medians out of which towering pine trees rose. They helped obscure the cross-street view and muffled the sound of passing vehicles. The scene would have been eerie, had "America's Last Hometown" been less benign.

The jade aftermath of the sun hung like a canopy over the town a quarter mile away. The writer had lost track of time, but guessed it to be shortly after dusk. "Slow down," he admonished, huffing to catch up, head still pounding.

"No harm in elevating your heart rate a little," his escort replied.

"What is it you expect to do?" he barked in frustration. "Push against the thrust of Predestiny in the hope of shifting its course? Change my fortune so we can live happily ever after? How heroic! Right out of a book!"

The string of laughter to follow was meant to be rough and roaring, but ended before it started. Ariel stopped and squeezed his bicep so tight the bone felt like it might powder. "I don't want to hear it, okay?" She pulled him close to her face. "You can make a difference in how this turns out!" She said it loud enough to catch the attention of a silver-maned couple walking arm-in-arm toward them, led by a leashed dog that looked like a shaggy rat. Their pet frenetically zigzagging before them, the pair regarded the writer and his companion for a few seconds too many.

"We're wasting time," Ariel whispered, and they began to stroll again, past small apartment complexes and pedestrian houses with million-dollar price tags. By the time they were greeted by the bright bombast of the Shell service station—a commercial beacon out of sync with the town's calculated understatement—the length of the walk had set the writer's teeth on edge.

Ariel took a deep breath. "Just smell that food. M-m-m."

"Overpriced," the writer growled, although he silently admitted the bouquet of grilled, spiced seafood would have been enticing under other circumstances.

They weaved toward the closely packed one- and two-story buildings spectrally illuminated by pinkish sodium lights. Ariel cut across the mostly empty avenue, pulling the writer along. They angled through the slanted row of parked cars and hulking SUVs that divided downtown

Lighthouse into lanes.

On the opposite side of the street they passed imposing old Victorians, a smattering of restaurants, and at least one clean, well-lighted place for liquor, slowing when they came to a dark brick building. Out front a covey of frayed-looking men, scattered among plastic chairs and tables, smoked cigarettes and drank coffee out of paper cups. A mongrel busily licked food remnants off a plate on the ground. A bike flaking paint leaned against a wall.

"Juice and Java?" the writer asked. In happier times he'd spent most mornings here satisfying his fix for coffee, scones and *The San Francisco Chronicle.* "My stomach can't handle caffeine."

"There's more to this place than coffee, and you know it," she said, then pointed to an ancient but well-kept VW microbus a few spaces away. "Oh, by the way, that's my car. Does it look like a figment of your imagination?"

He knew the cream-colored van with a certainty deeper than recognition and it disoriented him. He must have shown it, because she added, "That's what I thought. Anyway, hold on a second, I left my cell phone in the glove compartment."

The pounding in his head, which had begun to dull, started again in earnest. He regarded the cafe's tall windowed doors—it had been a stately bank in an earlier incarnation—until he became aware of a sibilation in his ears, like bacon frying. From nowhere, a short man with steel wool hair set free as if by an electrical charge moved in front of him, flickering like a malfunctioning hologram. The writer blinked. The flickering stopped.

One good hallucination deserves another.

"Hey, bro'!" Saliva soaked the man's salutation. Milky droplets dotted the corners of his mouth, which opened and closed amidst a patina of lines and peeling skin. Grime covered his checkered flannel shirt and, for a brief second, the figure dissolved into zigzagging bands like a scrambled video feed—

Huh?!

—before returning sharply into focus.

"Now ain't you lookin' all sure of yourself!" the man said.

The writer shook his head and, wishing to avoid a confrontation, took two steps toward the entrance of the coffee shop. The stranger stepped into his path. The gathering took no particular notice.

"Be that way!" the weathered creature exclaimed, sounding hurt. "Cats like you think they know it all. They don't know squat."

The man's fetid breath assailed the writer, who stepped back and noticed a snowy outline made the stranger contrast against his dimly lit background.

"Who the hell are you?" the writer asked.

"You can call me Tricky. I ride tandem with the random, my man, tandem with the random."

He reached out to touch the writer with a fingerless glove, a languid movement that looked almost sensual to the writer, who froze. The tip of the lowlife's tongue showed through his partly open lips as if he were in intense concentration.

The bizarre sizzling in the writer's ears grew louder.

"Hey, leave him alone!"

With a movement too quick for the writer to see, Ariel grabbed the vagrant's hand and bent it back at the wrist. He yelped in pain, losing his footing and crashing into a plastic chair. She let go.

The sound in the writer's head stopped.

Those in proximity chortled. The dog whimpered but kept on licking. The writer, speechless, looked at Ariel's victim who had lost his otherworldly aura. He expected to see an angry scowl, but instead saw a calm façade and a cool smile.

"Birds of a feather, flock together, yes they do. Seein' is believin'."

The writer might have asked him what he meant, but Ariel broke in with, "Keep your filthy hands off him!"

The writer felt Ariel's hand on his back, pushing him forward for the second time this evening. The itinerant stepped aside with a surprising grace.

With much effort, the writer pulled on one of the door's cylindrical brass handles. He made a small gesture with his free arm motioning her inside. After she passed through, he looked over his shoulder. The rims of the stranger's eyes burned like hot coals, mania pervading his toothy smile. "She's really something," he said. "Headstrong. Won't never see it comin'."

The writer kept moving. He wondered if the addle-brained dispatch was meant to be a threat, and shivered slightly before the restaurant lavished an envelope of warmth over him, one containing the aroma of coffee beans, cinnamon and amalgamated sweetness.

"He still bugging you?" Ariel asked him. "I'll go back out there and—"

"Let's go over there," the writer interrupted, knees feeling like red hot spheres, back beginning to clench. He pointed to an arrangement of sofas and plush chairs set before a large fireplace, the nexus of the cafe's floor space, centered among an even spread of traditional restaurant tables and chairs, all deserted.

Close to closing time.

They sat beside each other on the biggest couch. He couldn't help but comment. "That was quite a display out there."

She looked down and tried to stifle a giggle like a self-conscious ado-lescent might. "I guess I've got a bit of the warrior-woman in me," she offered, "or however it is you poured yourself into me. When it comes to taking things into my own hands, I get kind of compulsive."

"So you're saying I predisposed you to kick the ass of the Poor and Downtrodden?"

Her eyes danced with bright annoyance. "If you think that guy's downtrodden, you're a bigger ass than you've been acting."

"Did you notice something strange about him?" the writer asked hopefully.

She laughed. "You mean other than your every day street variety of derangement?"

"No, not exactly," he said. Her answer disappointed him. He *was* losing it.

"You're a victim waiting to happen," she continued. "I've seen plenty of hyenas like that waiting to take advantage of someone they think defenseless."

"Easy to fancy yourself noble, I suppose, in a world where everything is so cut-and-dried."

A blast of steam from the cappuccino machine suspended conversa-tion for a few seconds.

"Hey, you're the guy saying that the end is near and there's nothing nobody can do about it. Besides, there's nothing noble about me humili-ating myself to get your stubborn ass to change your mind."

The writer savored the potential irony in his companion's earlier com-ment. *If she were a fictional character, she, more than anyone, should under-stand the immutability of fate.* But he kept his mouth shut and surveyed his homey surroundings. They marinated in a golden ambiance, bursting with green flourishes spilling over from suspended planters.

His companion gave notice that she was ready to order.

"I didn't ask for food," the writer argued. "I didn't ask for anything but my pills. I'll regurgitate what you buy me, anyway."

"Fine!" she said, tossing her cap on the pile of discarded newspapers covering the long table before them. "It'll be a thrill to watch!" She stormed off between a pair of square pillars, part of the colonnade that ran down the establishment's center. The disheveled mop on her hatless head appeared out of character. She tried to smooth it as she looked up at the menu board suspended above the counter.

The writer wondered when it had gotten so hot. The urge to lie down on the couch flooded him, but he fought it. Behind the counter a young man with a shaved head and tattoos crawling up his neck tentatively stepped into sight.

The writer glanced at the front doors. "Tricky" peered through the glass, his figure once again frosted, looking backlit in the dull entryway light. The writer's eyes caught his and the figure disappeared. *Had* the derelict made a veiled threat aimed at his companion?

A blender whirred. Before long Ariel brought something over that looked like a strawberry milkshake. She placed the pink beverage in front of him next to a pile of napkins, keeping a tall tan coffee drink for herself.

"I can't drink sweet stuff," he protested.

"It's a fruit smoothie with a shot of wheat grass. It'll give you nutrients and coat your stomach."

She returned to the counter. The writer looked dubiously at the creamy concoction and took a sip. An explosion of tartness swelled through his tongue. It felt good as it rolled down his irritated throat and landed gently in his stomach. He took a little more.

Ariel returned, setting one bowl of steamed vegetables and brown rice down before him, keeping another for herself. "Should be bland enough for your ruin of a digestive system."

The watcher in the glass popped into view as he had popped out, crouching slightly, face and palms pressed against the door.

"You have an admirer," the writer informed Ariel.

She glanced over briefly. "He's lucky he doesn't have a broken wrist."

"And he doesn't look odd to you?"

She frowned at him. "What do you mean?"

"Nothing. Nothing."

She began to attack her food. By contrast, the writer picked at his, downing a smaller head of broccoli and a slice of carrot. "If I agree to do my best to ingest these tasteless victuals, can I have my pills back?"

"No." She swallowed the word along with her food. The rapidity with which she vacuumed down her meal amused him, but he found the smacking of her lips less pleasing.

A set of traits left to their own devices mutates in unimagined ways.

"Get serious," he said under his breath.

Bowl dishwasher clean, she took a napkin and swept it across her lips with gusto.

"Finished?" he asked. "Then let's get it over with. Pills, please!"

He decided he wasn't feeling so well. Droplets of sweat formed on his brow. A slight tremor wracked him. He dropped his spoon. It clanged on the table.

Ariel stood and stretched her long legs. "Moan and groan all you want but we're going to talk about what you've got going for you."

When had it gotten so hard to breathe?

Lines rutted her forehead as she blathered on. He only caught parts of it.

"... lot to live for. .."

"... make your own reality. .."

"... explore the mystery . . ."

The blood rushing to his brain was acid. "Tired . . ." he moaned, right before he spilled out of his sofa onto the floor, knocking against the table, catapulting a glass onto the floor where it crashed into pieces.

"What happened!" the barista cried from behind the counter. He looked squeamish and kept his distance.

Ariel knelt and patted the writer's cheek lightly. "Hey, are you okay?" she asked.

"Get . . . me . . . out of here." He dragged himself to an upright, seated position.

"Do you want to go to the ER?"

The writer coughed raggedly. "No! Take me home!"

"I have money . . . I—"

"Take me home!"

The counterperson tugged at his gleaming earring. "Lady, ya gotta do something," he whined. "I should be closing now."

Ariel glowered at him. "Thanks for the concern." She pulled out her phone and watched it for a second or two. "I can't get a signal in here. Watch him."

Bag in tow, she threw herself through the doors. The men loitering about scattered. The idler with whom she'd had the altercation slid-shuffled toward the bicycle leaning against the building, and hopped on.

The twin doors flew open again before Ariel had a chance to punch in "911". The writer appeared in the passageway, one hand on each door, wash hanging on the line. *"No ambulance!"* he gasped. "I won't ask for the pills, *just get me home!"*

"You need medical help—"

"I'll discuss it later, but for now, please—*take me home!"*

He delivered the last part with enough decibels that the indigents stepped back as he stepped forward and released the cafe doors. The sound of them locking from inside was analogous to the cock of a shotgun.

The writer spotted the bicyclist wearing that same halo and damnable grin. "Bet she learns something tonight," the indigent snickered. "Tricky-trick-trickmeister says 'word up'." He bumped down off the curb one wheel at a time, nearly falling before he wobbled away like a circus bear on fire.

"Look, I feel better," the writer said to Ariel, and he meant it until he lost his balance and folded up in one of the empty chairs.

"Not convincing," Ariel replied, but respected his wishes—a bit of a shock to him. She dashed to the van door and threw it open. "I reserve the right to take you to the hospital," she said coming back to get him. "But we'll try it your way first. Get in."

"Thanks." A pause. "Ariel."

There. I called her by name. And though doing so qualified as a significant concession from his standpoint, Ariel gave no indication she even noticed as she crouched down next to the clutch of plastic furniture and slid her arm around him.

"What's wrong with him?" a toothless man in a greasy hunter's cap asked.

"He's feeling a little less than himself," Ariel replied, looking up into his pudgy red face.

"He looks like he's drunk," a tall angular man in a beaten parka commented. "I should know," he added in a hoarse horn of a voice, smiling, black gums exposed as if they validated his standing.

"Sh-h-h," Ariel hushed, and in that moment the writer wondered what the harm would be in taking her at face value, because he was rapidly coming to the conclusion that she wouldn't make things worse.

And if she happened to be who she claimed to be, might his life have meaning and salvation be opened to him? Might he have accomplished something good? Something special? Thrown destiny a curve?

No. But she was growing on him. Somewhat. Maybe. The lightness of her touch felt soothing.

"Maybe you aren't such a . . ." he started, before a fit of rheumy coughing overcame him.

Her eyes glinted. "Such a what?"

He thought twice, but rasped it out anyway. "Such a bitch."

"Been called worse. Let's get you in the van."

"I can get in myself, thank you." But when he staggered to his feet, they almost slipped out from under him. Only the table and Ariel prevented him from falling backward and smashing the back of his head against the brick.

With reluctance, he let her escort him but insisted on stepping up into the passenger seat himself. With some effort he managed to twist himself into a semi-comfortable position, one in which a minimum of aches and pains racked his body.

Her vehicle was spartan, at best. A few inner trim panels had been removed or lost, revealing once-hidden metal bands, yellowish shreds of insulation and colorful strands of electrical wire. Other than these blemishes, the interior looked immaculate, though it reeked of spilled coffee and amaretto creamer. Didn't seem logical—you'd expect stickiness and spotting—but come to think of it, he may have written it that way.

Ariel climbed in and slammed her door. Outside, the band of street people waved to him. He returned the wave to the forlorn-looking group and melancholy welled up in him.

If I went on, that's what I'd be.

The aged transport lurched into reverse; its engine's grind and sputter underscoring the writer's misery. He knew he'd have to put his pain aside, however, for any sign of infirmity might give his driver the excuse to steamroll him through the hospital's front doors. She'd babble to the medical staff about his unstable emotional state and he'd find himself on suicide watch. That would never do, so he steeled himself for a vigorous walk up the stairs to his apartment.

Ariel drove with one hand on the wheel and a knuckle jammed in her mouth, which she removed long enough to shout over the vehicle's considerable cabin noise, "I'm going against my better judgment taking you home." The vehicle shook violently and he wondered how it held together.

Poorly conceived writing?

They rolled up to the feebly lit, semi-obscured apartment. The writer managed to slide out briskly. His feet crunched in redwood chips. Small pools of light from ground level lanterns guided him around calf high shrubs, helping him maintain his balance—barely.

He seized the moment to demonstrate he could walk through the breezeway without aid, and for the most part, he did. In fact, he felt modestly recharged, moving rapidly enough that he almost missed the bike some damn kid must've dumped at the foot of their communal mailboxes. He avoided tumbling over it.

Ariel caught up with him at the bottom of the Astroturf-covered stairwell leading up to his residence.

"It's not a race," she said, taking his arm lightly.

A fluorescent bulb threw a watery light onto the ground floor landing. He regarded the scene with momentary hesitancy. Without warning, the innocuous act of walking up to his apartment became fraught with significance. Something in his subconscious tugged down on him, heightening his cognizance of gravity's pull—as if the decision he made now would have implications that stretched beyond anything he could imagine.

Ridiculous! I'm simply returning to my residence to buy time until I can take fate into my own hands.

"Having second thoughts?" Ariel's voice sounded hopeful. The writer could have none of that.

"My God woman, you were just chiding me for moving too swiftly."

He took a deep breath and began his ascent with a surefootedness both pleasing and unexpected, but slowed when he reached the landing between the first and second stories—slowed, that is, and halted, not out of pain or dizziness, but out of deference to the thickening darkness collecting in the half-flight ascending to the topmost floor.

The lamp above his apartment no longer functioned.

The resulting murkiness commanded caution, and there was something else—a sliver of dark on dark, lining the perimeter of the doorway.

Had he left the door ajar a second time this day?

A blur whizzed by his ankles, upsetting his balance, but he managed to brace himself on the wall beside him.

"What was that?" Ariel said, breath catching between words.

"Neighbor's cat. Damned nuisance, it is."

He looked at her. Her mouth and jaw were set, resolute. "Are you okay?" he asked.

"Are you?"

Steadying himself, he climbed more steps, leaned forward and squinted. The door was, indeed, open several inches. He continued, figuring he had little to lose.

"Sure that's smart?" Ariel asked.

"What—think there's something in there?" he laughed cynically. "It can't be any more disturbing than the last entity that wandered in."

As soon as he said it, the hissing in his ears he'd experienced earlier started up again. He tried to disregard it, and tapped open the door with his hand. What he saw inside gave him pause. Even considering the drawn shades (another action he could not remember having engaged in) and the absence of strong light where he stood, the writer fancied the blackness inside the apartment as too absolute. It caused him to consider whether the dimensions of his apartment had greatly expanded.

Something in the dense darkness caught his eye. Floating, dancing, a spectral firefly at an undetermined point between foreground and background.

Disappeared.

Sizzling in his ears more intense, as if someone had turned up the flame.

Appeared again, closer, a discus-sized nebula of energy, of a still undetermined size and distance.

Disappeared.

A turbine's whine.

Back again, closer, the writer identified the aspect of a human torso.

Disappeared.

A roaring wind.

And then, flicked on like a light, a human figure stood in the doorway, looking at the writer.

"Tricky".

The checks of the invader's jacket undulated so rapidly that they blurred into a sheen alive with movement. The noise inside the writer's head had grown intense enough to send dull waves of pain through his entire body. The dead light in the stoop began to flicker wildly, causing the scene to play out in the strange syncopated motion of sequential, yet discrete, strobed images.

"You and her got me all feelin' like an imp," it said, "so don't misquote me and say I am a pimp." The vision passed by the writer before he had a chance to move, crowding Ariel, who eased back against the wall. It was hard to tell precisely what the invader was doing, as the confluence of his appearance and the flittering light caused him to fade in and out of view. To the writer it looked as if he might envelop her. Her bag dropped to the floor, and the writer realized that the pills could be his, if he but exploited the situation.

He made no move. The increments of light came so close together now that they blurred, transforming the surroundings into an oxymoron of blinding gray. The scene might as well have been playing out in silence, so loud had the din grown in his ears.

Was this it? Was he dying?

The entwined pair seemed to be struggling—the attacker appeared as a glimmering outline, when he could be seen at all—and the writer swore he saw a spasm rock Ariel.

As poorly as he felt, he had to do something. But just as he moved forward, the assailant disengaged himself. The fighter in Ariel exploited the opportunity and came forward, crouching, arms extended. The writer felt a force push him backwards and energy began to pulsate though his body and mind, discharging the vague thought: *He backed into me on purpose.* Then he and the interloper tumbled down the stairs, entangled.

The writer didn't feel the backbreaking pain or any of it; all sensation was cancelled. He again supposed he could be dying, or (again) perhaps losing his mind, but the point was moot. When the two of them reached the bottom of the stairs, they rolled right through the railing of the first landing. United, they plunged to the ground.

"A radioactive isotope decays into a stable daughter product." He didn't know what it meant, but it was his second to last thought.

His last was listening to Tricky's voice. "You were right all along, brother. Sort of."

Ariel looked on in horror as the tangled mass of arms and legs crashed through the railing, which must have been more rotten than it looked.

"My God!" she cried. As there had been no sickening thud, she held out hope that they had landed in something soft and life-preserving.

She dashed down the lightless stairwell to the landing with the broken rail, the sour breath of the deranged man still in her nostrils, the rough feel of his calloused hands still burning where they had clenched her throat. She'd never managed to get a good look at him in the darkened foyer, but she had seen enough of him for this lifetime and a few others.

Carefully, she eased up to the edge so that she didn't plunge over the broken barricade, too. What she saw set her back on her heels.

The man in the checkered jacket was nowhere in sight, but the man she had come to visit sprawled in plain view on the pavement, head crooked at an unnatural angle in a dark spreading puddle. His chest heaved. Ariel could hear his fits and gasps plainly; so, too, his words.

"Keep an open mind . . ." he managed between broken breaths, ". . . because it might just turn out to be the other way around."

With that, he and the expanding pool of blood faded before the startled woman's eyes, disappearing into a formless but eternal prison called memory. Ariel braced herself and waited her turn, but her turn never came.

A refugee from an imploded reality, Ariel found herself walking the gentle knolls of El Carmelo Cemetery at the end of Lighthouse Avenue, reeling in the aftermath of events recently completed. Unseen surf susurrued from somewhere behind the flashing beacon of the Point Pinos Lighthouse. The full moon outlined rustling cypress trees and century-old headstones in an icy blue, giving the objects a cast that looked delicate enough to shatter.

She'd held it together pretty well for the first few minutes after the "incident", until she got behind the wheel and started driving away from the apartments. With her need for vigilance receding, a combination of loss, regret and self-doubt had rushed in, hitting her squarely enough in those first few minutes that she almost lost command of the van. She supposed she should be grateful she'd been wrong—that he was gone and she was still here—but right now she felt more miserable than she could remember. *She'd been so sure.*

Then she spotted the cemetery. Graveyards had always calmed her, and here was a new one to explore. Perfect. As if scripted. She wasted no time parking, getting out and here she was, without forethought, moving deeper into the cemetery, settling herself, contemplating whether she should have left town altogether in case questions about the occurrence arose.

She doubted they would. In those first few minutes after his . . . death, she'd been operating on pure instinct, surveying "his" apartment, finding no evidence that anyone lived there. The expected gathering of concerned neighbors and neighborhood busybodies never materialized, a lucky break.

She figured the three of them must have made quite a ruckus—especially with the breaking wood and all—but maybe her mind had exaggerated the extent of the disruption. At this point, she was ready to believe anything. Anyway, if she did get questioned, she had little doubt she could handle it with a well-conceived lie. After all she was the . . .

Second oldest girl in a mystical family—with no supernatural powers of her own; mother a strong-willed practitioner of the mystic arts; empowered siblings that were troublesome and troublemaking; covering up for her relatives all the time, lest the household be found out.

Her destiny to fulfill.

She took long purposeful strides into the heart of the grounds, stepping deftly around the unseen slumberers, their eternal quiet a balm for her wounds. Up ahead a group of especially imposing headstones approached, some leaning, some crumbling, hemmed in by filigreed iron fencing, shin high. Here stood some of the oldest stones, with names like "M. P. Shiel" and "Fitz-James O'Brien". Gazing at them gave her the resolve to consider it:

God is dead and I'm still here.

What does one make of an individual who insists she's been haunted by a presence—be he god or ghost—who holds the key to her creation?

An emptiness so profound as to elude description—dappled with the poison certainty that she must have lost her mind for several months—proved too much for her to sustain. Cylinders of fluid memory emptied out of her, as if overturned by an invisible hand.

She's been lying on the cemetery grass for some time, in something akin to an alpha state. It's after midnight and the wind's kicking up, tossing dead leaves across the fenced-in patch beside her where they pile up in corners.

She knows she came to this town on a whim to investigate a presence, and is certain she felt something in that empty apartment, but the recollection is elusive. One might think that she would return to refresh her memory, but she feels relieved that the compulsion, the absolute craving to come calling upon—the "shadowy whatever"—is gone, a terrible obsession from which she's been released. She's not about to screw around with that. No, she's much relieved, and there's something else, too—a slight euphoria, as if she's taken in an oxygen rich mix of gases. Intoxicating, but energizing. Alive.

Alive, even though the strange life she leads with her family makes her feel like she's a storybook character going through prescribed motions.

The thought makes her a little homesick, so she decides to start back to the van and begin the long ride home to Palo Pacifica. A gust hits her, prompting her to pull the sweatshirt tightly around her, the sweatshirt she's never seen before in her life.

The boughs of the trees are really swaying now, but in between their groans, up there somewhere in the branches, her ears catch the rasp of a cough. And over near the mausoleum, out of the corner of her eye, she thinks she spots a twinkle of happenstance.

Finding Anna

by Byron Merritt

What is now proved was only once imagin'd.
—*William Blake,* The Marriage of Heaven and Hell

Anna Wooley shivered, feeling the coolness of the large room on her exposed arms and back. Lying face down on the sterile white table at Community Hospital of the Monterey Peninsula, she waited patiently for the focused radiation beam to administer a strong dosage to her small ten-year-old body.

"Okay," the technician's voice crackled through a speaker over her head, "we're going to start now. Ready, Anna?"

"Ready as ever," she said, almost cheerily, her voice bouncing against the distant walls.

"That's my girl," her dad's familiar voice echoed through the speaker.

Anna imagined seeing the red, dagger-like rays shooting out of the machine above her and spreading across her shoulder blades, the location of the bone cancer. When it was over, a smiling young candy striper came in, placed a blue gown over Anna's body, and helped her sit up.

She smiled and slipped her arms into the gown. ""Thanks, Fran."

"No prob. Wanna get dressed now?"

"No, I think I'll run around in this dorky hospital outfit the rest of the day," Anna said, rolling her eyes.

"Your choice, punk," Fran chuckled and tied up the back of the gown.

Finding Anna

Anna slid off the table and walked toward the control room that monitored patients' radiation dosages. She peeked around the corner of the open doorway and saw her father—a modestly built man with a small paunch-like gut, stocky arms, and rumpled clothing—talking somberly with Dr. Hildegard, a tall man with thinning brown hair and thick glasses who looked like he needed a few Big Macs to fill him out. They obviously hadn't noticed she was standing there, so she stood still, listening.

". . . hard to say," Dr. Hildegard was saying. "It could be a type of osteosarcoma that doesn't respond to radiation and chemo, or that her body isn't responding, period. I mean, she hasn't lost any of her hair and had only minor radiation burning on her back at some pretty high rad settings."

My final chemo and radiation treatment. Now what? Anna wondered.

"Then what the hell has this past year been about?" her father asked, his thick gray-black hair looking like an angry bird's nest.

"I know it's hard on you, Carl," Dr. Hildegard said. "I mean, losing your wife to it is one thing, and now you've gotta deal with it in your only daughter. But we've been tracking genetic links to cancers for years, and I've never seen anything like this. The shoulder nodules look identical to Barb's."

"I know!" Carl said, sliding into a chair. "This . . . this *disease* is eating her up." He placed his hands over his face and rubbed his bloodshot eyes. "What about surgery?"

Dr. Hildegard shook his head. "It's too late for that. We knew that four months ago."

Carl sighed and stood up. "So we keep going on like this 'til . . ."

Just then he saw Anna standing in the doorway and his face flushed. "Anna! Honey! Um, everything okay, Peanut?"

Anna nodded. "Better than everything in here," she snorted and headed to the changing room.

Anna and Carl crawled into their yellow 1970 International Scout with the dented, rusty, right front fender and drove, loud exhaust rumbling, down Highway 1 toward their Carmel home. It was usually a short trip, but today Carl moved along at a snail's pace, several cars skirting around them with short bursts from their horns.

Anna watched a semi-truck blaze by. Her dad seemed not to notice.

"You okay?" she asked him.

"Me? I should be asking *you*!"

Stands of pine trees stood like dark phantoms amidst the fog that lined both sides of the four-lane road, until the vehicle exited onto Carpenter Street where the sun forced itself through the haze. Their car leaned left as they swung down the divot-riddled road, between modest but finely manicured homes practically hidden amongst scrub brush and more trees.

"I'm fine, Dad. Don't worry about me." Anna smiled.

Carl ruffled her golden hair and admired how it shone in the afternoon sunlight.

Just like Barb's. Too much like her, he thought.

They finally arrived at their Third Avenue home, an old, blue two-story cottage with white shutters and a lone eucalyptus tree in the front yard. Anna's older brother, Bruce, came out of the house as the Scout thrummed up the drive. A couple of his teenage buddies piled out behind him wearing Carmel High letterman's jackets, backpacks slung over their muscular shoulders. They dispersed before Carl had gotten out of the Scout, leaving Bruce standing alone with his hands in his pockets near the front door.

"Hey, butthead!" Anna spouted as she walked past her brother, punching him in the ribs. The front door squeaked as she pushed it open.

"How was the extra sun today, Squirt?" Bruce asked, moving his heavy dark bangs out of his deep-set brown eyes, the spitting image of a younger Carl.

"S'okay," she called back to him from just inside the threshold. "Feels like a bad burn's starting on my back. It'll peel like the others," she added matter-of-factly, looking back to see her father approaching. He didn't look happy.

"Anna," Carl said, "could you give me and your brother a moment alone, please?"

Anna looked at her father, then at Bruce, and clicked her tongue, as if scolding them both. She stepped inside the house and pushed the heavy wood door shut.

Bruce stared at the ground and kicked an imaginary piece of dirt.

"How many times do we have to go over this?" Carl asked.

"What?" Bruce mumbled, not looking up from the walkway.

"You know damn well what! I'm at work 'til three and then I have to pick up your sister at three-fifteen to get her to her appointment by three-thirty on Sundays. I hate working the weekends, but that's the way it's gotta be until we . . ." His voice trailed off and he put his hand on his son's shoulder. "Look, I rely on you to keep things normal around here. And that includes keeping your friends from raiding the fridge and messing up the furniture."

"We were just studying." Bruce kicked at another piece of dirt.

Carl leaned forward and sniffed at his son's jacket. "Studying plants that can be smoked, huh?" He lifted his son's chin and looked him in the eye. "Please don't do this to me. I can't—"

"You know I wouldn't smoke that stuff!" Bruce yelled, drawing away. "Some of the guys do, but I don't! And don't give me that 'don't do this to me' thing again. What about me? I've gotta go to school, do football practice four times a week, then come home and keep everything neat and clean. What about time for me!"

Bruce brushed by Carl and hurried to the garage, manually lifting the broken automatic door. He grabbed his surfboard and wetsuit.

"Where do you think you're going?" Carl asked.

"I'm outta here. Gonna catch a few waves."

"And how are you going to get there?" Carl asked, jangling the keys to the Scout in front of Bruce's face.

"Come on, Dad! Dinner's not 'til five and the surf is supposed to be riotous today."

Carl sighed. *What the hell.* "Okay, but if I smell anything on you other than seawater when you come back, you'll be grounded for a year."

Bruce snatched the keys from his father and ran to the Scout, throwing his surfing gear into the back, then sliding himself behind the wheel. He spun the rear tires while backing out of the driveway and vanished in a haze of exhaust.

Carl walked into the house smiling, wondering if he had been so different from his son when he was that age. *Probably not.* Then he heard a distant yet familiar sound that caused him to stop and take notice.

Retching.

It came from the downstairs bathroom. He raced through the house and banged against a hallway table, causing a mountain of hospital bills to tumble onto the floor. Cursing the mess, Carl left the papers where they were and rushed to the bathroom. Anna sat on the brown linoleum floor with her head over the toilet bowl. He came up from behind, moved her hair out of her face, and grabbed a washcloth, quickly dampening it with cool water from the faucet. He started rubbing her neck and face, but a minute later, she pushed him away, her shoulders trembling, her hands gripping the toilet lid. A series of little *plunks* issued into the water.

"You okay, Peanut?" Carl asked. A wave of acid crept up his throat, causing his eyes to water.

Anna turned and smiled. "I'm barfingly wonderful, Dad."

Terrence Von Goodfeather puffed on a fat cigar at the Big Sur Filling Station as he topped off the tank of his silver and black 1957 Harley

Davidson XL Sportster. No one noticed the dangerous maneuver, even with the white hot cigar tip only a few feet away from the gas port of his perfectly buffed fuel tank.

Terrence's appearance matched that of the Harley perfectly—big, covered in black, and adorned with shiny fixtures—a contrast to the flowing wave of silky golden hair that spilled down from his head and across his broad shoulders to frame his colorless face; a white sheet upon which nothing seemed to be written.

After filling up, Terry got on the Harley and stomped down on the kick starter. The bike sputtered but didn't start. He repeated the action with the same result. "Start, you piece of junk!" He kicked down as hard as he could, and this time the bike coughed to life, releasing a belch of blue smoke. "Now that's my baby," he cooed, and stroked the chrome handlebars. He pulled up the kick stand and revved the engine, grinning at its roar.

Without paying for the gas, or the snacks he'd retrieved from the store, Terry *blat-blat-blatted* down Highway 1 on his noisy chariot, drawn toward Carmel for a special task, one that he'd performed before, a specialty he'd come to loathe.

"Bad way to take them out of their world," Terry muttered around the smoldering plug in his mouth. "And who has to do all the dirty work? Me!"

Terry felt the urge to continue north on the scenic snake-like highway, so he twisted the accelerator and the Harley lurched ahead, spewing more blue and black smoke. He enjoyed the ride until a disquieting thought grabbed him:

If Destiny and Fate find out what I'm trying to do, they'll make me pay.

He looked apprehensively behind him as the scenery whipped by.

"Come on, Dad!" Bruce complained while sitting at the kitchen table with his father. "It's only forty dollars and if I win, it'll make us a hundred and fifty buckaroos!"

Buckaroos? Barb used that word all the time, Carl thought. He glanced over at Anna on the living room sofa where she sat reading an *X-Men* comic book.

She stared back and shrugged. "He just wants to impress Paula Frazier," she smirked.

"Shut up, twerp," Bruce said half-heartedly. "She probably won't even be there."

Carl frowned. "Why haven't I heard of this Carmel teen surfing competition before?"

"Because it's the first time they've ever held it. It's so cool. Only locals can apply and you can't be a pro. Amateurs only." Bruce looked so excited Carl thought he might jump out of his skin.

"Amateurs like you?" Carl asked.

"And Paula Frazier," Anna added, thumbing through her comic book.

Bruce wadded up a paper napkin and shot it at Anna, then gazed pleadingly at his father. "I haven't asked for anything in a long time because . . . well . . . you know why. But this I really want."

Carl scratched his head. "I don't know. Forty bucks is forty bucks and we can't afford to throw money around. You know that."

"I thought about that, too," Bruce replied with a brief smile that faded to seriousness. "Um . . . Mike Tomlinson, down at Jib's Surf Shop, offered me a part-time job after school. The contest isn't for another month and if I start working right away, I'll have more than enough money. And I can start adding to our funds here at home, too."

"After school? What about football practice?" Carl asked.

"Dad, when's the last time I played in a game?"

"Well—"

"Two months!" Bruce exclaimed. "I'm a second stringer with no hopes for a scholarship. But surfing's cool, and Mr. Tomlinson says I have a lot of talent. He thinks I could do pretty good if I get started soon."

"You want to give up football, just like that?" Carl said, snapping his fingers.

The wadded up napkin reappeared, bouncing off Bruce's chest. Anna scowled at her brother, then looked down to read some more.

"It built a strong sense of commitment in me when I played," Carl continued, taking the napkin away from Bruce before he could fire it back at Anna. "It's also where I met . . ."

As if in response to his dad's softening voice, Bruce lowered his own. "I know. Mom saw you on the field and from there it's history. But I'm never *on* the field. How's some gorgeous babe going to notice me squatting on the bench?"

"It's not all about girls."

"But it *is* about doing what feels right. Right?"

Carl turned to Anna as she flipped another page. "What do you think, Peanut?"

She let the book fall onto her lap, her face aglow from the table-side lamp. "Sounds cool to me. Plus he might get lucky and get some from Paula."

Bruce bolted out of his chair and headed for his sister in mock anger. Anna squealed and dropped her book on the floor before climbing over the back of the sofa and hurrying toward her bedroom, all the while shouting, "It's all about Paula! It's all about Paula!"

Terry sat on his Harley in the city of Carmel sniffing the cool, crisp air. He didn't like seeing the trees lose their foliage—autumn's dying leaves on spindly branches reminded him too much of his job—but he knew he needed to find his quarry before they started going through "The Change".

He'd parked his bike next to Devendorf Park, near the ancient fire department building, and sniffed at meandering passers-by, young and old, but mostly old, dressed in expensive clothes and floppy hats. They shuffled obliviously around him and into the street as cars slammed on their brakes or swerved to avoid hitting them.

"Idiots."

Terry pulled out a shiny silver flask and took a swig of special sweet liquor, wincing as it went down. He burped and placed the flask back into one of two roughly-worn silver-studded saddlebags decorating the rear of his bike. From the other saddlebag, Terry pulled out a small silver rod with a tiny star on one end and sniffed at it.

A middle-aged couple strode by, the husband bitching about something the wife had just purchased at an antiques store. Terry inhaled the air around them as they passed.

Nothing.

He placed the wand back in its bag.

Jammed up in Carmel as he had been for the past couple of days, he was growing irritable at not being able to find this latest earthborn. With each passing moment, it became increasingly obvious that Fate and Destiny had drawn him here. They used him like a piece of expensive clothing, putting him on occasionally and then, more often than not, throwing him back into the proverbial closet, to be forgotten until they needed his services again.

Not this time. This time will be different. No more digging!

He looked at his callused hands and clenched his fists, but then his head shot up, nostrils flaring.

The odor!

It came from somewhere to his left, toward the ocean. After several curses and just as many kicks, the motorcycle rumbled to life and he rolled down Ocean Avenue.

"I will," he whispered to himself while darting cautious glances at his surroundings. "I will find this one before she goes to ground."

Carl finally relented, allowing Bruce to drop football and begin working at the surf shop. He didn't feel completely comfortable with his son working already—the boy hadn't even finished school—but he could tell Bruce truly wanted the job. Even so, Carl made him promise that his grades would stay as they were—or improve—otherwise his days at the surf shop would be history. Bruce happily agreed to the terms.

Today, though, was Wednesday—a non-workday for Bruce—so he'd decided to go to Carmel Beach and try out some of the wave action on a new loaner board that he'd gotten from Mike, the shop's owner.

Fortunately for Anna, she was feeling better, having finished her last round of chemotherapy over two weeks ago, which meant she could go out as her energy level allowed.

Unfortunately for Bruce, she always wanted to tag along with him! And being at Carmel Beach with girls his own age, he didn't want to be seen with his younger sister in tow.

"Go sit over there," Bruce ordered as they trudged down the steeply sloped white sand that led to the deep blue water.

"No," Anna said, crossing her arms defiantly. "I want to play in the water."

Bruce stopped and turned to her, a stiff expression on his face. "Look! I promised Dad I'd bring you down here today, but that's it! You do as I say or you're not coming along next time. Understand?"

"You don't scare me, you know," Anna said. She nodded at the people scattered along the beach. "There's lots of pretty girls here today. You don't want me to get upset. I might start throwing up again."

Bruce sighed. "Alright. Go in the water if you want. Just don't go deeper than your ankles. Okay?"

"Deal." Anna rushed the small breakers on the beach, squealing and splashing as she waded in up to her waist. Bruce laughed. *She's so happy all the time, even though she's sick,* he thought.

Paula Frazier was nowhere to be seen, but Bruce decided to walk along the beach anyway. He spotted a few surfers he knew, bobbing on the water about 30 yards out, and decided to join them. He skidded into the water on his board and paddled out, glancing back occasionally to see Anna splashing and playing with another girl about her age.

Bruce rode a half dozen small waves, nothing too exciting, casually shooting glimpses at the beach to see what Anna was up to. The first few times he'd checked on her, she'd been playing in the small waves. But now he saw her sitting on the sand and staring, not at the water, but up the hill at a lofty cypress tree.

"Hey!" he yelled toward her. He couldn't see her face, but he somehow sensed something was off. An image of the priest that had given last rites to his mother came to him and he swallowed hard.

He lay stomach-down on his surfboard and started making his way to shore.

"Hey!" he yelled again when he got closer. "Anna!" A couple of his surfer buddies pulled up beside his surfboard, asking if everything was okay.

"Yeah, fine," he said to them uncomfortably, and paddled away.

Bruce stumbled out of the water and onto the shore, brushing wet sand off his body. When he brought his eyes back up, Anna was kneeling in the sand, chin on chest. It looked as if she were sleeping on her knees. Then she toppled face-first onto the beach and lay still.

Bruce threw his board down and sprinted up the rising slope. When he got to Anna, he rolled her over. Even though the beach was active and lively with locals and tourists, no one seemed to notice the two of them. Anna's lips were blue, but she was breathing. Bruce was about to call for help when his sister's eyes popped open.

"Don't let him take me," she whimpered.

"Who?" Bruce asked.

Anna's eyes motioned over her head, toward the tree she'd been facing. Bruce scanned the area, but saw only the tall cypress, its branches lightly swaying in the ocean breeze, their shadows casting patterns of dark and light on the ground beneath.

"Jesus Christ, are you okay?" he asked and helped her sit up. "What happened?"

"He's coming for me. Didn't you see him?" She trembled.

Bruce frowned. "I'm taking you home," he said with worry and anger in his voice. "Oh man! Dad's gonna kill me for letting you in the water now!"

Bruce ran to where his surfboard lay, then back to Anna. He picked her up and carried her under his right arm while cradling the surfboard under his left. They reached the old Scout and Bruce shoved the board in before gently placing his sister in the front seat.

He noted that color had returned to her face and life had come back into her eyes, but her gaze darted around wildly, as if she were searching for something nearby.

Bruce got in the driver's seat and slammed his door shut before cranking up the car. "Feeling better?"

Anna nodded. "So you really didn't see him?"

"See who?" he asked, placing the car in reverse and backing out of the parking space.

"The man in dark clothes with the pale face."

Terry was ecstatic. He'd found her! He took out a fresh cigar, snapped his fingers near the tip, and watched it glow. He took a few puffs while keeping an eye on the beat up old vehicle as it muscled its way out of a parking space and started weaving between the unevenly spaced cars and trees that bordered Ocean Avenue. It wouldn't be a problem now. He recognized the smell of this one, and she had a brother with a unique car. Easy.

The Harley started on the first try, its tailpipe throwing out only the wispiest thread of smoke this time. He headed up the street, but before he could pick up much speed, a well-worn charcoal-gray Mercedes Benz slammed into him. His bike skidded to the curb, and Terry went flying over the hood of the car. He saw earth, then sky, then earth again, before crashing to the pavement, landing solidly on his butt.

The Mercedes screeched to a stop and both doors opened. An old lady stepped out from the passenger door and shuffled over to the driver's door, feedback from her hearing aid producing a migraine-inducing whistle. She helped the driver out—another elderly lady, but a blue-haired one—who held a metal cane with four prongs on it.

Seated on the ground, Terry was shaking his head, trying to clear it, when he saw four spindly legs approaching. One set sported a pair of drooping knee-high stockings that sloughed like shedding skin. Terry looked up to see identical flower patterned dresses ambling toward him, flabby arms dangling like soggy hornets nests from their short sleeves.

Destiny and Fate.

"Ah, thistle-crap," Terry muttered in recognition.

"Which is exactly what yew'll be if you keep this up, young man," said Destiny, carrier of the cane. She poked her "staff" at Terry's shoulder, nudging him backward ever so slightly. Terry winced.

"Yeah!" said Fate through the squawk of her hearing aid.

"I was just trying to speed things along!" Terry protested and stood up shakily, brushing off his black leather pants and his shirt. He noticed his motorcycle lying on the ground and his eyes widened. "My bike!" he yelped, and ran to it.

People streamed around the accident site. No one looked at Terry and his damaged motorcycle, or the two old women and their rickety Mercedes.

"Lucky you don't look just like it!" Destiny snapped. The two women moved over to Terry and his fallen bike. "You already look ridiculous as it is. No one takes notice of you anyway. And what's with this rebellious getup you wear and that stupid, noisy motorbike?"

Terry lifted his bike up. "It's a *Harley*, not a *motorbike*," he said between clenched teeth. "And you wouldn't understand. You're too . . . rigid." He cringed at the sight of his handlebars. They were angled all wrong, and there was a dent in the gas tank.

Destiny examined the bike before looking at him again. "Think you're the only one tired of his job? Hmm? We been determining everyone's fates and destinies a million times longer than you been doing your little chore. Don't see us dressing in animal hides and riding around on some shitty piece of machinery. For Nature's sake, you were a nobleman once! Now look at you. Just look at you!"

Terry showed them the thick calluses on his hands. "I've been digging up these folk forever!" he complained. "Why can't I just hang onto this one until she goes through The Change? Huh? Why not?"

"You sound like a five-year-old!" Fate yelled. "Quit yer squawking. Digging's not so bad. Least you don't have to see what we do!" She shook her head.

"Have you ever had to dig?" Terry protested.

"Nope," the women said in unison, ignobly smiling at Terry. Destiny looped her arm through Fate's.

"We gotta take our course," Fate said calmly, then her facial expression went flat and her voice took on a more threatening tone. "Personally, I couldn't care less what you look like and what you do, Terrence. Just as long as you don't screw with us!"

With their noses in the air, they hobbled back to the Mercedes and inserted themselves, seat springs creaking their disapproval. The car lurched ahead, then stopped. Destiny rolled down the driver's window, stuck her head out, and peered back at Terry. "The time's coming, Terrence," she said. "Save your strength for the dig!" She cackled and sped away, honking her horn and darting between pedestrians and cars.

Terry stared up the road where he'd seen the girl and her brother in the Scout. They had disappeared. "Piss on a leper!" he cursed.

Carl threw his hands up in the air. "What do you think you were doing playing in the water?" he asked Anna.

Anna lay on the sofa, thumbing through an old copy of *Spiderman*. "I just wanted to play in the ocean a little bit," she said, sticking out her lower lip. It disarmed Carl completely. Her innocence was infectious and, at times, terribly frustrating.

He sat down on the edge of the couch and rubbed her legs. "Look, Peanut. You can't do that kind of stuff anymore. You're not strong enough." Carl glanced at Bruce, who leaned against one of the living room walls.

"I know! I know!" Bruce said, throwing up his hands, too. "What am I supposed to do? Hold her down?" He stormed into the open kitchen and flopped onto a chair.

Carl followed his son. He sat down opposite Bruce at the small kitchen table and cupped his hands around a mug of coffee he'd been nursing. "You're supposed to be the voice of reason, Bruce. You're almost seventeen. You know better."

Anger and disbelief shot through Bruce's face. He glanced at his grinning sister and said, "I give up!" Then he stomped up to his room.

"I think he was a shadow of death," Anna said out of the blue.

Carl almost choked on his coffee and headed back to the living room. "What are you talking about?" he asked, wiping his mouth. Booming bass suddenly thumped from upstairs. "Turn it down!" Carl yelled. The volume retreated slightly and he returned his attention to Anna.

"That thing I saw at the beach," she continued calmly, still flipping through *Spiderman*. "I think he was some kind of weird death spirit or something." She shivered and tugged her sweater tighter around her shoulders.

Carl moved over to her and sat near her feet on the sofa. "Where did you come up with that?" he asked. He wondered if they were about to broach the mental wall that Barbara's death had helped him build, brick by brick.

"I saw it in one of my old comics," she said. "*The Spectre*, I think. He was this weird guy. A little dark and hard to figure out."

"So you think this guy you saw was the Spectre?"

"No, Dad! He's kinda like him, I think. He's sort of a puzzle waiting to be solved." She yawned and slid down on the couch.

Carl waited until she'd fallen asleep then covered her up with a colorful shawl Barbara had made in a knitting class at Monterey Peninsula College, so many years ago.

Bruce had been bouncing around the house ever since he entered the surfing contest. Apparently, Paula Frazier had promised to show up and cheer him on, providing enough incentive for him to practice every day after school (after he'd finished his homework, of course).

When the day finally arrived, Bruce awoke with a flock of butterflies in his stomach. He nearly threw up twice and refused to eat breakfast.

"You okay?" Carl asked him.

"Yeah. Just a bit . . . worried."

"You mean if you suck, Paula might not go out with you?" Anna asked between slurps of Cheerios.

"Shut up, turd!" Bruce spat and left the breakfast table. He went up to his room and slammed the door.

"That wasn't very nice," Carl said.

Anna dropped her spoon into the now empty cereal bowl and shrugged. "I know." She leaned back in her chair and looked toward the top of the staircase. "Sorry!" she yelled. Then she glanced at her father and whispered, "But it's true, you know."

Carl noticed that, while Anna's face was still a bit drawn, she had color in her cheeks and had actually put on almost two pounds during the past few weeks. After she'd finished her last round of chemo and radiation, the oncologist had told them to "wait and see what happens." Carl had heard those words before. They worried him.

"You sure you're feeling up to going out and watching the competition today?" Carl asked her as he walked over to the sink to wash dishes. She started to reply, but Bruce came barging out of his room with a rag and a bar of wax for roughing his board. It was about the hundredth time he'd waxed it in two days. He headed out to the garage and slammed the door.

"I wouldn't miss this for the world!" Anna said, bouncing on her chair.

Terry wove between cars rumbling down Ocean Avenue toward the Pacific. He'd been in Carmel for three weeks, but never had seen traffic this terrible. He parked his Harley near the tall, white and brownstone library and stared at all the vehicles. Most were VWs with racks on top and colorful surfboards strapped to their roofs. Buses and bugs streamed past, some with dreadlocked young people waving their muscular arms at other cars. A bunch of window-gawkers allowed their eyes to drift away from the pricey Carmel merchandise on display in store windows to frown at the swell of vehicles surging in the direction of the beach.

Then Terry saw the Scout. "Yes!" he exclaimed, and cranked down on the Harley's starter. Nothing. He kicked harder and, again, nothing.

"Not now!" *Damn you old hags!* He felt the unbridled power of Fate and Destiny dancing around him in the breeze, thwarting his efforts to get to the girl.

He kicked and kicked and kicked, but the bike refused to start. "Damn! Damn! Damn!" he cursed, getting off the bike and stomping around it in a semicircle. He stared down the street just in time to see the Scout disappear.

Terry shook a fist at the motorcycle, then turned and lunged down the

crowded sidewalks, dodging between the zombie-like street shoppers.
I won't do it! I won't dig anymore!

In the blacktop lot above the beach, Carl nudged the car into a parking
space next to a Monterey Pine and killed the engine. The kids scrambled
out of their seats. Bruce wriggled into his wetsuit and snatched his board
from the back of the Scout, while Anna—in a pink, one-piece bathing
suit—rested against the dented fender.

"D-a-a-a-a-d! That's enough!" she complained, as Carl began pouring SPF-50 sun screen on every exposed section of her skin.

"Can I go down to the water now?" Bruce asked, hugging his surfboard under his right arm and dancing as if he had to pee real bad.

"Both of you just settle down," Carl said, tossing the now empty bottle
of lotion into a nearby trash can. "You," he said, pointing to Anna, "will
stay close by and *not* go into the water unless it's with me." He turned to
Bruce and smiled. "And you . . . can go to the water."

Bruce started to bolt until his father said, "But with us at your side.
We're going down there as a family."

Bruce groaned and his shoulders sagged, but he obliged by following
his father and his sister as they slowly—painfully slowly—walked onto
the beach. When they passed the tall cypress tree where Anna had seen
her "shadow of death", she hesitated for a moment, looking up at the
tree's heavy boughs.

"You okay?" Carl asked.

Anna nodded and they continued walking. She glanced behind her at
her brother, who looked pitiful, and smiled at him.

"Bruce!" a young woman's voice called out as they strolled down the
sandy slope. She had long brown hair, a coppery tan, and wore a two-
piece bathing suit that left little to the imagination. Her blue eyes brightened as she trotted up to Bruce. "You made it!" she said.

Bruce puffed out his chest and stood straight. "Yeah," Bruce said.
"Told you I would."

Carl couldn't remember ever seeing his son so tall. He cleared his
throat loudly.

"Oh," Bruce said, nodding at his father and Anna. "Paula, this is my
dad and my kid sister, Anna."

Paula shook Anna's hand and then Carl's. "We've heard a lot about
you," Carl said smiling at Paula and his son. Bruce bore his eyes into his
father's.

"How's the water?" Bruce asked Paula in an obvious effort to change
the subject.

"Not sure," she replied. "I just got here myself."

Bruce looked at his dad, pleadingly. Carl waved at the ocean with his right arm, indicating that his son was a free man. Bruce shot down the beach with Paula beside him.

"She *is* cute," Carl said to Anna.

"Yeah. She's okay."

The competition started an hour later. The sun was warm and the waves high as the first group of five surfers entered the water. Competitors were called in alphabetical order, so Bruce—with the last name Wooley—would surf toward the end of the day's tide. He'd frequently break away from friends or fellow surfers and run up to Carl and Anna, asking if they'd seen this surfer do this maneuver or that one do that.

"Don't wear yourself out," his dad said. "You're running up and down the beach like a maniac. Stay calm."

"I am calm," Bruce assured him. "I'm as cool as a cucumber." Then something caught his eye, and he raced toward the volleyball net where Paula was playing with several other teens.

"'Cool as a cucumber,' right," Anna chuckled, and peered up at her father. "Mom used to say that a lot," she added softly, and nudged a seashell imbedded in the sand with her toe.

Carl realized it was the first time Anna had mentioned Barb since she'd died, and his eyes stung. He sat down on the beach and piled some sand into a mound with his hands. Anna helped until they had something that marginally resembled a castle. They were on their third building attempt when a group—last names starting with "W"—was called to the surf line. Bruce waved to Paula before hurrying past Carl and Anna.

"Good luck!" Carl yelled.

"Yeah!" Anna hollered. "Good luck, lover-boy!"

Bruce stuck his tongue out at his sister, but smiled as he ran to the water. He entered with his group, splashing into the surf as an official-sounding timer chimed through a loudspeaker.

Bruce was in fine form. He caught wave after wave and rode them many yards before plunking into the water and paddling furiously back out to catch another. Carl could see Bruce's wide grin whenever a wave brought him closer to shore. It looked to be the perfect day . . .

. . . until . . .

. . . from out of nowhere, a heavy wind picked up and the water became animated with a cluster of choppy white caps. Three of the surfers—not including Bruce and another boy—came hustling back to shore just before a horn sounded, indicating that their time on the water had ended. Odd, given that the other surfing groups before the W's had been given much more time.

Fate sat on the beach with Destiny by her side, a colorful and slightly ragged parasol spread out above their heads. Fate poured a cup of special hot tea she'd made while Destiny stirred in two lumps of sugar with a small wooden stick. Tiny flecks of debris swirled in the tea as she stirred it.

"Oh, how I love a good tea," Destiny said while gazing at the ocean, watching a whirlpool form in the relatively calm waters. "Perfect. And sweet. Could you resist something so sweet?" She stared down the beach at the young, blond girl holding her father's hand. Mixing the concoction a bit more rapidly, she turned to Fate and asked, "Seen Terrence around anywhere?"

Fate shook her head. "No. He's been sorta . . . delayed."

"Motorbike trouble?" Destiny asked with a smile. "Tsk, tsk."

They giggled like school children before focusing on the sea, Destiny stirring the strange brew faster and faster.

Carl pulled Anna over to a lifeguard tower and tapped on the wooden frame. A tan young woman looked down.

"What's going on?" he asked. "Why'd they cut the competition short?"

"Surf's changing," she said, bringing a pair of binoculars up to her eyes. She scanned the water wordlessly.

Carl shaded his face and watched a lifeguard on a surfboard try to paddle out to Bruce and the other boy, but his board remained practically static, despite his wide, powerful strokes. It was as if something were holding him back.

On the beach, several officials spoke into walkie-talkies. Squelching voices came in response. Carl caught only parts: "*Sorry . . . can't . . . Coast Guard's tied up . . .*"

He could see that Bruce and the other boy were paddling like madmen, trying to move toward the beach, only to be dragged further out. This went on for several agonizing minutes until the surfer out there with Bruce shot forward like a rocket, then made his way toward the beach. A lifeguard met up with him 100 yards from shore and towed the spent competitor the rest of the way. The boy collapsed in a heap on the beach, his chest heaving in and out.

Carl raced over. A crowd gathered.

A man—whom Carl figured to be the boy's father—ran over to the surfer and swept him into his arms. "You okay?" the father asked.

"Yeah," the boy gasped.

"What's going on out there?" Carl asked.

The lifeguard who'd helped bring in the teenage surfer pulled Carl aside. "Riptide. A big one. And it doesn't just pull you out to sea, it pulls you down, like a drain. Freakiest thing I've ever seen."

"My son's still out there," Carl said. The lifeguard gripped Carl's shoulder and appeared ready to say something when a loud voice interrupted, crackling through a bullhorn.

"Hey! Get her out of the water! Now!"

Carl realized Anna's fingers were no longer laced in his. He spun to face the ocean, but the mass of spectators blocked his view. Apprehension squeezed the breath out of him. He bulldozed through the crowd, knocking people aside, and emerged out of the tangle of humanity in time to see a group of orange-vested officials waving madly at something in the distance. Halfway out to where Bruce still lay on his board, a whitish form with pale arms paddled toward him with surprising swiftness.

Anna! Carl muscled his way in between a group of people.

"Hold it right there, pal," an orange-clad official said. "No one goes in the water." The man held onto Carl's right arm.

Carl pointed and yelled, "That's my son and daughter out there!" He shook himself free of the man's grip, but more hands came from behind and held fast to his shoulders and clothes.

"Hold on, sir!" the official said. "We can't risk sending anyone out there right now. I don't know what your daughter was thinking, but you'd better get her to come back in." He handed Carl the bullhorn.

"Anna!" Carl shouted. *"Please! Come back!"*

She either couldn't or wouldn't hear, and continued paddling out to sea.

"Bruce can take care of himself!" Carl continued. *"Come back in now! Please!"*

Anna continued her steady course toward her brother until, without warning, she shot away from the beach in one giant movement, a motion decidedly opposite that of the rescued surfer. The crowd gasped.

"She's in the rip!" someone yelled. Carl again tried to break free, but heavy hands still restrained him and voices—trying to sound soothing, but ending up more aggravating than anything—told him to "hang on" and "wait and see."

The radios crackled again: *"Sorry, Coast Guard's still tied up . . ."*

Bruce's arms were on fire. He'd always heard that you should never fight a riptide, but this one came from three different directions. He seemed to be near the center of it, and off to the right he could see a foaming maw of . . . something . . . sucking down froth and bits of seaweed. Occasionally he heard garbled words coming from a bullhorn, and maybe his dad's voice, too, but calling out to . . .

Anna? Was he yelling Anna's name?

The sunlight reflected off something in the water, a spot that moved toward him. Someone was coming for him! Bruce relaxed and slowed his paddling.

"About time!" he called out when the figure got within hearing range.

"Hey! I'm going as fast as I can, butthead!"

Butthead? No one called him *that* except . . .

"Anna! What are you doing!"

His sister's head popped up above the waterline, an alarmed expression on her face, like she'd just awakened from a bad dream. She gazed at him briefly, before her eyes rolled back in her head—as if she were in a trance—and the lower half of her face dipped under the surface, her open mouth filling with seawater. She gulped it down. It looked to Bruce as if she were savoring the ocean's flavor. Her eyes scanned the water for a moment, then locked back onto Bruce. She started paddling toward him again.

"Anna! You gotta go back! There's some *big* riptides off to your left!"

In horror, Bruce watched her suddenly spin into the center of the whirling water.

"No! Anna!" he yelled, but her head now swirled below the waterline. "Anna!" he screamed. Bruce sobbed and thrashed his fists upon the sea's surface, a burst of angry adrenaline coursing through him; anger that quickly changed to confusion as something tugged on the leg strap that attached him to his surfboard.

The board pivoted 180 degrees and, with Bruce still on it facing away from shore, began moving inland. He glanced back and saw an intense circle glowing behind him, underwater, as if it were pulling the board. He punched out of the riptide seconds later. Applause erupted from the crowded shoreline.

About 100 yards away from Carmel Beach, Bruce's forward motion slowed and the seawater around him began bubbling as if a submarine were surfacing from beneath. Looking to his left, he saw the back of Anna's head float to the surface, her golden hair flaring out on the water. Her back followed, then her legs, as she rocked slowly, face-down, in the swell.

Bruce's bottom lip trembled, and he wept and screamed as he dragged

Anna onto his board. He looked at her face, glowing impossibly bright, as if lit from beneath by molten sunlight. She seemed so calm, so peaceful, he was almost afraid to touch her. He brushed a lock of hair away from her face. Her eyes remained shut, her chest still. The glow from her face dimmed. He felt someone next to him reach over, a female lifeguard. She grabbed Anna by the shoulders, pulling her onto another board.

"CPR!" the lifeguard yelled as she paddled into shore. She turned back to Bruce. "Come on! Keep paddling!"

Bruce stumbled onto the beach and found his father standing over a group of orange-clad people, one of whom was pressing on Anna's little chest and performing mouth-to-mouth resuscitation. Sand flew everywhere as rescuers and helpers ran up and down the beach, bringing equipment and placing it next to Anna.

"Dad?" Bruce said as he approached.

Carl pulled his son to his chest, keeping his eyes on his daughter's prone body. "You're okay," he said firmly, hugging him tightly.

A siren penetrated the cacophony of voices and an ambulance gurney appeared. A mob of helping hands thrust Anna onto it while wires were connected to her chest. The rescue team placed a clear bag with a mask on it over Anna's mouth and compressed it, forcing gusts of air into her lungs. With great effort, the paramedics wheeled the gurney up the sandy hill, Anna's body bobbing and shaking with its awkward movements. Father and brother marched alongside Anna all the way to the awaiting ambulance, Carl holding on to one of the gurney railings while Bruce stroked her face.

"You have to let go," said a voice. Carl looked up to see a young paramedic who motioned to the back of the ambulance. "We have to get her in there now, sir. You have to let go of the gurney."

Carl wrenched himself and his son away as two men lifted the bed into the ambulance. Three people crowded into the back of the small, medical compartment and swung the doors shut. The siren screamed back to life. The ambulance's air horn blared and the driver stuck his head out the window, yelling at a slow moving gray Mercedes in front of them, "Get out of the way!"

Carl swore that he heard a gruff voice cursing just beyond the crowd.

Anna Wooley's funeral, a surprisingly large affair, took place two days later at San Carlos Cemetery. It received quite a bit of press, with some reports claiming the young girl had saved her brother's life by dragging him and his surfboard out of the riptide. The competition's officials said such an effort was impossible from a child so small, but Bruce felt there was some truth to it and told any newspaper reporter who would listen that he believed Anna had somehow rescued him.

"She looked beautiful in that little casket," Carl said, as the services ended.

Bruce nodded. "Yeah. She had a bit of the glow I saw when I pulled her onto my surfboard."

Black straps slung under the coffin began letting out as small electronic motors on either side of the grave hummed to life, sliding the tiny hardwood box into the hole. The cemetery's perfectly-trimmed grasses shined almost neon-green. The joyous sound of play floated overhead from Dennis the Menace Park just behind them.

Carl smiled, ruefully. "You know, the lifeguards aren't too happy with you and those claims you made."

"But they're true, Dad! It *wasn't* just the sun reflecting off the water. This was completely different, like there was a bizarre power source under the ocean. And then, when Anna . . . came up, she had that glow, too. It was inside her. I saw it."

Carl nodded. "Perhaps you did."

They said a prayer that was cut short by the sound of the casket clunking against the bottom of the grave.

Old Father Roberts, clad in black, his threadbare stole hanging askew, stayed behind after the services. He patted Bruce and Carl on the back, indicating it was time to go and let the gravediggers finish their job.

Carl meandered a few feet away with the priest and turned back to see his son grabbing a handful of dirt from under a green tarp. Bruce went over to the hole and tossed the dirt in. "Thanks," he whispered, and jogged over to his dad and Father Roberts.

After some kind words from the clergyman, Bruce and Carl got into the old Scout. Bruce hung his head out the window with his chin on his crooked arm, looking at a group of screaming blackbirds scattering from the cypress tree that shaded Anna's grave.

A backhoe lumbered across the grass.

The Scout struggled to life, as the hole in the ground started to disappear.

Perched 30 feet up the cypress tree—above the earthborn's grave—and chasing away pesky birds that landed on his shoulders, Terry cursed the gravediggers. They'd filled the hole in a matter of seconds!

The old hags did it again! And now she's buried six feet underground. Just like all the others!

He sighed, descended to the ground, and gazed up at the sky. It was still full daylight, but the lunar orbit was off; he could feel it. There wouldn't be a full moon for another seven days. He wanted her out of the ground, but unearthing her now would only mean that he'd be hanging onto a corpse until the correct moon-cycle came around.

She won't go through The Change for a week! he thought. *And either way I'm still* digging, *again!*

Terry went over to his Harley and started it on the first try.

"Now you start!" he yelled, and snapped another cigar to life.

For Terry, the next few days crawled by like a glacier. He monitored the grave site, and watched the father and brother come and go several times, putting fresh flowers on her headstone. By the sixth day, their visits had slowed.

Good, Terry thought.

On the evening of the seventh day, as the sun began to set, he fetched an ancient, rune-covered, golden shovel from one of his saddlebags and commenced digging. He worked steadily for over three hours until he heard the end of the shovel *thunk!* against the top of the coffin. *About time!* he thought, blowing on his inflamed hands.

He pushed the remaining dirt out of the way and made a groove around the edges of the dirt-encrusted casket. *At least this one is somewhat fresh*, he mused as he lifted the lid. It swung open easily and revealed a sticky chrysalis inside, a walnut-colored shell with thick criss-crossing layers of something resembling spider silk. The sphere pulsated, but the dense matrix blotted out whatever might be inside. Terry smiled and crawled out of the hole, leaving the lid of the coffin open. The full moon arced its way across the dark sky. In another hour or two it would be in the correct position.

Terry sat on the edge of the hole he'd dug, and scraped the dirt from underneath his fingernails with a twig before going over and plopping down next to his bike.

When the brightness from the moon finally touched the edges of the grave, he walked over. Silvery rays of light spilled into the hole and seemed to be absorbed by the structure in the coffin. Terry puffed on another thick stogie and sat down, his legs dangling over the sides, his eyes wide and expectant. A faint tapping sound came from the cocoonish glob. It grew louder and louder until, finally, a luminescent, doll-like hand punctured through. The hand tore at the chrysalis and quickly ripped open a wider hole. Then, like a giant lightning bug spat from the earth, a pale, winged form burst out. Its speed and trajectory caused it to smash into a nearby tree, sending sparks showering to the ground.

"Ouch!" cried the petite creature, holding its head.

Terry looked up and grinned. "Haven't got your air-wings yet," he said, puffing smoke.

Anna shrieked and edged up higher into the sky, an ethereal image of pale light against the inky blackness. "I've seen you before! You're that dark shadow of death . . . um . . . thingy! You want to steal my spirit or something!"

Terry chuckled, chewing on his cigar. "Yeah, right."

Anna lowered herself a little, although she wasn't exactly sure how she was doing it, and stared at the strange man in dark leathers.

"How did I get here?" she asked Terry, and then stared at the ground twenty feet below her. "And . . . up here!"

Terry didn't answer, but continued smiling strangely.

Anna frowned and was about to demand a response when she heard an insect buzzing behind her. It sounded big, so she cautiously twisted her head around to look. Out of the corner of her left eye, she noticed a crystalline form vibrating quickly. What was it? Was it attached to her back? She glanced at her right shoulder and saw the same thing.

"O-o-o-k-k-k-a-a-a-y-y-y," she said, high above Terry. "I'm a bug."

Terry laughed heartily, fell into the hole, and grumbled angrily as he pulled himself out. "No, no," he replied. "You're not a bug. Not exactly."

She glanced at the strange shapes fluttering on her back again, and a brief image of herself lying on a cold, hospital table flashed in her memory.

The chemo. The radiation therapy to my shoulders, she thought. *The cancer.*

Her eyes filled with tears as she landed lightly on the ground. Terry rushed over to her and opened up his flask, catching the droplets as they fell. "Ah, fairy tears. The best."

Anna rubbed her eyes. "Fairy tears? I'm a . . ." She looked at her hands and noticed that she could see through them, as if she were a self-lit transparency. "What happened to me!" she screeched.

Terry's flask suddenly zipped out of his hand and hovered above Anna's glowing, tapered feet. "Hey!" Terry yelled. "Be careful. I don't get those everyday. They're extremely potent." He went to pick up the container, but it burst into a bright-orange flame under Anna's angry glare. Then it vanished.

"Oh, just great! Gone!" Terry said, hanging his head. He eyed Anna for a few moments and frowned. "You're a strong one, you are. I've never seen a Newfay manifest so early without instructions."

Anna lingered over the grave site and peered down at the cracked open shell within the casket. "Is that me?" she asked pointing at the chrysalis.

"That's what you used to be. A shell. Now . . . well . . . you're a powerful creature of Mother Earth. She can be a real pain in the ass at times, too, if you know what I mean."

A clap of thunder rang out.

"Sorry!" Terry yelled up into the clear night sky. He leaned over to Anna and whispered. "She doesn't like being called names."

Anna sat down heavily next to the grave. She rested her head on her drawn up knees, her new wings folded limply against her back, and she sobbed.

They always do this to me! Terry thought. *Why do they always have to cry or do something cute?* He sighed and put his arm around her.

"Hey, it isn't so bad," he said. "This is a special privilege. One that I'm—"

"And who are you?!" she blurted, shrugging his arm off her shoulder.

Terry moved away quickly, waving his arms in front of his chest, as if warding off some evil attack. "Calm yourself, will you? I'm a Finder. It's my job to seek out folks like you and help them . . . uh . . . find their way into this new existence." He cautiously stuck out his hand for Anna to shake. "My name is Terrence Von Goodfeather, but most fairy-folk call me Terry."

She shook his hand carefully, then walked around him, inspecting. "You don't have wings," she said.

"No, I *don't*." He gazed enviously at Anna's new form. "I was Mother Earth's first attempt. A proto-fairy, if you will. Then she made 'new and improved' versions and I was . . . reassigned."

"Reassigned? Do you mean downsized?"

Terry's colorless face went beet-red for a moment. He looked away from Anna and counted to ten, then turned back to her. He explained his role a bit more—in a monotone voice, as if he were a flight attendant discussing a flotation device—using bizarre terms like "moonlife" and "earthcycle photonics".

As he blathered on, Anna gazed up at the full moon, and the comprehension of what had happened to her flooded in. Terry's words were painful, yet helpful, the way a stomach feels when it's fed after being empty for a long time. He began speaking in strange tongues, and she understood. She understood! The words streamed into her. Memories old and new clashed, some obstructed, others rearranged. Head aching, she doubled over, clasping her hands to her temples. "Argh! Too much information!"

Terry stopped talking and smiled. "Painful, isn't it?" He helped her to her feet. "Fly up into that tree," he said, pointing to a massive eucalyptus a few yards away. "It'll help clear your head and give you a feel for your wings."

"How do I do it?" she asked.

"Just think about it. It'll happen."

Anna thought about her wings and they buzzed to life, lifting her off the ground. She darted skyward at incredible speed and zipped far above the top of the tree.

"Overshoot!" Terry yelled.

She hovered high in the night air. "How do I get down now? No. Let me guess. 'Just think about it.'"

Terry nodded.

Clearing her mind, she concentrated and shot toward the ground, an explosion of dust billowing out of the hole as she crashed into the coffin. Terry snapped another cigar to life and laughed as though he were enjoying his favorite show.

Anna hoisted herself out of the grave and sat next to Terry. "This is hard to learn."

Terry shrugged. "Life's tough when you're entering a new realm." He went over to his motorcycle, sat on it, and lifted up the kick stand. It started on the first try—again—and he sighed heavily. He looked over his shoulder at Anna and the grave. "Fill in the hole before you leave, okay?" With that, he gunned the throttle. The Harley spewed grass and dirt at her before vanishing into the night.

"Wait! What do I do now!" But there was no reply except for a devious little laugh.

She brushed herself off and thought about his parting words. "Fill in the hole before you leave . . ." Okay. She'd be leaving, but to where? She kicked at the mound of dirt and wondered why Terry hadn't used some magic spell or something to put it back in the hole. Then she remembered his filthy, caked fingernails, and his equally gross clothes. *Maybe he can't move earth*, she thought.

But I can!

She tried to will the dirt into the grave first. But the mound just shook, only a small portion sliding into the hole. Then she took a deep breath and closed her eyes, thinking about what she'd like her grave site to look like. When she opened them, the entire area shimmered with silver and gold sparkles. The dirt mound winked out of existence, soil and green grass and beautiful flowers suddenly covering the grave. She clapped her hands together excitedly. *Yes! That's my grave!* she thought. And then: *How twisted is this?*

Her wings tugged against her back and then began fluttering. Her feet left the grass, and she found herself speeding through the air only a few inches above the ground. After ripping through a thorny rose bush and some thick lavender plants, she began to get a "feel" for how to adjust her altitude. She brushed flecks of plant material off her arms and kept moving. Before long, she understood she was following a trail of some kind. Her mind zeroed in on a smell, the warm exhaust from one particular motorized vehicle.

Terry's guiding me somewhere.

Her senses heightened, she found she could easily track him. Other sensations came to her, too. She could feel the moonlight on her skin, and smell the action of the waves on the nearby water.

Buzzing above Highway 1, using it as a southerly route, she gazed down at the occasional car rolling by below her. When she'd passed the Carmel Highlands, where the highway began to twist and turn, she spotted Terry's solo headlight. She dipped down closer to the road and sped up in an attempt to pull next to him. Terry caught sight of her out of the corner of his eye and accelerated. By the time they'd reached the Point Sur Lighthouse, they were neck and neck.

When they entered Big Sur, Terry locked up his brakes and came to an amazingly quick standstill. Anna zoomed ahead. She hadn't seen the big redwood tree nearly sticking out into the road, and slammed into it amidst another shower of sparks that scattered from her body upon impact. She bounced lightly onto the pavement.

Terry laughed himself into hysterics, holding his belly as he staggered away from his bike.

Dazed, Anna shook her head as she got up. "Not funny!" she yelled. But he continued to laugh, stumbling over to her and placing his hand on her shoulder.

"That's one of the best fairy bumps I've ever seen!" He wiped away tears of mirth and cleared his throat. "I'm okay now," he chuckled. Catching his breath, he went over to his bike, withdrew the long silver rod with the tiny star on the end, and handed it to Anna.

"Let me guess," Anna said. "My wand?"

Terry nodded. "It'll help you focus your energies. I found this one near my workshop up in the Ventana Wilderness. That's how I knew you were coming." He sniffed Anna and the wand. "A perfect match."

Anna admired its glittering colors. "Where do wands come from?" she asked.

Terry shrugged. "I'm not entirely sure. But I *think* Destiny and Fate plant them and Mother Earth helps them grow."

Anna screwed up her face. "Destiny and Fate?"

"Sisters. They wander around the world and occasionally visit this area whenever a Newfay is due."

"You mean there are other fairies around here?" Anna asked, her eyes filling with wonder.

Just then a soft tinkling came from the forested area behind Terry. After a few seconds, it became the recognizable sound of water, trickling somewhere back in the clump of trees. It gained in volume, and a beautiful, white light flooded the openings between the thick branches.

"What's that?" Anna asked and moved around Terry. She squinted, looking at the dense foliage, trying to see the source of the light and sound.

Terry stood behind Anna and put his hands on her shoulders. "There's a meadow, a beautiful meadow back there. The fairy-folk visit it during full moons or whenever a Newfay is born. Tonight, both have happened. Someone's waiting for you back there."

He let go of her shoulders as she flittered up and forward. She brushed aside the Spanish moss hanging from lower branches and continued toward the warm light.

As she flew deeper into the forest, the sound of traveling water became more prevalent. The meadow Terry had mentioned came into view, carpeted with silver grasses and bordered by a small rivulet. Very old and tall redwood trees sat like giant guardians along the border of the stream. She hovered near the edge of the meadow for a moment, seeing a fine-winged figure dancing in the moonlight on the opposite side.

The luminescent creature spun toward her, and Anna recognized it.

A wave of joy flooded through her as she raced into the field yelling, "Mom! Mom!"

Lavinia

by Walter E. Gourlay

*F*irst she heard the rain rattling on the windowpanes. Next she noticed the clammy sheets, wrinkled and smelly. Awareness rushed in; her head was clear for the first time in days. She was in her third-floor room at the Point Sur Light Station, a mighty fortress some 300 feet above the Pacific Ocean, about 30 miles south of Pacific Grove and her mother's suffocating presence. *Thank you, Lord. I'm going to get married. Hallelujah! Not bad for sweet little Lavinia.*

She forced herself out of bed, walked shakily to the marble-topped dressing table, sat down, struck a match and lit the kerosene lamp. She peered warily at the sallow image in the slightly tarnished mirror as she brushed her thick, dark shoulder length hair.

Her face stared back, dark smudges beneath her eyes, cheeks sunken and devoid of color. *How awful I look,* she thought. *If Theo sees me like this . . .* She bit her lips and pinched her cheeks to restore some color. *I should make myself pretty for Theo. I must have lost twenty pounds fighting the fever.* "Probably pneumonia," the doctor had said. He hadn't been quite sure.

A wave of dizziness hit her. She rested the hand with the brush on her lap and put her head on the table. Her white nightgown, embroidered on the bodice with figures of tiny flowers, was damp with perspiration. *No,* she thought, rebelling against her mother's fastidiousness, *sweat. Dank, unlady-like smelly sweat.* She shivered. A chill? The fever returning? No, the room was cold. The rain had stopped but an angry wind poked at the window. She had to change into dry, clean clothes. Parched throat and dry lips told her she needed a drink of water.

Steadying herself with one hand, she rose from the dressing table and peeled off her nightgown. She took her pink woolen dressing gown from the wardrobe and slipped it on, then made her way to the chinaware pitcher on the nightstand by the window, and drank a glass of tepid stale-tasting water. She looked out over the ocean, shrouded in dense gray fog. As she watched, the fog lifted, unveiling sparkling waves just for her.

So beautiful, she thought, watching the white breakers. *Life is so beautiful.* And she felt a wave of joy and a surge of strength as she realized she'd survived her terrible illness. Soon she'd be seeing Theo again and beginning a wonderful life with him. *Theo, Theo, come back to me*, she cried silently.

Her eyes rested on the blue notepaper and the envelope with its pink two-cent stamp, from the Hotel International in Mansfield, California. "Just this one trip in the mountains and I'll come back to you," he'd written. *But Theo, I've been ill, deathly ill, and I've needed you.* She stood still for a moment, listening to the roar of the ocean, then threw open the window and let fresh cool air into the room.

Mother would have a fit, she thought, shivering. *Or at least a snit.* "Fresh air is good for you," the doctor had said.

She inhaled deeply, sat down at the table again and poured another glass of water. As she drank, she hacked a cough, then another, and soon was doubled over by a loud, painful spell that came from deep within her lungs. She grabbed the brown flask sitting on the table, poured a portion into a small china teacup and gulped it. *Laudanum. Opium, really.* In a moment the coughing stopped. *Thanks, Dr. Roberts,* she thought. *"You'll recover," he'd said. "A strong young woman like you with everything to live for."*

She took another deep breath, pulled several sheets of good paper to her, picked up a pencil, and began to write:

Point Sur Light Station
Monterey County, California
Wednesday April 19, 1905

My Dear Millie,

Please forgive my tardiness in replying to your so welcome letters. You have no idea how important they are to me, to hear of you and your family and my other dear friends in Pacific Grove.

The truth is, I've been a bit ill lately and haven't had the energy to write anyone. Please do not say anything to Mama! I fell ill just before my twenty-fourth birthday last month, but all is well now, and I'm about to resume my teaching duties. Our lighthouse is about thirty miles south of Carmel, on a high, rocky promontory, almost entirely surrounded by the sea. It can be a lonesome, dreary place, with frequent storms when the winds howl like banshees.

We have little contact with the outside world, except for mail (once a week) and for the lighthouse tender (a boat—or should I say a ship?) that brings us supplies every so often. My quarters are in a rather forbidding Gothic stone structure, much like a medieval fortress or castle. Sort of ghostly. Millie, I can just about see Count Dracula climbing these walls! B-r-r-r! I really think I should get some garlic to hang in my room!

Other than that, I'm comfortable enough. My room is pleasantly, if a bit heavily furnished, and I have my own coal-burning stove to keep off the chill. The walls are of thick sandstone, so I'm pretty well insulated from the chill and fog. A window looks out over the sea, and when we're not fogged in I can actually see the water. Luckily, indoor plumbing has been installed recently, so I have my own bathroom. I can imagine what it must have been like before to have to go outside in a strong, chilly wind!

And now, dear Millie, I have a surprise for you. I cannot contain myself any longer. I must tell someone! And you're my dearest friend! I rely on you absolutely to keep this a secret until I give you permission to reveal it. And you must not tell Mama until I say so! Your awkward spinster friend is about to become Mrs. Theodore Stevenson of Carmel!

In my next letter I'll tell you all about how I met Mr. Stevenson— Theodore (isn't it nice that he has the same name as our beloved President? But he doesn't like to be called "Teddy." He prefers "Theo"). Millie, when two people are destined for each other, The Fates bring them together, don't you think?

And now, dear Millie, I must stop for weariness. I will write you soon and tell you all about Theo, and about my life here in Big Sur (or, as the residents call it, "The South Country") later. And, of course, I'll invite you to my wedding. You absolutely must be my Maid of Honor!!

Please give my regards to all my dear friends in Pacific Grove. I'm so grateful that the awful war is over, and that the Spanish navy didn't attack California, as the papers predicted. But I do think it dreadfully ungrateful of those brown savages on the islands. They don't appreciate that we've liberated them and given them freedom, and they are even killing our boys.

And remember, not a word about my illness or about Theo to Mama until I've had a chance to tell her myself!!!!

Your devoted friend, Lavinia

Lavinia

She folded her letter and sealed it in the envelope, addressed it and affixed the two-cent stamp. She sat with it in her hands. *Just wait until I tell Mama*, she thought.

Since her childhood—ever since her father had died—she'd been the sole companion of her mother, who'd kept her almost a prisoner in the strait-laced community of Pacific Grove, where they actually had laws against pulling down your window shades at night, and where the biggest excitement was watching the Southern Pacific trains come into town.

She'd so yearned to be free to leave old fuddy-duddy Pacific Grove; to travel; to someday meet a man who'd share her thoughts and the dreams she'd always had, dreams of being a writer—not just a writer, but a great writer. Free to get married and have children of her own. But under her mother's vigilant eye she'd felt doomed to die a spinster.

Then one day she saw an advertisement in the *Monterey Express* that would change her life.

Educated Christian lady of neat and tidy habits
and good upbringing needed to teach young children.
Modest salary, room and board included. Must be single.

Well, thought Lavinia, *I'm certainly single enough and educated. And I never got the chance to have bad habits. Mama sure saw to that. And I do love children.*

About a week later, without telling her mother, she went down to Calle Principal in Monterey for an interview. The job, she discovered, was at the Light Station at Point Sur, and the children would be the one son and three daughters of the first assistant lightkeeper, Mr. Thurman (the big, florid redheaded man who was interviewing her) and the son of another keeper.

"We don't have a county school, you see," Mr. Thurman explained, "and so the remuneration will be modest, as we have to pay for it ourselves, and the income of a lighthouse keeper is rather less than generous, to say the least. But the food will be good, and the room cozy. There's no regular school year, and you'll be off Saturday afternoons and Sundays, and national holidays, of course." He searched her face with his eyes. "Do you think you can live in isolation, with no city frills or . . . um . . . gentlemen friends? It can get quite lonely out there on The Rock, as we call it."

"I've no need of social distraction," she answered. "I've led a quite decorous life in Pacific Grove."

She was hired on the spot. Lavinia strongly suspected she'd been the only applicant. It wasn't surprising. The pay was low, and the Big Sur country, even now in the modern twentieth century world of 1905, was untamed, notorious for mountain lions, huge bears and (if you believed all the stories) a lair for bandits. Everyone had heard about Notley's Landing down near Palo Colorado, and its riotous brawls, drunken mayhem and bawdy women. And some told eerie stories of mysterious murders and ghostly apparitions.

But these tales thrilled rather than dissuaded her. She'd be safe at the lighthouse, she figured, and what great material for the novels she'd write!

The session with her mother was stormy, but Lavinia defied her.

You only live once.

Along with her workaday clothes, she'd packed two good dresses, ecru muslin with lace insets, and a pink dotted Swiss.

"Why pack *those*?" her mother had asked. "You don't need to dress so fancy just to teach school."

"Mama, we're not in the wild and woolly West," she answered. "Maybe I'll be invited to dinner by some family wanting to meet the new teacher, and I should dress up."

Her mother sniffed. "A place filled with vagabonds and ne'er-do-wells from what I hear. Ruffians. Miners. Chinese. Mexicans. Indians. Cutthroats. Where the women are no better than they have to be. I've heard the stories."

"Mama, I'm going to live at a lighthouse owned by the government of the United States. Of course I'll be safe."

"And what'll become of me, all alone here? You don't care, do you? After all I've done for you."

"You'll be all right Mama. You have your church and your friends here in Pacific Grove. And with the money Daddy left you, you're almost a rich woman. You'll be able to take care of yourself, Mama."

Her mother stamped out of the room.

I'm not an old spinster, Lavinia thought to herself. *Not quite twenty-four; not yet withered on the vine.* She knew she was nice looking, with wavy brown hair, blue eyes, fair, clear skin and a slim body.

She finished packing, said a hasty goodbye to her glowering mother, and taking the money she'd earned giving children piano lessons, went to the depot on Lighthouse Avenue just in time to catch the afternoon train to Monterey.

In the city, she walked to the booking office by Ordway Pharmacy, and paid ten dollars to reserve her place on the coach to Big Sur the following morning. Then she went to the nearby Pacific Ocean House, entered the lobby — which reeked of cigar smoke and cuspidors — and paid for a room overnight, arranging for a wake-up call before sunrise.

In her room, Lavinia sprawled out on the big bed and relished the unfamiliar feeling of independence. Her money was all but gone, but this was the beginning of her new life!

Excitement and anxiety about missing the stage prevented much sleep. She'd barely dozed off before a knock on the door told her it was time to get moving.

A Spanish-looking couple was already in the coach, taking the two seats facing forward. After exchanging polite nods with the couple, Lavinia sat facing backwards with an empty seat beside her. She felt a bit uncomfortable riding backwards and trusted she wouldn't get sick. Wanting to savor her new-found freedom and to avoid polite conversation, she hoped no one else would get aboard.

But to her disappointment, the coachman, a short, wiry man with a heavy Spanish accent, announced that they'd be stopping at the Pine Inn in Carmel to pick up another passenger.

The newcomer turned out to be a sun-tanned stocky man slightly taller than average, blue-eyed and dark-haired. He reminded Lavinia of pictures she'd seen of General Grant, except he was younger and had a neater beard and haircut. His navy blue jacket with brass buttons, lighter blue trousers and well-polished boots spoke of good taste. Smiling amiably, he nodded to all, doffed his soft felt hat to the ladies, deftly climbed aboard and sat in the empty seat next to Lavinia. He smelled, not unpleasantly, of bay rum and cigars. *A manly smell,* thought Lavinia, feeling vaguely attracted and uncomfortable.

He introduced himself. "Theodore Stevenson, late of San Francisco."

The Spanish-looking couple spoke English, and they began to converse with him. Lavinia listened silently at first. Mr. Stevenson had returned recently from the gold country in the Klondike, he said, where he had struck it "moderately rich," and had gone to Carmel to invest in some property. He had seen Mr. Devendorf, who was developing the newly-settled area, and had bought some sites near the beach. "Some day it'll be valuable property," he claimed. "Devendorf wants to create a community for artists and writers." He smiled at Lavinia, who summoned up the courage to speak.

"Are you an artist or writer, Mr. Stevenson?"

"Oh, I've tried to paint a little. Landscapes mostly. Some figure painting. Strictly an amateur, I assure you. And you?"

"Just an ordinary old maid schoolteacher," she said somewhat defiantly, swallowing a desire to tell him she was going to be a writer.

"A schoolteacher, I accept," he said, looking at her searchingly. "And a fine one, no doubt. But certainly not an old maid. And I very much doubt that you are ordinary. May I inquire as to where you teach?"

She told him about the job at the Light Station.

He nodded. "I know the place well, and the assistant lightkeeper, Mr. Thurman. A good man." He was silent for a moment. "It can be a lonely place for a young woman."

"Are you from the Big Sur country?" she asked.

He smiled. "Oh no, my dear. I'm from New York by way of San Francisco. I'm thinking of prospecting in the Los Burros District." He noted the puzzlement on her face. "In the Santa Lucia Mountains. They're mining gold and silver down near Mansfield. A mining town. Who knows? Maybe I'll find the Lost Mine of the Padres." He laughed. "Actually at the moment I'm going down to the Cooper Ranch to attend the engagement party of a dear friend of mine, Jim Ramey. The ranch is near your Point Sur."

They passed the Carmel Mission, dull amber stone in the morning drizzle. *How sad,* thought Lavinia. *All that beauty, all the piety and good works of the padres come to naught.* They plodded past Point Lobos on a narrow muddy road leading into the Big Sur country.

Suddenly the stagecoach jolted down a decline, gave a lurch, and jerked to a halt. The driver turned around and said, "*Senores* and *Senoras,* I'm afraid I must ask you to get down and lighten the load until we can go on."

"Malpaso Creek," Stevenson said. "'The Bad Pass'. I'm afraid we must help push the stage."

She was glad she'd worn her bad weather boots. Theo jumped down and extended his arms to her as she stepped from the coach on to the soft ground. She felt the blood rush to her face and broke away from him.

The three men pushed, and got the stage moving again. Stevenson lifted her back into the coach. They passed through gloomy dripping forests of redwoods and oaks, up and down canyons, across creeks forded by narrow planks or nothing at all, often along rocky cliffs looking over the restless Pacific, between forbidding, hostile peaks. *An unfriendly country,* she thought, and wondered whether she'd made the right decision in coming here.

Suddenly she saw, or thought she saw, outlined on a ridge, a dark figure, short, squat, eerily unmoving, watching them. "Who is that?" she asked, her voice a whisper. Stevenson looked at her questioningly. She described what she'd seen.

The Spanish couple crossed themselves. "A Watcher," the man said. "One of the Watchers."

"A local superstition," Stevenson said, dismissively. "Sometimes they're called the 'Dark Watchers'. They're supposed to be guarding the so-called 'secret' of the Lost Mine of the Padres. Or according to whom you ask, they're the spirits of a race that lived here long ago. Before the Spanish or even the Indians. Others say they're survivors of that ancient race, hiding here in the mountains, waiting to take back their land. It was probably an Indian you saw. A Rumsen, a member of the local tribe."

The Spanish man shook his head. "No. I saw him. No Rumsen. A Watcher." He crossed himself again.

"I don't believe in superstitions," Lavinia said. "This is the modern world, after all. The twentieth century."

"Don't be so sure," Stevenson said. "There are things in these mountains . . ." He fell silent.

"The Lost Mine?" Lavinia asked.

Stevenson grunted. "Maybe it's a legend, maybe not. There's supposed to be a fabulous lode somewhere in these mountains. Some stories say it's in the Los Burros district, well to the south of here. Others say it's up on Pico Blanco. That's a limestone peak just inland from Point Sur. The story goes that the Indians used to bring quills filled with gold and silver dust to the padres in the Carmel Mission—or maybe it was to the San Antonio Mission on the other side of these mountains—but they never would tell the priests where it came from. The 'secret' has been lost, and one legend is that the 'Watchers' stand guard to see that no white man ever comes close to the mine."

What a wonderful plot for a novel, thought Lavinia, wrapping her cloak more tightly around her.

"There's even more to the story," Stevenson went on. "A fabulously beautiful lady all dressed in white like an angel, or by some accounts dressed in nothing at all, guards the mine. The Watchers warn her when any unwary white man comes too close, and she kills him in a blaze of fire."

"Surely you don't believe such nonsense! Do you think the mine really exists?"

"Who knows? Pico Blanco does exist. But the Rumsen were pretty primitive—not like the Aztecs or the Incas—and I doubt they'd recognize gold or silver ore if they saw it, or think it of value."

"Not Rumsen," the Spanish man insisted. "The Old People. Watchers."

"Whoever. Whatever," Stevenson said. "If the mine exists, I wouldn't mind finding it, and I'd take my chances with the naked woman." He grinned. Lavinia turned her face away and looked back to where she'd seen the Watcher. *No. What had Stevenson called him? A Rumsen Indian.*

The drizzle had ended and a wan sun showed signs of breaking through the fog. For the rest of the journey they chatted as new acquaintances do. She was thrilled to discover that Stevenson liked poetry, and that he shared her love of Browning and Shelley. *Too bad I won't be seeing him again,* she thought.

She brought out the sandwiches she'd packed before leaving Pacific Grove, and offered to share them with the other passengers, who declined and unpacked their own. Stevenson produced a bottle of wine and small pewter cups and shared the wine with the Spanish couple, Lavinia having declined.

After an uncomfortable journey that seemed interminable to her, they forded Bixby Creek and a few other muddy places where they all got out and the men pushed the coach. Then, almost at sunset, suddenly ahead of them was the ocean, and in the distance a huge rock seemingly planted in the water.

"That's Point Sur," said Stevenson. "You can just make out the Station." The buildings stood, sharply etched atop the rock, like a fortress in the dusk. A narrow isthmus led to it, reminding Lavinia of pictures she'd seen of Mont-St.-Michel.

A small wagon with a driver had been waiting for her by a narrow road leading to the Station, and Stevenson walked her over to it. He lifted her hand to his lips and bade her goodnight.

"Goodbye Mr. Stevenson," she said. "I enjoyed our conversation very much. I wish you luck in your hunt for gold."

"I trust we'll meet again," he said, grinning. "People usually do in the Sur. And when we do, my name is Theodore, but you must call me Theo. We don't stand much on formalities in these parts."

The drive in the wagon up the narrow road to the Station was unnerving, with narrow turns along the cliffs, the ocean roaring below. Lavinia wondered how they could ever make it in heavy fog or a strong wind. *Well, Lavinia, you wanted adventure,* she thought. But the horse was surefooted and the driver, a taciturn Mr. Beck, seemed content to let it lead the way to the stone buildings at the top.

Mr. Thurman gave her a warm welcome, and then introduced her to the other lightkeepers and their wives who had gathered in his quarters to greet her. Donny, his towheaded son, scampered out to tell the other children that the new teacher had arrived.

Lavinia deposited her small trunk in her room, and joined the Thurmans at dinner. To her delight, she learned that the people of the Station had been invited to the festivities at the Cooper Ranch tomorrow, a Saturday.

"Of course," said Mrs. Thurman, a fussy plump woman with pursed lips, "you've had such an exhausting trip you'll be too tired to go. I'm certainly not going," she proclaimed self-righteously. "There'll only be a lot of drinking and such with those Spanish people and cowhands and you had better stay here with me. After all, you're a schoolteacher and you have to set an example. You don't want to set tongues a-wagging."

Lavinia's heart sank. *Oh dear, it's Mama all over again!* "Oh, but I'd like to go," she said, raising her chin. "If I'm to make a living here I need to know the local customs. I need to meet the families who live here."

Mrs. Thurman made as if to object but Mr. Thurman broke in. "Let it be, Clara. The young lady's absolutely right. I'll be there to see she comes to no harm. And they're not all a bunch of ruffians, despite what you and your sewing circle may think. Most of them are damned fine folk." He leaned toward Lavinia. "If you'll pardon the profanity, miss." Mrs. Thurman glared at him.

"I'll be ready with the buckboard at noon," he said.

He left the table. Mrs. Thurman gave the younger woman an angry look, got up and refused Lavinia's offer to help with the dishes. It occurred to Lavinia that the older woman might see her as a threat to their marriage, she being drab and homely. And Mr. Thurman was not unhandsome. He was well put together and had a gentlemanly air. She wished she could pretend to them that she belonged to another man, but of course that would be prevaricating. *Oh, Mama, what would you think of me now. Not here a day and already a home wrecker.*

Mr. Thurman gave her a quick tour of the Station. "It was completed sixteen years ago, in 1889," he explained. "To keep ships from running up against the rocks. And as a warning that if they don't change course here they'll wind up in Russia."

The three assistant keepers had apartments of their own in a three–story sandstone building, a "triplex", while the head keeper lived in a two-story structure nearby. Lavinia would have a third story room in the Thurmans' quarters. The keepers' apartments shared "the Rock," as they called it, with a carpenter-blacksmith shop, a barn, and, of course, the lighthouse and fog signal building.

Mr. Thurman showed her the gigantic lens in the lighthouse. "It's called a Fresnel lens," he said. "Made in France and we're monstrous proud of it." A simple weight mechanism operated it, like a gargantuan grandfather's clock that had to be wound by hand every four hours. "The beacon can be seen as far as twenty-four miles out to sea. With no fog, that is. When it's heavy, like we reckon it's gonna be tonight, we blast the foghorn. Don't get too close to it or it'll blow your ears off!

"Even so, we had a tragic shipwreck right off the Point ten years ago. The *Los Angeles*, it was. Took five or six lives, maybe more. Had the bodies lined up in the barn below until a wagon could haul 'em to Monterey. Kind of mysterious, too, that shipwreck. Nobody's quite sure how it happened."

That night Lavinia slept well in her small apartment, despite the mournful sound of the foghorn blowing at intervals. It should have made her feel comfortable and protected. *But it was a little spooky,* she thought.

Her first morning of teaching, in the one-room shed used for a school-house, went well. A day so sunny, and the children such darlings (even Donny, the mischievous one) that she almost forgot about the celebration at the Cooper Ranch. She'd put on the ecru dress, and enjoyed the admiration of the children, who doubtless had never seen a party dress before.

Little Jenny, aged five, took her hand and asked if she were going to be married. Lavinia laughed. "No, but I'm going to a party for a lady who *is* going to be married."

"What's her name?" asked Susie, a little older. Lavinia, embarrassed, had to admit she didn't know.

Susie wore red knit stockings. One sagged and needed repairing; the other looked new. The girl noticed her looking. "I have three stockings," she boasted. "My mother is mending one of them. When she's done I'll put it on and then she'll darn this one. So I always have three stockings." Lavinia kept a straight face and wondered how much a lightkeeper earned. *Not much,* she thought. *Probably only a little more than the teacher.*

Donny wanted to tell her about the "ghosts" in the area, and the others chimed in. It turned out that all the children had a story to tell about the "Watchers" in the hills. They also spoke of spooky horses that galloped in the night, "Chinamen" buried in ghostly mines, and most chilling of all, the spirits of those who'd drowned in the shipwreck of the *S.S. Los Angeles*, just off the Light Station about ten years ago. "The bodies were all over the beach over there," Donny said with relish. "It was real scary."

"Did you see them?" Lavinia asked.

"No, not exactly. But somebody told me."

"Don't you know that there are no such things as ghosts, children?" Lavinia asked. The youngsters looked at her in disbelief. She changed the subject. "Now let's do some history. Children, who was the first president?"

"George Washington," they all recited, even the youngest.

"Wonderful. Now who's the president today?"

Silence. "All right, children, repeat after me: 'The-o-dore Roos-e-velt'."

Mr. Thurman and another keeper, Mr. Haskell, both in dress shirts, string ties, jackets and neatly pressed trousers, brought the wagon around at noon as promised. Even though it had springs, the buckboard was uncomfortable, so Mr. Thurman had provided a cushion for her. Mercifully the ride would be short. No more than thirty minutes, Mr.

Thurman said, to the Cooper Ranch near the mouth of the Big Sur River.

Along the way, Lavinia repeated to Mr. Thurman the stories she'd heard from the children. To her surprise, he didn't discredit them. "There are weird things in these hills, Miss Lavinia," he said softly. "It's a strange country. Before the Spanish were the Indians, and before the Indians, who knows? When the fog rolls in from the sea you may hear strange noises and it's best to stay indoors. And the 'Watchers'? I've seen them myself."

It seemed very odd to be talking of ghosts and spirits on such a glorious day. For the first time, Lavinia began to really grasp the unique beauty of this Sur country. Under an amazingly blue sky, golden poppies, wild lilacs, lupine and other wildflowers wove tapestries in the meadows. Purple iris peeked from shaded glens under the oaks and redwoods. The aroma of brush and blossoms merged with the scent of salt spray. Gulls circled overhead, and intermittently jays squawked and hawks soared on outstretched wings. Her uneasiness had disappeared and she felt so glad to be here!

When they arrived, the party was already going strong. Ceanothus and lupine in bloom surrounded a dance platform near the willow-lined bank of the Big Sur River, shaded by giant sycamores with mottled bark. Huge redwood logs and planks made benches and tables, and a roaring fire roasted slabs of beef, pork and chicken, enough for about a hundred guests, more than Lavinia had imagined lived in all the Sur country. Couples of various ages and lineages danced to the strains of a mazurka, played by a lively band of accordions, harmonicas, guitars, a violin and a flute. Children of various ages and sizes scurried about, some dancing by themselves to the beat of the music. And over all, a magnificent azure sky.

The women, young and old, were clad in finery, some in Spanish garb. The men wore denim jeans or buckskins, or were dressed as *vaqueros* wearing wide-brimmed black hats. Some, like Mr. Thurman, wore conventional jackets and ties. On the edge of the crowd sat a Chinese in buckskins wearing a queue. *Suitably inscrutable,* Lavinia thought. Several men and women looked like Indians. There was even a black man or two dressed in ranch clothes. *America in the raw,* Lavinia thought. *Just like the old frontier days!*

Mr. Thurman gadded about introducing her to his friends, a succession of names and a mélange of individuals she'd never remember because her mind and eyes were elsewhere. *Where was he?*

A shift in the circle about the musicians gave her the answer. She saw Mr. Stevenson. *Theo.* And he was . . . he was . . . playing a violin!

He caught her gaze and smiled widely, as the band began to play a varsoviana.

She felt a touch on her elbow. Mr. Thurman. "Care to dance, Miss Lavinia?"

Under her mother's careful supervision she had never really learned to dance, but with Theo watching, she decided not to betray her lack of sophistication. Besides, she'd always heard that all a woman had to do was to follow the man's lead. She nodded, and Mr. Thurman led her out to the dance floor. She felt awkward at first, and stumbled, but the lightkeeper didn't seem to mind.

At the end of the dance, Theo came to her side and Mr. Thurman vanished into the crowd.

"The *cascarones!* The *cascarones!*" someone shouted.

The crowd joined in. "The *cascarones!*"

"Jim Ramey is marrying a lady from a Spanish family, so they follow Spanish customs," Theo said. "For the *cascarones*, each guest is given an eggshell filled with scented confetti, which you're supposed to break over the head of the one you prefer to dance with." He saw the other musicians waving at him. "I'm sorry, but they expect me to play for this number." He excused himself ruefully and walked over to the musicians' stand. Someone handed Lavinia an eggshell embellished with a paper fringe.

A friend of Mr. Thurman's, a Mr. Lowery, hurried over and raised his eggshell above her but she ducked away and rushed over to Theo, breaking her egg on his head while he played. Several spectators applauded and he smiled broadly. At the end of the piece he joined her. "They didn't give eggshells to us musicians. But I'll take this as an invitation to dance."

It felt so good to have him standing behind her, the back of her head touching his shoulder, his hands holding hers as he led her through the simple but graceful steps of the varsoviana. Then came mazurkas, polkas and waltzes. After a while fiddlers took over, playing Stephen Foster music and popular tunes of yesterday, the crowd bellowing out the words of *Oh! Susannah, John Brown's Body, Shenandoah* and *Red River Valley*.

"I didn't notice you had a violin on the coach," she said.

"No," he said. "Jim Ramey keeps it here at the ranch for me. That's so I can play at their parties."

"Where'd you learn to play so well?"

"My family paid for lessons." He changed the subject. "Let's get some food."

Lavinia decided there was much to learn about this man.

They walked to the tables holding the tremendous repast—various meats, soups, salads, hot and cold vegetables, buns, cakes, fresh cider, tea, coffee, and even lemonade made from a powder bought in San Francisco. No alcoholic beverages could be seen, but men were going behind the barn and coming back with flasks in their hands.

"The rule is no alcohol at these shindigs," Theo explained. "A show of propriety for the ladies. But there's always a barrel or keg behind the barn."

The music stopped. Voices called for Theo. "Sorry," he said. "I promised my host I'd play a duet." He sat down on a bench next to a lovely Spanish-looking woman who held a flute. They played something slow, nostalgic and beautiful. Obviously, from the way they looked at each other they had performed together before, and Lavinia felt a tiny twinge of jealousy. The crowd cheered and demanded more. This time they played something lively, and a woman got up and danced flamenco style, while a man dressed like a *vaquero* sang the words. The duo played and played to the plaudits of the crowd until finally they took a bow. Theo excused himself and joined Lavinia, the flutist following him with her eyes.

By now the first stars were out, and a half moon floated among wispy clouds. The air turned chilly. People began to light pitch pine torches and to build a bonfire.

A harmonica player sitting on a bench led the crowd in singing *Meet Me in St. Louis*, the "rage" of the year.

Meet me in Saint Looey, Looey,
Meet me at the fair.
Don't tell me the lights are shining
Any place but there.

Lavinia decided one day she'd have to visit St. Louis.

We'll dance the hoochie coochie
I'll be your tootsie wootsie . . .

She wondered what the "hoochie coochie" was. It sounded deliciously sinful. But not dreadfully sinful of course, or they wouldn't allow it at the fair, would they?

Mr. Thurman came up and suggested they leave.

"But we've just begun," Theo protested. "This party'll last another two days! The Coopers would be happy to put Lavinia up here at the ranch."

"No," said Mr. Thurman firmly. "I have to bring this young lady home tonight or my wife will have my head."

Lavinia decided it was time to make her own decisions. "I'll come back here tomorrow," she said firmly. "That is, if I can borrow your wagon." She looked at Mr. Thurman.

Theo broke in. "No, I'll bring a carriage to pick you up."

"No," said Lavinia. "I'll borrow the wagon."

"But then you'd have to drive back alone at night," Mr. Thurman said. "I can't have that."

It really would be nice to be alone with Theo in the carriage, she thought. "I accept your kind offer, Theo. Can you come fetch me at noon?"

The tongues would surely be a-wagging all the way from Point Lobos to San Luis Obispo. *So, let 'em wag!*

As Mr. Thurman drove her back to the lighthouse, she fantasized a life with Theo. An end to loneliness. A friend to share her innermost thoughts. *But, of course, that was only a dream.*

Theo showed up as promised the next day, driving a spanking surrey. He looked dashing in his blue coat with the brass buttons. As she climbed into the coach and sat next to him, she asked him about it. "You know, when I first saw you I thought you might be a sailor. Is that a seaman's jacket?"

He nodded. "As a matter of fact, it is. At the moment I'm filling in as First Mate on the *Mabel G.*, a small freighter picking up tanbark along the Sur coast. That's how I got to know so many of the people here in the South Country."

She sighed. "It must be wonderful to be a man. You've done so many things. I wish . . ." She fell silent.

"You wish what?"

"I wish I could have some adventures. Like men do."

He looked at her. "You're a woman alone in the Sur country. That's pretty adventurous for a starter, isn't it?"

"I mean . . ." Then she began to tell him everything about herself. About Mama. About her aching loneliness. About her dream of becoming an author. She told him about the journal she'd kept hidden from her mother, about the scraps of stories and poetry she'd written, about her gray cat, Tennyson, who'd been her only consolation when her father died when she was twelve. She let it all pour out, desperately wanting to share, wanting him to know her.

When she had finished, he stopped the horse, reached out an arm and pulled her to him. He kissed her, at first gently, then more ardently. She pulled herself away, trembling.

They looked into each other's eyes, silently.

"Lavinia," he said, his voice husky. "I've been needing someone like you. I'm not getting any younger, and I want a companion and a family. I hope you'll marry me."

She sat silently for a moment, her head bowed. Then she looked up at him, her eyes filled with tears, and smiled. "This *is* rather sudden, but I will marry you, Theo. As soon as the Thurmans can find my replacement." She kissed him. The first time ever she'd kissed a man. Except her father when she was a child.

They decided to get married in three months, after the *Mabel G.* regained its regular First Mate.

"How would you feel about living in Carmel?" Theo asked. "We'll build a house and hobnob with all the 'swells'."

"And Los Burros?"

He laughed. "Maybe later. I'll be too busy loading tanbark for a while. If there's still unclaimed gold there it'll probably all be gone by the time I get to it. But if I ever do strike it rich"—he hugged her—"if I do, then what would you say to a honeymoon in New York, or Paris? Or London? Or Venice?"

"All four," she answered.

"Greedy! OK, all four. But some day I'd like to live in Paris to study painting. Maybe before Carmel. And I want to do your portrait. You must model for me."

In the nude? she wondered. *Yes, I'd be willing to pose for him in the nude. Just wait until Mama hears about this!*

So in a few months she'd be Mrs. Theodore Stevenson of Carmel (or of Paris, London, Venice, or New York or all of them). And while Theo painted in Paris she'd live in a garret with him and write her novel. And they'd have a cottage in Carmel. They'd get to know the Bohemians and the "swells" there. She'd call her novel *Christine Finds Life,* and it would be the story of a not-so-old maid schoolteacher who found life and love in . . . the Sur? No, some place more romantic. The Scottish Highlands, perhaps? Or Paris? Of course she'd have to visit them first. For authenticity.

After they reached the Cooper Ranch, they decided to leave the party for a while and drove down for a walk on the beach where the sparkling Big Sur River emptied gently into the Pacific. Lavinia spied a strange object glinting at the water's edge, a twisted piece of yellow wire the size of a pin. She plucked it from the sand and handed it to Theo.

He studied it and shook his head.

"You know, I think it's gold," he said slowly. "An unusual shape for a nugget. Maybe someone lost it or . . ." He looked up at Pico Blanco. "This river flows down from the mountains. I just wonder . . ." He gave the object back to Lavinia, who clutched it in her palm.

"I'll keep it as a memento of today."

Fog pushed in from the ocean and turned the sky gray, causing Lavinia to shiver. They drove quickly back to the party. Somehow she felt uneasy, as though she were being . . . watched? She glanced up at Pico Blanco, but saw nothing in the fog.

Later, as Theo drove her back to the lighthouse, Lavinia rested her head on his shoulder. She felt so fine, so secure.

The next three months were the happiest of her life. The *Mabel G.* made frequent stops at Notley's Landing, and Theo called on her at the Light Station often. They went for walks or for rides in the buckboard or a carriage. He bought her a beautiful diamond engagement ring in San Francisco. But even more precious to her, on each visit he presented her with lovely sketches or watercolors he'd done just for her. And she gave him poems she'd penned, declarations of her love, bound with pink ribbons.

Mrs. Thurman was annoyed that Lavinia had decided to leave her teaching job "to marry a sailor," she sniffed.

"He's really an artist," Lavinia protested.

"That's even worse."

Mr. Thurman began looking for Lavinia's replacement.

She still hadn't written to her mother about Theo. *Am I afraid she'd somehow spoil the cloud of happiness I've been living on? Don't be silly. I'm a big girl now. I must write Mama.*

Everything seemed to come together on the night of Jim Ramey's wedding reception.

Theo showed up at the Station wearing a big grin, a bouquet of pink roses in his hand. "Eddie's back. The First Mate. We can get married whenever and wherever you say."

She squealed, threw her arms around him and nuzzled. "Oh, Theo. Let's get married here, in the Sur. I'll invite my mother. And my friend Millie will be my Maid of Honor."

Lavinia hardly remembered the drive to the Cooper Ranch that evening. If anything, this *fandango* was bigger and more boisterous than the engagement party. To one side stood Jim Ramey and his slim dark-haired bride, resplendent in Spanish dress, each of them looking triumphantly at each other and at the crowd.

Theo, as expected, was pressed into playing his violin. After an hour or so of traditional favorites, Mexican, Spanish and American, he raised his arms and called for attention. Then, to Lavinia's astonishment, he announced their engagement. The guests cheered and toasted the couple in both Spanish and English. Lavinia was hugged by the women and kissed by what seemed innumerable men, many with too much whiskey on their breath.

Theo jumped up on the table. *"Amigos!* Friends! Before I have played for you the music you know. And now I ask you to be patient and be quiet for me while I play some of the music I love for my Lavinia."

As the guests gradually shushed each other, Theo picked up his violin, closed his eyes, and played Mozart's *Eine Kleine Nachtmusik,* then a selection from Beethoven's *Violin Concerto,* and the melody of *Ode to Joy,* followed by Bach's *Air on a G-String,* Saint-Saen's *Pavane,* and finally, Schubert's *Ave Maria.*

Lavinia cried from the sheer joy and beauty of it all. As Theo finished, the guests broke out in prolonged applause, accompanied by enthusiastic whistles and hooting from some of the ranch hands.

By now Lavinia felt tired, and asked Theo to take her home. As they said their good-byes she noticed on the fringe of the crowd a beautiful woman dressed all in white, who seemed to be observing them closely. *Part of Theo's past, perhaps,* she thought. But she was too happy to want to ask him.

On their way to the lighthouse he told her he wanted to visit the gold mines in Los Burros, and they had their first disagreement. A vague premonition of trouble tugged at her, and she pleaded with him not to go. But he was set on it, and promised to be back before her birthday in three weeks.

Lavinia felt a cough coming and took some more laudanum. *Time to go back to bed, Lavinia.*

But she dreaded the night. Ever since Theo had left, she'd been having these disturbing dreams. It had started when she'd become ill. She'd imagined a Watcher in her room. He'd awakened her and stared into her face. Then came other Watchers, crowding about her bed silently, while Lavinia buried her head in the covers and whimpered. And once a lady all in white stood and regarded her despairingly.

Hallucinations. A bit of delirium from her illness. If she could dwell instead on Theo and the wonderful life ahead of them. If only Theo were here! *Where was he?* He'd promised he'd be back for her birthday. *When would it be her birthday?* She'd lost track of time during her illness. But never mind. He'd written to say he was surely coming. She had his letter. *How long ago had it arrived?*

There was something terribly wrong about this room. No, it was her. The illness had made her subject to illusions. Scary, unsubstantial things. Like visitors to her room whom she didn't recognize, who didn't see her or hear her speak, visitors who were themselves just shadows or transparent beings. *Ghosts*. Perfectly normal looking people—but they weren't there!

Voices on the stairs leading to the ground floor, but only flickering shadows when she looked. Voices of children playing outside, when it was the middle of the night. And the sounds of a boy next door in a perfectly empty room. *I don't believe in ghosts!*

She heard the rain pouring on the roof above, and got up to look out the window on a perfectly sunny day.

She reached in the drawer where she'd kept the piece of gold that she'd treasured as a symbol of their betrothal. It wasn't there!

Where was Theo's letter? In the reassuring blue envelope. From the Hotel Cosmopolitan in Mansfield. It wasn't there either. Where was it? Her hand touched another envelope. Her letter to Millie. But she distinctly remembered posting it. *When was that?*

She sat at the table again and picked up a pencil.

> *Dear Millie,* she started to write. *There is one thing I have kept from you because it sounded so silly. I think this place is haunted. Just the imaginings of an over-age schoolgirl, I know. But there is something terribly wrong here.*

She heard someone coming up the stairs. It must be Dr. Roberts. Had he promised to look in on her today? She couldn't remember. She dropped the letter to the desk and stared as the door opened . . . It was Theo. *Theo!*

She got to her feet and cried his name. But he didn't seem to see her or hear her! His eyes ranged vacantly about the room until he closed the door and lumbered downstairs. She heard him question Mrs. Thurman and heard clearly the response:

"No. I'm so sorry . . . about a week ago. Just after her twenty-fourth birthday, poor thing. She kept asking for you. Her mother sent down for her body."

Lavinia went to the window and looked out to watch Theo leave. But saw nothing except swirling white fog. *Theo, Theo, come back!*

Again she heard someone coming up the stairs. It must be Dr. Roberts. Had he promised to look in on her today? She couldn't remember. She dropped the letter to the desk and stared as the door to her room slowly opened . . . A boy, about eight years of age, peered into the room. *Oh, dear. Another hallucination.* She shut her eyes.

She heard him go down the stairs.

"Mama!" he yelled. "Who's the lady who coughs all the time in that room up here next to mine?"

A woman answered. A low, sweet voice. "There's no lady there, Billy. That room is empty."

"But I saw her. You mean she's a ghost?"

"There are no such things as ghosts. Why don't you go out to play, dear? It's such a nice warm day."

Lavinia looked out the window and saw only the gray, cold fog. She drew her robe more tightly around her.

"OK, Mom."

His feet clattered down the stairs. Then she heard the creak of his toy wagon as he pulled it outside.

A male voice: "I don't believe in ghosts, but they do say there is one in that room. That girl who died there years ago. Every so often, when the room is vacant, somebody claims they hear her coughing."

The woman: "It was so sad. A schoolteacher, wasn't she? Died just before her twenty-fourth birthday, they say. And then her fiancé came up from the gold fields to marry her and she was already gone. Poor thing."

Male voice: "So I've heard. Do you remember her name?"

Silence for a moment. "No, I don't remember it."

Lavinia put down her head and cried. Then she screamed. But nobody, she realized, could hear her. *Ever.*

Author's Note:

There's reputed to be a coughing ghost in the Point Sur Light Station, which is now maintained and preserved by the Central Coast Lightkeepers. However, my story takes place a quarter century earlier than the appearance of the "real" ghost. Lavinia, like all other characters appearing in this story, is a fictional character.

For information on the Light Station I am indebted to Lighthouse Quarterly, *the newsletter of the Central Coast Lighthouse Keepers. Thanks to Paula Walling of the Central Coast Lighthouse Keepers for helping with the artwork for this story.*

Many thanks to Dawn Cope, docent at the Light Station, for telling me about the "coughing ghost", for giving me a tour of the Station, including the building housing the rooms occupied by Lavinia, and for proofreading, editing and encouragement.

All errors of fact, however, are my own.

For further information about sources, geographical information and references, please see my "Author's Note" at the end of the following story, "Theo."

Theo

by Walter E. Gourlay

Jf Theo hadn't returned to the Cooper Ranch after escorting Lavinia back to the Light Station the night of Jim Ramey's wedding *fandango,* he might never have met Al Clark or the woman he would always think of as The White Woman. And his life wouldn't have been changed forever.

And Lavinia might still be alive.

Now, at about two in the morning on the night of the festivities, a string trio—fiddle, banjo and guitar—sat by the dying embers of the fireplace, playing *After the Ball.* Boisterous, bleary-eyed ranch hands and settlers sang the words off-key while swigging hard liquor from their flasks. Confetti from the earlier *cascarones* littered the rough planks of the dance floor. The children were long gone, packed away to sleep in the barn. The Big Sur River murmured from behind its screen of willows. Mountains brooded over the demise of the party. A cold half moon, peering through fog, silhouetted the massive limestone block of Pico Blanco.

Theo breathed deeply, savoring the aroma of wood smoke, charred beef and sizzling fat. Grabbing a glass from the rough-hewn table, he drew a beer from the almost empty keg behind the barn, took his silver cigar case from his pocket, bent over to ignite a twist of paper from an ember, and lit a hefty Havana cheroot. He puffed on the cigar and thought of Lavinia, his bride to be. *Dear Lavinia.*

She'd worn a pretty dress of pink dotted Swiss, her dark hair caught up by a pink ribbon, like a schoolgirl instead of the teacher she was. Around her neck there'd been a gold locket. Being near her gave him a sense of peace he hadn't known for years.

Lavinia had felt tired so he'd taken her home to the Light Station. *Probably too much excitement,* he thought. As they said goodnight, he told her he'd decided to visit the Los Burros gold field the next day.

"No. Please, Theo." She drew back and looked into his eyes. "I've only just found you. Please don't leave. I'd be so worried about you."

He patted her shoulder. "Nonsense, my dear. I'll be perfectly safe. This is California after all, not the Klondike. There's even a post office in Mansfield and daily mail through Jolon. How civilized can you get? I'll stay in a hotel and drop you a line as soon as I get there. In a couple of days. In any case I'll be back for your birthday in just three weeks." His eyes brightened. "Just think, my dear, maybe I'll be lucky again. Maybe even find enough to retire on, and we can live wherever we like. Then we'll get married. Here in the Sur, if you like."

She appealed to him with her gaze. "I just have this awful feeling." She clutched him as they kissed goodnight. "You'll write to me? And be back for my birthday?"

He promised. After another long kiss he tore himself away, got back in the wagon, and drove to the Cooper Ranch. In the morning he'd rent a horse and a burro from Ramey and set out for the Los Burros gold fields.

Just one more strike.

The Wall Street Panic of 1893 and the ensuing depression had wiped out most of the Stevenson family's wealth, leaving Theo, his widowed mother and two sisters almost destitute. Then in the summer of '97, when the headlines screamed "GOLD! GOLD! GOLD!" he sold their sailboat and their summer house on Long Island's North Shore and used the money to go to the Klondike.

His family objected, strenuously. He'd been trained as a concert violinist, they reminded him, and had a promising career as a watercolorist at New York's Art Students League. And, most importantly under the present circumstances, he was practically engaged to Clarissa Conway.

"Marry her," his mother and sisters had chanted. "She'll make a wonderful wife for you." *And she's going to be very rich,* they didn't need to add. He and Clarissa had practically grown up together, and he really was fond of her, in a comfortable sort of way. Pretty, demure, polished at the best schools, and heiress to millions in gilt-edged bonds. Desirable and willing. A good pal, but . . . he had no desire to marry her. Too conventional, too Fifth Avenue, too dull. Life had to have more excitement than what Clarissa offered. He'd chosen the Klondike instead.

Poor Clarissa. I'll have to decide about her later.

He booked passage to Skagway, then by river steamer up the Yukon to the Klondike and raw, bustling Dawson City. But after discouraging months in the summer heat, battling mosquitoes and biting black flies, sluicing and panning to no avail in Bonanza Creek, he'd been about ready to call it quits, go back to New York and, maybe, settle down with poor wealthy Clarissa. Then, one day he spied ruby-tinted dust glinting in his pan, went upstream some yards, found a few shiny nuggets, and staked a claim. He continued panning until winter froze the banks, then he swung his pickaxe into the hard earth nearby and hit a small lode.

It made him moderately rich, but not enough to let him join the leisure class in New York. He sent some money home to keep his family solvent and to pay off debts, but kept enough to stake him for further prospecting.

He'd caught "gold fever". The precious metal was there, and if he found the mother lode he'd be able to retire for life.

For four more years he remained in the Klondike, prospecting, making small strikes but never a really big one. When the gold petered out, he stayed at the Fairview Hotel in Dawson City, making side trips near old worked-out mines, still hoping to find the elusive big lode.

It wasn't so much the gold that held him there, but the game. The gamble. The thrill of the hunt. The fortune that could be found in the next pan or with the next blow of a pick. But as the days rolled past, his confidence waned, and so did the fever. The artist, the musician whose spirits soared with Beethoven's *Violin Concerto* or a piece of poetry or a painting by Gauguin, emerged again.

Finally he left the gold fields and wired his sister Emily to send his violin and watercolors to him at the St. Francis Hotel in San Francisco. What he would do with himself he didn't know, but he didn't feel ready for New York just yet.

On the ship from Skagway the first mate suggested he visit John Ogilvie, skipper of the *Mabel G.*, a little stern paddle steamer that carried supplies and freight between San Francisco, Santa Cruz, Monterey, and San Luis Obispo. Presently in Monterey, Ogilvie urgently needed a temporary replacement for his first mate, now serving 90 days in the local pokey for being drunk and disorderly and assaulting a police officer. Under the circumstances, Ogilvie needed little convincing that Theo's years of sailing on Long Island Sound qualified him for the berth.

As they sailed out of Monterey, Theo reclined in a deck chair, watching the sun go down, enjoying the cool salt air. He took his violin out of its case. His hands, roughened by years of the pickaxe and shovel, were a bit clumsy. A little practice, he knew, and he'd be ready for Beethoven and Mozart.

Theo

He relished the smell of salt in the air, the gentle rolling and pitching of the vessel, and the swish of water along its sides. With his pencils and watercolors, he tried to capture the brilliant azure Pacific, the white breakers and blue skies, the gulls and the occasional otters, the gamboling dolphins, and the sheer cliffs and grassy plateaus of the Big Sur coast. New York was far away.

The vessel's first stop was the "doghole port", as Captain Ogilvie called it, of Notley's Landing, nestled on a narrow bluff overlooking the sea. Nothing more than a dismal cluster of weather-beaten wooden shacks, it didn't even have a dock. Heavy ropes moored the ship to huge iron rings driven into the rocks, and a cable on pulleys lowered a ramp from the bluffs above to the deck. Theo and most of the crew went ashore on the rickety ramp while a small shipment of food, staples, and light equipment was unloaded. On its return voyage the *Mabel G.* would pick up redwood poles, planks and shingles, and valuable rolls of peeled tanbark for use in the leather factories in Santa Cruz and San Francisco.

A small group of people, mostly men but with a few women, all in ranch clothes, rushed to greet the crew. "Hungry for gossip," Ogilvie said. "They get newspapers and books through the mail, and even the latest music from Tin Pan Alley in New York. But they still feel isolated, like they're on another planet down here."

Theo walked about a half-mile from the landing to "West" Smith's Westmere Saloon, notorious all along the coast for all-night dancing, harlotry and mayhem. The place reeked of beer, spilled liquor, sawdust, spat tobacco and sweat. The crude barstools were all occupied, so he stood in the sawdust between two of them and ordered a brandy.

Two rowdy ranch hands staggered in. The man on Theo's left, a middle-aged Chinese dressed in black with a long, carefully tended queue, got up from his stool. He picked up two large canvas sacks he'd had at his feet and walked toward the door. Theo slid onto the vacated stool and picked up his drink.

The ranch hands blocked the path of the Chinese. The place went silent. "Hey, Sing Fat, watchee got in them sacks, huh? You gotchee some gold dust?" The Oriental blinked, smiled blandly and tried to walk between them. They remained in his path.

"Hold it, you fellers!" yelled the bartender.

Theo got up to intervene, but the man on his right, a young sandy-haired fellow with a full beard, put out a brawny arm to stop him.

"Just wait, my friend. Just watch this."

As smoothly as though it'd been choreographed, Sing Fat put down the sacks, reached into one of them, pulled out a sawed-off shotgun, and still smiling, cocked it and pointed it at the pair. They swallowed hard and sullenly stepped aside. The Oriental gentleman waved to the bartender, hoisted his sacks and walked out. One of the ranch hands made as though to go after him, but the other one pulled him back. They swaggered to the bar and shouted for whiskies. The noises of the saloon returned.

The man to Theo's right chuckled. "Old Sing Fat, he just don't let *nobody* peek into his pokes. He claims it's only seaweed, but some people think he's got gold dust stashed in there." He reached out a leathery paw. "Jim Ramey. Top hand at the Cooper Ranch a few miles south of here."

"Theo Stevenson." They shook hands. "What's this about gold dust?"

Ramey laughed. "From the 'Lost Mine of the Padres'. That's what they believe. Or some of them, anyway. Don't worry about it. It's a myth, a legend."

"Why so secretive about his sack? Seaweed? That's not worth a plugged nickel."

"Who knows? All part of being Chinee, I guess." Ramey studied him. "You're new around here, aren't you? But I have this feeling I've seen you some place before."

Theo took a sip of his brandy, and laughed. "Not likely. Unless you've been to New York. Or the Klondike."

The other man slammed his fist on the bar, rattling the bottles. "I'll be damned. Dawson City, right? Bonanza Creek? Klondike Kate's? Diamond Tooth Lil?"

"Yeah. Ever been in Mattie Crosky's Bathhouse?"

"The cleanest place in Dawson. Of course that ain't sayin' much. Hey, did you ever stay in that so elegant Fairview Hotel? White linen tablecloths, fine crystal, real chamber music?"

"Yeah. Yeah. And walls of canvas covered with paper."

Ramey ordered a couple more drinks and slapped Theo on the shoulder. "Well, my old sourdough friend, did you ever strike it rich?"

"Almost."

"Almost," Ramey repeated and laughed. "We all did *almost*, didn't we? So what're you doing here?"

Theo explained his berth on the *Mabel G.*

"Hey, then you'll be passing by here now and then. Next time drop in on us. If you can stop over I'll put you up at the ranch."

For the next few hours, while the freighter unloaded its cargo, the two drank and swapped tales of the Klondike. Ramey had been less lucky than Stevenson, and had returned home no richer than he had left.

"You know, they've been mining gold south of here," Ramey said. "In the Santa Lucia Mountains, the Los Burros district. I took a look-see down there, but most of the mines are played out already. They never did find the mother lode. I'm cured of gold fever, anyway. Never want to swing a pickaxe again.

"You know where I'd put my money if I had any? Go to Carmel, my friend. Buy some property there. The lots are selling fast. That's the only gold mine around here."

By the time the *Mabel G.* blew her whistle, the pair, abetted by liquor, had become fast friends. Ramey insisted that Theo come to his engagement party in a couple of months. "To a beautiful Californio *senorita*. And we'll have a big *fandango*. That's what we call a dance party in these parts. Any excuse and we have a *fandango*. Especially at the Cooper Ranch. Everybody around here's always invited. Drop in any weekend. But mine'll be something special. Come alone or bring a lady friend. We'll put you up at the ranch house. No trouble."

Theo promised to come to Ramey's *fandango* and, walking a bit unsteadily, wondering about the Los Burros mines, he managed to navigate the perilously swaying ramp to board the *Mabel G.*

A pearl-gray fog had crept in as the freighter chugged out to a rolling sea. A mournful foghorn sounded a dirge. Captain Ogilvie joined him at the rail and pointed his pipe ahead. "The horn's at the Point Sur Light Station. It warns of the rocks near Cooper Point, out there. Tricky in a dense fog. Even in clear weather, as a matter of fact. Just a few years ago a passenger steamer, the *Los Angeles*, crashed and sank near here. Nobody ever figured out why. Plain goddam incompetence is my guess."

The fog cleared barely enough for Theo to see the lighthouse and other gray buildings on top of a massive rock protruding into the sea. As the promontory fell astern of them the fog engulfed it until nothing could be seen.

During the next two months, Theo visited Ramey whenever the *Mabel G.* stopped at Notley's Landing. Occasionally, between trips, he came down by coach from Monterey. His violin was welcome at the lively parties, where he became acquainted with many of the locals.

He particularly enjoyed his stormy but friendly arguments about politics and the state of the world with the legendary "Doc" Roberts, who drove his buggy down from his practice in Monterey to respond to local medical emergencies. Roberts was a rock-ribbed Republican, and Theo was amused to find that they disagreed about almost everything, from the gold standard, to the war in Manchuria, the Filipino insurrection, and the recent revolution in Russia.

The good doctor had friends in the Republican administration in Sacramento, and was making a pest of himself by lobbying for a hare-brained scheme to build a paved highway along the coast with bridges spanning the rivers and canyons. It would cut the distance to Big Sur by more than a third and make medical care more accessible, he urged. When Theo observed that the small population wouldn't justify the immense cost, Roberts responded, "Just wait. Just wait, my boy. Build the highway and open the coast to automobiles and they'll come." He was going to buy an automobile himself, he said, to help him with his Monterey practice.

Theo soon felt completely at home in the Sur. Lovely dark-eyed Juanita, the sister of Ramey's intended bride, was accomplished at the flute, and they practiced duets together. Theo realized he'd been lonely for female company, and for the first time seriously thought about marriage. Maybe with Clarissa, after all. Or he might settle down here. Hadn't Jim Ramey suggested he invest in Carmel?

One sunny day in March he walked into the plush office of the Carmel Development Corporation in the stately Pine Inn on Ocean Avenue. A tall broad-shouldered man with a tanned smiling face stood up to greet him, motioned him to a leather chair by his desk and extended his hand.

"Mr. Stevenson? It's a great pleasure to meet you. I'm Frank Devendorf. My friends call my 'Devy'. May I offer you some coffee?"

Stevenson declined, but accepted a panatela, clipped its end, and lit it with his silver lighter. He drew on the slender cigar with a contented sigh. It was good Havana tobacco. He asked Devendorf the name of his tobacconist.

"The Ordway Pharmacy in Monterey. Here, have another." Theo accepted it gratefully.

"Is this your first visit to Carmel, Mr. Stevenson?"

Theo nodded.

"From the Klondike country, I understand."

Theo nodded again.

"And I understand you want to invest in Carmel real estate with a view to settling down here."

"I do mean to buy here, yes."

"You couldn't do better. Did you see all those tents in the vacant lots around here?"

"I did indeed."

"Those are people who've come from the Valley to escape the heat. We have the perfect climate, Mr. Stevenson. And that's why our lots are going so fast.

"My partner, Mr. Powers, has the deeds all drawn up as you requested. We need only your signature to transfer the title. And your check or cash, of course." Devendorf chuckled. "Five lots near the beach, sir, on Camino Real south of Seventh Avenue. All prime property. The president of Stanford University is building a home right next to you. We call it 'Professors' Row' because that's the high quality type of neighbors you'll have."

Stevenson smiled, glanced over the papers, took the gold-embossed fountain pen extended to him and signed. He drew from his billfold a sheaf of banknotes and handed them over.

"Will you be building on any of the properties immediately, sir? If so, I can recommend a crackerjack architect for you."

"No. I'm afraid I have to go back to New York to settle a personal matter. I don't know yet where I'm going to live. I intend, in any case, to hold the properties as an investment."

"A safe investment, sir. Those properties are as good as gold."

As good as gold, Theo thought. Sound investments, to be sure. Given time, enough to keep his mother and two sisters on Easy Street. But as good as gold? Not quite. Dammit, he missed the search for the yellow stuff, the lure of the hunt, the excitement of discovery. If the fields hadn't played out he'd still be up there. But he wasn't really eager to return to New York. Not yet, anyway.

"Will you be staying in Carmel for a while, Mr. Stevenson?"

"I'll stay here at the Inn a few days just looking around, and then I'll go down to the Big Sur country to celebrate the engagement of a friend of mine, Mr. Ramey." *And maybe I'll go down to Los Burros. "Take a look-see,"* as Ramey put it.

Two mornings later, Theo sauntered down to the restaurant at the Pine Inn, and sat at a breakfast table covered with thick white linen and gleaming silver. He ordered fried eggs, potatoes and bacon and a cup of strong coffee. As he sipped the bitter brew, the front desk clerk walked over and deferentially held out an envelope. "Just arrived, Mr. Stevenson."

A letter from his sister, Emily, who hated to write letters. She'd sent a clipping from the *New York Tribune*, which he read with some amazement: *Mr. and Mrs. Thomas A. Conway announce the engagement of their daughter, Clarissa of New York City, to Mr. Henry Dowling of Stamford, Connecticut.* And with it a note from Emily: *Faint heart never won fair lady. Now you can come home, you big coward.*

He felt relieved but at the same time a slight nostalgia mixed with some regret. Had he missed an opportunity? He had really liked Clarissa, that tall, willowy brunette. Had his family been right all along? Had he been prospecting in the wrong places? He sent Clarissa a telegram with best wishes and signed it "Love, Theo."

The next morning, Theo paid his bill at the Pine Inn—nine dollars for three nights—and boarded the coach headed to Big Sur. Already seated were a Spanish-speaking couple and a pretty, slim, dark-haired young woman whose name, he learned, was Lavinia.

And his life got turned around.

He was attracted to her at first glance: a pretty, unpretentious young woman, intelligent but shy, with a bit of mischievous adventure in her eyes. By the end of the journey he'd been thoroughly smitten, captivated. And then, during Ramey's engagement *fandango* when she'd opened up her heart to him and poured out her dreams he'd felt a warm surge of kinship and fell deeply in love for the first time in his life. *Lavinia. The woman I've been waiting for.*

After Theo had taken Lavinia back to the Light Station following the *fandango* celebrating Ramey's wedding, it was about two in the morning. At the Cooper Ranch the wind had turned chilly. Theo shivered, and looked about for Ramey's assistant, from whom he would rent the horse and the burro for the trail south along the coast.

He passed a trio of musicians. The banjo player, a tall, thin disheveled fellow maybe in his fifties with white scarecrow hair and an unkempt beard, abruptly stopped playing. He raised his hand, and stared at Theo. Then, after a few seconds: "I'll be damned. I'll be double-damned."

Theo stopped. The man looked oddly familiar.

He walked up to Theo and studied his face. "Teddy Stevenson, or I'll be a horse's ass. The image of your father! I heard somebody mention your name t'other day an' I been hopin' to meet you in the flesh." He extended a knobby paw and dropped his voice almost to a whisper. "Al. Albert Clark, from back East. You don't remember me, I guess, and don't let on if you do. But your father saved my life." He led Theo to a bench away from the fire.

Theo had heard stories about "Crazy Al", the hermit who lived in the woods near the base of Pico Blanco. "A bit daft but harmless," they said. "Pixilated on the subject of gold." Rumor had it that he mined a secret lode of silver near his cabin.

Theo stared at Al and suddenly recalled from his childhood a thin, poorly dressed college student who had inexplicably lived with them for a few months before disappearing. "Albert Clark. Now I remember you. You were a student at . . . ."

Al put a finger to his lips and shook his head. "I never talk about that. About being educated, you know. My past is past. Here I'm just Al Clark, the crazy man. But I'm not crazy, you know. I know things. I know things. I know about gold." He shook his head again.

"About gold? What do you know about gold?"

"Oh, I know where to find it. Gold is so beautiful, but it's evil. I know. I know." He looked in Theo's eyes. "Are you looking for gold?"

"Maybe. I'm going to visit the Los Burros mines."

"Oh, but there's a curse on gold." He dropped the subject. "Your father. He saved my life, did you know that? I was a stupid kid. I wanted to be rich, played poker, fan-tan and whatever. I gambled on the races. I lost all the money I'd inherited from my family, and more that I didn't even have. They came after me and were going to kill me if I didn't pay up. Your father paid them off for me, and never told anybody. He believed I had promise, you know. Put me through Columbia and then Harvard Medical School. I even got a medical degree. Nobody here knows about it, except Doc Roberts."

"What happened? Why did you leave?"

"I did a terrible thing. Never mind what. I had to leave the city. I came west to look for gold."

"So did you find it?"

"Oh yes, I found it. But that's a secret."

He gazed toward the mountains. "What I've told you—about your father and Harvard—I haven't told anybody. I don't want anybody to find me. Here I'm just Crazy Al, who lives alone in the woods. I like it that way."

Then the White Woman walked into Theo's life. A tall, striking woman, perhaps in her thirties, wearing a long flowing white gown. She was almost an albino, with platinum blonde hair and a classic profile that could have graced the Acropolis. She sat on an empty bench across from them on the other side of the fire. Theo had never met her or seen her before, yet felt a nagging wisp of recognition, nostalgia almost, as though he should know her, or had known her elsewhere.

She was astoundingly beautiful, but none of the men nearby seemed to have noticed her. Except for Al, who got up quickly. "I'll see you later," he said, picked up his banjo, and joined the other musicians. They began to play a catchy mountain tune.

The woman came over to sit down close to Theo, giving him a friendly smile. Her eyes were a deep gray. Flickering light from the fireplace revealed a slender well-formed body under the diaphanous dress—was she wearing anything under it? She was easily the most beautiful woman Theo had ever seen, the very definition of feminine perfection. Sexually desirable, but you couldn't imagine bedding her. He wondered whether she was lonely in her perfection, whether it was a cocoon around her.

"Mr. Stevenson, who are you, and why are you here?" Her voice was a silvery contralto.

None of your damn business, he thought. But he found himself compelled to explain. "I've just bought some property in Carmel, and I came for Mr. Ramey's wedding party."

"Property? Carmel? Tell me, Mr. Stevenson, do you really think anyone can truly own that land or any land?"

She didn't wait for an answer, and had a mocking but not unfriendly smile on her lips. "This is very strange country, Mr. Stevenson. The Rumsen Indians believe that Pico Blanco, just over there—" she pointed to the peak now obscured by fog "—is the center of the universe. They say human history began there when Coyote, Hummingbird and Eagle greeted the first humans after creation. They believe that Pico Blanco is the tip of the world and the souls of every living creature must pass by it when they die. And that deep in that very mountain is the womb of the world, where the earth mother lives."

Her eyes searched his face. "And before the Rumsen there lived a race much, much older. Some call them 'Dark Watchers'. They guard Pico Blanco and protect its secrets from the 'men from the south', meaning the Spaniards and other white men who come to destroy, with their dynamite, their engines, their dams, their deadly chemicals. They're watching you, Mr. Stevenson. You must be careful where you tread. Be careful what you look for and what you may find."

She smiled and her voice turned soft. "I heard you play the violin this evening. It was so very beautiful, like a song from the gods. And the young lady you were with. Are you in love with her?"

Theo nodded.

"Then her fate is bound to your own. For her sake take care where you tread. You are an artist and have beauty in your soul. Treasure what beauty you may find and do not destroy it."

"What do you mean?"

She didn't answer, but rose and shook hands with him. Her touch was cold, almost freezing. "Who are you?" he asked.

She looked past him at the sky. "I have many names. Here they call me Blanca, 'The White Woman'. In other places, far away, I've been known as Parvati. The Indians of the south call me Ixchel. It makes no difference, my name. Good night, Mr. Stevenson." She walked swiftly into the gloom, not looking back.

Al returned.

"She talked to you."

"Who the devil is she?"

"Her name is Blanca. She's here to guard secrets. Secrets of the people who were here even before the Indians. Secrets so secret only she knows them. I've seen her once before. She came to warn me. She means no harm but mind what she says."

Theo

Al extended a calloused hand. "Come see me when you get back from Los Burros. Ask anybody where my cabin is." He walked away.

Somewhere nearby an owl hooted. The river chattered over its bed. A few of the Cooper Ranch hands were collecting trash and unused food to keep the bears away. *All in all, an interesting evening,* Theo thought. *Ghosts. Curses. Warnings from the most beautiful woman I've ever seen. You couldn't take any of it seriously, of course. After all, this is the twentieth century, isn't it? The U.S.A. Modern medicine. Physics. Darwin.* He lit another cigar and puffed on it.

Several days later, Theo sat in the Gem Saloon in Mansfield, California, nursing a snifter of cognac and penning a letter to Lavinia. He watched the frantic life and death struggles buzzing on the ubiquitous flypaper and studied the unshaven and odoriferous denizens of a bar presided over by a toothy portrait of Teddy Roosevelt. He finished his letter to Lavinia, vowing again that he'd be back for her birthday, kissed it, folded it and sealed it in the embossed blue envelope supplied by the local hotel.

Mansfield huddled itself in the Santa Lucia Mountains in the southern Big Sur country, accessible only by narrow trails winding through the craggy mountains. Except for the climate, it reminded Theo of decrepit mining towns in the Klondike. Five saloons, a hotel, a general store, a stable, two restaurants, a barber shop, about forty homes, a bank, a post office, and a jail. The obligatory whorehouse had three women ranging in age from "Who Knows?" to "Who Cares?" The fifteen-room hotel, sagging like the harlots, badly needed a paint job. Grandiosely named The Metropolitan, it had no bath or running water, and a fetid outhouse in back—so primitive that Theo wished he had rented a room at the Dutton Hotel in Jolon, but that was almost a day's ride away. Originally called Manchester for some forgotten son, the town had been rechristened Mansfield for a deservedly obscure politician.

He'd spent a week or so in the hot sun, probing around the smaller mines that had already been worked out, their entrances gaping, some filled with oily water, most with abandoned rusting machinery. It stood to reason, he reckoned, that somewhere nearby was the mother lode, the great primordial river of molten gold that had fed the veins and fissures in the white quartz that miners picked and crushed. But nobody had yet discovered that great bonanza. The big mines, owned by corporations such as the *Oregon*, the *Cool Springs* and the *New York*, were fast petering out. Someday someone might make the lucky strike, find gold where no one had looked, or even hit the mother lode and become fabulously, fantastically rich. *What a great wedding gift that would be for Lavinia.*

Reluctantly, Theo came to the conclusion that the Santa Lucia gold rush was already history. He gave Mansfield a few years—ten at the most—before it became a ghost town. He got up to post his letter and to make arrangements to reclaim his horse and burro from the stables early the next morning. *Lavinia, I'm coming back to you.*

Perversely, his thoughts kept returning to the legend of the fabled hidden mine and the Indians who had brought gold dust to the mission fathers in Carmel, until both the mission and the padres had become extinct. The Lost Mine of the Padres. The legend said no white person could ever find it. But he'd heard rumors that Indians even today had access to it.

And what about that Chinese puzzle, Sing Fat? Not a white man, certainly, and his wagon went up and down the coast, collecting seaweed—a clever camouflage, some said, for his visits to the mine. "You know how devious Orientals are," they said. "Who in creation would buy seaweed?"

And "Crazy Al". What did *he* know?

Theo walked briskly to the stable where he told the boy in charge to have his horse and burro ready in the morning.

He found Al's cabin surrounded by redwoods at the foot of Pico Blanco near a branch of the Little Sur River. Al welcomed him in; the cabin was surprisingly well kept; bookcases lined the walls and there was even indoor plumbing, a rare and expensive amenity in these parts. Theo remembered that Al was supposed to have a silver mine he was secretly working. *This is not your run-of-the-mill madman,* he thought.

Over good coffee served in fine china, Theo asked Al to relate what he knew about the Lost Mine of the Padres.

Al shook his head. "I don't know anything about that. It's just a story. A myth."

"But you said you know where there's gold."

"I do. But it's a secret. There's a curse on it."

"Can you tell me where it is?"

Al shook his head again. "No. I promised Blanca."

"I can keep a secret." Theo thought a moment. "Like not telling anyone that you had to leave the East."

Al stared at Theo. "You won't tell anyone?"

"Not if you tell me about the gold."

Al frowned and bit his lip. "All right. I'll show you. But just to look. You must promise not to touch it or tell anyone."

"You have my word." *This could be it. The lucky strike to end all strikes.*

Theo

He brushed away a vision of the White Woman. *I won't fall for this super-stitious crap. Just this one more try.*

The morning dew soaked their boots as Al led Theo through the undergrowth and scattered stands of madrones and redwoods. They came to a bank where a small creek gurgled. Theo's practiced eye noted the white quartz pebbles in the streambed—often found near gold. Instinctively, he wanted to pan the sands, but quietly followed Al along the banks of the stream. He could come back later.

Various birds whose calls Theo didn't recognize trilled and chirped. The air was wonderfully cool and fragrant with aromas of the forest. Gradually he became aware of the sound of a waterfall ahead. They stopped just below a cascade of rushing water that seemed to gush from a rocky cliff above the stream. "I think this is where the Indians used to gather gold dust," Al said, "by panning the sand. They'd put it in quills and carry it to the padres. But there's no 'lost mine'. Those Indians didn't mine. There's a small pocket of gold up there above the falls, but I doubt the Indians ever found it. Maybe an earlier people, before the Rumsen, Blanca's people maybe. Come, I'll show you something marvelous, far more precious than gold."

Theo gazed at the surrounding forest. He had an uneasy sense that they were being watched. *Just show me the gold. Just show me the gold, crazy man, that's all I ask.*

Al led him to the top of the falls, which raced over a gigantic boulder worn smooth and polished by the timeless flow of incessant water. An ancient redwood clasped the boulder with great gnarled roots.

"Here," Al said. "Something wonderful." He put a finger to his lips, slipped behind the tree and disappeared. Theo followed through a crevice in the rock just wide enough to admit him. He slid through the opening, then stood awestruck by what lay before him: a colossal cavern, filled with stalactites, stalagmites and cascades of calcite in a myriad of wondrous colors and fantastic shapes.

"Is it any wonder," Al said, "that the ancient people kept this a secret? This is a sacred place. It's the center of the world, you know." The waterfall put a musical emphasis to his words. He raised his hand and pointed at Theo. "Don't touch anything. This place is protected by the gods."

Stupefied, Theo gazed around. Wall paintings in ocher and blue, superbly executed, decorated the cavern. Some portrayed mammoths and saber-toothed tigers. Others were intricate abstract designs. Stick figures depicted men hunting. As an art student he'd visited the Cantabrian caves in Spain, but paintings there were not nearly as beautiful, or as skillfully rendered as these. So far as he knew, nothing like this had ever been found in America or anywhere else.

The artist in him was hungry to study these paintings. He could spend a lifetime here. But where did this light come from? He couldn't see any fissures to the outside. The illumination seemed to be a radiance from the cavern itself. Blanca was right. This was too precious to reveal to the outside world. Thank God Crazy Al had kept this secret, hadn't shown it to others the way he'd revealed it to him.

On the wall, under a magnificent depiction of what seemed to be a ferocious jackal, a painting of a hand in red ocher caught his attention. He pressed his palm against it to compare sizes. Oddly, it felt warm to his touch, and then hot. He pulled his hand away.

"There's some gold in here. Come." Al led Theo to an adjoining cavern, littered with huge bones and tusks of animals certainly long extinct. Part of the wall had been hollowed out. Exquisite figurines of terra cotta, of jade, of gold and silver, of crystal, lapis lazuli and turquoise, equal to or surpassing anything ancient Europe had ever produced, sat on ledges sculpted from the rock. Treasures beyond price. This had been a culture of stupendous aesthetic achievement. Centuries, if not millennia of magical artistic inspiration were displayed here as though in a museum.

A tiny figurine caught his eye. It was a representation in gold and ivory of Blanca, perfect, like the woman it depicted. As much as he tried to resist the impulse, his hand reached out to it. He shoved it into his pocket while Al wasn't watching. *My birthday gift for Lavinia*, he told himself.

He felt a buzzing in his ears and then a roar. The ground began to tremble under his feet.

"Earthquake!" screamed Al. They scrambled out of the cave and made it some distance away just before the tree guarding the cave shuddered and collapsed in a roaring avalanche that effectively sealed the entrance under hundreds of tons of boulders. Theo tripped on a mossy root, slammed his head on a rock, and felt ribs crack. Darkness engulfed him.

Things and people came slipping in and out at the edges of his consciousness. He seemed to be at the Cooper Ranch. Dr. Roberts was treating his bruises and telling him he had a concussion. Al Clark asked him how he felt. Jim Ramey told him to rest. Then from a distance he seemed to hear Lavinia's voice calling him. He found it hard to concentrate.

Then the White Woman, speaking to him. "I had hoped to spare you, Mr. Stevenson, because you understood the beauty of my people and because you are a friend of Mr. Clark, who has already paid for his crimes and is innocent in his soul. But mostly because you can play the kind of music that lifts my heart and soothes the spirits of the gods. However, when you took that figurine you violated an ancient taboo. Whoever defiles that site must be punished by losing whatever is most precious to him.

"I am sorry I did not come early enough to warn you. But what's done is done. I suggest you leave the Big Sur country forthwith. Do not ever return here. As for your lust for gold, it has been cured. At a terrible price to you, as you soon will learn."

Crazy Al had no memory whatsoever of the earthquake. "All I know is we were out walking and suddenly you tripped and fell." And he claimed no knowledge of the cave, shaking his head when Theo mentioned it.

Roberts also dismissed Theo's mention of an earthquake. "No one around here felt any tremor. It must be a product of your concussion. And Al has no memory of the cave you mention. He may follow his own music, but is perfectly sane. I've known him for years."

"You knew him Back East?"

Roberts nodded. "We attended medical school together."

"What made him leave?"

"He never would say."

Theo found it hard to think, to remember. Soon his memories of the cave began to fade.

Then, suddenly one day, the haze in his mind began to clear. Against Roberts' protests, and without explaining, he pulled himself out of bed and dressed. He borrowed a horse and buggy from Ramey and with his head buzzing, made his way to Point Sur and up the winding road to the Light Station.

His heart pounding, he raced up the stairs. Lavinia's door was unlocked, her room deserted, hollowly, horribly empty. Even no covers on the bed.

He stumbled downstairs and knocked. Mrs. Thurman opened the door and glared at him.

"Lavinia?" Theo's voice stuck in his throat.

"I'm sorry."

"Where is she? What's happened to her?"

"She passed away about a week ago. Just after her birthday, poor thing. You should be ashamed. She kept asking for you. Her mother sent for her body." Mrs. Thurman shut the door in his face.

Tears streaming down his face, Theo staggered down the front steps.

He drove to the beach at Cooper Ranch, where the Big Sur River emptied into the Pacific, and where Lavinia had found that small nugget in the sand. *A memento of our betrothal, she'd said.* He walked up a bluff overlooking the ocean. He took from his pocket the little statuette he'd taken—stolen—from the cave. *My birthday present to Lavinia.* It seemed to burn his fingers. With all his strength, he hurled it into the sea.

On his way back to the buggy he saw a small dark figure on a neighboring ridge. And he sensed the presence of the White Woman watching him from the top of Pico Blanco.

Author's Note:

All the characters in this story are products of my imagination, with the exception of (in the order of their appearance) Sing Fat, Dr. Roberts, Frank Devendorf, and Albert Clark, although the scenes I described probably never took place. For the real Albert Clark I have invented a fictional past.

Mansfield and Notley's Landing did exist, but are no longer, although some of the ruined mine entrances near Mansfield can still be found.

The Pine Inn, of course, still stands majestically on Ocean Avenue in Carmel, and Ordway Pharmacy still does business in Monterey. The Pacific Ocean House did exist, as did the Westmere Saloon at Notley's Landing, the Gem Saloon and Hotel International in Mansfield, but all four are long gone. "The Lost Mine of the Padres" still exists in the folklore of Big Sur, as do the "Dark Watchers" and the "White Woman", although I have given her a more sympathetic personality.

Diamond Tooth Lil, Klondike Kate, Mattie Crosley's Bathhouse, and the Fairview Hotel all existed in Dawson City at the time of the Klondike Gold Rush.

I am indebted to Dr. Alan Rosen for supplying historical information, and to Jeff Norman for answering questions about Notley's Landing and distances on the old Coast Road. Thanks to Professor Sandy Lydon for his helpful comments on "Lavinia" and "Theo". And to Byron Merritt for his careful editing of my story.

To Dawn Cope, docent at the Light Station, thank you for helping me to keep my geography straight, for information on the flora of the Big Sur country, and for your patient, perceptive critiques and proofreading.

Any errors of fact or fancy, of course, reflect my own ignorance.

Theo

Final Sentence

by Linda Price

n and out of consciousness for hours, I had served as a reluctant witness to Diane Davies' suffering. The blood from her head, mixed with my tears, had seeped into the wide plank flooring of the Boronda adobe. Her blue lips looked as if they'd been drawn with charcoal on a pale canvas face. The blood that had drained onto her thick blonde hair gave it the texture of painted straw. As the miniature reflection of ceiling fans rotated in her unseeing eyes, my thoughts turned, too. My life has revolved around that warm August night exactly one week ago. As it turns out, her death has led to my end.

The green-eyed brunette judging me from my dresser mirror has led me to this conclusion. Freshly cleaned up, her tomboy haircut, white collared shirt, blue blazer, black wool slacks and leather loafers testify to her impeccable character. Dark gray Tahitian pearls sum up her good judgment and taste. She reminds me it's getting dark.

The two-tone Rolex on my wrist confirms it's close to eight. It was a gift from Aunt Helen and Uncle Harry for graduating from Law School. My Berkeley degree hung in the Monterey County District Attorney's office, where I had practiced meting out justice for over ten years.

Justice.

I pushed the .38 Ruger aside and pulled the small Sony tape recorder close. I put in fresh batteries and a new cassette before setting it up on its little metal legs, just as I had seen my secretary do a thousand times before an interview or deposition. I faced my mirror and pushed record. "My name is Stephanie Black . . ." I choked on the force of words that erupted from the pit of my soul. I drew circles of tears on my mother's gold-leaf mahogany dresser, my heirloom. I had to face the past seven days. Indeed the past twenty years.

I had planned to stay home last Sunday night. I basked in the late afternoon sun on my deck overlooking the ridge off Tierra Grande Road. The heady fragrance of roses near the pool heightened the caress of the sun that had lulled me into Carmel Valley bliss. I suppose I could have ignored the ringing telephone. When I grudgingly answered it, the voice of Diane Whitehead Davies, known by all as "Di," insisted we revisit the past—again.

"I finished my research on the Gibson case," she said. "The report will go off to the insurance company tomorrow, and you won't believe what I got from the Gibsons."

I hit my knee against the chaise jumping up. "A confession, I hope."

"No, photos from our senior year homecoming. I'd like to go over a couple of them with you." She always had to sound like a detective. I had pushed bittersweet memories away when she mentioned our senior year. Fresh Monterey Bay salmon and a Greek salad had to satisfy my appetites tonight.

"Di, I'm very disappointed to hear that you're taking gifts from suspects. Besides, I don't want to drive all the way to the forest."

"Suspects at your office, not mine," she retorted. "And, you can meet me in Carmel Valley. I'm on my way to feed Mumsey's cats while she's in San Francisco for a few days. Now you have no excuse."

I stretched back out on the chaise. "I'm in the middle of . . . cooking dinner."

"Stephanie," she instructed, "finish your dinner. Meet me at the adobe at eight. Humor an old friend."

"Okay, Di. Consider yourself humored." I sighed, reluctant to leave the sanctuary I had created after two failed marriages. They say you never forget your first love. Neither the aspiring filmmaker nor the successful mortgage broker had made me forget mine.

After eating, I put the top down on my green BMW roadster and cruised along the lazy Carmel Valley Road. The evening sun cast the mountains' shadows over the Valley. The warm summer air tossed my hair around my face. But my thoughts became clouded as I drew closer to Di and her photos.

Di had been creating drama with her journals since our freshman year at Carmel High. The Carmel Unified School District provided diversity for her. It was the largest geographic district in the United States when we went there. The kids from the cozy grammar schools in Carmel, Carmel Valley, and Big Sur, as well as private schools, merged into the Carmel Middle School. Two years later, add in the kids from the Monterey and Pacific Grove Districts who faked a Carmel address, and we all melted into the high school pot having earned a spot in a designated peer group. I ran with the "intellectuals", the brains, who studied the rest: the surfers, the jocks, the heads, the cowboys, the geeks, well . . . the rest.

The journals were safely stored at Gloria Whitehead's home in Carmel Valley. She was Di's mother whom we had affectionately called Mumsey since we were ten. An appropriate place, I mused, as the original building on the site of her home had been a respite for traveling Catholic priests and nuns. They recorded inspirational thoughts as well as warnings about dangers on the trail in a journal kept by the small altar. The California missions and small churches were situated a day's walk apart and the smaller churches deteriorated from lack of use when riding replaced walking. While some deteriorated, interesting inhabitants moved into others.

Señor Boronda and his wife and thirteen children were among the people who first lived in the Boronda house on what is now Di's mother's property. He had lost a leg in a bullfight. His wife sold her homemade cheese to help feed the family. A friend named Jack kindly delivered the yellow cheese that became known as "Monterey Jack". During high school, we held séances and tried to call forth these spirits and other past inhabitants.

Diane's parents had purchased the neglected property in the early sixties and restored it to its original beauty . . . and mystery. Di was proud of her family home's history and encouraged her aging mother to stay on, helping with the expensive upkeep and the string of uninvited "historians".

Di and her husband, Grant, lived on the Pacific Grove side of Pebble Beach. After passing the bar, she had rejected a job with the Monterey County District Attorney's office in favor of work that better fulfilled her talent for gathering information and ordering chaos. Her firm, Salinas Private Investigations, had grown from spying on unfaithful spouses and unethical business associates to specializing in suspicious deaths involving large life insurance payouts. Rich people seemed to love to knock one another off for money.

One of her cases that potentially interested my office involved the Gibson family. The family patriarch, Howard Gibson, had died in a mysterious boating accident off Mulligan Point near Moss Landing. Evidence had surfaced that prompted Franklin Insurance and Trust Company to withhold ten million dollars from his son and heir, Chuck Gibson. Di's report was crucial to the outcome.

I would love to prosecute the Gibsons.

I squeezed the steering wheel and pressed the accelerator thinking of Chuck and his silly society Barbie wife behind bars. I careened into the driveway and parked in the back. Di greeted me with pursed lips and furrowed blonde eyebrows.

"What's up?" I asked.

"These photos are . . . interesting. Revealing, in fact. You have some explaining to do," she said, as she gestured for me to come inside. I never dreamed that she would stumble upon my deepest secrets. Both of them.

I watched the breeze from the fan stirring Diane's hair. I patted the photo in my pocket and twisted around to look at the burned pictures in the fireplace. The pain that pulsated from my neck to my leg completed my misery. As I lost consciousness, I thought I heard gravel crunching under the weight of a car on the drive.

I awoke on the mustard yellow sleeper sofa we had used for high school slumber parties. The intermittent red flashes on the living room wall and the cool cloth at the back of my neck confirmed the urgency of the evening's events. A siren screamed. The shrill noise grew louder as it neared the house, then stopped abruptly. Nauseated, I tried to sit.

"Steady, there Steph. You've got a pretty big bump on the back of your neck and that ankle looks bad." I swallowed back salmon and feta cheese, soured with fear, and turned my attention to Captain Redmond of the Monterey County Sheriff's department. Neil Redmond was one of the best investigators in town. He was also my cousin, but more like a brother. His parents, Aunt Helen and Uncle Harry, had raised my brother Don and me. I never knew my dad, and my mom had been murdered when I was nine years old. Neil and Don both studied at Berkeley in the late sixties. Later they served together in Vietnam. They'd come home on the same plane. Neil helped carry my brother off in a box.

"See who did this?" Neil asked.

I fell back on the sofa. "Di? Did you see . . . her?"

"Shh, yes, honey, I saw. We'll get the bastard," he rubbed my shoulder with his thumb just as he'd done since we were kids. The way he'd search out the knots in the middle of my back on either side of my spine and work his fingers up to the tightness in my neck was an especially comforting gesture tonight. He'd always been protective and I loved the way our lives had continued to intertwine.

Grant's tall angular frame appeared before me.

"Steph, Steph, I don't understand. What's happened here?" He pulled me to my feet and planted his chin on top of my head repeating, "I don't understand," in a quivering whisper. I pushed him away as I fell back on the sofa, clutching my ankle. The pain didn't stop me from looking at his face. Curly blonde hair, gray at the temples, blue eyes that turned hazel when he wore dark colors, full, firm lips. Handsome. Irresistible to women of all ages. His latest lover was reputed to be Charlene, Chuck Gibson's wife. Diane had been his trophy wife. Beautiful. Smart. Time apart in pursuit of separate interests had created a gulf between the two lovers. I always thought they were the perfect match, but then who knows what goes on inside a marriage. What *really* goes on. Even best friends can't know that.

How did we get to this place?

Carmel Valley Village had been a community of contrasts even before the movie stars and tourists discovered it. Sex, drugs, and rock and roll flourished side by side with the blooming physical fitness movement. Recovering alcoholics shared their experience, strength, and hope at the Chatterbox on Saturday night while drunks toasted themselves at the Stirrup Cup. Cowboys rode horses and wrangled livestock. Artists painted and sculpted. Teachers, mechanics, domestics, doctors, and stockbrokers lived side by side. Sitting on the ballpark fence, perched like birds on telephone wires, my friends and I would watch our parents. They'd be drinking booze out of paper cups in the bleachers at the Little League Park down by the river. Jabbering away like crows, they'd stagger down to the river to share a joint. The cops looked the other way back then. Everyone partied together.

Diane captured all of it and continued to track the community in journals over the years. She'd show up at parties, races, ball games, weddings and dinner parties with her camera and notebook. She rescued tickets, napkins, and other memorabilia out of trashcans from the smallest gathering to the Monterey Jazz Festival. Even off the musicians! She had secured a lock of hair from a guitar player. Her journals took on considerable sophistication with the advent of digital cameras. Naturally, as her investigative business grew, and people changed, her penchant for data gathering became unsettling for some. There would be many suspects for Di's murder.

"God damn it!" Grant pulled at his curls, "Will somebody tell me? What in the hell happened here?"

Neil motioned a uniformed officer over and whispered to him. The officer nodded and approached Grant. "Come with me, sir." He skillfully guided Grant out one of the many adobe doors to an inside courtyard and maneuvered him into a green chaise longue. A sheet of tears covered Grant's face. He pounded his fists on the arms of the chair. The officer listened intently, taking notes and nodding sympathetically.

Moments later, the stretcher on which I found myself was guided by attendants to the waiting ambulance, where they simultaneously mounted a blood pressure cuff on my arm, checked my pulse, and placed an oxygen mask over my mouth and nose. Neil appeared, picked up my hand, and squeezed it. "I'll be up to CHOMP shortly," he whispered, then he disappeared under the arched gateway to the courtyard. The ambulance's siren screamed the entire trip. Even though I couldn't see out, I recognized every turn, every stretch of pavement. The long driveway to Boronda Road, then Carmel Valley Road to Highway 1, to Highway 68, to Community Hospital of the Monterey Peninsula.

CHOMP. Not a place I wanted to be . . . under any circumstances. I recalled Diane had recorded my stay here for a broken leg just before our senior year. Her laughter rang in my ears as it had the last time we took a trip down memory lane in one of the journals.

The ambulance doors opened and the stretcher moved under me.

"She's been talking and laughing the entire trip," the young female quipped from beneath her cap.

"Really? Trippin' during the trip?" the driver queried sarcastically.

"We get some crazy ones, don't we?"

"Sure do."

They wheeled me into the emergency room and switched to professional mode as they reported my condition to the calm male nurse who was already checking my pulse and shining a small flashlight into my eyes. He was a big guy, gentle, concerned, studying me. I closed my eyes and when I reopened them, Diane hovered above me. She was angry. I reached out to touch her cheek and my fingers felt a scratchy beard. Someone was screaming and I could feel the big nurse's strong arms holding me down. More green smocked nurses, clucking comforting sounds, joined him. Diane's eyes stared vacantly at me. Lifeless, except for those tiny little fans rotating methodically. A blissful oblivion followed the prick in my arm.

I awoke to the antiseptic smells of suture kits and sterile gloves in my small curtained stall. The white X-ray screen behind it highlighted the blurred form of an oxygen tank. The tube that traveled from the bag hanging on the IV pole to the catheter in my arm pulled at my skin when I turned toward the opening curtain. Neil's eyes met mine and our quick tears acknowledged our loss. Within moments, he squared his shoulders, stretching to his full six-foot-two inches. My friend disappeared and Captain Neil Redmond stood before me. He looked serious.

"If you're up to talking, while you wait for the doc, I need to hear what you remember. Details. While they're fresh in your mind." He pressed my forehead gently with the back of his hand and continued, "I know you want this bastard caught. So do I. Nevertheless, we can't be effective if we let our emotions take over. I'm setting mine aside for now, so must you. Steph? Steph!! Nurse, nurse, she's passing out!"

"Officer, you have to leave."

"Okay, okay. I'm going to post a uniformed officer outside. She may have witnessed a murder."

"Certainly, go ahead."

I struggled to sit up. "Wait, don't leave. Nurse, I'm okay. I don't want him to leave."

"Relax, honey. He'll be back. The X-ray confirmed that the ankle is not broken, but the doctor's going to wrap it for you."

I fell back onto the narrow ER bed. Nodding agreement, I closed my eyes in the hope of shutting out the multiple levels of pain in my body and soul.

"Neil, we'll get this investigation on track as soon as I'm out of here. Okay?" I whispered.

He clicked his heels together, saluted like a Boy Scout, and backed out of the enclosure.

Two days later, Neil delivered me to my sanctuary. He held up his finger indicating that I should wait while he searched his coat pockets for his ever-evasive notebook before the interview began. I downed a Percodan.

"Ah, here we go," he said. "Start at the beginning, Steph, and take me through to the best of your recollection. I'll just take a few notes. We'll do this formally later."

"Okay. Di called me in the afternoon to say the Gibson report was about finished. And that she wanted to meet at her mother's place around eight to go through some pictures she had acquired. When I arrived—"

He interrupted, "What time was that?"

"Ummm, around eight. When I arrived, she didn't answer so I let myself in . . ."

"No, I meant, what time did Di call?" he asked.

"Oh, sorry, I think late afternoon, I was already thinking about dinner. Yeah, late afternoon," I said.

He wrote in his notebook, and then continued. "So, you arrived at eight?"

"Oh, wait, I was running late. I think it must have been closer to nine. I wasn't paying much attention."

"Okay," he said as he scribbled, "then what happened?"

"I saw Di on the floor."

"Wasn't it dark?"

"Dark?"

"You said you arrived around nine, it must have been dark. There were no lights on when the neighbor found you. So maybe you arrived closer to eight?" he asked again.

"Yes! No, closer to nine," I cried.

"And it was dark? No lights were on?" he asked.

"No lights were on, it was dark," I mimicked.

He put the notebook on his knee and clicked his pen open and close. "Didn't that seem odd?"

"No, Neil. Mumsey kept all the lights on a timer or some sort of sensor. The moon was going to be full. It was very bright late so maybe the lights didn't go on."

"What happened next?"

"Di was covered with blood, slumped on the floor. I ran and knelt next to her. Someone pushed me while I tried to hold her. Her blood was all over me by then. Someone pushed me and I fell over the coffee table into the fireplace. Then when I looked up he was running away," I said.

"So you caught a glimpse of him. What do you remember about him?" Neil asked.

"He was tall, thin. He wore a hat pulled down over his face," I answered.

"What kind of hat?"

"Oh, I don't know."

"Felt? Knit? Baseball cap?"

"Oh, well, it was, I think, it was a cap, a baseball cap."

"What makes you think so?"

"I don't know, Neil, it was a cap." I could feel the Percodan smooth out my nerves.

"What happened next?"

"I, uh, woke up. I had been unconscious off and on. Diane was on the floor in the dining room near the table. I think she was still alive, but I'm not sure. I couldn't help her; I thought my ankle was broken. I felt blood on my neck and didn't know if it was Di's or mine. I was worried that the man would come back, that maybe he had an accomplice and they'd both come back. I was afraid, confused. I passed out, finally, and the next thing I knew I was on the sofa and the place was full of uniforms, and you were rubbing my shoulders."

"Okay. Where was Mumsey?"

"I don't know. Out to dinner with a neighbor, I think. No, no, Di said she was out of town."

He jotted down a few notes and put the notebook in his shirt pocket. "Okay, that's enough for now."

The next day, Neil and I drove to Di's cozy P.I. office near the courthouse in downtown Salinas to meet with her partner, Kate Bishop. Formerly a police officer, the six-foot 145-pound marathoner quit the force to work with Di. She was a high school chum, too, representing the Big Sur contingent in our group of "intellectuals", although she had a well-earned spot with the jocks at a time when it was still difficult for women athletes. She stifled her tears and busied herself studying the top of Di's desk. "Di was up to her eyeballs in the Gibson case. She was just about ready to finish the report and submit it to you on Monday, the day after . . . after she was murdered."

She took a long drag off a cigarette. "Damn bad habit. But what the hell, you only live . . . once. The other investigators already took pictures and went through her desk thoroughly. They're coming back with a court order for the computer files. Help yourselves." She motioned us closer. The three of us surrounded the Queen Anne antique as if it were a shrine.

Finally, I reached down and moved some of the files around. I held up a photo.

"What's this, Kate?"

"Let me see," Kate said, "I don't remember that."

"Look at the license plate on the car in the photo. F-A-N-T-A-S-Y-2. This is from our senior year, homecoming. Old man Gibson is driving, looks like Chuck and that girl who was murdered in the back," I said.

"No kidding," Kate said, handing the photo to Neil. "Poor Chuck. Some of the parents were reluctant to let their kids hang out with him because of his dad's 'movie' business. Then he had to deal with Gracie's death." Kate rolled her eyes and put out the half-smoked cigarette. "I gotta start running again and get off this shit."

Neil put the photo back on the desk as he shuffled through the desk drawer. "Nothing here except pens and paper clips. When is the officer coming with the warrant to review the computer files?"

"Tomorrow, I believe."

I took out a tissue and blew my nose, waiting for an opportunity to speak. "We need to meet with the Gibson family, don't we Neil? Don't you think that photo is significant? Investigators do miss things."

He nodded in my direction. "Maybe. You should go home and get some rest, young lady."

"I'm good to go," I assured him.

Kate lit another cigarette. "After your officer comes with the warrant, I'll start on the contents of the computer. I'll let you know what I find.

Remember I can't reveal confidential information about clients who have nothing to do with this case."

"Kate, right now everyone's a suspect," Neil sighed, and gave her a quick hug on his way to the door.

"Stephanie, you are a wonder on those crutches," Kate said adding a mock one-two boxer jab at my arm.

"Not my first time. Remember homecoming our senior year?"

"Oh, right. Bye. Be careful." She and Neil exchanged their customary two-fingered salute.

The Gibson mansion hung from cliffs above the Pacific Ocean in Pebble Beach. The private security guard made a call as we drove through the heavy wrought-iron gates. Neil observed him through the rear-view mirror and we weren't surprised to find Charlene—Chuck's wife, Grant's lover, my suspect—standing outside the imposing entry door. Her arms folded over her perfect breasts, a perfect smile exposing her perfect teeth complimenting her perfect features. Neil parked the car, and then walked around to help me. He took the crutches out of the back seat and held them firmly while I pulled myself out of the passenger seat. Sweat dampened my entire body.

"I suspect the murder has something to do with this family," I whispered to Neil as I stood up. He smiled and motioned for me to hobble aside so he could close the car door.

Charlene's manicured fingers reached out to welcome us. "I am so very, very sorry for the loss of your colleague and good friend. Diane was a unique person in our lives. Her loss is personal to the entire community." A solitary tear trailed down her cheek. I gagged back my breakfast.

"Come in, please. Chuck and I want to assist in the investigation in any way," she cooed. She led us through the massive entry. "Chuck, CHUCK!" Turning toward us, she wrinkled her perfect nose as if smelling Gruyere. "Chuck and his computers. He'll be right in. Please sit."

Neil cleared his throat. Ice, from a glass pitcher of tea, clinking into large goblets, cut off his words. Charlene handed him a glass and fixed him with a level stare. "Our family is eager to put the rumors about my father-in-law's death to rest. We're leaving for our place in southern Italy soon. Of course, our attorney will keep us informed, unless we're not allowed to go. Is that possible? Will this, uh, tragedy delay the proceedings?"

Neil took a sip of iced tea. "Yes, delaying your trip is a possibility. As soon as Di's partner, Kate, can review and submit the report on your father's accident, you'll get our decision. I'm, I mean, we're here today in an effort to retrace Di's footsteps the weekend of her death. Kate told us that Di planned to come to see you on Saturday."

Charlene tipped her chin up accepting the change in topic. "Yes, she was here. I was away from the house, but Chuck was home. He'll tell you what he knows. And, speak of the devil, honey, they're here to ask you about Di's visit last Saturday."

Charles Winfield Gibson III was a large, but unimposing man. He had made an art form of not being noticed. I wondered how long he had stood in the doorway before we became aware of his presence. Chuck hesitated for a few moments before he lowered his eyes and walked across the floor. He shook hands with Neil, then me. His fingers were long and soft.

"Good afternoon," he said. "Diane's death has us both in shock. She was here the day before. She wanted to look at my dad's collection of cars so I asked our driver to show her into the garage. I think eight, maybe seven, remain of the original fifteen. Dad and I have been donating them to charity auctions. Taxes! Anyway, Billy, our driver, let her in, then left to pick up Charlene at the Beach Club. I went back to work and didn't see her again."

Neil searched through his coat pockets for his notebook.

"It's in your shirt pocket," I said.

"Did she say what she wanted in the garage?"

"No, but she seemed to be in a hurry. When I started to walk to my office, she, she, oh, never mind, I guess I'm grasping at straws."

"What size straws?"

"Uh, well, let me see if I can put together a bale."

Neil laughed at the lame joke. "Would you mind if Steph and I looked around the garage?"

"Not at all," he said. "Follow me." Chuck led us to a side door. Charlene waved good-bye and disappeared up a wood staircase that wound its way to the mezzanine. A mezzanine. Rich people! I stifled my envy and followed unsteadily, the rubber tips of my crutches squeaking on the white marble floor.

Chuck escorted us to the front of the impressive stone structure that housed the estate cars. I couldn't keep up with them on my crutches and fell behind. I heard Chuck whisper to Neil, "I need to speak to you privately." I caught up to the two and, having found my pace, swung past them and said, "I'm on a roll here. Meet you inside Neil." I negotiated my way inside, pushed the door part way shut, and made a lot of noise pretending that I was heading toward the adjacent room. I leaned on my good foot so I could peek through the doorjamb. I swallowed down a Percodan and heard Chuck say, "Diane asked me about Gracie Jordan."

"Gracie?" Her name hung in the air.

"Yes," Chuck responded, "Gracie was my date for homecoming dance the night she was murdered. Di wanted to know how well I knew her."

"What did she want to know?" Neil asked as he fished for his notebook again.

"She wanted to know if Gracie ever talked about her . . . relationship with Stephanie."

"Stephanie?" Neil snorted, "my Stephanie?"

"Yes," Chuck confirmed.

"And she used the word . . . relationship?"

Chuck nodded.

"Well, what did you tell her?" Neil asked, lowering his voice.

"Nothing much. Gracie was somewhat weird, always kidding around. I never listened to her when she rambled on about this person and that. God, Neil, that was twenty years ago. But, yeah, Diane wanted to know if I thought they were involved. Do I have to paint a picture? I hate saying it. She's like your sister."

Neil's face corkscrewed. "Well . . ."

Chuck cut him off. "Charlene had given Diane some old photos from our senior year. I think some of them were of homecoming, you know, when Gracie died."

Neil let out a long, slow breath. "Here's my card. My cell's on there, too, that's probably the best number to reach me. Stephanie's inside waiting for me. Call me if you remember anything else. Even if you think it's unimportant, call me anyway. Thanks."

I watched them say good-bye, but my thoughts were somewhere else. Gracie Jordan's thin pale face framed by those dark flirty tendrils from her constantly moving hair invaded my mind. An enviable free spirit, not really belonging to any group, she skirted the edges of Carmel High society. I scampered to the adjoining room on both feet when I saw Neil approaching the door. The Percodan was working.

"See anything of interest?" Neil inquired.

"No. Get anything from Chuck?" I tried to sound normal.

"Um, no," he said fingering his notebook.

I turned my face away as I digested his lie. I put on my most innocuous prosecutor face. If he didn't volunteer information, I knew better than to push him. Every time an opportunity presented itself, I'd tried to implicate Chuck in that twenty-year-old murder. Over the years, I had used my position against his family. His father paid a high price for a drunken driving incident. When he drowned with a five million dollar double indemnity life insurance policy in force, I was the influence behind creating doubts so Chuck couldn't collect.

"Hey, snap out of it!" Neil tousled my hair as he squeezed between a 1955 Porsche Spyder and a yellow 1967 Lamborghini, being very careful not to leave a fingerprint on their beautifully polished surfaces. Pictures of the Concours d' Elegance featuring one or another Gibson posing near a Bentley hung on the walls.

"Neil, look at this," I said.

"Where?" He looked at the wall where I was pointing.

"Here, where the wood is a darker shade. Doesn't it look like something's been removed?"

He scrunched down and examined the spot. "Could be. Maybe a picture?"

"Or, a license plate!" I pointed to the others on the wall. "Look at these plates. They're from all over. This shaded area is the same size as a license plate. F-A-N-T-A-S-Y-2?" I wondered aloud.

Neil made a note in his book.

"I wonder what Di was looking for out here?" I said. "Old man Gibson died in a boating accident. Cars don't figure, Neil. Unless, she found some clues to an old unsolved murder. Gracie's murder."

He put his notebook and pen away. "Let's go. I'm expecting to hear from Kate."

Neil helped me to the car. We rode in silence until Kate called Neil on his cell phone. I could tell by his frown that he didn't like what he was hearing. The pieces weren't fitting neatly into this puzzle. He shut off the phone and focused his attention on the turn from Highway 1 to Highway 68 toward Salinas.

"Well?" I finally broke the two-mile silence.

Neil seemed to take time to think while he swallowed down some bottled water.

"Kate just told me that she found extensive research on Gracie Jordan's twenty-year-old unsolved murder case," Neil said.

I affected my most confident prosecutor voice, "I wonder if Di found clues that tied Chuck to it. She probably went out to confront him. And the next night he beat her to death before she could reveal the new clues. I always thought he was guilty. Gracie's body was found at Whaler's Cove in Pt. Lobos, I think. Raped, too, wasn't she? They interviewed a lot of us kids. I was on crutches all fall that year from a water skiing accident at Lake Tahoe. Remember, you were up with the family."

Neil kept his eyes on the road as he spoke. "Chuck had nothing to do with Gracie's murder. I was a rookie on the force at that time. Gracie and Chuck sneaked down to the beach with two other couples. Chuck left with the others but Gracie refused to go with them. They took Chuck to his car in the school parking lot. Ten minutes later, he was at his parents' home in Pebble Beach. He admitted having sex with her, but all the evidence said it was consensual."

Cold sweat oozed from every pore of my body. "What if he went back?" I said. "What if his father lied for him? That old pervert was always eyeing the young girls. Maybe *he* killed Gracie. It makes sense. Di found a clue and Chuck killed her to protect himself, his father, or, or both!"

"Okay," Neil growled, tossing his cell phone on my lap. "Call Di's mom and let her know we're coming. We need to find the negatives to see what's in the rest of those photos."

"But Neil, we have the photo that counts . . ."

"I want to see all of them. Call Mumsey."

I punched the numbers. The machine answered. "Mumsey, it's Steph. If you're there, please pick up. Neil and I are on the Laureles Grade on our way . . . Damn it! I've lost the signal."

He skillfully guided the car over the curvy grade to Carmel Valley Road that would take us to Mumsey's. Several neighbors were leaving by the courtyard gate as we turned down the long graveled driveway and parked in the back.

"Good evening," a stooped, frail woman whispered. "Mrs. Whitehead is very tired. We've fed her and taken out the garbage for tomorrow morning's pick up. We heard you on the machine and picked up, but only heard static. You were calling from the Grade, weren't you?" She looked at me carefully. "You remember me, don't you Stephanie?"

"Yes, I remember. You're Nancy Jordan, Gracie's mom."

"That's right. You used to tutor my Gracie in English. Carmel High School? Seems so long ago." She scribbled a number on a pad Mumsey kept by the door with a pencil tied to it for people to write messages.

"Here's my number. Please call when you leave so we know to come back. Good-bye." Gracie's mother disappeared down the driveway like a ghost. She used to leave soft drinks and chips for Gracie and me to take into the guesthouse when I . . . tutored her. A sweet pang shot through my stomach as I remembered my moments with Gracie in those cozy quarters. I remembered how vibrant I'd felt then . . . how alive!

Neil had already gone inside. He came back to the door and stared at me. "Are you going to stand there on those crutches all night? Get in here and sit down." He helped me in and called out, "Mumsey, it's Neil and Steph."

Mumsey appeared at the end of the long hall dressed in an ankle-length black bathrobe and black leather slippers.

"Stephanie and I want to go through some items that might have been overlooked. Do you mind if we look at the journals she has stored next door in the upstairs bedroom?"

"No, honey, I don't mind. Go. Go do your investigating. Leave me. I'm fine. I'm not alone." She kissed the cross that hung around her neck and held it up for us to see before she turned to climb the stairs to her bedroom.

We left the office through an interior door, crossed the courtyard, and entered again through the old kitchen. We passed through the dining room to a narrow staircase in the living room. We climbed up and walked to the back bedroom. A journal lay on the dressing table. We studied the cover decorated with cotton cloth in Carmel High's red and white. A graduation tassel with a little gold '84 was pinned in the center.

Neil slid the journal toward me. I touched the cover with the tips of my fingers, reverently, as if it were holy.

"Di put her heart and soul into these journals. I think because she loved us all so much. And she's dead because of . . ."

Neil held me like he did when I was a child. "Everything's going to be okay." We sat quietly until the evening chill nudged us into motion.

"Come on," Neil said. "Let's brew a pot of coffee, start on page one, and look for the negatives."

I nodded, wondering if I had the energy to stand. He helped me down to the kitchen then went to check on Mumsey. I ground fresh beans and started the coffee. Neil returned to report that Mumsey was sleeping peacefully. I poured a cup for him and watched him add brown sugar and cream. God, how did that man stay so slim? I drank mine black but waited, as was customary with us, until he stirred his to readiness so we could take our first sip together.

"Mmm, good, let's work on the dining room table. Stay here, I'll bring down everything we need."

"Okay, I'll put out some snacks."

Neil returned with boxes for us to go through. We sipped our coffee while we turned pages and emptied boxes. Outside the wind rustled the trees and shrubs. Neil pulled the collar of his coat up. "Spooky place."

"Di and I used to pretend that the spirits of people who used to live here could be called upon to protect us from evil. We believed all the answers we needed were here, carried on the wind." I didn't say anything to Neil, but I could feel Diane's kiss on my cheek. Or was it the breeze from outside sneaking in through an open window?

"I thought you found all your answers in the law library." He intended to make a joke, but his eyes looked sad. He shook his head quickly, as if to refocus his thoughts. "We need the missing negatives. I'm waking Mumsey to ask her if she knows where they are." He stood up and stretched his back. "How're you doing? Maybe you should climb on the sofa for a nap."

I yawned. "No, I want to help."

As he left the room, he looked over his shoulder and said, "Steph, you're injured, you're still traumatized, and you're exhausted."

My neck *was* stiff. Di smiled at me from decades of family photos covering the wall. Neil ran back into the room a few minutes later.

"What's wrong?" I asked.

"The negatives may be gone. Let me have the Jordans' telephone number."

I searched my coat, located the slip of paper, and handed it to him. "I don't understand."

"Mrs. Jordan took the box out for tomorrow's trash pickup," he said as he dialed the number and waited for an answer.

"Hello, Mrs. Jordan? This is Detective Redmond. Yes, yes, that's right. No, we're not leaving. No, it's not an emergency either. We are looking for a box of negatives and understand you may have taken it out with the trash." I could hear her voice buzzing in Neil's ear. "You did. Thank you. Yes, good-bye. I'm sorry to call so late." Neil gave me the thumbs up as he hung up the phone. "Good news. She remembers putting out the box of negatives. I'll go get them."

I sat down on the sofa to wait for him. But the coffee was no match for fatigue and Percodan and I didn't hear him return.

The smell of fresh coffee awakened me. For a brief moment, I stretched, relaxed, rested. The clock on the wall chimed twelve times. I sat up searching for my crutches and purse with my pills. I swung into the kitchen. Mumsey was dressed and pouring herself a cup of coffee.

"Good morning, dear," Mumsey said.

"Good *morning*?"

"How about some coffee and something to eat. Eggs?"

"Uh, no. Where's Neil?"

"Kate called. He went off to meet her. He wants you to stay put until he calls for you," she said and placed a glass of orange juice on the small kitchen table, motioning for me to sit.

I sat down and picked up the glass. "What did Neil say, exactly?"

"Just for you to wait."

"That's all. Did he say . . . what Kate wanted?"

"No. But this will cheer you up. Chuck Gibson phoned him early this morning about some of the negatives you two were searching for last night. Relax, dear, Neil will be back soon."

"Mumsey, please let me borrow your car. I'm going home to clean up. I'll phone Neil." I pressed my lips against her temple. "I love you."

I jumped when the phone rang. Mumsey excused herself and went into the dining room to answer it. I finished my orange juice, washing down another Percodan and a Xanax, and leaned toward the door to listen.

"Hello? Yes, Neil. She's up and she wants the keys to my car . . . home to clean up. What? Speak up. Yes. Yes. What?" she whispered. "What is happening? Okay. Okay. But please hurry." Mumsey walked back into the room clutching the portable phone. She stood silently in front of me looking pale and miserable.

"Give me the keys to your car, Mumsey," I said firmly, trying not to frighten her. I felt guilty. Ashamed.

"No," she said. "You have to stay here until Neil gets back."

Mumsey turned abruptly toward the dishwasher. A roaring filled my ears and the room darkened around me.

My mother was quoting a line from the movie, The Godfather. *"Your sins are terrible. It is just that you suffer so." Shame washed over me like the water rinsing the dishes she cleared from the table to the sink. Spellbound, I marveled at how Mother would both ignore and engage me at once. Her contempt for the scraps of food that clung to her Limoge was amusing and alarming. Was I a little piece of leftover that clung to Mommy's fine person?*

Mother faced me but her dark blue eyes looked past me. She reached up behind her head to adjust long hair captured by a pearl studded clasp. As she lowered her arms, she walked past my chair to straighten the picture of her parents that hung there. She pulled a white linen hanky from her apron pocket, touched it to the end of her nose as she finally allowed her eyes to fall onto my face. I couldn't look away, I never could. I breathed as slowly as possible, finally holding in too much and the breath exploded out of me.

"What did you say?" she demanded.

"Na, nothing, Mo-Mo-Mo-Mommy . . ." I stuttered.

"Don't you lie to your mother. You stupid little shit!" Her shriek assaulted my ears while the back of her hand loomed dangerously close to my face. She postured like a snake as she spoke in a low hard voice. "Look what you've done. You've made me speak the devil's language. I never swear, never. You're very bad."

I tried to flatten my face so it would be void of expression in the hope of pleasing her, or at the very least distracting her. Tears burned my eyes. Hold them back, hold them back, hold them back until she stops, I prayed over and over. They were an admission of guilt—guilt means punishment. I held on until they were scalding my brain. Finally, I had to let a few escape to relieve the pain. Her bony knuckles cracked across the front of my face. She walked behind my chair and stood for a moment. I could feel her breath on the back of my neck. Blood trickled from my nose decorating my white pants with little red dots. She continued walking around the entire dining room table checking each chair to ensure it was perfectly aligned. Finally, she returned to stand in front of me. She folded her arms around her slim waist and leaned down, putting her lips next to my right ear. "When will you learn?"

A small child and a teenaged boy appeared to me from behind our green sofa. The boy, about sixteen, folded his arms over his muscular chest, his eyes glared at mother. He was big. The little girl clung to his legs, peeking from behind him. She was small, maybe two years old. She was a good little girl. She would sit on the tiny little wooden potty for hours until she did her duty. Then her mommy would let her out to play. The boy floated over to the side table and studied the utensils mother had carefully polished and laid out. Finally, his eyes rested on a long slender pair of shears mother liked to use for cutting skin off fowl.

I felt Uncle Harry's hand on my arm guiding me to Aunt Helen. "Get her out of here," he said. I looked over my shoulder at my mother's crumpled and bloody body. People in uniforms rushed into our house while my Aunt rinsed blood off of me with the water hose outside. She hugged me close and walked me across the street to her house. I glanced up into the large sycamore tree in Mother's yard. The little girl and the boy smiled down at me through large green leaves from their perch on a great round limb.

Mumsey's groaning brought me out of the past. I looked in horror at the bloody knife in my hand and dropped it next to her body. I screamed and pressed a dishtowel into the wound on her back.

"Stephanie," she whispered, "did you kill my daughter?"

I held her close.

"What have you done?" she gasped.

I wondered if Mumsey, or anyone for that matter, could understand. When Di had confronted me with her "evidence" at the adobe, her scornful and abusive attacks had shamed me worse than my mother's used to. She would not shut up about the handholding and the looks between Gracie and me captured on those photos. The more she accused and judged, the more I'd felt myself slipping away. Again, I'd watched, as if in a movie, while the teenaged boy came to help me, and Di's hateful words were beaten out of her. Di's screams had awakened me, and I found the bloody hammer in my hands. I'd carefully cleaned and hid it in the trunk of my car. Later I dropped it into the water off Fisherman's Wharf. I burned all the pictures . . . but I forgot about the negatives.

I knelt down by Mumsey and rocked her in my lap. I don't remember how long I sat with her. The late afternoon breeze was blowing up the valley by the time I slid my arm from beneath her neck and put her car keys in my pocket. I washed the blood off my hands, straightened my hair, and put on some lipstick. I knew where to go.

The persistent fog rolled in to protect the forest from the late afternoon sun. Deer stood on the side of the road, disinterested in passing cars. The Gibson mansion, across the highway from where I'd parked, faded and reformed like a large stone ghost on the water's edge. I finally grew tired of watching and wondering, and started the car. I downed a Xanax, saving my last Percodan for later. I pulled out of my hiding place in a grove of trees and steered toward the Carmel gate, the air through the car window heavy with the scents of cypress and salt. I drove along Carmel Beach, past Mission Ranch, and the Carmel Basilica, south on Highway 1. I parked on the shoulder outside the entrance to Point Lobos.

Gracie and I first explored one another with our eyes during tenth grade in gym at school. I tutored her in English and she tutored me in love. We worked in her family's guesthouse where, when I finally gave in to her probing fingers and tongue, I experienced a human connection like I had never known in my life. Her tender touching, searching, and demanding loving gave her absolute control over my entire being. My time, my life was completely organized around anticipating moments in her presence. When she announced she was inviting Chuck Gibson to the homecoming dance, I tried to be supportive and understanding. I followed them to the beach that night. After he left her, alone, naked, wrapped in a blanket, I hobbled down to her. She said mean things and told me to go away. The boy who had helped me with mother jumped from behind a rock and shut her up with one blow of my crutch. The crutch burned to ashes quickly in Aunt Helen's fireplace.

I turned the car around and drove north toward home. I knew what to do.

I turned off the tape recorder and walked from the dressing table to the bedroom window overlooking Mid-Valley. A silent procession of police cars, lights flashing, had turned up Tierra Grande. My smiling reflection calmed me when I returned to sit down. The black handle of the .38 was smooth in my hand and the silver barrel cool as I pressed it firmly against the soft flesh under my jaw.

Final Sentence

Snakeskin Jacket
by Mark C. Angel

Al wasn't much of a conversationalist, but he could sure sling trash. He woke up at o'dark-thirty every morning in his Carmel Valley home, eyes fluttering open even before the alarm sounded.

Today was no exception. He went to the bathroom, shaved his cheeks smooth and dried his face, regarding himself thoughtfully in the mirror. He pushed back his thinning gray-streaked hair and ran his fingers along his strong jaw line, accented—since his late twenties—by trimmed sideburns and a well-manicured goatee.

It was the same man he'd seen every day of the week for as far back as he could remember. *Well, almost the same,* he mused, adjusting the sturdy prescription safety glasses that framed his clear brown eyes, and gazing disparagingly at his swell of a double chin. Back in the day, when garbage men had to heave trash over their shoulders and haul it to the trucks, he was as strong as an elephant, but now, with mechanization and automation, slinging just wasn't the workout it used to be.

Al dressed in clean blue Dickies, a neatly-pressed uniform shirt and steel-toed leather boots, then pulled on his blue knit fisherman's cap and roused Betty, his wife of 25 years, just long enough to kiss her good-bye. As he made his way toward the kitchen, Parrot stirred in his cage hoping for a treat. Al dropped an animal cracker through the bars, and then pulled fresh ground coffee out of the freezer to fill the drip filter. He added water to brew what he considered a perfect cup of coffee, making enough to fill his thermos with some left over for Betty. Soon after, he headed out the door.

"Bye-bye!" Parrot squawked.

Al waved over his shoulder, a Pavlovian reaction to the bird's salutation. "Damn bird got me again," he snickered aloud.

When Al and Betty first got married, they lived in the city of Marina, just ten minutes from work. The move to Carmel Valley had turned the drive into more than a half-hour commute, but Betty craved the warmer temperatures in the Valley where the air was crisp and clear and changed with the seasons. Al thought it even smelled different than the moist salt air he had grown up with in his coastal home.

The garbage man hopped into his '78 Chevy pickup, which he fondly referred to as "Old Blue," and headed west on Carmel Valley Road, driving deep into the fog. Climbing over the Carmel grade, he hugged the coast for twenty miles on Highway 1 before exiting in Castroville to pick up his rig at the Waste Management corporate yard.

The yard bustled with activity, as it did every day, and before long he had fired up his International Harvester and joined the brigade of sanitation engineers rolling out to invade the communities of the Monterey Peninsula. It was a good living, and Al found it refreshing to work in the outdoors. The smell of cold wetness dripped from Monterey Pines and eucalyptus trees. He savored the brilliant red-orange sunrise, which backlit dawn's vaporous bands of clouds and contributed to the golden glow of daybreak.

As the day progressed, Al slung bin after smelly bin of refuse into his truck's rear hopper: wet household waste, construction waste, garden waste, the worst being restaurant waste—a veritable smorgasbord of rotting leftovers. Familiar hydraulics whined as the blade rose up and over the hopper to cram each container's worth of trash into the compressor box.

Though some rubbish was separated out into curbside recycling bins, it never ceased to amaze Al that—in addition to all the really repugnant garbage—people often discarded stuff that seemed perfectly reusable. He pulled half a dozen perfectly good bricks out of one trash can and put them in the front cab. For the next few miles he contemplated how to use them in his yard.

At the end of the day he returned to the corporate yard, refueled his rig and parked. Other drivers who finished early left early, but Al always spent a few extra minutes washing his rig down. He was a "regular waste management chauffeur" as some of the fellows would say.

"See ya later, Al," one called out to him. "You better ease up on that paint job. The way you rub on it all the time, it's gonna wear out!"

Al smiled and waved off the comment. Then he called back, "Four o'clock, Mario, like always?"

His coworker acknowledged him with a nod as Al began to transfer the bricks to his truck.

Al arrived home early in the afternoon and smiled when Betty greeted him, her summer dress swishing as she walked toward him. Their relationship had its ups and downs, and he was happy to say that now was an up time. He embraced her.

"You look chipper today," she said, pushing back her fine, gray hair. She unclipped his suspenders and began to unbutton his shirt.

"I feel good, Sugarplum," he replied, tenderly kissing her on the lips.

"Oh? Then how about proving it, big man?" She kissed him back deeply.

"I missed you," he said, pulling her closer, grasping her soft, firm backside and feeling her body pressed against him. He breathed in her freshly washed sweetness, and she squealed as his hands squeezed her bottom. When he kissed her again, he tasted the spaghetti sauce she had been preparing for dinner, one of the few meals she regularly cooked from scratch.

"H-h-hello!" Parrot squawked, vying for attention. Al and Betty laughed.

"Hello, Parrot," Al said, looking over Betty's shoulder at the generically-denominated bird.

Betty gave him a frisky push. "You smell like you've been working hard all day," she said, then added teasingly," now go get cleaned up and I'll be there in a minute."

Al headed toward the shower, peeling off his boots and pants while Betty took his dirty clothing to the laundry room. Then she went to help him scrub down in the shower.

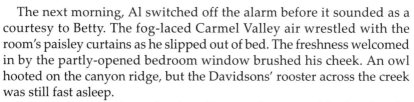

The next morning, Al switched off the alarm before it sounded as a courtesy to Betty. The fog-laced Carmel Valley air wrestled with the room's paisley curtains as he slipped out of bed. The freshness welcomed in by the partly-opened bedroom window brushed his cheek. An owl hooted on the canyon ridge, but the Davidsons' rooster across the creek was still fast asleep.

By nine that morning—the time Al normally stopped for lunch—the overcast in the Valley would be gone and the canyon oaks with their long-tasseled yellow blossoms would be bathed in the morning sun's nurturing warmth. For now, though, Al chose to relish the hazy glow of the moon as it beamed down through the mist.

His day progressed uneventfully through the end of his first set of rounds. He emptied his truck at the Marina landfill and headed for the sorting station, a model facility designed to maximize the reuse and recycling of waste. The state-of-the-art complex had even incorporated tons of recycled materials in its construction.

Al appreciated the conservation efforts. After the construction dumpsters were emptied, their contents moved along a conveyor belt to be sorted for recyclables, a nice alternative to a landfill, which was the case with most dumps.

He drove past the huge warehouse-like structure and parked next to the concrete platform and reclamation conveyor belt. It was his regular visit to the pile of salvageable goods pulled out for resale at Last Chance Mercantile, the thrift shop run by the facility. Al liked the fact that he could get first crack at Last Chance goods. It was one of the more unusual perks of his job.

As he foraged through the buffet of discarded treasures, part of a scaly olive green object with black spots caught his attention. Something of a reptile enthusiast, Al didn't take long to recognize the skin of a giant Amazonian anaconda resting in a loosely stacked pile of reclaimed curios. The stack settled, giving the impression that the object—a piece of clothing?—moved. A shiver traveled down Al's spine, but his apprehension soon changed to curiosity. He reached slowly into the pile to disentangle it.

It was a jacket—a snakeskin jacket.

Holding it by its shoulders, Al gave it a good snap and fought off another shudder. He'd seen a lot of discarded clothes, from dirty diapers to lipstick-stained silk shirts, but he'd never seen anything like this. It sported a wide collar, broad shoulders and a single-breasted tapered cut to the waist. The sleeves ended in cuffs folded back with faux buttons and elbow patches. Al examined it closely, admiring the hand-stitched craftsmanship of its interior, but found neither a label nor any other kind of identification.

"Pity such a majestic creature had to be slaughtered just for dress-up," he muttered, bringing the coat up to his nose to take a sniff. The sweet, but biting odor—mixed in with something that smelled like marijuana—made him think of anacondas. He then recalled what he knew about anacondas. How the female of the species grows to be five times as large as the male; how they live among the hyacinth blossoms in the black water rivers of the Peruvian rainforests; how they love to bask in the sun along the banks of a river while digesting their prey.

He moved the jacket away from his face and took measure of it, yet again. It looked as good as new, but for a couple of dark, sticky spots, one on the left cuff and the other on the oversized collar. It had an uncomplicated European cut; for a moment, he imagined it had been made just for him.

Al felt a certain amount of regret as he contemplated what to do with the jacket. The flamboyant vesture scarcely conformed to his simple, even mundane life. *When could I ever wear this?* he wondered, turning it over in his hands. Despite such doubts, he placed it on the seat of his truck. As he did so, Al had every intention of stopping at the Last Chance Mercantile on his way out to pay for it, but after turning over the engine, he reconsidered.

I can't let anyone see me buying this thing.

He stuck with the decision, although a pang of guilt shot through him as he drove away. A wave of excitement then washed over him generated by his successful getaway. The latter feeling overcame any remorse. As he traveled between pick-up points, he glanced repeatedly at the jacket, coiled in a neat pile beside him. Its uniqueness clung to his mind: the soft, smooth feel; the musky, sweet smell; to whom it might have belonged.

Al finished his final rounds, dumped his load, and hurried back to the corp yard where he quickly cleaned the rig. He rolled the jacket tightly and tucked it securely under his arm. Once home and in the privacy of his own garage, he tried to put it on, but it was too tight. He pulled at the collar of his undershirt, but found no relief from the constricted feeling until he completely removed the jacket.

It might have fit me twenty years ago.

He grimaced at it, feeling fat and tired. Folding the jacket neatly, he wrapped it in a clean towel, slipped it into a paper bag, and in an unconscious attempt to hide it, laid it behind the seat of Old Blue. He again felt guilty for having taken it without paying. But the exhilaration . . .

Al met up with his buddies, as usual, at Eddie's off North Fremont after work. They clanked mugs of beer and talked sports and politics as if the two held equal significance, but when the second round of drinks was called for, Al decided to pass. "I've really got to get going," he said. "Betty is planning an early dinner."

"Oh, come on, Al, since when have you skipped a beer for Betty's sake?" Mario asked.

"Must have gotten lucky for a change," someone else jeered.

"I got to change my eating habits," Al replied. "We're not burning calories like we used to." He patted his belly and nodded toward the beer nuts. "Better go before I start packing in the snacks."

They applauded his intention to lose weight, raised their mugs to salute his speech, and went right on poking fun at his born-again determination to regain a fragment of his youthful physique. Over the next several weeks, he managed to defy their skepticism.

In the weeks that followed his discovery of the jacket, Al tossed and turned in his sleep so often that on many a night Betty sent him to the couch. So when the warm Valley air and bright moonlight awakened him even earlier than usual one morning, he got out of bed readily, made his silent preparations, and left the house without arousing Parrot.

In the garage he took the snakeskin jacket out of the truck. Unfolding it carefully, he decided to again explore its fit, but first attempted to clean the sticky stuff off the lapel and sleeve. He moistened a white handkerchief with spittle and firmly wiped the lapel. Not until the cloth turned dark red did he suspect the substance to be blood. Instead of recoiling at the thought, he sniffed the stain. Then he tucked the garment back behind the seat.

At lunch, Al opened his pail and surveyed the fare Betty had packed — the usual Tuesday menu. For years he'd been satisfied with his daily lunches, and understood that the limited weekly variety made it easier for Betty to shop. But now, as he poured his coffee and despite his hunger, the lunch seemed much less appetizing. Almost reluctantly, he took out half a liverwurst sandwich and nibbled at it. The tang of mustard once so pleasing to his taste, now irritated him; the crunch of celery sticks, previously refreshing, now struck him as obnoxious; and the slimy banana pulp in his cheek made him nauseous.

He looked back on the past few days and took note of certain other facts. That the smell of beer had begun to disgust him. That he never felt satisfied with a regular meal. That the sight of all that raw meat at the grocery store got him salivating.

He shook his head and put the rest of his lunch away.

"How was your day?" Betty asked when Al walked through the door shortly after noon.

"Fine," he answered abruptly.

"Are you alright?" she asked, unclipping his suspenders.

"Yeah, I'm okay." He slipped out of his dirty trousers and shirt. "I just feel a little more tired than usual."

She took both his wrists in her hands and placed his arms around her neck. "Don't you want to . . .?"

"Nah, not today, don't think so." He moved his hands to her round hips and gently pushed her away. "I'm just going to hit the shower and get some rest."

Betty's disappointment made her look older than her 50 years. She grimaced as she gathered his dirty clothes to put them in the hamper. He headed toward the bathroom realizing that over the past few weeks, a small distance had opened between them. Was it something he had done?

"Al!" Betty called through the bathroom door.

He didn't answer.

"Maybe I'll go next door to Donya's house for a while! I'll be home about five, okay?"

"Fine!" he called back, relieved to have the time to himself.

The alarm sounded and Al tumbled out of bed collecting his clothes from the closet. Betty had cleaned and pressed them the night before— one of the little domestic things he seemed to have appreciated more in the past. He went into the bathroom and shaved, but then varied his routine by undressing and stepping into the shower.

After languishing in the water until it ran tepid, he stood before the mirror and saw himself in a new light. He placed his hands on his hairy belly, turning to view his pear-shaped figure from the side. He never thought much about his diet before, but he sure did now. Even with the exercise he got at work and his cutting back on beer and salty snacks, his abdomen still bulged. Disappointment washed over him.

I'll never fit in that jacket!

"Who am I fooling?" he said laughing with a hint of bitterness. "What am I going to do with a jacket fit for a rock star or a pimp?" He threw his clothes on carelessly, and headed for the kitchen. As he ate his cereal he heard a soft curse and the slamming of the bedroom door. Parrot fluffed his feathers nervously. It then occurred to Al that he had left the closet light on.

The autumn days were passing too quickly for Al. Summers in Carmel Valley had always seemed too hot to him and its insects—flies in the daytime; mosquitoes at night—far too annoying. But he now found he couldn't get enough warmth, and the sounds of the insects made him feel alive.

Each day, he removed the snakeskin jacket from behind the seat of Old

Blue and tried it on, but unsatisfied with the fit, he would wrap it up again and put it back.

The wax on his rig began to dull from lack of care, making it look like the rest of the garbage trucks. Al's friends had come to expect him to leave the bar early or not show up at all. "He's whipped!" they would say.

Betty accused him of being aloof. "You're spending too much time out with the guys, and not enough time around home," she'd say. But it didn't faze Al; in truth, he was spending most of his time wandering through the wild golden wheat of Garland Ranch Park, or soaking in every ray of the lingering Indian summer sun near the watering hole in the high meadow.

There was more: colors were brighter and smells more defined. His sight was so sharp he stopped wearing his glasses. Garbage that had once repulsed him, now intrigued him. Years on the job had honed his skill at gleaning information about a household based on the contents of its refuse. His increased awareness furthered the art. *Someone got kicked out of this house,* he'd muse, seeing a barely-used pair of men's running shoes and high-dollar warm-ups. *The rats must really like this alley,* he thought, tasting their stringent odor on the air. *Another baby at 2301 Third Street,* he noted, taking a whiff of dirty diapers.

But despite the transformation Al's life appeared to be undergoing, one behavior didn't change. Each day after work he carefully removed the snakeskin jacket from Old Blue, tried it on, found dissatisfaction with its fit, then wrapped it up and put it back.

"Is that you, Al?" Betty called from the kitchen one warm afternoon after he had come home from work. She wore her hair long the way he used to like it, but Al felt nothing—said nothing.

After receiving a customary peck hello, he expected her to start rebuking him for his moodiness, something she did almost every night now. But she surprised him. "You look great! Are you wearing contact lenses?" She didn't wait for an answer. "You are! Your face looks slimmer."

She must have noticed more had changed than his physique, because, as she unhooked his suspenders, she added, "Everything okay, Al? I feel like you've had something on your mind lately. Do you want to talk about it?"

"I'm just a little tired." He made a move toward the bathroom.

She caught his arm. "Well I wish you'd *stop* being so tired," she complained, lips tightened into a small pout. "Maybe you should see a doctor."

Impulsively, she wrapped her arms around Al and kissed him.

He accepted her tongue, but without arousal; he was more fascinated by the tactile sensation, although it *did* feel good to squeeze her warm body. Filled with the sensation of her touch and smell, the alien compulsion to squeeze her until she couldn't breathe boiled up within him. He sought to repress it, evidently not soon enough.

"You're hurting me!" Betty cried. "Let me go!" She writhed out of his embrace and stepped back angrily. "I've just about had it with you!" She started to sob. "You better spend . . . a little more time cleaning up around the house." She paused to sniff. "You've been leaving your junk all over the place. The neighbors can see it, and it's embarrassing! And I can't even walk through this house without tripping." She kicked at a pile of newspapers and stormed back into the kitchen where she put the dishes away. She did it with enough ferocity that Al was sure some would break.

As he headed up to the bathroom, she called after him. "Don't use up all the hot water! Your new obsession with hot baths is costing us a fortune!"

The next time Al tried on the jacket, the red stain on the left cuff and collar had faded and the smell of marijuana was completely gone, although a trace of some mysterious cologne lingered. The jacket still felt tight, but he resisted his impulse to struggle against its fit. Eventually it relaxed and shaped itself around him.

After fastening the buttons, he caressed the jacket's scales and turned up its collar. Its weight settled onto his shoulders in a right-fitting way, nicely snug around his midriff.

Imagine the beast that once lived in this thing.

Al pondered the experience of being an anaconda: slipping through the murky river water in search of prey; wrapping the coils of a muscled tubular body around a struggling creature and tightening until movement stopped; basking in the sun on the riverbank after a good feed. As his imagination wandered, he continued to admire the jacket's fit, until a sudden pang of anxiety gripped him, compelling him to quickly remove it. He couldn't quite articulate it, but it was as if his instincts and sense of humanity rebelled against certain . . . reptilian thoughts. He quickly returned the jacket to its hiding place.

The rest of the week he couldn't free his mind from the experience he had wearing the jacket. It had taken him into a world of a Paleolithic predator and he had liked it; it excited him. He began to work quickly and carelessly, not stopping to eat lunch or hose down his truck, anxious to find a quiet place by a river where he could sit in the sun and daydream until the afternoon shadows drove him away. By the end of the week he was grateful for the prospect of a full day of rest. Once home, he hurried through the front door, wiping the sweat off his forehead with his sleeve.

Parrot squawked. Al slipped in to the kitchen for a cold drink. A note on the refrigerator read, "Gone next door. Back soon." He squeezed out a sigh of relief, and shed his clothes without thinking to place them in the hamper. He showered until the water ran cold and shaved off his beard for the first time in twenty years, cutting his upper lip in the process. He studied the red fluid that oozed out of the wound and tasted its salty essence. The tang stayed on his tongue as he surveyed the rest of his body. Double chin, less prominent; and he could suck in his belly with a meaningful result.

He dressed himself quickly but deliberately, picking his way through his wardrobe, selecting a crew neck T-shirt fresh out of the package. He tucked it into his best black jeans and tightened his belt. Now would be the perfect opportunity to wear that pair of alligator boots he had rescued and resoled. He got them out and rubbed the thick leather—not nearly as delicate as the jacket—with a soft flannel rag. Finally, he returned to the dresser and opened his wife's jewelry box which contained an item of worth from his bachelor days: a thick gold chain. He placed it gently around his neck, and then looked at his wedding ring, which also rested in the box, which he immediately snapped shut. He left the room to get the jacket.

After retrieving it from Old Blue, he returned to the bathroom and slowly placed one arm into a sleeve after the other. It fit even better than it had the last time. He watched excitedly in the mirror as the garment adjusted to him with a snugness that went much further than its tailored cut. It caressed his body. *Must be the pliability of the material,* he reasoned, but didn't ponder it. A stranger looked back at him; he didn't care. Al lost himself in the jacket's scent.

When he entered the living room with the jacket on, Parrot had a fit, making a racket and sprinkling bird seed and water around his cage and out onto the floor. Feathers littered the air like dust mites. Al's first inclination was to rush the cage and rip Parrot's little blue and yellow head right off its body, but he resisted. The intensity of the urge surprised him, but not as much as it should have.

He went out onto the sunny back patio, closed the French doors and leaned back against them, listening to Parrot catch his breath.

The jacket's fit seemed to further improve with each photon of sunlight. It had the aspect of warm wax, Al thought, softening to blend into his figure. He dozed off for a moment before waking abruptly when his chin dropped to his chest. He headed back to Old Blue.

Al drove west toward the coast, barely glancing at the rolling hills on either side of him. When he got to the Highway 1 interchange, he headed north as if on autopilot, exited onto Munras Avenue, and turned into the Del Monte Shopping Center. Macy's—normally Al hated that sort of place—pulled at him, and before he knew it, he was sniffing around in the mall.

Near the courtyard fountain his eyes flicked toward its central sculpture, a sea otter ostensibly held aloft by a spurting stream of water. For a time, he paced back and forth in semi-circles around it, unsure of his own intentions. Then he decided on a course of action: off to Macy's.

He entered the store and went directly to the perfume counter. "Do you have men's cologne here?" he asked the young attendant with an unusual urgency.

"Sure, we have lots of 'em," the girl, probably in her mid-twenties, replied with a smile Al found infectious. She had bobbed black hair and wore a black miniskirt that effectively revealed her smooth and firm white thighs. A pink, frilly top peeked out from under her clerk's vest.

"I need one like this," Al said, leaning over the counter, pushing the lapel of his jacket toward her face. Her name tag read, "Trish".

"Trish" hesitated, caught off guard, but played along. She bent forward awkwardly, and tried to smell the lapel. As she felt the jacket with her outstretched hand she flushed, her eyes widened, and Al could sense her increasing heartbeat. He smelled a change in her. Or did he taste it? Her palms moistened as she stroked the shiny soft skin; her scent sweetened as gooseflesh formed on her arms, her face showing internal struggle. She began to push him away, but then grabbed both lapels and pulled Al and his jacket close to her. She buried her face in the olive-colored skin. It was hard yet soft, smooth yet scaly, sensual . . .

"Well, do you know what scent it is?" Al swallowed into a dry throat.

Her silky hair brushed against his nose as she sniffed the lapel. The hunger that had been simmering inside him for so long now raked him, and he knew that this tender creature could satisfy; he resisted the urge to instantly take her, and instead placed his hands over hers to gently peel her white knuckles off of the lapels.

Free of the jacket, Trish wiped her forehead with the back of her hand and pushed her bangs into place. Then she straightened her skirt and gasped softly. "Let me get some testers," she said sheepishly, pulling her eyes away from the jacket. Clumsily, she selected a few blank paper cards. Al's eyes fixated on the throbbing pulse in her throat. His stomach tightened.

"How about this one?" Trish seemed to have forced a semblance of control back in her voice. She sprayed a mist of fragrance on one of the rigid squares and waved it in the air by Al's face.

He winced and pulled back slightly. "Hmm, not quite." Frankly, he felt suffocated. "Maybe we should go outside, away from all these other odors. I'm very sensitive to s-smells . . . occupational hazard, you know."

Trish cocked her head and lifted the corner of her lip. Her creamy forehead broke into parallel lines that may have signaled skepticism.

"I'm in waste management," he added, trying to sound innocent.

Her lips curled up as if she suddenly *got* it, but she still eyed him dubiously. "Let me take another whiff of that." She reached for the jacket and Al didn't resist, leaning forward over the counter as she took hold and inhaled deeply, brushing her cheek against the material. He reveled in her pungent odor—seasoned by a full eight hours behind the counter—and allowed it to flood his olfactory senses. A metallic tang clinging to the top of his tongue excited him. He struggled intensely against his desires, or were they cravings?

"My shift is almost over," Trish blurted, "but I'll bring a couple of test cards out." She let go of him abruptly and picked four scents, labeling the paper squares before spraying them. She ignored the other customers, now waiting impatiently, and left the counter to head for the exit. As Al followed her out, his eyes darted around the store. Suddenly he found himself suspicious of everyone in sight.

Out in the open air, Trish made no effort to maintain any semblance of decorum. "Let me see." Forcefully she took hold of the lapels again, tugging against his weight and yanking the garment to her face. Al's body followed, and crowded up against hers. She turned the collar out and took in the scent from the inner side of the fold, sighing loudly when she exhaled. Then she passed a card by her nose. She repeated the action several times, her nose getting closer each time until it touched Al's neck. A quiver shot through him.

She finally settled on a card. "I think it's this one." She held the paper up without letting go of the jacket. Al fought off another tremor.

"Don't you agree?" she asked with more than a hint of insistence, fanning the card in front of him a second time.

Al pulled himself together enough to reply, "I-I think you're right."

"*Poison*. One of my favorites . . ." Trish looked into his eyes for the first time. She must have seen something there, because she quickly averted her gaze.

"I'll take it," he whispered.

She pushed him away reluctantly and turned to go into the store. Al followed her back to the fragrance counter. Another employee at the counter scowled. Al fumbled for his wallet and quickly paid cash.

"Cool jacket," Trish growled as he took the bag containing his purchase. She reached out and touched it more confidently, caressing the lapels with both hands. *Almost lovingly,* Al thought.

"Must be going somewhere pretty special to wear a piece like that," she asserted through two full rows of teeth.

"Nowhere in particular. At least, not yet."

"What a waste." She made a clicking sound while scanning his torso and shoulders. "I know people who would kill to wear a skin like that for just one day." The guttural quality in her voice caught Al off guard, but it added a fearless quality to her that excited him.

"I don't think I want to meet any of them." Al tried to sound light. It worked. They both giggled. "Maybe you'd like to get some coffee or something after you get off . . . Trish?"

She touched the name tag on her vest. "That's not fair; I don't know *your* name."

A new surge of excitement saturated him. "Ah . . . B-B-Bo," he stuttered, trying to pick a name that would fit a guy in a snakeskin jacket.

"Ah-b-bo?" she teased. "Sounds African."

Al flashed a tight-lipped smile. "Just Bo."

She tilted her head, exposing a creamy swath of neck. "Alright, 'Just Bo'. You seem like a nice guy. I'll see you outside in a minute, near the fountain, okay?"

"S-sounds good."

"I just got to change and clock out first."

"Okay."

She turned and headed off the floor, leaving three people abandoned at the counter. She looked once over her shoulder at Al as she disappeared around a corner.

If Al at first had been unsure about asking Trish out for coffee, he now couldn't imagine leaving the mall without her. It wasn't sex appeal; he couldn't put his finger on *what* it was.

Coffee can't hurt, he reassured himself.

Avoiding shadows in the manicured walkways, Al returned to the central fountain where he huddled in a light-splashed corner. On the bench-seat of a planter, where he enjoyed the cocoon of soft warmth from the sun-baked concrete, he looked like a middle-aged mall rat.

The movement of water in the fountain captivated him. He stared into it with a growing sense of anticipation, accompanied by the desire to sneak into the pond, slither up to the smaller pool on top, and clutch the playful otter. His stomach grumbled. He brushed his tongue over his upper lip.

"Hi there," Trish said from behind. It startled him and he whipped around to face her, relaxing when he saw who she was.

"I'm glad you came," he said.

"Yeah, sure," she replied flippantly. The top she now wore under her black blazer displayed her tight but soft midriff. Fishnet stockings and red heels set off her black miniskirt. Her eyes looked a little bigger than before.

"Do you want to follow me or should we drive together?" Al asked.

"Better follow you."

"Do you think you can keep up?"

"Sure. But go easy on me, okay?" She tilted her head and smiled in the cutesy way she had several times before, but he hardly noticed. A different appetite drove him.

Trish turned toward the parking lot, hesitantly reaching for his hand.

Al started to pull away, "My car's the other way," but he reconsidered and clasped his fingers firmly over hers. "I'll walk you to yours, though."

"I'll drop you back," Trish offered with a girlish lilt. She searched the lot near where she had parked her car, then pressed the alarm button on her key chain. A yellow Miata chirped in the distance. "Oh, there you are," she said, and hauled Al off in that direction.

Al squeezed into the passenger seat. The car smelled like Trish. Al's whole body felt alive. Every pore seemed to tingle.

"I'm famished—missed lunch," he said matter-of-factly, as Trish navigated through the parking lot. "Would you like to get something to eat, instead?"

"Sure, I guess."

"How about Greek?" he asked. "There's a place around the corner from Morgan's that's pretty good, and it's close."

Trish's face softened into a languid smile of acquiescence.

He pointed. "My ride's right there." For the first time, Old Blue embarrassed him.

In a few moments, Al was driving down Motel Row on Munras, making it easy for Trish to follow, but then, overcome by the thought that—*this is all wrong!*—he whizzed through the yellow light at the five cornered intersection of El Dorado Street, almost hoping he might lose her. Before long, however, he found himself maneuvering into a parking place on Tyler Street. The Miata rolled in behind him.

"Ya miss me, Bo?" Trish asked playfully after she stepped out of her convertible.

"Like dessert." He reached for her hand and led her toward Epsilon restaurant.

Trish cleaned her plate, but Al ate sparingly. Nothing on the menu appealed to him. He soon asked for the check, eager to get on with the engagement, wherever it might lead.

They got up and the sly smile crept across Trish's face again. "With a jacket like that, you gotta be able to dance," she said, putting one hand around his elbow and stroking his arm with her other.

"It's been awhile, but I suppose I could try."

She laughed as if he didn't mean it, and said, "D'you wanna go back to my place? We can slip in a disk and give it a whirl."

"S-s-sounds perfect."

The sun was setting in a spectacular display of purple-and-orange-streaked clouds, but Al didn't see it. The yellow Miata had become his sole focus as it turned off Del Monte Avenue toward the beach. While Trish pulled into her condo's carport, Al parked in the street. The sound of breaking waves and crashing surf filled the saline air.

He left his vehicle and sidled up to open her car door, offering her his hand as she emerged. She pressed up against him, wrapped both her arms around his waist and buried her face in his chest. Before he knew it, she was clawing at his scaly back with her fingernails and he felt the temptation to engulf her. Finally she managed to push him away. She gasped like she had almost suffocated. "Easy, mister!"

Wasn't really me, he thought, following her inside like a trained puppy at heel.

Trish slipped in a CD of soft music and took Al by the sleeve, leading him into the living room. The apartment was sparsely furnished, but revealing in its own way: gypsy bead-strings hung in the doorway between the kitchen and living area; beside the couch, a sequined silk scarf draped a lampshade; and a faux bearskin rug spread across the floor. Trish lit several half-spent candles and returned to Al, who still stood close to the door. She looked up at him coyly as she extended her arms toward him. He gathered her into his chest and she practically melted into his arms. They began to sway in soft embrace, Trish fondling the jacket while Al first caressed her hair, then moved his arms slowly down her back. The music stepped up a beat and they found the sofa. Al felt Trish exerting her allure over him, but couldn't quite find a place of ease with it.

She seemed to sense his discomfort.

"Shot o' Gold?" she asked, raising a neatly plucked eyebrow.

"With a shaker of salt and a lime," he answered glibly, but realized by her puzzled look that she wasn't old enough to make the connection with Jimmy Buffett. Nevertheless, she squeezed his arm and sprung up like a kitten, returning with a half-empty fifth, two crystal shot glasses, half a dozen lime wedges, and a salt shaker.

They licked, chewed and sucked in unison for the first round. The burning liquor calmed his nerves, but did nothing to dull his craving.

She took the second shot alone, sprinkling salt on his fist and putting the lime between his fingers. Then she took his large hand in both of hers, licked the salt off of it, chewed the lime he was holding and lowered her head towards the table. Al stared at the soft dark hair at the nape of her neck, then his gaze traveled under the collar of her blazer along her upper spine. She took the shot glass in her mouth and tossed her head back to empty it into her mouth, sticking her tongue up into the clear glass to lick the remnants of the distilled agave juice. Before he knew it, she had lowered her head back to the table to place the last glass next to the other empties.

"Your turn now, Bo," she said breathlessly, a dribble of Gold on the edge of her mouth.

He obeyed, grasping Trish's hand and placing a lime between her thumb and forefinger. He pulled her hand close to sprinkle it with salt, surprising her when he leaned forward to flick out his tongue and lick the drop off the corner of her mouth. Without missing a beat, he bowed his head and bit down on a shot glass before tossing back his head.

They did the third shot the same way, only together, nearly bumping heads as they put down the empties. This caused a spontaneous outbreak of laughter, after which Al stole a long, wet kiss, probing Trish's yielding mouth with his tongue.

I haven't ever been this drawn to someone, he realized and then discovered he couldn't recall anything of consequence from his past. He gave in to the irresistible urge to lick her throat and taste her skin, nuzzling her sensually.

"You wouldn't happen to have a Jacuzzi, would you?" he asked smoothly.

"Would a hot bath do?" She sounded puzzled, but enticed.

"Lead the way."

Trish stood in front of him. She took off her shoes, slipped out of her jacket and pulled down her miniskirt to step out of it. He watched transfixed as she removed her top. Now naked but for her thong, her bra and a smile, she reached down and grabbed the lapels of the jacket like she had at the store, pulling him to his feet. She unbuttoned the jacket and reached inside, squeezing Al softly. One of her arms slithered into a sleeve with his arm in it. Winding herself around him, she worked her hand down to the cuff, ducked her arm under and rolled her body around his back, peeling the skin off him and putting it onto herself. Her other arm crept into the other sleeve finally stripping him of the prize.

Trish felt the garment shrink to fit her figure. Before her guest could protest, she led him to the bathroom.

"Draw the bath and I'll be right back," she commanded, kissing him again, nearly sucking his tongue out of his mouth before pulling away.

She stepped in front of the large bathroom mirror. He ran the bath water into the claw foot tub, and stripped out of his clothes. She pulled the jacket tightly around herself, buttoning it slowly, her eyes slits, experiencing the throes of a consuming new passion.

She nearly forgot about Al, but when the roar of the bathwater abruptly stopped, she remembered. She saw him watching her keenly in a corner of the mirror, eyeing the jacket, no doubt. She didn't want to take it off, though, not even to bathe, and his desire for it sent a mixture of fear and anger through her. She couldn't bear the thought of returning the jacket and huddled it around herself more tightly than ever. Only after she heard the soft splash of Al entering the water could she bear to turn and look at him directly. He had submerged himself, his eyes closed beneath the film of water.

She considered what to do next. The thoughts passing through her mind made her uncomfortable. *Where do they come from?* she pondered, but soon felt nothing but desire to keep the jacket.

Someone . . . something . . . was in her way and lying vulnerably before her.

She crept toward him and braced herself to step into the tub. Straddling him she—gently at first—took hold of his throat and pushed down hard to keep his head under. He didn't respond at first—*he thinks I'm playing rough, this is going to be easy!*—but soon he began to struggle wildly. She fought to keep him under, but with a lurch, he shifted his position and pulled her down to one side. It was her turn under the water, which sloshed out of the bath and onto the floor in a wave.

Al, now half out, broke her death grip on his neck and scrambled to stand, one foot in the tub, one foot out. He almost slipped and fell as he left her slithering in the water. "What the hell's gotten into you!" he yelled.

Trish floundered around like an angry serpent, frustrated that she had failed so completely in dispatching her adversary. "I won't give it back!" she cried. As she struggled to her knees, grasping the rim of the tub, she

Snakeskin Jacket

hissed, "I . . . want . . . this-s-s . . . jacket."

Trish watched Al grab up his clothing and boots as she wallowed in the tub, hair stringy and wet, the skin of the jacket shrinking to fit even more tightly around her frame. As she watched Al leave the bathroom, she saw him look back at her in—was it pity or disgust? She didn't care, she decided, and sunk under the steaming water, smiling triumphantly.

Al sighed deeply after closing the door to his truck. Only then did he realize he was dripping wet. He pulled away from the curb and headed home looking forward, for the first time since he had found the jacket, to seeing Betty and Parrot.

"What got into me?"

He shook his head and enjoyed the evening drive out Carmel Valley Road.

As a Bird

by Frances J. Rossi

"They have a rocky coast connector here, Zoltan," Elizabeth said, filing her nails as Zoltan shaved in front of the bathroom mirror over the blue and white tiled counter top.

"What did you say, my dear? A *connector*, you say?" Her remark had come out of the blue, unrelated to anything he could think of. He worried, at her age, lest her mind fail. Lately there were more of these "senior moments", and you never knew . . .

His wife of 45 years stopped filing and frowned at him, left hand poised with fingers curled up. "*Connector*? No, Zoltan! Pay attention to me! I said, 'THEY ARE LUCKY TO HAVE YOU AS THEIR CONDUCTOR!'" She heaved an exasperated sigh and rearticulated her words in Hungarian, which they often spoke when they were alone, even after half a century in the U.S.

Zoltan's long-fingered hand guided the shaver over one last section of jaw where his thinning skin rippled under its pressure. He noticed that Elizabeth spoke less clearly these days, but he usually tried to interpret what he could make of her words with a humorous twist. "You should have said it so distinctly in the beginning, my love," he replied, shifting his focus to his trim moustache. "If you were a singer, the audience would never understand you unless you pronounced the consonants more clearly." It was what he'd been telling his choirs for years.

He turned off the shaver. Elizabeth had gone back to filing her nails, her face like an archer's about to loose an arrow from a tensed bow. "Zoltan Dalmady! Please! You must consider a hearing aid! Do you want to end up like Beethoven—unable to hear his own music?"

"I've told you before, a hearing aid would not help me." His voice scraped the edge of anger as he spoke. He fumbled trying to coil the cord. "How many times must I tell you, it would just magnify the background noise and I would hear even less than I do now?" It was the first time she'd brought up Beethoven's deafness—the embodiment of every musician's greatest fear. His hand shook as he stroked his smooth, pink bald head, smoothing down its aureole of silver.

"No, Zoltan! You use that as an excuse. You could at least try one."

He pushed the shaver into the open drawer in front of him and slammed it closed. Turning away from her, he strode heavily toward the kitchen. She followed him and caught his arm just inside the door of their pine-paneled kitchen, pulling him gently toward her. He stiffened back against the refrigerator.

"Listen, Zoltan! I've always known you to be a man of courage." She looked up at him through brown eyes that glistened with tears. "When we met back at that dance in Los Angeles—1956! It seems like yesterday! —I was so impressed that you'd come alone from Hungary. And such ambitious plans! Those years at U.C.L.A. you worked like nobody I'd ever known for your doctorate. I was so proud of you, my dear."

He'd asked her to marry him during his second year of grad school, after she'd supported him with her love and trust during those years of study. After the wedding, they'd left for his first position, with the Indiana University music department, where he'd conducted the university symphony and chorale.

Yielding to her hold, he said, "I'm sorry, my love. You have always believed in me, I know. But perhaps now it's better to admit that my career is over." He'd just put words to the feeling that had gnawed at him all week, ever since he'd begun preparing for the upcoming Bach concert.

"Nonsense, my dear!" She moved quickly to the Mister Coffee that snorted noisily by the stove. "Come, let's take our coffee out on the deck! It's a beautiful day." She poured two china cups of the strong German coffee, and put them with matching cream and sugar set on a tray along with a basket of biscotti. Zoltan led the way out through the French doors to the deck that looked down across Skyline Forest to Monterey. At 7:30 that May morning the sun had just risen, gilding the city in a shimmer of rose-gold. Beyond it the bay stretched blue toward Moss Landing and Santa Cruz, a bank of fog barely visible farther out at sea.

In the pine tree closest to the house a gray-blue scrub jay squawked its raucous greeting. Zoltan spooned sugar into his coffee.

"Why do you say your career is over, Zoltan? You have this opportunity to conduct a concert as part of the Bach Festival—at the Carmel

Mission Basilica. That will be beautiful!"

"Only this is one time, Elizabeth. If I do badly here, there are plenty of other directors in this area. They do not need me. I am 'the new kid on the block,' as they say it in English."

"But you have a reputation, Zoltan. You have conducted around the country, even in Europe. They will call on you—"

"Not if my hearing goes. My hearing is everything . . ."

"Well, as I said, there are hearing—"

"No!"

"Well, of course, you could also give lessons."

"I would give lessons? *What? Deaf?*"

"Or you could write, or teach . . ."

He grunted and crunched down on one of the biscotti. The trouble with women was they would not let a man be morose. They insisted on trying to cheer him up. He saw no reason not to stay gloomy at this point, however. Writing or teaching was not the career that had given him joy over the years. It was conducting, molding a piece of music as it came to life in your hands, that fed his spirit. But for that he needed his hearing.

Zoltan strained his ears for the faint sounds of waves or of barking sea lions, carried up from the bay below. Were they always so difficult to hear, he wondered? Earlier he had barely heard the bugle tones of *Reveille* wafting up from the Presidio.

He glanced at Elizabeth as she watched a jay on the railing ogling the biscotti. The sun shining through her silvery hair turned it into a golden halo, floating loose above her deep pink robe. Zoltan let his knee lean against hers momentarily, then straightened up to take one more of the biscotti—his last for the morning.

Elizabeth threw a piece of her cookie to the bird. "Zoltan, please . . ."

Zoltan knew she wanted him to confide in her, but he wasn't one to spill out his troubles, even to his wife. He swirled the rest of the coffee in the cup to mix in the undissolved sugar and checked his watch. "My dear, I must be going to the college now . . ."

"Not yet, please." She laid a restraining hand on his arm. "Is it the music director over there? That Dr. T . . . Tar . . ."

"Taravella. Head of the department. No, no, he's quite happy to have me there. A very fine man," Zoltan assured her, downing the last of his coffee.

"And your soloists?"

"Yes, I see them this morning." He ran his fingers over the table's redwood grain, focusing his awareness on the ridges and valleys, slight as they were. His fingers encountered a loose splinter, which he began prying loose with shaking fingers.

"And you are happy with them?"

"Enough!" He softened his tone. "If I don't leave now, I won't have a parking place." Getting up from the table, he added, "You should see how the students park over there—up on the grass, down in the woods! There is not enough space."

Zoltan bent to kiss the creases of concern on Elizabeth's brow. "Everything will be okay, my dear." But he had a bad feeling.

Zoltan grabbed the well-worn leather briefcase the musicians in the Omaha Symphony had given him as a going-away present, and got into his little Subaru. Heading downhill, his thoughts flew to the problem he'd avoided telling Elizabeth about. Alexis Townsend, daughter of a music patron for both the Bach Festival and the very fine college choir, Cantadores, was a contender for the soprano solo. Alexis sang passably well thanks to thousands of dollars worth of voice lessons, but her voice simply did not have the quality of the other possible soloist, Caroline.

It was like the difference between young wine, no matter how perfect the grapes, and one that had aged. Caroline was only 36, but she'd been singing all her life—this, she'd told him at the audition. Although she had taken a few lessons, she'd managed to get most of her training at the college—thanks to Dr. Taravella. Mike Taravella had told him about Caroline over coffee one morning.

"Amazingly, she learns all her music by ear," he'd said. "Records it during rehearsals and listens to it at home—blind, but she has a repertoire of over one thousand pieces, including masses and oratorios."

Zoltan believed Caroline to be the best choice, but Alexis' father, Geoff, had already called to determine whether his daughter had been chosen. Veering sharply onto Mar Vista, he recalled the conversation.

"I've given my daughter voice lessons for the last five years," Geoff Townsend had announced in a judicial-sounding voice, "plus she's attended the summer music institutes at Indiana University for three summers now." Zoltan remembered picturing the man in a courtroom offensive as he went on. "None of the other kids here, I regret to say, can hold a candle to Alexis, and, well . . ." He'd paused, seemed to regroup, then switched to a breezily genial manner, "Well! With your experience, do I even have to tell you any of this? You'll have heard the difference."

He'd waited expectantly, but Zoltan disappointed him, saying, "I will certainly give your daughter every consideration, but I must hear all of the applicants before I make my decision. The soloists themselves will be the first to know."

Anxiety now made his foot heavy on the gas, and the tires squealed on the next corner. Townsend had blustered at being given the runaround. Well, he'd find out at the Board meeting this afternoon that Alexis hadn't gotten the part. He could make trouble if he chose to. His money was important to the Festival and to the music department. At the very least, he could embarrass Caroline. Zoltan's years as a teacher had taught him how ruthless parents could be. "The Mother Bear Syndrome" he called it.

Zoltan braked sharply, coming up to the stop before turning onto Soledad Street. Today he had appointments with Caroline and the other soloists to announce his selections. Later he would rehearse with the group from the daytime choir. Then in the afternoon he would meet with the Board. And perhaps the proverbial "shit" would "hit the fan", as they said so colorfully in English.

He slowed for the light at Munras and managed to get through without stopping. There, he continued straight on, taking the back road that threaded under Highway 1 through a secluded stretch of forest and down into the deeply wooded Iris Canyon.

Feeling tense, he turned on KBOQ, the Peninsula's only classical music station, where he heard—what was it? Brahms' *Sextet*, it must be. He allowed his mind to focus in on the intertwining melodies, while the underlying turbulence of the rhythms melded with those of his own spirit.

Minutes later he was winding up the hill to the music and arts parking lot at the college.

"Your stop," the bus driver said to Caroline, who sat in the seat right behind him. She already knew, accustomed as she was to the rhythm of the route, ending in the sharp turn off Aguajito onto the campus of Monterey Peninsula College. She extended her collapsible cane and gripped the pole next to her. When the bus stopped, she stood, and, using her cane, negotiated the stairs and stepped onto the curb. Once on the sidewalk, she reached for her cell phone to alert the campus assistance program that she needed a ride in one of the small electric shuttles that carried students to their classes. She could walk if she had to, but the ride was faster and easier, and it was available. *So who needs to be a hero?*

Before she could punch in the speed dial number "3", a familiar lilting voice greeted her and she heard light footsteps approaching.

"Hi, Caroline! Can I walk you to the music building?"

"Sure! Are you going that way anyway?" She didn't relish the long walk up the path from where she was near the new library, over to the fine arts and nursing area on the far side of campus, but with company it would be more fun than riding.

"I am!" Alexis Townsend said in her usual little-girlish head voice. A voice she used in order—she frequently reminded her friends—to protect her vocal chords. She was friendly in a gushy kind of way, and pretty much a kiss-ass in class. They sat together in Dr. Taravella's daytime choir, where Alexis sang in a rather shrill soprano voice, often noticeably flat. She threw Caroline off sometimes, but Alexis was fun to talk to, with her humorous comments about various members of the class and observations about Dr. Taravella.

Now Alexis took her arm and Caroline automatically adjusted to the movement of her body as she led the way.

"It's so nice to be walking on a beautiful day like this," Caroline said. "I love all the spring sounds and smells. I miss that on the electric shuttle."

"So, have you heard who they chose for the soprano solo on the cantata?" Alexis veered to the right to avoid an oncoming bicycle, its wheels whirring an airy whistle as it passed.

"No, I haven't. Did you try out?"

"Yes. Did you?"

"Umm-hmm." When she'd explored its words with her fingers, Cantata 14—her try-out solo—had struck a sympathetic chord in Caroline. "Were not God with us all this time, we would have surely lost courage . . ." began the choral part at the beginning of the piece. Blindness had been a struggle for her in her early years. Still challenged her.

"I didn't expect to get it or anything," she found herself explaining to Alexis. Why was she saying this? It was her habitual way of preparing herself for the expected failure, even though, with the encouragement of Dr. Taravella she'd really come out of that protective shell and discovered her—rather outstanding—talent. She had to guard against falling back into the old defeatist attitude. "Our own strength is called too weak . . ." went the words of the solo part. At one time, *that* had been her song, she remembered, as the tune tugged at her vocal chords.

But the words of the chorale movement at the end of the cantata spoke most clearly for her now—*Vie ein vogel* . . . "as a bird from its snare comes free." Music had set her free, had given her wings to fly.

"I mean, I'd like to get it, of course," Caroline said, adding, "but you'd do it well, too." *But not as well as I would, because it's my song.*

"Well, I ran into Chris Zarillo making some copies in the library. He'd met with Dr. Dalmady a little while ago and found out he's going to sing the bass solo." Alexis paused, as if waiting for Caroline to volunteer some information, then went on. "So I guess the choices have been made. He said Dalmady is meeting with the soloists this morning."

Caroline felt an air pocket form in her insides. She drew in a sharp breath, but said nothing. Was that what her appointment with him was about?

Alexis pulled her to the left abruptly. "Damn goose shit! Pardon my French, but there are too many geese around here." A sea of honking to their right signaled the birds' presence. "Somebody oughta call Fish and Game," she grumbled.

Caroline heard a hissing nearby. "Somebody thinks the same way about us, I think," she said, feeling a certain solidarity with the goose.

"Humph! Yeah, well it's *our* campus." Alexis had slipped into a deeper tone of voice. "And ya know, I think Dr. Taravella ought to conduct this Bach concert. I really do *so* not care for that Dr. Dalmady. He's way too particular. 'I vant to hear dose consonants!'"

"Hey! Watch those vocal chords!" Caroline tried to hold back a sly grin.

"Oops! Well, sometimes I forget. Yeah, so, you haven't heard anything? I bet it was probably one of the 'divas', don't you think?" Alexis referred to several sopranos who managed to land most of the meaty parts, although she herself was often among them.

"I just figured he'd bring in an outside soloist like Lana. She tried out, too." Lana Carmody had graduated from San Jose State as a music major and volunteered her rich soprano voice to various vocal productions around the Peninsula.

"Hmm. Maybe so, but I think it should have been one of us. I have to say, my dad will be pretty pissed if I don't get it—and I guess I didn't." Her voice had lost its perkiness. "It would have looked good on my record when I apply to Juilliard."

Alexis tightened her grip on Caroline's arm. "Careful now, this is a step." As they traversed the bridge behind the old library, the sweet fragrance of buckeye rose up from below. In spring this was Caroline's favorite part of campus, aside from the choral room.

"You going to class now?" Caroline asked.

"Yes—Theory. How 'bout you?"

"Dr. Dalmady—um—wanted to meet with me about something."

"Really!" Alexis' voice dropped back into her chest. "Do you know what it's about?"

"No. Maybe he wants me to do some recording for him or something." It felt lame, and, sure enough, Alexis picked up on it immediately.

"So it *is* you!" Alexis stopped abruptly. "Why would he choose *you?*"

"It's not me! I'm sure it's not." Caroline suddenly needed to go to the bathroom. "Can we go to the ladies' room, please, Lex?"

"Sure!" Her voice sounded like the rasp of a dry oak leaf under foot. She saw Caroline into the small restroom. "You okay now?" She waited for Caroline's murmured okay. "While you're in there I've got to make a phone call."

Caroline used this moment of privacy to collect her thoughts, which had taken off like a flock of startled black birds. The possibility of performing this solo, now hovering close to reality, sent chills through her. Outside, Alexis could be on the phone with her dad—she could imagine his reaction to his little darling's disappointment.

I wish I could just wash my hands of the whole thing, she thought, groping for a towel.

Alexis met her just outside the door, grasping her upper arm with a tight hand. "Well, you must be on time for your *appointment!*" She emphasized the word in a patronizing way. Caroline winced as Alexis squeezed her upper arm, maneuvering her to the music room. Then she released her grip and left without a word. Caroline stood momentarily in the silence of the empty choral room, then felt her way over to the music office door and knocked. A rustling on the desk inside, then steps coming to the door.

"Ah, Caroline, come in, please!" Dr. Dalmady's voice was like dark chocolate. Touching her back lightly, he guided her to a chair. Then he rolled out the desk chair, squealing on its castors, and sat down in front of her.

"Thank you, Dr. Dalmady." Sitting felt good after the long walk. "By the way, I want you to know, I like the cantata we're doing very much."

"That is good, because you will be singing the soprano solo, and I would want you to love what you are singing." She noticed that at times he spoke with almost no accent at all.

"Me?"

"Are you so surprised? I told you at the audition that you performed v–well."

"I figured you said that to everybody." Her throat tightened with emotion.

"Oh, the others performed it well enough, but you . . . you did it with feeling. I could tell you already loved the words." He patted her arm lightly as he spoke. "Let me tell you, the words are more important than the notes in this music. Bach wrote these as a prayerful meditation on the Scripture, so they must be sung meaningfully. You were the only one who sang them with real excitement. And, of course, your voice quality is nice, very nice . . . as a bird, you sing."

"I just had no idea . . ." Caroline felt in her pocket for a handkerchief to dab at her eyes.

"No, and that was the other thing I liked about you—your humble spirit." He cleared his throat and rustled some papers on the desk. "Did you say you had the music?"

"Yes, and the recording." She noted the smell of the dusty air and the close feel of the room.

"Okay, when you are ready you can begin singing it with the choir during our rehearsals. I'd like to work with you a little on it first, though." His voice sounded tired, she thought. The phone rang.

"Music office, Dr. Dalmady." The caller's words crackled angrily from the receiver. "Ah, yes, Mr. Townsend . . . yes . . . yes, we have. Well, it was a departmental decision . . . whoever told you that was misinformed. Yes, well, I'm very sorry, we could choose only . . . we, ah, did what we had to do, sir."

Caroline tried to focus on Dr. Dalmady's voice, which sounded like a stretched rubber band, but couldn't avoid overhearing the caller's voice, ". . . can't support this sort of thing. My money has sustained . . ."

Dr. Dalmady was choosing his words so as not to let on what the caller was saying, but Caroline understood what was happening. The words of the Bach aria came back to her in the German—*ihre Tyranei*, "Surely would their tyranny . . . threaten our very being." He is living it, too, she thought.

She heard students coming into the choral room. Her speaker watch said, "Eleven o-three." She got up and felt her way along the bookshelf, brushing against papers protruding past the edge. Dr. Dalmady was still on the phone with Alexis' father, and she didn't want to hear any more right now.

Her friend Julie, who had just come in, took Caroline's arm and guided her down to her regular seat in the soprano section, talking about a jazz group she wanted Caroline to join. On her right, Caroline heard the chair next to her scrape slightly. She could tell from her breathing it was Alexis.

"Oh, I wish you could see this, Carrie!" Julie said. "Bird nest straw is coming right through the wall."

"From the woodpeckers?" She'd been told how the outside wall was full of holes hammered by the industrious birds, and they often heard them hammering away during practice. Sometimes Dr. Taravella went out and pounded on the wall to chase them away.

"No, these are starlings, but they nest in the same holes. Oh! I just saw the straw moving!"

"Ve begin!" Dr. Dalmady boomed from down in front. "Please stand, everybody. Can we start with an F major, *yah, yah, yah, yah, yah?* Remember to keep your jaw loose, mouth rounded."

The pianist played the chord, and as they started singing the warm-up exercise, a loud cheeping resounded through the wall from overhead. Julie snickered.

On the other side, Alexis muttered, "Stupid birds!"

"Yes, I would ask you, ze birds are bad enough. Please let's not have conversations going in here. Now, let us sing, *ni . . . ney . . . noo.*" Concentrating on relaxing her vocal muscles, Caroline pushed thoughts of the phone call from her mind. She did wonder about the starlings, though. She'd heard that they were related to mynah birds, and mynahs could learn to talk, like parrots. So did that mean the starlings might learn to sing Bach? Just a wild thought . . .

After warm up, they sat down and Dr. Dalmady said, "I would like to present to you our soloists for this cantata. We have our soprano and bass here with us today. Miss Caroline Vigil—Caroline, would you stand, please?" She stood, head held high, feeling her thick hair hanging against her hot cheeks, and listened to the applause from around the room.

"And our bass will be Mr. Chris Zarrillo." She knew his voice well. Chris also sang with the Bach Festival chorus.

"Later you will meet our tenor soloist."

When practice was over, Caroline turned off her small tape recorder and slipped it into her purse. She already had the music memorized, and the recording would remind her of things to listen for in singing it.

"So it *was* you! Why didn't you tell me sooner?" Alexis asked, a tone of accusation in her voice.

"I didn't *know* this morning when you asked me." She felt defensive, almost guilty for having been chosen.

"Yeah, well I know he wanted to make you feel good—I mean, like, give you confidence—like . . ."

"I know *exactly* what you mean." Caroline felt like the floor had dropped out from under her and her stomach had gone with it. *You mean that he chose me because I'm blind. Sure, why else would he bypass you, with all your training and connections?* She knew Alexis had tried consciously to make her comment sound positive and encouraging. She probably had no idea how condescending and dismissive it sounded, or how it played havoc with that very self-confidence this was supposed to be giving Caroline.

After a quick sandwich at the student center, Zoltan started off for Carmel's Sunset Center, where the Festival Board would be having its meeting. Rummaging in his pocket for a piece of mint gum, he tried to envision various meeting scenarios. Geoff Townsend would have made known his opposition to the choice of soloists, and the Board would face him in angry opposition.

He turned off Highway 1, taking the route down Carpenter Street that Elizabeth had shown him . . . or maybe they would not be against him. Perhaps Townsend had one of those quick tempers that calmed down once he'd thought things through. Think positive, Zoltan! Elizabeth would say. It's going to be a routine meeting.

He turned off San Carlos into the parking lot of the Sunset Center, locked the car, and walked over to the office where the meeting would be held.

When he entered the room, he noted that several Board members standing over by the window had abruptly ended their conversation. They were now discussing something in lowered voices. Zoltan caught a few words—"ticket sales," "donors"—but couldn't make out the rest. One of them, a woman in her mid-sixties wearing a long flowing rust-colored skirt topped with an East Indian print jacket, was looking at him, but averted her eyes when she caught his gaze.

Fred Mannheim greeted him at a side table where a woman was serving coffee.

"This is Agnes Lell, Dr. Dalmady. If you'd like coffee, she'll pour you a cup."

"Thank you. Well, Miss Lell, I am trying to remember where I know you from."

"I see you on Sundays at San Carlos Cathedral, and I am so glad to know you now as Zoltan Dalmady." She took his hand and squeezed it supportively before handing him his coffee.

The meeting slowly came to order and, sitting down at the table, Zoltan turned to the gentleman to his left—whose head of white hair and sagging florid face identified him as the senior member of the group.

"Harvey MacMillan. Glad to meet you, sir." Harvey offered a weathered, slightly shaking hand in greeting, meeting Zoltan's eyes with a look that probed uncomfortably.

"It is my pleasure, sir." Zoltan took a quick drink of his coffee, burned his tongue, and splashed a few drops on his tie. Dabbing at the wet spots with his handkerchief, he chuckled, commenting to MacMillan, "You vould think after almost seventy-five years, I vould know not to gulp hot coffee."

MacMillan fumbled in his breast pocket. "My, uh . . . my . . . there we are! Now, may I ask you to repeat? My hearing aid was turned down."

"Oh, it was nothing. Just the coffee," Zoltan said, brushing at the drops on his coat front. "So, how does that thing work for you?"

"Just fine! It's made a world of difference for me—except when I forget to turn it up. You know, sometimes I enjoy the quiet . . ." His eyes crinkled with mirth.

"My wife thinks I should get one. Otherwise, she says, I will end up like Beethoven."

"In good company, you mean! Yes, I expect I wouldn't have one now if Edith hadn't kept hounding me about it. She was right, of course. Hate to admit it . . ."

The conversation helped Zoltan relax, and he felt the black cloud of the unspoken soloist question dissipate. Mannheim came back into the room, checking his watch, and took his seat. "Well, I guess we'd better get started here." The group by the window drifted to the table and sat down.

He looked toward the door, then began. "I've asked Zoltan Dalmady to be here with us for part of this meeting to tell us about his program for the Festival." He straightened the papers on the table in front of him. "The Mission Basilica, as many of you know, has allowed us an additional night of the week for a concert this year, so we've decided to incorporate an all-local chorus, performing one of the Bach Cantatas. And as our conductor for those concerts, we've chosen Dr. Zoltan Dalmady, a widely-respected conductor whom we have the good fortune to welcome as a rather new resident on the Peninsula." He went on to give a short biography of Zoltan's career, and the members nodded as he spoke, although Zoltan observed some furtive looks as well. "Dr. Dalmady is officially retired, I believe," he looked to Zoltan for a nod of confirmation, "but we hope he will continue to grace our community with more of his conducting as time goes on." His eyes moved to the door, then back to Zoltan. "Dr. Dalmady, would you tell us something about your program, please?"

Zoltan, beginning to watch the door himself, told them a little about Cantata 14, and then spoke of the chorus he would be working with. "Most of them sing with one of the local choirs here, and several are students at our local colleges. As for our so—"

"Thank you, Dr. Dalmady! And now we, uh, need to continue with our agenda for today." Again, his eyes nervously flicked toward the door. They were expecting someone else to arrive, it seemed, or dreading that person's arrival.

Zoltan began to perspire, picking up the general discomfort of the group. Did he really need to remain there for the rest of the meeting? As if reading his mind, Mannheim looked over at him. "Uh, the rest of our agenda may not be of great interest to you, Doctor, so if you have other things to do, you need not stay.

Once outside, Zoltan drew a breath of relief, allowing the warm Carmel sunshine to soothe his ruffled spirits. He must not allow these troubling suspicions to upset him.

A week had passed since the first of the daytime rehearsals, and now, in the last week in May, chorus members were coming in for the first of the evening rehearsals. John Harriman, designated choir librarian, was signing out packets of music to the accompaniment of a din of choir member conversations. Zoltan had heard no more from Townsend, and hoped the incident could be forgotten. He thought he'd handled it well enough. The man had been insistent, but Zoltan had not given in. Once you start doing that, everybody thinks they can manipulate you, he thought. It wasn't the first time, and wouldn't be the last, he guessed, that money would try to run things.

As he began the warm-up, the starlings began their loud chatter. Maybe we excite them, he thought. A good sign.

Before starting on the cantata, Zoltan said, "Cantata 14 was used at a Sunday service in Bach's time. 'War Gott nicht mit uns diese Zeit. Were God not with us in this time, we would surely have lost courage.' These words, my friends, are more profound than you may realize. They were the words that got me though my escape from Hungary during the revolution. You must feel them, my friends. Now, let us look at the music, and, please, I hope everyone here has a pencil. If ever I see one of you without a pencil, I will embarrass you. Why? Because without a pencil, you cannot make notes of what I say, and if you are normal, you will forget it by the next time we practice." Tote bags rustled, as people fished for pencils.

"You may notice that this music is written in three-eighths time. A dance rhythm!" He looked out at them, noting the surprise on some faces. "People think Bach was so serious, but many times he took the same tunes he had just written for the Sunday service and used them in the dance hall. It is upbeat music, so we don't want it to sound like a dirge, even if the words are serious."

Lifting his arms to begin, he felt lightness in his chest and his hands throbbed with anticipation. He raised his eyebrows and gave the upbeat. It was like taking a dive, that final bounce on the board before soaring into the air. Then the thrill of running with the singers. Conducting was a little like turning the crank on a music box and hearing the melody come out. Also a bit like coaching a basketball team, except that there the coach remained on the sidelines, whereas here he was . . . *at the helm*, yes! It was more like sailing, he thought.

The rehearsal passed quickly. Several of the students stopped afterwards to introduce themselves and tell him they'd enjoyed the practice, and it was after ten when the last one left. He'd heard the phone ring during class, so he went into the office to listen to the messages. The first was from Geoff Townsend. "Dr. Dalmady, I'm afraid I'm going to have to insist that my daughter Alexis be given a solo in this Bach concert. She needs this for her acceptance to Juilliard, and, well, she deserves it. I don't want any unpleasantness . . . click."

The next message came from Fred Mannheim of the Festival Board. "Dr. Dalmady, I've had a call from Geoff Townsend, and we're going to have to discuss this. I'm afraid he's going to make things unpleasant here . . ." Again, the machine clicked off.

Zoltan seethed. He'd said no, but his answer had not been accepted.

All was silent when he emerged from the office into the empty choral room and locked the door behind him. Even the birds had apparently settled down for the night. Taking his briefcase, he turned off lights, turned down the heat, locked the outer door and left the building. His car stood alone in the dark lot, where the streetlights produced dim auras in the fog. He hastened his steps. As he aimed the key at the lock, his hand shook so badly that he had to steady it with the other hand before he could get it in. Nerves, he thought.

Once in the car, he saw that the fog was heavy enough to have condensed on the windshield. He turned the key and the car started up right away. Thank God! He switched on the wipers. *Why is it so dark?* He'd forgotten to turn the lights on. *There!*

He turned left from the lot and took the road leading down into Iris Canyon. Tonight the oaks danced eerily in the mist that twisted among their slouching trunks. He turned up the heat.

Up the dark road he wound, under the trees. The road was rougher here than he remembered. He was now beyond any of the streets leading to residential areas, and the forest seemed to close in around him. Abruptly the car began bumping along. Zoltan pushed down the brake, then released it, allowing the car to drift back into a safe position off the road. A flat tire? He got out and bent to look at the wheels. The two front tires seemed okay. Going around to the right rear tire, he saw that it lay collapsed, seeming to accuse him of negligence. "Have I not had the rotations done?" He tried to remember. Surely he'd taken it in a few months back. "Well yes, so what do we do? I could call Triple A." He reached for his phone, but didn't find it in its usual place on his belt. Had he left it charging at home? Suddenly frustration cracked his shell of composure, anger charging through. "*Fene!!*" he shouted in his native Hungarian. Hell! "*Fene egyen meg!*" Hell and damnation! He kicked the tire as hard as he could and felt a throbbing in his toe. The futility of this hit him immediately, simply infuriating him more. Tears burned at the corners of his eyes, and his throat clutched. "I will walk then! Maybe it will do me good. Shit!" This came freely in English, after Zoltan had heard it from students over the years. In Hungarian, he was still uncomfortable with the word. He slammed the car door and started walking up the hill. After a non-stop day, he had to will his leaden feet to move, and the memory of the two phone messages weighed heavy in his mind. A cold, misty gust of air set him shivering. Quickening his pace, he pulled up his collar and buttoned his sport jacket. He hadn't dressed for walking.

There was a Union 76 on Munras. Maybe a mile? He could make it there in half an hour. Did they do tires? Well, at least they would have a phone. A rustling sound in the black undergrowth next to the road made his hair stand on end, until his eyes, acclimating to the darkness, picked out the silhouette of a deer above a clump of manzanita. *You are fearful over nothing!* he chided himself. Twenty feet beyond him, a couple of raccoons waddled onto the road and paused to look back at him. He stopped. *Recent articles in* The Carmel Pine Cone *had documented raccoons attacking people.* The animals continued to fix him in their gaze, and he remained frozen in place. *This is crazy, Zoltan! They are much smaller than you!* In frustration he bent down to look for something to throw at them. A stick. He launched it in their direction with all the force adrenaline could fuel and they resumed their lumbering trajectory across the road. Zoltan quickened his step, his heart pounding. *People had seen mountain lions in this forest, too.*

So, what had caused the flat? Could it be a nail? How would there be nails in the parking lot? The phone messages boomeranged back into his mind. *No, Zoltan, let us not be paranoid!*

He'd been staring at the ground and at the brush beside the road as he walked, but now he looked up, his attention drawn by a small sound. An obscure figure, maybe 100 feet away. It was tall—he could see that much already—and coming toward him. In his befuddled state, and knowing something of the possibilities the population of this forest offered, Zoltan stiffened in fear. He'd seen the homeless walking bikes loaded down with possessions, others bent under heavy backpacks. Most, he imagined, were benign, but one didn't know. Could this place also harbor criminals?

The sound increased in volume as the figure approached, now distinguishable as a high-pitched rapid clicking. Mesmerized, Zoltan watched a dark-clad cyclist bearing down on him, only feet away now. His mind directed his body to jump, but the message came too late. The impact threw him to the ground, and something hit him on the head. Pain spread from his shoulder and right leg into his entire body, and then faded into a cold yellow fog that moved across his view, obscuring everything.

When he opened his eyes, he saw a dark latticework of tree branches overhead against the gray sky. The pines dripped steadily as the fog hung in their branches. Ghostly forms flapped to and fro. Bats, he thought. In his curiously detached state, he wondered about vampires. Back in Hungary as a child he'd heard terrifying stories about them. The pain in his shoulder had merged into the cold that reached up from the hard pavement below him. *Maybe I could get up,* he thought. *The pain is not so bad now.* As he tried to roll to the right, his shoulder sent throbbing spasms down his arm and across his chest. *Is it my heart?* He sank back down.

So, you win, Townsend! he thought. *I will die here. Someone else will conduct the concert—and you will convince them to let your daughter sing. Or they will cancel it. Yes, that's what they'll do. And neither girl will sing.* The Bach's St. Matthew Passion he knew so well played in his mind, and his thoughts swirled like the agitated turbo choruses of the cantata's angry mob scenes. He felt cold sweat running down his cheeks. Finally, the swarm of dark thoughts drifted away into the clouds above him, and he lay still, caught in the spell of the bats and branches.

Click, click, click, the rhythm of their flapping wings. Humming in the branches, a whirring sound. And a whispering. A slight breeze chilled the dampness of his face and rustled the leaves—*above or below?*

Crunching, approaching from behind. "Man, why'd ya hafta bring me back here!" whimpered a man's voice. "I didn't do nothin' bad. Just knocked a bum down."

"Shaddup! There he is, up there," answered a hoarse whisper.

"Is 'e dead?" the first voice grated.

"Shhh! You tell me. Has he moved?" This time the voice sounded brittle.

"Hey, hey, you gonna tell me I can't go get some crank when I need it? Huh? Huh? I heard Billy down by the waterfront had some, and I was needin' it right then." He barked a brassy cough. "This dude was in my way."

The conversation hung above Zoltan like a bright bubble that might burst or float away. He lay still, disconnecting from the unfamiliar words, but tuning in to the sounds of the voices, that grew into mental images of their owners. *Owner!* Yes, that was an interesting thought. Could you really *own . . .?*"

Suddenly the voice solidified into a dark form looming above him, and Zoltan closed his eyes. "Let's move him, dude. I don't want nobody t' find the body just yet. C'mon!" cried the gravel voice.

"Wait! I think his eyes moved!"

Rough cool hands seized Zoltan's ankles, lifted his legs and began pulling him. The dormant pain awoke and charged into his consciousness.

"I'm movin' 'im!"

"Stop that!" Rapid steps; the hands let Zoltan's feet fall back to the pavement, releasing more waves of pain through his body in a frenzied *agitato. Maybe my finale?* He heard the thunk of flesh against flesh, heavy staggering footsteps beyond his feet, and sounds of a fight. From a distance, the narrow whine of a siren wafted through the trees.

"Ya dropped a dime on me, Chink Face! Yeah! Well, if ya wanna interfere in things that ain't yer business, then why don't you just take responsibility for 'em!" The speaker hacked out a phlegmy cough. Zoltan heard the clinking of a bicycle being lifted. "I'm outta here!"

A distant siren grew louder, and the bicycle clattered back onto the ground uncomfortably close to Zoltan's side. He cracked open his eyes and saw the two men struggling. Shock was numbing his body once more, but he struggled to remain conscious, riveting his gaze on the thin man with his dark mop of hair, who had locked his emaciated-looking opponent's wrists in his own. Then Zoltan saw himself holding the crank addict by his bony wrists, and the harder he gripped, the louder the wail of the siren became. "I will not let go!" he groaned from between clenched teeth.

"Did he get away?" When Zoltan lifted his hands from the white sheet on his hospital bed to check them, his arm hurt.

"You were clenching your fists so tightly when they found you, that they could hardly get them to relax!" Elizabeth's voice came from his right side. His neck hurt when he tried to turn his head, but he managed to move enough so that he could see her sitting there. She put down her knitting, and he tried to reach for her hand, but felt pain in his shoulder when he moved his arm. Now he saw that it was imprisoned in a cast. A cacophony of memories from the past days swarmed over him. "Rehearsal . . . I was leaving . . ."

Elizabeth squeezed his hand. "You will be okay, Zoltan. They say you were very lucky. Blessed, I think." She turned and reached behind her, bringing out a floral arrangement. "See, this is from your choir." She squinted to read the card. "Get well fast! We need you!"

Zoltan tried to reach for the card without thinking, and again pain gripped his imprisoned arm. "They need me! Fine! Just fine! What can I do without this arm?" His neck hurt from craning to see Elizabeth, and he felt with his left hand for the button to raise the head of the bed.

"What do you want, Zoltan? Raise the bed? Here, let me do it." She found the button and the bed bent upwards.

"So . . ." The effort to remember was too much. He wanted to stay in this peaceful cloud of oblivion, holding Elizabeth's hand. It was enough for now. He drifted.

He'd just wiped his face with a napkin after a left-handed meal when he saw two familiar faces at the door. "Can he have visitors?" asked Julie—that was her name, wasn't it?—the little blond soprano who always sat next to Caroline.

Now Caroline stood next to her, holding her arm, that lovely peaceful smile on her face. "We didn't know if this was too soon, Dr. Dalmady, but we thought we'd try anyway."

"I think Dr. Dalmady would enjoy seeing you for a few minutes," Elizabeth said, squeezing Zoltan's fingers. "Please sit down."

"We were so worried, Dr. Dalmady," began Caroline, settling back in her chair opposite him under the suspended TV. "You had a close call."

"Yes, I know." He saw himself once again wrestling with the pale man on the road and felt, all the while, the sharp gravel biting into his back. "For a while there, I thought it would be the last movement of my life." Brushing aside the hornet's nest of memories, he focused on the girls' bright young faces. "But I should have remembered that Bach does not *end* his Passion with such turbulence, but in calm."

"Zoltan, dear, I do wish you'd had your cell phone along. Lately you are so distracted!"

"Yes, I had some things on my mind. But someone found the car, I assume?"

"They found *you!* That's the main thing. But only in the nick of time." She pressed one hand against her forehead as if to iron away the lines.

He remembered the siren, giving its one last yelp as it stopped near them on the road. "Who called the ambulance? Did you guess that I was out there?"

"No, not I, Zoltan." Her voice cracked, and she yanked on the tweedy yarn she was knitting with. "I . . . uh . . . let these girls tell you."

The little blond began, straightening up in her chair as she spoke. "Your wife called me after eleven, freaking . . . she was all, 'When did he leave?' And I told her I didn't know. I left right at ten with Carrie."

Elizabeth put down her knitting. "So Julie—this girl is an angel!—told me she would go over to see if you were still at the office, but I told her I'd called and you didn't answer . . ."

Elizabeth paused, and Caroline prodded, "So, you were about to call the police, right? But you asked Julie to make a few calls first? That's when I found out."

"Yes, I didn't want to jump to conclusions." Of course, Zoltan thought, she knew how he sometimes met with students after practice back in the old days. He imagined this flurry of phone calls vibrating in the air above his head as he lay out there on the road.

"But finally . . ."

Julie took up where Elizabeth had trailed off. "I called everybody and nobody knew where you were—even Alexis. I mean, she's been so negative, but she was all, 'Omigawd! What do you think happened?' all freakin' out. So I called your wife back. I was pretty worried by that time. And while I was on the phone, the police arrived."

Elizabeth dabbed at her eyes, her knitting abandoned in her lap. "A homeless man called 911 from a convenience store, and they sent an ambulance."

"And the guy who did it was a speed freak, right?" Caroline chimed in.

"He came down the hill very fast, if that's what you mean." Zoltan was fitting the pieces together now. "Those are two wasted voices! A tenor, the one . . . what a shame!" He raised his left hand to flex it. "Two? Or were there three?"

"The police found two men there, Zoltan," Elizabeth said. "They had been struggling."

"Ah, yes. Two, it must be." He bent his wrist, felt its stiffness.

Caroline sat forward on her chair now. "I suppose it's too early to know how soon you'll be back with the choir, Dr. Dalmady?" Her eyes were closed more tightly than usual, her brow wrinkled.

"Oh, I don't think he's going to be able to work for quite some time," Elizabeth answered for him. "They will have to find someone else to take his place. In fact, one of the Board members was in yesterday, and he said maybe they will cancel this concert."

These words struck Zoltan as though they were about some other concert that did not concern him. It would be so easy to cancel the whole thing, he thought. He could just take the leisure—when had he ever taken real time off, away from music?—to recover, and maybe do a concert next year instead. Maybe his fears had all been for a reason. He was not meant to do this. And Townsend would be vindicated. But it would have to be so.

Trying to shift positions, he leaned on his left arm, but immediately felt the pang in his hand and wrist.

Caroline's smile had faded, and Julie's forehead wrinkled in a frown. "Not do the concert?" Julie spoke. "But we have to perform! This is such an opportunity for all of us, Dr. Dalmady!"

Then her head turned toward the door, and Caroline cocked her head slightly.

The rosy-faced nurse stood there with Alexis Townsend, her dark red curls swept back from her face. She held a pot with a yellow orchid growing on a long graceful stem. "How do feel about one more visitor, Dr. Dalmady?" asked the nurse.

"Let her come in," he said, his voice so dry he could hardly get the words out.

Alexis came to him, her face paler than he'd remembered, and held the orchid forward with thin hands. "Dr. Dalmady, I brought you this and I want you to know I'm *so* sorry this happened to you." She spoke in a slow normal tone, almost rehearsed, unlike her usual flippancy.

"Thank you, Alexis. It is very kind of you." His words felt stilted too.

She moved to stand by Caroline. "Um, my father says the Board is thinking of canceling the concert now." Her voice shook slightly.

"That's what we just heard," Caroline answered, her voice in a decrescendo to almost no volume.

Alexis cleared her throat and swallowed. "No, that can't happen. We can't . . ." She covered her face with her hands, drew a sobbing gasp, then went on, "I feel responsible for what's . . . what's happened to you, and I don't want that to ruin the concert for everyone. We can't let my father defeat you . . . us." She looked at the other girls, as if for their absolution.

"Your father?" echoed Julie.

"My father. He is angry that Caroline was chosen for the solo instead of me, and I was the one who complained to him about it. The thing is, I'm not upset any more." Her face relaxed now into semi-composure. "I think your voice is perfect for the part, Caroline. But my dad is still mad. It's the Juilliard thing. And then, he can't lose face with the Board."

The room was silent, except for the bubbling and beeping of the hospital equipment. Grasping Caroline's hand, Julie looked at Alexis.

Alexis twisted a piece of her hair. "I want us to go ahead with the concert," she whispered.

Zoltan looked at Elizabeth, whose face had tightened with concern.

"Oh, Zoltan," she said, as if on cue, "I worry . . ."

Caroline was biting her lip, fingering her purse strap nervously.

Zoltan stretched his legs out in the bed. His hip hurt when he moved, but he could wiggle his toes. "When do I see the doctor?"

"He will be in later this morning, I think," said Elizabeth. "Yesterday he said you would survive, but . . ."

"I will do more than survive, Elizabeth. I think we will perform the cantata and other numbers at our concert. Yes, I think we can do it. I think I see two young ladies who can help conduct the rehearsals until I get this arm going again. Maybe the hospital will have some therapy for me. Maybe I even look into a hearing aid." He glanced at Elizabeth as he said this and chuckled at the incredulous look on her face. "Yes, a hearing aid!" he went on. "I've been wanting to get one for some time now."

Elizabeth shook her head and lifted her arms in exasperation, but the broad smile that grew on her face told him he'd said the right thing.

Fred Mannheim stopped in briefly the next day." Well, sir, I am glad to see you looking better."

Zoltan was sitting up comfortably in the bed, the *Herald* still spread over the blankets." Please, sit down." Zoltan gestured to the chair. "Yes, I go home tomorrow," he continued, wondering whether this was purely a social visit.

"Good t'go, eh!" Mannheim eyed the cast on Zoltan's right arm. "But I must tell you quite frankly that the Board is, uh, concerned . . . that you might not be able to go through with this concert. If there is a possibility of that—that is, a chance—we must know before the program goes to its final printing. It would, of course, be disappointing to the chorus—to all of us—but these things do happen."

Zoltan straightened. "My chorus and I will go ahead with the concert, Mr. Mannheim. We can do it."

"Well, yes, I suppose you think you can, but if you find you can't . . . it could be embarrassing for all of us"

"Let us be frank with one another, Mr. Mannheim. I realize you are dealing with an angry donor." Zoltan felt his heart beating faster. "I also realize that this accident of mine could allow you to avoid losing that donor's support, but as it turns out, his daughter wants very much for us to go forward with the concert, and so do I."

Beads of perspiration now glistened on Mannheim's tanned face and a vein throbbed near his temple. "Of course, of course! But the Board wishes to reserve judgment until they see how well you can handle the rehearsals. We will see how things go."

"When will you have to know?"

"By June Fifteenth."

"Very well."

As Mannheim left, a nurse entered the room carrying a blood pressure cuff. She checked Zoltan's vital signs, removed the cuff, and marked his chart. "My goodness, but your vitals are looking good this morning, Dr. Dalmady." Her voice sounded genuinely surprised.

Caroline felt giddy as Julie guided her down the steps to her seat in the front row, for the first evening rehearsal after Zoltan's return. "He's coming," Julie whispered, "but he's still going to let me and Alexis conduct most of it."

"Do you think he's ready?"

"I think he's still pretty shaky, but the thing is," she added in a confidential tone, "he really doesn't have to conduct much, because we follow him so well as a group that he only needs to just—how did he put that?—*shape it,* just shape it with one hand."

"Or with his eyebrows!" Caroline settled into the seat next to Julie, squishing her tote bag under her chair and pulled out her water bottle.

The idea of shaping music fascinated Caroline, for this was something she could easily imagine—sounds being carefully molded like clay, so that they fit together as something you could feel.

Alexis slid into her seat next to Caroline, leaned over and whispered, "High five, Caroline." She slapped Caroline's up-reached palm.

"What does your dad think about your conducting?" Caroline asked.

"He doesn't know. He doesn't even want me to *be* here."

<hr />

"Tonight I will ask my two ladies to warm us up," Zoltan said, beginning the rehearsal. "I hear they have done a very good job leading the group over these past two weeks. Of course, tonight I will try to conduct a bit myself, but my doctor says I must still be careful."

He took a turn conducting, and the group followed his minimal movements exactly. Very quickly, though, he began to feel woozy, and went to the back of the room, leaving Alexis to carry on. He watched as she directed the group in small, stiff movements. Her timing was exact, and her strokes increased in size to indicate a crescendo. The group responded to her surprisingly well, although they were dragging this number. He suppressed an urge to jump up and hurry them along.

She stopped abruptly. "Hey, guys! I'm not going to be your metronome! You've got to feel the pulse and keep this up to tempo. One-two-three . . . like that!"

Was she quoting him? He beamed. They had actually been listening to him.

The door scraped open. He glanced over, expecting late singers, but saw instead Fred Mannheim and Geoff Townsend. Fred looked around the room, then at Zoltan, giving him a quizzical grin. Zoltan indicated the chair next to his, and Fred came over to sit down. Townsend remained rooted by the door, staring at Alexis. She'd been so wrapped up in directing that she hadn't seen them come in, but now she looked up momentarily. Zoltan watched her ivory cheeks turn bright red, her mouth tighten, but she kept going. Was there greater fluidity now in her gestures? Some people would have frozen in fear, but Alexis now moved with liberation, almost defiance. The music became hers.

Zoltan saw Julie lean over to Caroline before she stood for her solo, undoubtedly to tell her who had arrived. Caroline stood with her shoulders back, chest lifted, and sang as Zoltan had not dared to hope she would do.

Townsend's eyes didn't veer from the front of the room, where his daughter carried through to the end of the cantata. Finally, as she dropped her hands after the last chord, he slipped out the door, letting it slam behind him.

Fred Mannheim, seeing him leave, stood awkwardly and went down to the front. He shook Alexis' hand, and then each of the soloists'. "I must thank you all for an impressive performance. I, uh . . ." He looked up at Zoltan, then over at Alexis. "I can't speak for the Board, of course, but my recommendation will be that this concert go forward as planned." Cheers and foot stamping erupted from the group.

Zoltan stood on the top step of the sanctuary in the darkened mission nave, leaning on a four-pronged cane, but steady on his feet. By his side stood the three soloists. Elizabeth sat in the third row, and in the second row he noted Dr. Taravella and his wife. On the opposite side sat a very sober Geoff Townsend and his family. At least he'd deigned to come.

Zoltan became aware of his right arm, still painful, but which he'd managed to get into the sleeve of his tux with Elizabeth's help. The memory of that night in Iris Canyon swept over him like a cold breeze. He concentrated on the candle lighting. As he watched, one by one the candles in their sconces began to cast their golden light on the ancient walls, warming the faces of the audience that was crowding into the church, filling all but a few places.

Caroline stood waiting a few feet from him at the edge of the sanctuary, dressed in a long flared black skirt of tulle, over which she wore a draped white crepe blouse with sleeves that hung down from the wrists. As he turned to whisper a word of encouragement, he became aware of a whistling sound. *Perhaps a siren?* He stiffened.

Carolyn turned slightly, edged toward him, and whispered to him. He leaned over to hear her better. "Your hearing aid is whistling, Dr. Dalmady," she said, her voice quavering as if on the brink of laughter. His hand shot up to the new device, his fingers feeling for the volume adjustment.

The choir, waiting at the back of the church, had lit their candles. He signaled to them, and they began to file up the aisle singing an ancient Gregorian processional. The pure unaccompanied tones of the choir seemed to join with voices of the past reverberating still within these walls.

Alexis and one of the young tenors led the procession, bearing banners that would hang at the mission during each of the succeeding concerts there. As the singers approached the front and began mounting the risers, soft lights went on in the altar area, bathing the entire nave in a soft, amber radiance.

Zoltan raised his hands ignoring the twinge in his shoulder. He heard the first majestic notes of the pipe organ, clearer and more resonant than he'd heard for years. The program continued with a few shorter pieces of Bach's and his contemporaries.

Then came Cantata 14—*Wär Gott nicht mit uns diese Zeit*. The soloists came down from the risers and went to the front next to Zoltan. Despite the pain in his shoulder, he felt better overall than he had for months or maybe years. Primed by the successful first half of the program, his whole being now poised itself for the cantata. Shutting his eyes, he felt for the beat, and then raised his left hand. Black music folders lifted in synch, all eyes upon him.

He gave the downbeat; the organ sounded the somber first B minor chord, followed by the tenor and then the bass entrances. This music was so organic to his being that, amoeba-like, he had only to draw the singers into that oneness with him. That was the exhilarating thing about music. A Rembrandt was always the same painting; a piece of music lived a new life each time it was performed.

Now the altos began the statement, "*Die so ein armes* . . . for we were but a feeble band . . ." and the basses took it up. We *were* a "feeble band" for a while there, he reflected, and I was the feeblest of them. And truly, *wär Gott nicht mit uns* . . . had God not been with us . . . thanks to the girls and their determination; thanks to . . . to that homeless man, whoever he was; to Padre Junipero Serra, who lay buried just feet from where he now stood conducting, for this place, where sound shimmered in the most perfect way for all to hear. His tears mixed with the drops of perspiration running down his cheeks as he guided the music out of the repetitious fugal movement that pushed on to the movement's conclusion on a major chord—a note of hope.

As Caroline began her aria, he saw how radiant she looked, standing there in readiness, hands together in front of her. This movement began on a more positive B flat major chord, and she sang out the first bars, "*Unsre Stärke heist zu schwach* . . . our own strength is called too weak." Her voice dipped and soared, lightly, as if on wings. Some might have said her own strength was too weak, but she'd shown them the power of her voice and of her determination and hope.

Coming up was the high A she'd had a problem hitting, but there she was, right up there on the words, "their tyranny . . ." They had all risen to meet the challenge, and in that effort had grown from a collection of singers into a choir that sang with one voice. And Zoltan could hear that one voice clearly.

The tenor sang the runs of his short recitative, followed by the bass aria. Zoltan had told Chris to let every phrase in this movement move inexorably to the word "*frei*—free" that ended almost every phrase. This is the message of the whole cantata, he'd told him, that God's protection sets us free.

He glanced up at the reredos behind the altar. Knowing something of the history of the mission's restoration, he realized that this building, too, was a triumph over difficulties of various kinds, from Father Serra and the Indians who first built it, to Father Casanova, who longed to see its ruins restored in 1870, and finally to Harry Downie, who completed the project, so that today it provided a beautiful place of worship as well as a concert venue having some of the best acoustics in the area due to the elliptical arch in the ceiling.

Then began the triumphal recessional, "To God be praise." The first row left the risers to file across the sanctuary step and down the aisle singing, "As birds fly from foes . . ." He looked up then, and saw, catching the light of the candles on either side, the fluttering forms of bats mounting and diving above the singers, as if in rhythmic ecstasy—soaring up into that vaulted ceiling, and back down toward the audience. *Just as that night . . .*

Amid the applause echoing from the ancient walls, the choir returned to take its bows. Zoltan acknowledged the soloists, the organist, and the flag-bearers. The crowd went on clapping. There was an empty space next to Mrs. Townsend. How could a man carry such unrelenting anger, he wondered?

Raising his hand, Zoltan tried to silence the exultant throng, as the timpani rolled a call to attention. In the silence, as they continued standing, Zoltan said, "As many of you know, there was some question whether we would be able to go through with this concert." He patted his shoulder, finally managing to smile at the memory. "God was with us—as the name of our cantata tells you—but without my choir members, we would not be here now." He hesitated, then continued. "I must thank my three angels, Caroline, Julie, and Alexis, who gave me no choice but to go on, when I was about to give up. Come over here please, ladies!"

As he embraced the girls, he looked up to see a hesitantly smiling Geoff Townsend bearing three bouquets. Zoltan stood aside to allow Geoff to present them, and as he gave Alexis hers, he put his arms around her. Then, moving to the other girls, he hugged them in turn.

Zoltan took his hand then and raised it with his own." So, we see you at the rest of the Bach Festival," he cried. "Viva Johann Sebastian!"

Author's Note:

Zoltan Dalmady and all other characters in this story are fictitious, as are all events described herein. However, I must express my gratitude to William Jon Gray and David Gordon, chorus directors for the Carmel Bach Festival, Sal Ferrantelli, professor of music at Monterey Peninsula College, and, of course, Bruno Weil himself, Festival Conductor and Music Director, for the wisdom I was able to impart to my characters. Caroline, though she belongs only to the world of this story, was inspired by Frances Avila, who blessed this community for many years with her vast from-memory repertoire and her lovely lyric voice.

A Break in the Trail

by Byron Merritt

idden. I have to stay hidden.

H   Sitting twenty feet up a stately oak tree, perched on a small platform that passed as a makeshift tree fort, thirteen-year-old Lottie listened to her "Daddy" thundering around the yard, cursing the pig as it lapped up the spilled milk. Lottie hadn't meant to knock over the pail; she just hadn't seen the escaped pig lying in the middle of the path between their windswept barn and the hapless cabin. The fact that she was budding into womanhood hadn't helped either, her lanky build resulting in unsure footing at the most inopportune times.

If her mother were here, Lottie felt sure that she would have protected her. But such thoughts were futile, Mama having died two years ago in 1823 from what Daddy called "The Fever". The man shared no paternal blood with Lottie—her real father having been killed by a flash flood six years ago in the swollen Connecticut River that flowed behind their cabin—but he'd insisted on being called Daddy anyway.

Now I'm alone. Alone with him.

Lottie hugged her knees to her chest, looking down at the weather-beaten cabin. The failing barn, with its slight lean to the east, shadowed the poorly constructed pig pen which sat framed off on its south side. The garden, located between the cabin and barn, sprouted a few greenish clumps of vegetables but desperately needed weeding.

"Where are you!" Daddy yelled. Ignoring his calls, Lottie focused on the flower-patterned dress she wore, flayed out against the fort's hard-wood boards. It had a fraying lace hem that she mended from time to time. *I wonder if it'll last another season,* she thought, picking at the edges.

"Are you up there!" he yelled up at the tree fort.

She held her breath and trembled, but kept still. *He won't care that the stupid pig tripped us up.*

The wind whipped a lock of her long, black hair into her brown eyes, stinging them. She reined it back into place and stared at her left hand, then put both hands in front of her face. The calluses were mountainous, with ridged peaks and valleys that told of a rough life lived on a demanding farm.

"I can see your dress through the cracks, Lottie," he said, more calmly this time. A thud echoed through one of the boards, maybe from a volleyed acorn.

A cloud crawled across the sky, momentarily blotting out the sun and dipping the temperature of the already chilly spring day. Black crows sprung up in a distant field, cawing objections for reasons known only to them.

Are they near Mama's grave?

"Don't make me come up there and get you!"

Knowing that if he did have to "come up there and get her" he'd be all the more angry, she smoothed out her dress, tightened a lace on one of her black work boots, and shimmied down the trunk of the tree. He met her at the tree's base, blue eyes cold, crooked nose flaring, brown hair a tangled mesh of sweat and carelessness. He grabbed her by the arm and wordlessly dragged her back to the cabin.

The poorly hung knotty pine front door swung open under the force of Daddy's muscular arm, developed from years of loading and unloading freight and baggage off stagecoaches.

Lottie's right arm ached in his feral grip as he dragged her through the cabin and into her room. He pushed her in and, instead of removing his thick leather belt in preparation for punishment, cursed and slammed the door shut, causing dust to settle from the ceiling.

Alone in her room, she could hear him on the other side of the door rummaging through their meager kitchen supplies. *Looking for a new weapon to beat me with,* she thought. Then came the sound of a cork being forced from a bottle and the tinkle of glass on glass. Drinking. He was drinking again. The last time he drank he'd beaten her so badly that she couldn't get out of bed for two days.

A grimy little window that graced one of the walls in her room projected a dull patch of sunlight onto the bed, and she felt its comforting warmth touch her right leg. It was the little things that pleased her now, like beating the town boys at their own games.

The teenage ruffians of Lebanon, New Hampshire, just up the road from their outskirt cabin, had taunted Lottie about her dirty hair and her secondhand shoes and clothes. The insults made her dislike going into town, even when her mother had been at her side.

But that changed quickly. After her mother passed away, Lottie had been forced to do much of the work on the farm. She stacked hay, milked the cow, fed the chickens, cleaned the cabin and barn, and tilled the garden with the help of Goldie, an aging mule with the mentality of a boulder. These activities made her lean and firm. Her hands hardened into stone and her forearms bulged with large muscles; muscles obscured by delicate female apparel and the first bloom of womanhood.

One warm summer day, Willie, a brash blonde boy whose father owned the stables—and who always boasted about how much he won betting on himself when he arm wrestled—kicked at Lottie's fraying outfit and said, "Your dress looks like a rotten dish rag!"

Lottie'd had enough. She challenged him then and there to an arm wrestling match.

A chorus of laughs and exaggerated "ooohs" surrounded her.

"What's the bet?" one boy snickered, picking at a scab on his elbow.

Chin held high, knowing the amount wasn't important, Lottie pulled out two pennies.

"Boy, I don't know if I can afford that!" Willie squawked, pulling a pile of coins out of his pants pocket and thumbing through them. He plopped down five cents. "You can keep the extra when you win," he laughed. The other boys clapped and shouted in anticipation of a certain massacre. No one bet against Willie.

Lottie took up her position on a bench facing an overturned water barrel whose underside served as the focal point of the competition. Willie moved to the opposite side and pulled up his right sleeve, revealing an impressive tan bicep.

Jimmy, a teenager with gapped teeth and short-cropped brown hair, took hold of Lottie and Willie's hands as they locked into place on the flat surface. The other teenage boys gathered around. Willie winked at Lottie. "This won't . . ."

"One," Jimmy intoned, his brown eyes darting between the two combatants.

". . . hurt . . ." Willie continued.

"Two."

". . . a bit."

"Three!"

It was over so fast that the boys hooted and hollered before they realized Lottie had won. Willie's eyes went wild and he stripped his hand away from *the girl*. The jubilation of the others changed to gasps of wonder as Lottie picked up her winnings and went into the local trade store to buy herself some penny candy.

After that the Lebanon boys whispered to themselves whenever they saw her in town, but they never harassed Lottie again.

"Charley! Charley, wake up!" shouted Buster McGeorge, a lean Irishman who rode shotgun on the stagecoach. He threw on his shirt and green bowler hat as he stomped around the small shack looking for his coat.

"What is it!" Charley responded in a guttural growl, half-filled with sleep. He turned over on the makeshift cot, its metal frame scratching against the dusty wood floor, and glowered at Buster while trying to rub the sleep out of his eye.

"It's startin' to rain," Buster said, nudging Charley with a well-worn, pointed boot. "We need to put the tarp over the carriage or the luggage'll get soaked."

Charley slapped Buster's boot away. "Get that damn foot away from me, boy, or I'll shove it up your ass." He pushed the blanket off himself and stood up, fully dressed in his buffalo skin coat and cap.

Buster stepped back from Charley even though he stood a full head taller than him. You didn't mess with Charley; his reputation preceded him. One infamous story told of a raunchy mare that Charley had freed from a nightmare encounter with some barbed wire. The mare, once freed, had kicked out with her rear feet, one of which landed squarely on Charley's face. A rumor circulated that Charley had been knocked to the ground, but retained enough of his wits to pull his pistol and fire a shot between the horse's eyes.

As a result of the encounter, Charley wore a large, faded, black patch over his left eye, an accessory that had earned him the nickname, "Cock-eyed Charley". Many other tales about him drifted amongst stage drivers, and Charley gained almost a legendary reputation as the best stage whip in the West. And tonight, although not too happy about being awakened, the best whip would have been even more upset if Buster had let him sleep through the storm and allowed the passengers bags to get wet.

Buster opened the rickety door to the way-station where the Pacific Coast Stage Company staff slept. He gazed out at the misty Santa Cruz evening as silhouetted bursts of lightning turned distant clouds over California's central coast into flickering, pale ghosts.

Buster put on his heavy coat and hat, and the two men raced outside just as the drizzling rain changed to a powerful downpour. After putting a tan canvas tarp across the back and top of the red and yellow Concord stagecoach—covering the precious bags—they returned to the poorly ventilated way-station.

"Jesus!" Buster exclaimed. "We wasn't out there three minutes and I'm soaked to the bone!" He began peeling off his clothes and setting them in front of the small, black stove. "You should dry out your clothes, too."

"Think a little rain's gonna hurt me?" Charley grinned while cutting out a wedge of dry tobacco and putting it in his right cheek. He chewed firmly, his craggy face scrunching up with each movement of his angular jaw. Then he tucked himself, damp clothes and all, back into bed and was asleep in seconds.

Buster scratched his head as he lay down on his own wobbly cot. *I'll never understand how he can chew tobacco in his sleep.*

Evening had spirited away the warmth of the sun from Lottie's bedroom, leaving a darkened window and an empty coolness that had nothing to do with the chill running up her spine. When her bedroom door creaked open on rusty hinges, she sat up quickly on the bed. Daddy's head peered around the corner, a movement that reminded Lottie of the thin, green snakes she occasionally ran across in the garden. His nose and cheeks were flushed, and he wore a dull grin. He slid into her room and closed the door. She glanced at his hands, expecting to see the familiar sight of the belt, prepared to snap to attention and procure its punishment, but it wasn't there. Instead his fingers curled around a two-thirds empty bottle of rye whiskey, its liquid contents looking like dirty laundry water.

He half shuffled, half staggered toward her. Lottie scooted to a corner of the bed, and its wooden frame squeaked in protest as he sat down opposite her. After taking a long swig from the whiskey bottle, he placed it on the small night stand, then turned toward Lottie and smiled. She could smell the choking odor of the whiskey on his breath, even from the other side of the bed.

"Come 'ere," he slurred.

She didn't move. *Was he trying to be friendly?*

"I ain't gonna beat you!" He slid his right hand across the bed and grabbed her arm, pulling her easily toward him. His bloodshot eyes fixed on her face for a moment, then he blinked and stared down at her chest.

"You're turning into a fi-fine young lady, you know that? You just need some . . . refinin'." He licked his lips and lifted his left hand up toward her face. She flinched and scrunched her eyes close, expecting to feel a slap or heavy blow. But he didn't strike her. He simply moved some of the hair out of her face and slid his hands to the top of her rose-patterned blouse, where he unfastened the first button, then the next.

Blood rushed to her head and pulsed in her ears, nearly deafening her. A cold sweat broke across her forehead. She tried to stand up, but he forced her back onto the bed. She fumbled against his fingers, trying to push them away, but he tore open the front of her blouse. Pretty green buttons skittered across the floor like glossy cockroaches looking for a place to hide. He forced her back onto the bed, and lay against her. She squirmed to get out from under him, but couldn't. His bulk and superior strength were too much for her.

"No. Please," she whispered.

Daddy reached down to unbutton his britches.

"No! Please don't!" Louder this time.

A clap of thunder shook the cabin as the spring storm pounded down, driving raindrops through the cracks in the leaky roof.

The next day was bright and clear, quite a change from the night's storm. Charley and Buster hitched up a six-horse team—two extra to help with muddy spots they knew they'd encounter—and guided their guests into the stage compartment's interior before setting out on the Santa Cruz/Monterey trail.

Buster and Charley had been paired for six months now, making the treacherous route over the Los Gatos/Santa Cruz pass and then on to Monterey. Indians were rarely a problem anymore—most having been killed by lead or disease, others having been sent away to reservations—but bandits still frequented the area, and Charley was glad to have someone as sharp as Buster along.

Although the typical shotgun rider carried an actual shotgun, Buster didn't care for that weapon. Coming from Ireland, Buster had learned about firearms from his grandfather, who picked off Protestants at great distances, a skill that eventually got him hanged. When that happened, Buster's parents dispatched themselves and their children to America, where Buster's learned talents with a rifle came in handy for the stage driving companies. He'd quickly proven himself with a .56 caliber Walker Rifle as well as a Colt .45 pistol, taking care of some nasty bandits on the rocky Carson's Cañon Pass. Charley, already a well-established driver, had been a passenger on that trip and knew immediately he wanted Buster to come work with him. When Buster found out who'd requested him for the new job, he'd accepted instantly.

Now here they were, sitting next to each other on the *Yodeler*—the name Buster and Charley had given their coach because of the repetitive warbling sounds it made—splashing along the muddy road, heading down the Santa Cruz/Monterey trail. Charley drove; Buster gazed into the highly-polished, reflective wood stock of his Walker rifle, checking between his teeth for breakfast leftovers, listening to the excited exclamations of their passengers as the coach passed scenic vistas, or spotted deer and bears grazing—on grass or each other.

"So I saw that you voted in Soquel last week," Buster said matter-of-factly.

Charley gave him a questioning look. They usually didn't talk much, especially about politics.

"Yep."

"Who'd you vote for, if you don't mind my asking?"

The horses slowed momentarily, but speeded up when Charley slapped the butt strap. "Ain't that s'posed to be private?" he asked Buster with a twinkle in his eye.

"Just curious. It's a close contest. I voted for Grant."

Charley grinned. "Congratula . . .oh, shit."

Buster looked over at his partner who didn't usually curse with such highfalutin customers in the stage. "What?" he asked, sitting up straight and swinging his rifle around so that it sighted above the horse team.

Charley pointed ahead to where the road traveled up a rise then vanished from view. "Trail's washed out."

"So?" Buster said. "Ain't the first time for us."

"No it ain't," Charley agreed. "But there's no side trails 'round here. At least none that I've seen. We'll have to blaze our own." He clicked his tongue.

They stopped the coach and Charley got off, wandering up the trail until it dropped away to reveal a raging milky-brown river below that shot out toward the Pacific Ocean.

"Where's he going?" a young man inside the coach asked Buster. He wore an expensive-looking suit. "Why are we stopped?"

"Wash out," Buster replied.

"Well that won't do," said a more mature voice, a woman's. "My sister is getting married tomorrow and I have to help with the final preparations. I paid an extra three dollars to get from Santa Cruz to Monterey and I must get there soon."

The other three passengers groaned, sounding like they'd heard one too many times about the wedding and how important it was that she—Mrs. Wilson, of the Washington D.C. Wilson's—get there on time to help the proceedings along. Ignoring the other travelers, Mrs. Wilson asked, "Will there be a delay, driver?"

"I ain't the driver. Charley there is. And if anyone can get us there on schedule, he can."

After a few minutes, Charley returned to the coach. He looked at the ground before focusing his eye on Buster. "Not good." He pointed east of the trail where a long, round meadow, about a quarter-mile in diameter, sat surrounded by pines glinting with moisture in the daylight. "Looks kinda boggy over there, but we might have to chance it. Hand me the pistol."

Buster handed him their company-issued Colt .45.

"You know how to handle that?" Buster quipped. "Ain't no bridled mare in your hand now. That there's a Colt."

"Yeah, maybe I oughta shoot you to find out if it works right 'n' proper," Charley grinned. "Might not coming from a slipshod like yourself."

With that, he turned and walked out into the meadow, weaving between sink holes and mud, finding the smoothest and least damp areas of the field. When he reached the forest, he disappeared into it.

Buster remained on the stage, picking at some scrambled egg and a swath of sausage wedged in between two back teeth. He was digging for the prize with a firm blade of grass when the sound of the Colt sliced across the meadow. Buster's head snapped up and the makeshift toothpick fell from his hand. He knew the sound of his own gun all too well. Jumping down from the driver's bench, he swung the Walker rifle off his shoulder.

"Was that a gunshot?" the young man's voice asked.

"Stay here," Buster ordered.

"Well this just won't do," came Mrs. Wilson's voice again.

Lottie awoke to find herself alone in bed, the sheets and holey blanket twisted, the mattress nearly dislodged from the bedframe. She tried to stand, but her legs gave out and she collapsed to the floor. Crying out in pain as she hit the hard wood, she forced herself into silence, then jumped when she felt something crawling on the inside of her left thigh. She looked.

Blood.

Trembling, Lottie crawled to the door and pressed her ear against it. No noise. She pulled herself up by the doorhandle and peered out into the empty living area. *Where was he?* She staggered into the washroom as quietly as she could and grabbed an old sponge, scrubbing herself again and again until her white thighs glowed red.

This didn't happen! Didn't happen! Didn't happen!

But it had. And things would be different now. *Everything* would be different.

Lottie carried the washroom bowl toward the front door, ready to empty its filthy contents, when she heard snoring. She peeked over her shoulder and could see *him*, asleep on his bed, his clothes on, his pants unbuttoned, his face stilled into a dreamy sense of peace. She continued to the door, flung it open, and threw the water out in a great curving arc.

Out of habit, Lottie sloshed over to the well and pumped out more water, filling the washbowl again. The storm was letting up, the deluge easing into a drizzle. She carried the filled basin carefully back to the cabin and placed it in the tiny washroom. A little mirror that her mother had given to her sat poised on a thin wooden shelf, and Lottie looked into it, staring long and hard at her reflection.

It did *happen! How could we have let this happen? What went wrong?*

The reflection didn't reply. But a thought did come to her, warming a recess of her mind the way the blurred patch of sunlight had warmed her leg earlier. She went into her room and pulled out a pair of scissors from her cherrywood dresser before coming back to the washroom mirror. She grabbed her hair, pulling it taut.

Snip, snip, snip.

Mindlessly, she chopped off long locks of hair as a baleful song filled the suddenly blank spaces in her mind:

This is the way we lose our hair,
lose our hair,
lose our hair.
This is the way we lose our hair,
so early in the morning.

This queer grooming went on for what seemed like an eternity, and Lottie could hear a strange noise bouncing back toward her. It sounded like a whining, injured dog. The mirror displayed a face foreign to her. Tears streaked the image's cheeks, and its lips quivered as a long, slow moan crept out of the reflection's mouth. She hadn't felt the tears or heard the sound of her own weeping, and it struck her that this was happening to someone else in another cabin, somewhere far away.

The room began to tilt, making her feel queasy, and she dropped the scissors to the floor. She latched onto the counter that held the washbowl and heard popping in her ears, like giant balloons bursting.

That's when the voices started, all of them whispering to her at the same time.

Why don't we just kill him, a husky voice said, above all the others. It reverberated through her skull as if her head were deep in the metal milking bucket. It wasn't her voice. It wasn't Daddy's.

"Who . . . who's there?" she asked, her eyes wandering around the cabin.

Does it matter? The voice sounded powerful and fearless and right on top of her.

Lottie spun around quickly, as if she might see this person if she moved fast.

"Who are you?" she asked. The room tilted again and she felt sure that her feet would go out from under her, but she held fast to the counter, digging her fingernails into the board and clenching her teeth.

We're friends, it said. *We* can *kill him, you know. That's what we want, isn't it?*

Charley had been concentrating on the meadow and forest floor, trying to find the best and most accessible ground cover for the stagecoach wheels, when he smelled something familiar. Campfire. He lifted his head and found himself face to face with an ugly, disheveled man wearing ragged denims and a toothless grin, an ancient-looking flint rifle in his right hand.

Charley brought up the Colt .45 and the man's grin turned to a frown, his eyes blazing in anger and surprise. The stranger's finger slipped toward the trigger on the old flint.

Too late. Charley fired the Colt point-blank into the man's chest. He staggered back then collapsed onto the ground with a *thump*.

A plume of campfire smoke wafted toward Charley and, as if by some dark magic, three more men drifted out of it. One held a long wooden pole, while the other two had more conventional weapons: a knife and a small pistol. Charley swung the Colt toward the tallest man, the one with the pistol, but the stranger holding the pole extended the wood-beam forward and gave Charley a painful smack on the right arm. Charley's hand reflexively opened, releasing the .45. It tumbled to the ground. He was about to reach down and grab it, but another blow from the pole struck him in the center of the chest, knocking him backwards and expelling the air from his lungs.

"He done shot Tobey!" spouted the smallest man, the knife-wielder.

Charley sat up and gasped, flexing his right arm. Not broken, thankfully, but definitely bruised to the bone. The tall man snatched the .45 off the ground, then moved toward Charley and picked him up by the lapel of his thick muffler jacket, shoving a pock-marked nose into Charley's face, his breath a malodorous combination of burnt bacon and dog crap.

"Why'd you shoot, Tobey?" the man demanded.

"Because he was gonna shoot me!" Charley retorted. He frowned at the three men. "What're you all doin' out here in the middle of nowhere? You the welcoming committee?"

The tall man threw Charley to the ground and walked over to "Tobey", turning him over. "Didn't much care for him anyway," Tall-Man said, taking the rifle off the dead man and a few other items from his coat pockets.

"Hey!" Knife-Man yelled as he watched items being lifted from the corpse. "Those is my dice! How'd Tobey get those?"

Tall-Man tossed the dice to him and smiled. All of the men, Charley noted as he stood up and brushed himself off, had *very* bad teeth. *A dentist could make a fortune out here.* Not that Charley couldn't have used a dentist himself, but these men looked as though they'd been eating mud.

Tall-Man stood up and tossed a smudged pocket watch to Wood Pole-Man and then looked at Charley. "You driving that stage on the road up yonder?" he asked.

"What stage?" Charley asked.

"Don't get stupid on me, stage-hand. We fanned out along the tree-line when we heard your noisy coach coming down the road. Can hear that thing a mile away! I saw you looking for a side trail."

So much for playing dumb. "So you *are* the welcoming committee 'round here," Charley quipped.

The pole came down again and caught Charley across the left shoulder, knocking him back to his knees. "Don't be nasty now," Wood Pole-Man said. "We's just asking some questions."

Knife-Man wrestled Charley back to his feet and pushed him toward a tall redwood, tying him to it. He bound Charley's hands and secured his torso to the tree's trunk. Charley smelled food burning and heard the crackling of a fire.

"Didn't mean to disturb your breakfast," Charley muttered, initiating another smack from the pole, this time on his right thigh. Charley winced but didn't cry out.

Tall-Man stared admiringly at the Colt Charley had dropped and tucked it into his belt. "Nice weapon," he said. "What kind of valuables you carrying, stage-hand?"

"Tain't none of your business," Charley replied angrily, his muscles throbbing where wood had met flesh.

"Well it's my business when that kind of waste takes place!" Tall-Man yelled, pointing at the forever silent Tobey a few yards away.

"Yeah," Charley said, grinding his teeth. "Probably shouldn't've wasted the lead on him."

Tall-Man stripped the gun out of his belt and slammed its butt into Charley's right temple. A dancing spectacle of light burst across his vision and then—like the falling of a dark curtain—blackness came.

Lottie sat in her room, thumbing through her mother's tattered diary, the only item she had left of her since Daddy had sold everything else to help pay for whiskey, women, and other cheap pleasures.

The popping in her ears had stopped but she still felt off-balance, as if the floor had shifted and remained at an unnatural angle. She thought reading about her mother would take her mind off the disturbing sensation—and off the voice that buzzed around her like a horse fly—but it hadn't helped.

"Why are you here?" Lottie finally called out.

She heard a short noise. A laugh? Then: *It's time that we took care of ourselves, wouldn't you say? Daddy's not going to take care of us. Not in the way that we need to be taken care of.*

Lottie looked across her bed. She'd smoothed out the blankets and covered the stain on her sheets from the encounter with Daddy, but the memory burned like a glowing coal. She listened to the wind whistle an unknown melody past her window, the last evidence of the passing storm. The odd tune matched her feelings; new, unfamiliar . . .

She stared unseeing at an empty page in the back of the diary. Her legs tingled. A thin line of sweat formed on her upper lip. She sat up and scanned the room for the hundredth time. *Why couldn't she see this man?* It was a man, she was sure of that.

Lottie looked up toward the ceiling and touched the delicate silver cross that hung around her neck. "Are you a . . . a spirit?"

Goodness no!

It made her wonder if the invisible speaker was a thing of evil, but she didn't sense it. The voice and what it said—filled her?—like something solid had been poured into her, making her less breakable. Felt good.

The floor stopped tilting.

"Why are you here?"

It's for us. We have to take care of ourselves.

Lottie nodded and put her mother's diary on the nightstand.

"So how do we take care of . . . us?" Lottie asked, feeling a rush of excitement whirl through her body.

The voice was flat; no emotion, filled with common sense. *Easy. We just kill him. It's not hard, you know.*

Lottie got up and walked toward the fireplace. A few embers twinkled in between the ashes thanks to a draft coming up the chimney. The coals flickered like eyes opening and closing as gusts from the storm swept past the cabin.

Lottie watched her hand come down and grab the cast-iron fire poker. She felt the weight in her hand, but only slightly. She turned it carefully over in her hand, admiring how it ended in a sharp hook.

Very nice, the husky voice said excitedly.

She turned and walked to the bedroom where her mother had once slept with this man, this creature, who'd violated her. Her insides ached from the act, but the only thing she really felt was the need to prevent it from ever happening again.

The wood floor creaked as she approached Daddy but he didn't stir, except for his lips which fluttered with each wheezing breath. She noticed that her shuffling feet were stirring up small particles of dirt. She grimaced. *When was the last time he'd cleaned up in here?*

The snoring stopped.

She saw his head lift off the brown-stained pillow and fix her squarely with his gaze. In his eyes she saw the same terrible thing she'd seen only hours ago.

He won't stop, can't stop.

She felt something kindling within her, like the red-hot embers of the fireplace. Power. The power to keep herself safe.

"Need something, honey?" Daddy asked, his voice sweet syrup. He looked down at the object she held. "Why'd you—"

Lottie heard a scream. She wanted to turn around and see where the outcry had come from, but before she could, her right hand shot up toward the ceiling and flew back down, the cast-iron whistling through the air as it came crashing toward Daddy's head. Though drunk, he was able to move sideways, but only just. His left shoulder took the blunt of the blow. Lottie heard a fleshy thud and the snapping of bone.

Very satisfying.

"Shit!" Daddy screamed as Lottie tried to free the imbedded poker from his shoulder. He bolted upright and grabbed the end of the weapon with his right hand while his left arm hung limply at his side, blood streaming down his forearm to his fingertips. He ripped the poker away from her with surprising strength. "What the hell's wrong with you, girl!"

His teeth were clenched in pain and anger as he swung the poker at her, its end finding the left side of her face. The impact sent her flying backward and crashing to the floor. Amazingly, there was no pain.

Daddy stood over her with the poker. "What'd you do that for? And what happened to all your hair?"

Lottie's hands touched the stubble on her head, feeling a mixture of joy and pain. *Men will never find us attractive like this,* the voice had said proudly.

Daddy's lips grew pale, the alcohol-saturated blood flowing freely down his left arm to form a crimson puddle on the floor. Then his eyes glazed over and he stumbled backward, dropping the poker. It clanged to the floor, ringing through Lottie's body. Dreamily, she touched the left side of her face. Blood poured down it and soaked her dress. The stream ran down her arm to join the red pool on the floor that Daddy had started. She swept her arms wildly across the floor, scattering her own tributary of blood as it streamed across the boards toward his. Anger flared up in her to think that their blood might meet.

The bed creaked as Daddy fell onto it, and his eyes rolled back in their sockets. Lottie found an old shirt on the floor and wrapped it around her head, tamping down the bleeding. Crawling over to the poker, she picked it up and stood. Her legs felt strong. She walked over to the bed and shuddered at the sight of him. His eyes remained glazed, but life flickered across his face. He raised his right hand, a plea of some kind.

"We can't stop now," she said as she swung the poker down again and again. Except it didn't sound like her own voice anymore.

Lottie stood emotionless on the banks of the river behind the cabin as the water swept his body away. A firm wind whipped the blood-soaked shirt that remained wrapped around her head.

"It's over," she whispered. Did the passing storm carry off her voice? It sounded so far away.

She walked back to the cabin and tugged off her dress and undergarments, throwing them into the fireplace. The fire licked the stained and tattered dress, before consuming it like a hungry orange beast.

Lottie found herself standing in front of the dresser in *his* room. Did she walk in here? She couldn't remember. Picking up a shirt and a pair of jeans, she pulled them on, then found an old straw cowboy hat crumpled under the bed and placed it on her head. She went to the washroom and checked herself in the mirror. The hat covered most of her head wound and shaded the rest of her features. Hiding under the hat and clothes felt so good it startled her, but then she'd always enjoyed hiding, and was good at it, too. Even her mother had trouble finding her when they'd played hide and seek.

Lottie moved to the front door and opened it. Puddles littered the walkways between the cabin and the barn. Above her, streams of blue crossed the sky; the storm was drifting away, spirited to the east by strong winds.

Lottie pulled the hat down firmly, stepped out of the cabin, and closed the door, making sure that it latched tightly.

Then she walked toward the setting sun, leaving the storm and her secrets in the East.

Charley's blurred vision returned. He felt blood trickling down his forehead.

The three men still stood in front of him.

"Shit, he's tough," Tall-Man said, and put the Colt back in his waistband. "What's your name, stage-hand?"

"Eat dog balls," Charley growled, licking the blood out of the corner of his mouth. The metallic taste heightened his senses. He became acutely aware of the ropes knotted around his wrists and tied across his body. A terrible sense of imprisonment closed in on him and his mouth went dry. Something deep inside was forging its way forward, something terrible, struggling to break the surface. The ground shifted beneath his feet. He shook his head trying to shoo away the feeling.

"Why don't we just kill him and then go and take everything off the stage?" Wood Pole-Man asked.

"What good will it do to risk our necks trying to rob something if there ain't nothin' to take?" Tall-Man said.

The other two bobbed their heads in unison

"I guess we best find out then," Knife-Man said. He turned toward Charley and held up the large hunting knife. It gleamed in the sunlight filtering down between the thick tree branches.

Charley felt its tip touch his chest, just below his neck, where the muffler jacket made a scant V-shape opening.

"Now," Knife-Man said, "what's your name?"

Charley smiled and said, "Donkey Shit."

Knife-Man pushed harder on the hilt. The blade dug into Charley's chest. He gritted his teeth and moaned.

"That don't sound like your true name to me. So why don't you just tell me and I'll pull back on ol' Shiny Glory here." He twisted the end of the blade.

"A-h-h-h!"

Charley felt blood winding its way down his stomach.

"Don't hurt us!" a meek voice said.

Knife-Man stopped and looked up with a start. "He sounds like a whimperin' little girl!" Then he pushed harder on the hilt of the knife and it dug deeper into Charley's chest.

Charley screamed again and panted, trying to get out a few painful words.

"My . . . name's . . . *Lot* . . . Charley."

"Charley?" Tall-Man said and stepped closer, pulling the blade away from Knife-Man and out of Charley's chest wound. He stared at the black patch over their prisoner's left eye, nudging it with the tip of the knife. "You're a stage driver and your name is Charley?"

Charley nodded.

"Charley Parkhurst. That who you is?" Tall-Man asked.

Charley nodded again, and the two other bandits glanced at each other and shrugged their shoulders.

"You the same Charley Parkhurst who drove the Diamond Springs stage route in '61?"

Charley's face went slack. That had been a bad year. He'd identified eight men who were involved in the murder of stage personnel, then watched them hang for their crimes. Charley never liked to see hangings. He thought it was cruel. *Just shoot 'em!* he exclaimed whenever hangings were arranged. *There's no wait time and the guy won't even know it's coming, probably.*

"You might remember my brother," Tall-Man continued. "They used to call him Smokin' Sammy."

Charley scowled. "Yeah. I remember him. Used to burn bodies to hide what he'd done to 'em before-hand."

Tall-Man's mouth twisted at the corners and he moved closer to Charley. "You identified him as one of the one's to be hanged, didn't ya?"

"Had to," Charley said.

"Well, if you had to, I guess you'll understand that I *hafta* spit you like a pig and throw your guts to the animals!"

The veins in Tall-Man's eyes filled with deep red, as did his nose and cheeks. He slid the knife back to Charley's chest and dug the tip into the wound, but before any pain began, the tip trembled and pulled out of the hole. Charley heard a *Pop!*

Time slowed.

Charley blinked.

Warm blood shot onto his face.

The thundering boom of a gunshot echoed as it caught up with the bullet. A gruesome third eye sprouted like a scarlet flower in the center of Tall-Man's forehead. His other two eyes instantly glazed over. On his way to the ground, he harmlessly sliced open the front of Charley's heavy clothing with the knife.

The two remaining outlaws spun around, and things began to happen very fast.

The next bullet caught Wood-Pole Man square in the chest and knocked him back ten feet. He moaned, arching his back as he hit the ground. He lay silent as the final thief turned and started toward Charley, his eyes bleeding rage.

"If I'm gonna die, so are . . ."

He stopped cold and gawked at Charley, mouth hanging open, angry scowl replaced by a look of utter disbelief.

"What the hell are you?" he asked, staring at Charley's chest. The delay allowed a third shot to find purchase in the center of his back and send him flying forward. He landed at Charley's feet and looked up with a not-quite-lifeless smile. "How can you have tits?"

Buster came running up to the gory scene. He looked at the dead men, his handiwork, with a modest grin of satisfaction as he passed them. But when he saw Charley, his prized Walker rifle slipped from his grasp.

"Charley?" His hands shook.

"Untie me, Buster," Charley said in a stern voice. His partner's eyes were locked in on his chest, but Charley refused to look down.

Buster pointed. "Can't be," he whispered. "How can you have . . . those!"

"Buster!" Charley yelled.

He looked up at Charley's face.

"Untie me. Now."

Buster blinked, then went around behind the tree and cut the ropes, muttering, "Can't be. Can't be."

Charley grabbed the .45 out of Tall-Man's belt then pulled the dirty shirt off the body and put it on with his back to Buster. "Let's get going," he said calmly, but firmly. "Gotta get those folks to Monterey. We're already behind schedule."

With long strides Charley burst out into the meadow. Buster—who couldn't, or wouldn't speak—followed him. He ran up beside Charley, glanced at his profile, opened his mouth as if to say something, then seemed to think better of it and fell back.

"Is everything all right?" the young man in the stage asked as Charley and Buster approached. "We heard shots."

"Everything's fine," Charley said as he hopped up onto the driver's bench. "Buster here done took care of some nasty men. Bandits. Lucky for ya'll. If they'd gotten past us, they surely would've killed you and taken everything."

"Oh how exciting!" Mrs. Wilson said, the meaty story having apparently improved her mood. "Did you dispatch them, sir?" she asked eagerly, staring at Buster.

Buster looked at Charley, then back to the woman, then back to Charley. "Yes ma'am."

Charley put his hand out to help Buster up, but Buster climbed onto the driver's bench unaided. Buster took off his jacket, wadded it into a ball, and placed it between them as if it were a safety barrier of some sort. Charley turned the horse team toward the meadow. He navigated the stagecoach past several muddy sink holes and soon entered the forest. They passed within a few hundred feet of the dead bandits, but not close enough for any of the passengers to get a good look, causing the young man to voice his disappointment.

They crossed the newly-formed river after finding a rocky streambed that was wide enough and shallow enough for the coach, and picked up the Santa Cruz/Monterey trail on the other side of a low rise as the trees thinned out. Buster remained silent during the remainder of the trip, darting only an occasional glance Charley's way.

They pulled into Monterey shortly after sunset. Charley used the light from the city's gas lamps—visible because of the curving arc of *Punta de los Pinos*, the southern projection of the Monterey Bay land mass—to guide them the final few miles. Main Street's dirt road was packed solid from the previous night's storm, keeping dust down in the wake of the stage. The shadows of the tiny post office with its newly constructed pine porch soon came into view, and lights streamed out the windows of the Monterey Saloon, the only two-story building in town. The sound of men whooping it up at the local tavern got louder as they approached the city. Captain Harloe's schooner, *The Wild Pigeon*, sat bobbing in the bay, his men obviously enjoying their shore leave. Timmons, a short, plump man with a handlebar mustache and thin spectacles came out to greet the travelers as the *Yodeler* approached the stagecoach station next to the post office and saloon.

"Oh thank goodness you made it!" Timmons exclaimed. He pulled open the side door to allow the passengers to disembark. "Mrs. Wilson? Your sister has been hounding me nonstop about the arrival of the coach. I told her that Charley and Buster here were our best team on this trail, but she wouldn't listen. She could only say, 'If they're not here tonight, I will personally blame you and your little stagecoach company for the failure of my wedding!'"

When all the passengers had disembarked, Timmons came out of the office grinning broadly. He shook Charley and Buster's hands. "Thank you, gentlemen! Thank you so much!" He handed them each two dollars. "A bonus. From Mrs. Wilson. She said . . . well, all of them said, that you two took out a band of ten bandits on the trail. Wonderful work!"

Charley spit on the ground and wiped the dribbling tobacco juice off his chin. "Were only four of 'em," he said. "And Buster here took care of three." Charley started unloading the bags and placing them on the porch.

Timmons praised Buster and shook his hand again and again, saying that the main office would hear how they'd protected the passengers from bandits and still managed a timely arrival.

Charley took the team of horses to the livery and unhooked them. Then he went to the saloon for a drink, like he always did at the end of a haul. Buster, who usually joined him, was nowhere to be seen.

The rambunctious crew of *The Wild Pigeon* surrounded him, but Charley didn't mind. The saloon was a safe-haven for him. He loved the smell of stale cigars, the card games, the drinks, everything; he blended in.

Charley was downing his third beer when Buster finally entered and strode up to the rail. Buster put his green hat on the bar and ordered a whiskey.

"Whiskey? No beer tonight?" Charley asked over the din piercing the saloon.

"Beer ain't strong enough for what I seen today." The whiskey arrived and Buster shot it down. He ordered a second.

Charley sighed and slammed his beer glass down hard onto the counter. No one but Buster seemed to notice. "Alright! I get it! You don't want to ride shotgun with me no more!"

Charley picked up his duffle bag and stalked upstairs to the room above the main hall that he'd rented for the night. He tore open his bag and found a semi-clean handkerchief and bottle of moonshine. He dabbed the wound at the top of his chest, put on one of his own shirts, buttoned it to the neck, then stretched out on the bed. He was fidgeting, unsuccessfully trying to sleep, when a soft knock sounded on his door. He got up and opened it.

Buster brushed past him, bumping Charley's left shoulder. "How?" Buster asked as he flopped into a flimsy chair with his arms folded across his chest.

"It's . . . kinda hard to explain," Charley said and pulled the bottle of moonshine back out of his bag.

"Try me," Buster said angrily.

"I wasn't trying to hide nothing from you, Buster. Honest." He poured them each a shot glass.

"Honest! Honest?" Buster slugged down the shot and poured himself another. "You can't do this no more, Charley. You can't!" He downed the second shot. "I mean, you're a—"

Charley stood up, knocking his chair over in the process, and moved toward Buster. "Stand up," he ordered.

Buster stood.

"Now hit me."

Buster's eyes went wild. "Those bandits must've given you brain damage when they smashed you over the head!"

Charley cocked his arm back and swung at Buster, landing a perfect blow on his chin. Buster went flying halfway across the room and crashed into the corner. He shook his head and stood up, nose flaring, face reddened.

"I said hit me or I'll plow you again!" Charley demanded, stepping toward Buster and cocking his arm for another assault.

Buster moved to his right and connected with a stiff blow to Charley's jaw. Charley's head snapped back but he didn't fall.

"Damn!" Buster yelled, as Charley's right hand came up and landed hard on Buster's face a second time. Buster reeled back and sank to one knee in the corner, blinking away spots in his vision.

Charley walked over to him and extended his hand. Buster winced for a split-second, then saw that the hand was open, palm up. He looked at its calloused, rough surface and, swallowing hard as if he'd eaten a piece of stone, took it. He stood up tall but unsteadily, teetering over Charley.

Why hadn't I ever noticed how short he was?

Buster wobbled over to his chair and sat back down. He slugged down another shot of moonshine as Charley tucked some tobacco into his left cheek and resumed his seat.

Buster tried to think of something to say, but everything felt either awkward or like complete nonsense. Then a thought came to him. "You voted!" he blurted.

Charley looked eerily calm. "I know," he said. "And do you think that they would have let me vote, or do any of the other things I've been doing, if they'd known about . . . about me."

"Hell no!"

Charley slammed back his own shot glass. "Are you going to tell anyone?" he asked, rubbing his knuckles, as if warming them up for another round.

Buster thought for a moment, then stood up and started pacing. He stopped and massaged his sore jaw. "And what, exactly, am I supposed to tell them? That my partner, the toughest man I've ever known, is a . . . a . . . Jesus! I can't even bring myself to say it!"

"You can't 'cause it ain't true, Buster." Charley stood up and, for a moment, Buster believed that Charley might tower over him. "I'm a man. I've been a man since I was thirteen years old. And I'll be a man 'til the day I die."

Buster cleared his throat and laughed uncomfortably. Shaking his head, he stepped away from Charley and toward the door.

"Look at me Buster."

Buster turned.

"Am I a man or not?"

Buster didn't answer, but reached for the knob and swung the door open.

"We pullin' out in the morning?" Charley asked as the door started swinging close.

The door stopped when it was only open a crack. "Yes . . . sir," Buster whispered, and closed the door.

Author's Note:

Charley Parkhurst was a real person. He worked for the stagecoach lines in the Santa Cruz area in the 1850s and 1860s. He drove the gold country routes for years before moving to the Santa Cruz area where he drove the dangerous Santa Cruz/Los Gatos trail, among others. Charley died on December 29, 1879—his cause of death noted as tongue cancer, probably from years of using chewing tobacco.

Only after Charley's death did the truth about his unusual past come to light: He was a woman! The fact shocked many who'd known Charley (Charlotte), since she'd acted exactly like a man: drinking, chewing tobacco, using coarse language, driving horse teams and, so it appears, voting! She voted in Soquel during the close election of 1868 between Ulysses S. Grant and Horatio Seymour (52 years before the right was guaranteed to women by the Nineteenth Amendment). Grant won the election by a small popular margin. Whether she voted for Grant or not shall forever remain a mystery.

Charley's grave site can be viewed at the local cemetery in Freedom, California.

For dramatic purposes, this story took some liberties with historical fact. The most notable concerns the stagecoach route. In reality, the commonly-used stagecoach trail went down Old Stagecoach Road from San Francisco to Los Angeles with the usual stop being the small—and now absent—city of Natividad (some ruins of this city can be seen six miles east of Salinas, California). At Natividad, mail was usually dropped and picked up, and the stagecoaches continued on to Monterey or south to L.A. Though some old stagecoach maps show a trail leading from Santa Cruz to Monterey, it is unnamed and appears to be a seldom-used side trail. For purposes of this story, however, I incorporated it as a stagecoach line. In addition, it is a known fact that Charley (Charlotte) Parkhurst was orphaned at a young age, but what caused her to masquerade as a man for the rest of her life remains unknown.

I am indebted to Dennis Copeland, archivist at the Monterey Public Library, and Lowell March for aiding me immensely in the researching of this fascinating historical figure.

Time Pieces

by Mike Tyrrel

"**I**t's not fair!" Katy loudly complained, as only a twelve-year-old could.

"Arghh! I know," whined Dot, her year-older sister. "No one's throwing out anything good; it's all junk. This is a lousy way to start summer vacation!"

So the two blondish sisters, each a head shorter than their classmates, trudged home empty-handed after spending three fruitless hours scrounging through the boxes and bags stacked along the curb of the Indian Springs subdivision in Salinas, California. Their Dad let them scavenge on the eve of the subdivision's annual garage-cleanout day. But only what they could bring home in one trip. And it all had to stay in their special places. If he found anything overnight in the yard or deck, it went to the dump.

With Black Mountain blocking the evening sun, the shadows grew and the air started to chill. Their red wagon was empty as they passed their next door neighbor, John Kelly, who was pushing his trash container to the curb.

"Why so glum, girls?" John asked. "Summer's here, school's out."

"John, is everyone fixing or selling their junk at the flea markets? We couldn't find . . ."

Maybe they complained more than they explained, but John, their adopted grandfather, understood. During World War II he had flown Mustangs and had brought home his share of war booty that cluttered his garage.

"Maybe I have something that'll make your summer more interesting," John said. "Follow me."

In the corner of his garage he pulled away a heavy canvas tarp exposing a Leica binocular periscope, mounted on a four-foot tall tripod. He dragged it to the middle of the garage.

"Looks cool. What is it?" Katy asked.

John retrieved a rag to wipe off years of accumulated dust. "During the war, the Germans would use this to measure distances. Up to six thousand meters, as I recall." He put his eyes to the instrument, showing the girls how it worked. "Because of these offset eye pieces," he said, pointing to them, "their spotters were accurate in directing artillery on our guys."

Crossing her arms, Dot stated, "I don't want anything that killed people!"

"This one was never used. I found it in a warehouse in its original box."

The girls looked at each other and nodded their heads. They liked the idea of having something no one else had. "We'll take it. Thanks, John," they said in unison. They loaded the periscope into their wagon and pulled it home.

Their house was set back from a canyon that during the summer held a dry creek bed. Using ropes anchored to hundred-year-old oak trees, they hoisted their treasure into their tree fort.

The next morning they started their measurements. "Horse stable, eleven-hundred meters," Katy said to Dot, who marked it on her self-made map of their subdivision.

"How far is the stable from the baseball diamond?" Dot asked.

"Home plate, or the benches behind it?"

"Home plate's good enough," Dot replied.

"Six-hundred meters."

Consumed by their mapmaking, that first week of summer vacation flew by. When they'd finished, they showed their map to John. He studied it intently. It had elevation points of the canyon and distances to landmarks. The Spreckles sugar factory was 2,400 meters away. The distance from the canyon's bottom to the top of John's house was 35 meters. He drew his finger over certain points and looked at them in the distance.

"Girls, you made a good map. In the war, maps were drawn from memory. Sometimes they were right, many times they weren't. If we'd had maps like this, we could've beaten the Germans quicker."

The girls accepted the compliment. "Thanks, John, we'll use the periscope to watch the ballgames. If you have any more stuff you don't want, we still have room."

John rubbed his chin and glanced along the wall. "You know, I do have that old trunk. When the war ended, my unit had taken over the air base, where Hermann Goering maintained his backup command post and jet airplane research center. When I got there, the Nazis had already stripped the base for parts. But inside a hidden underground bunker, I discovered two trunks. I took one and my buddy Bertie took the other. You can see if you want anything that's in it."

Katy didn't want oily rags and dusty old college books, so she asked, "What's in it?"

"Don't remember," John said with a twinkle in his eyes. "After the war I went to Alaska to build the railroad and forgot all about it."

"Sure John, we'll take it!" they both said.

The trunk was buried under a pile of lumber. That corner looked worse than Dad's section of their garage, Dot thought as they removed the boards and bundles of newspapers. John brought out a handcart. Wedging it underneath the trunk, he lifted, then rolled it out of the garage. Dot helped push the cart while Katy ran to their house to open the garage door. They placed the trunk in a corner of the garage that was their indoor play area.

Upon hearing the commotion, their dad came into the garage. "What's going on?" he asked.

"Look what John gave us, it's from Germany!" Katy exclaimed.

"Interesting," Dad said, staring at the faded swastikas on the trunk. He motioned to John to follow him out to the front yard. When they were out of ear shot he asked, "Any guns, grenades, or gross things in the trunk?"

John answered, "It's all safe. Just dials, switches, and electrical drawings from World War II. This might give them the adventure they need for their summer vacation."

Dad nodded in agreement.

The trunk's padlock was rusty; the hinges corroded. Katy lifted, twisted, and then shook the lock trying to open it to no avail. She opened the tool drawer, removed the hacksaw, and started sawing. When she tired, Dot took over. After an hour they looked at the padlock and could see only minor scratches from their effort.

"This is impossible. It'll take all summer," Katy said glumly, dropping the hacksaw on the garage floor. The girls' first rule was, "Never give up." Their second rule, one that helped the first, was, "If something is impossible, try a different way."

"We need to try something else. Go get a mallet," Dot ordered.

As the older sister, Dot was the boss and Katy obediently listened to her. She opened the tool cabinet, found several mallets, and asked, "Do you want a rubber, wooden, or metal mallet?"

"Metal, silly!" came the exasperated reply.

She brought it to Dot, who aimed the mallet's pointed end at the lock then whacked it a few times. After the fifth swing, the latch separated from the trunk lid and fell away. Together they lifted the lid. Musty air escaped and they stood back marveling at the stuff inside. Their Mom wouldn't hesitate to call it junk, while Dad would call it, "interesting." For the girls, it was treasure.

On the top lay an oblong object wrapped in thick, greasy paper. They unwrapped it and discovered a most peculiar device. Closing the trunk, they placed the device on top to study it.

It was two feet wide and a foot high, basically a tarnished brass box with three large clock-faces across the front; each face rich with mother-of-pearl inlay. The left face was definitely a clock. The center face appeared to be a stopwatch with a start button. The right face had numbers reversed from a normal clock, starting at twelve then going backwards to one.

Katy pointed to the right face. "Dot, does that look right to you?"

"John said he found the trunk at an Air Force base. Maybe the right side is for showing how much flying time is left. The left clock tells you what time it is," Dot responded, not really knowing, but as the big sister she needed to have a plausible answer for every question little sister asked.

"Go get the magnifying glass," she told Katy. "I'll get some brass cleaner."

Katy sighed and went upstairs to locate the magnifying glass. On the way, the latest copy of *Ranger Rick* magazine distracted her and she fell on her bed to read it.

When she finally returned to the garage, Katy saw that Dot had polished the clock to a glowing shine. "Yuck!" she said. "I don't like those Nazi swastikas on the sides. But that eagle on top sure is pretty."

"I agree." Holding out her hand, Dot commanded. "Gimme the magnifying glass!"

But Katy kept the glass and started examining the clock's face. She too, knew how to give orders. "Dot, write this down: M E S S E R S C H M I T T GmbH." She looked up, clutching the magnifying glass. "What does 'Mister Schimtt' mean?"

"Remember, John said he flew against Messerschmitt airplanes," Dot replied. "Is there anything on the back?"

Katy carefully scanned the back. "All I see is zero, zero, zero, one. Maybe it's a serial number."

Just then they heard John's garage door open. Dot stepped out of their garage and shouted, "John, do you have a second to look at this?"

"I see you opened the trunk," John said, joining them in their garage. "You find this inside?" He lifted the polished clock and turned it in his hands.

Katy replied, "It's a clock made by the Messerschmitt Company for their airplanes. Right?"

John shook his head. "It's too big and fancy to put into a cockpit." His eyes brightened. "It would look good on a fireplace mantle. You say Messerschmitt, huh? I didn't know they made clocks. Maybe it was a present for their boss, Hermann Goering. You girls might have a valuable piece of history." He tapped the trunk with his toe. "If you find any gold in there, we split it fifty-fifty, right down the middle. Everything else is yours to keep."

The girls looked at each other and replied, "C-o-o-o-o-l."

As he left, John added, "If you need anything, just knock on the door."

Dot picked up the rag and continued polishing. "Well, what's next?" she asked.

Katy knew what to do. She pressed the button under the stopwatch. The second hand swept around, stopping after one minute. The hands on the left face started moving then, and as they did, those on the right face started moving backwards; its minute hand sweeping as fast as a second hand. The right face registered an hour backwards for every minute the left face went forward. Fascinated, they watched for six minutes. Their vigil ended when Mom called them for dinner.

"How do you stop this contraption?" Dot asked.

"Dot, there's only one button," Katy said as she depressed it. The clock stopped. "See? Real simple."

After they'd cleared the table and finished the dishes, they went upstairs and logged onto the Internet. They Googled "Messerschmitt," and found the company was part of Focke Wolfe Corporation, now owned by the Daimler-Benz car company. They logged into the Daimler corporate site and composed this message in an e-mail:

```
We have uncovered a two by one foot brass clock having
three faces and the serial number 0001 that was manu-
factured by the Messerschmitt Company. What can you
tell us about this clock?
```

After they sent the e-mail, they logged onto a free game site and became engrossed in a game of 3-D Tetris. After playing for two hours, they heard the familiar, "You've got mail."

They suspended the game and clicked on the mailbox. The incoming e-mail was from the Daimler-Benz Corporation.

They opened it.

```
Dear Sir:

The clock you described has historical significance.
We are interested in purchasing it. Depending upon its
condition, we are prepared to pay $100,000. Send a
picture of the clock and your phone number, or call us
at 121-321-245-22334.

Dieter Meiter
President
Daimler-Benz GmbH.
```

"Wow! Now we can get horses," Katy said jumping up and down.

Frowning, Dot said, "Doesn't it seem strange to you that they replied this fast?"

"Well, they've been looking for the clock for fifty years," Katy said, imagining the horse she'd get. "They probably want it before someone else gets it."

"Maybe if they had replied two or three days from now I wouldn't be suspicious," Dot said. "Maybe if a clerk replied to our message. Maybe if they'd offered ten thousand dollars. But the big boss replied quickly . . . with a lotta money. We can't even get Duncan Yo-Yo to answer our questions about sticky bearings. If we call this Deiter guy, he can trace our phone back here to the house. Right now they can't trace us through the Internet. But in case they can, we'll have to be careful when sending e-mail. We need to go into research mode to figure out what's going on."

Katy agreed and realized the horses would have to wait. "Dot, if the clock is valuable, then maybe the rest of that stuff is as well. Let's check it out in the morning."

They resumed their game of Tetris, and set a new high score. For their name, they entered, "Girls rule Dad!"

Dot had trouble going to sleep that night. Nothing made sense to her, but like in Monopoly, when someone offered you a lot of money for your property, it's time to say no because you're about to lose something important.

After breakfast, they emptied the trunk's contents onto the workbench. They found eight dials, four switches, seven square metal boxes, two copper tubes, bundles of labeled wire with rings soldered on each end, one lab manual, and a folded sheet of thick blue paper, that when opened, was huge. Except for the copper tubes, each component bore an imprinted serial number, red swastika, and the words: "Messerschmitt Research".

They took the blue paper inside the house and opened it on the dining room table. It looked like a wiring diagram. They studied the numbers and hieroglyphics, trying to understand them. In the top center of the diagram, written in large print was "Reichsmarschall Hermann Goering". Underneath his name was written:

☠☠ZEIT BEWEGUNG MASCHINE☠☠

"Looks like we're missing a lot of pieces," Katy said.

"Yeah, I count twenty-one gauges and nineteen boxes that are wired to the gauges and the clock," Dot said, trying to make sense out of it all. "This clock controls something. It has wires going to the copper tubes, and this smaller tube is placed inside the bigger one."

Pointing to the skull and crossbones, Katy said, "Maybe the Nazis were developing a ray gun to shoot down airplanes."

"Yeah, that's possible," Dot said excitedly. "But what's the clock's purpose? And why is it worth big bucks?"

Katy thought for a moment, and then said, "Maybe there's more to . . . whatever it is . . . than just the clock."

Both girls became silent, trying to hear if anyone was in the house.

"Let's not mention the money again," Katy said. "It might worry Mom and Dad."

"Okay."

They refolded the diagram and returned to the garage. They opened the lab manual and thumbed through it. Two diagrams clearly showed the copper tubes facing two mirrors. The first diagram depicted a concave mirror; the second a convex one. Both rendered distance and calculations with arrows running from the mirror through the copper tubes.

Each page had a numbered item with more electrical diagrams, math formulas, and numbered notes in German that seemed to correspond to the numbers on the blue engineering paper. A few notes extended into three pages.

The girls wondered just what it was that they had. They knew one thing for sure, though. It was their secret, and they were going to unravel its mystery.

"I'll call Frank and ask if he can see us," Katy said, picking up the garage phone. Frank taught her Sunday school class and knew *everything* about clocks.

The phone rang twice before Katy heard her teacher's voice. "Frank's watch repair."

Time Pieces

"Hello Frank, it's Katy and Dot. Do you have time to see us today?" It was her favorite pun and she liked pulling it on Frank. She didn't know that he heard it from everyone.

"For you girls, I have time to spare."

"See you in thirty minutes," Katy said, and hung up. They wrapped the clock in a beach towel and lashed it inside Katy's bike basket. Mom had gone to the store, so Dot left a note saying where they were going.

They used the bike trail. After crossing the Salinas River, they traveled the dirt road that separated the strawberry fields on their way to Old Town Salinas. They locked their bikes to a lamppost outside Frank's store.

Katy carried the clock. As they entered the store, a tall, skinny and completely bald man greeted them, his glasses hanging on the end of his nose.

"What did you girls bring?" Frank asked.

"Our neighbor gave us a clock from World War II," Katy said. "But it works funny. Could you look at it?"

Frank studied the three faces before unscrewing the backing for a look inside. He whistled when he saw the intricate diorama, and put on his loupe for a closer look. It was a long time before he said anything.

"Amazing!" he exclaimed. "I've never seen anything like this!"

"What is it?" Katy asked.

"Most clocks have eight or more adjustment screws. I can't find one. It's perfectly built." He adjusted his glasses and peered at the clock. "This will keep perfect time for hundreds of years," he said, pointing to the gears inside.

"The timepiece on the right is connected to a motor that appears to generate an electrical signal. The face on the left is connected to a series of gears that moves the earth, moon, and stars diorama you see right here. Any master clockmaker would display the diorama on the outside, but this one has hidden it inside. It takes skill to make the planets and moon move correctly for hundreds of years. With something this sophisticated you'd expect the maker to proudly display his work." Frank paused then said, "This is a most peculiar clock."

"Watch this, Frank," Katy said, as she pressed the button under the middle face.

The three watched the mechanism spin. When the stopwatch stopped, both clocks came to life and the generator spun, creating sparks.

"Amazing!" Frank marveled again. "I think the planets are moving backwards! See this counter shaft, it's the opposite gear drive for the right face."

Frank continued to explain the intricacies of the different gears as the clock spun. He looked at the front and his mouth dropped open when he noticed the right clock hands spinning backwards. He timed it for three minutes, then placed a small dental mirror inside, behind various gears and spindles. He let out a low whistle.

"Girls, you have a unique timepiece here. Its accuracy is unsurpassed." His voice seemed distant as he carefully replaced the back plate. "Would you like me to research it?"

Dot frowned and Frank, used to her facial expressions in Sunday school, knew it meant she didn't want any help. "Thanks Frank," she began, "but Dad said money's tight, so we're not going on any vacation. This is a good summer project. We'll do the research ourselves."

After tightening the screws, he carried the clock to their bikes.

"Thanks, see ya Sunday," they said, peddling away.

"Good answer, Dot," Katy said. "We need to keep this to ourselves."

On their way home, the girls stopped at Ruth's, their favorite used bookstore. The girls had an agreement with the owner's daughter, Sarah, who had taken over for her mother—the original 'Ruth'. They helped Sarah dust and organize the stock in return for the loan of books, just like the library.

They stopped outside the bookstore and looked at the clock. Katy volunteered to stay outside and guard it while Dot went inside, breezing past Sarah who was busy with a customer. She found a German-English dictionary. Then she went to the military history section to look for Messerschmitt or Hermann Goering. She found several books, scanned them, picked out three, and walked up to the counter.

"Hello, Dot. What are you looking for?" Sarah asked.

"World War II. Our neighbor John flew Mustangs against the Nazis. I want to understand what he says when he talks to Dad. Can I use your phone to call Mom?"

"Sure. Are the deer still feasting on her garden?"

Dot snickered before she answered. "We scare them, but we really need a dog to keep the deer away. And you know what Mom thinks of dogs."

Dot rolled her eyes as she dialed the phone. She never understood why they couldn't have a dog. But that didn't stop her from reading every book Sarah had about dogs, preparing for the day when Mom would change her mind.

"Hi, Mom. We're at Ruth's and coming home now. Yeah, okay." She handed the phone to Sarah. "Thanks Sarah. See you Sunday."

On the way home Dot thought about all the unanswered questions. Why was this fancy specialized clock built? Why was it so complex? Who really owned the clock? Why was it left behind if it was so important?

Could there be another clock? Too many questions and too few answers! John had given them a mystery to solve.

When they got home, Dot read about Goering, while Katy tackled Messerschmitt. Together they examined the jet airplanes, bombers, fighters, and giant six-engine transports that Messerschmitt had produced. Using the magnifying glass they studied each cockpit looking for a clock like theirs and became engrossed in reading fascinating tales—like the fact that the first airplane Israel bought to shoot down Egyptian bombers that had bombed Tel Aviv daily had been a surplus Messerschmitt.

After two weeks and numerous trips back to Ruth's, the girls became experts in the air war. But in all their research they found no reference to a clock like theirs. Dismayed, they again emptied the trunk onto the garage floor and tried to arrange the parts according to the big diagram.

"We need to translate this diagram," Dot said. "Where's that German to English dictionary?"

"On my dresser, I'll get it."

Dot looked at all the strange writing that covered the diagram and shook her head. "Like Mozart said, 'Too many words.' Let's start with the title."

It was tedious work. They had an idea what the skull and crossbones meant, but they were surprised when they finally converted the words in the title and read: *Time Movement Machine.*

Katy repeated the words several times; they made no sense to her.

Dot said, "Remember reading about the Germans broadcasting radio beacons for their bombers to follow when they bombed England? They used the same radio beacons to guide their rockets. Maybe this is that device."

"Wait! Throw away the middle word!" Katy cried out. "It says 'Time Machine'. Maybe this is a machine that moves things through time!"

"I don't think so! That's only in the movies."

"It doesn't matter what you think, Dot!" Katy said, pointing at the words. "What does it say?"

Dot ignored her. The parts they had seemed to form an outer ring. The stuff in the middle was missing. She traced her finger over it, before saying, "The mirror, at an exact distance, focuses on the copper tubes. The other side of the tubes has another measurement but there's nothing there. Maybe this is another device to control the world. Let's ask John about the other trunk. And I think we should show this lab notebook and all these formulas to Russ on Sunday."

The girls had met Russ Durham, a double Ph.D. and instructor at the Naval Post Graduate School in Monterey, at a weekend class he'd taught on rockets.

"In the meantime, we need to create a laboratory in this garage," Dot said. "Go get the picnic sheets."

Dot set up the ladder and strung twine through the eyehooks in the ceiling. Katy handed her the sheets. Soon they had changed their garage play space into a semi-private area. They erected a worktable out of saw-horses and a sheet of plywood.

Katy opened the diagram on the new workbench. When she'd trans-lated the words under the clock, her mouth fell open and she looked at her sister. "The clock is called a 'Time Accelerator'."

"Of course," Dot said. "You don't want to go back in time slowly do ya? You might get old before you get anywhere!"

Katy enjoyed having a sister who was smart, but she didn't like snappy answers. They arranged the components on the worktable and attached the wires according to the diagram. When they'd connected all the com-ponents, they went to John's house and rang his bell. Katy stood behind Dot, letting her sister do the talking.

"Hi girls, how are you coming along?"

"This is the best project we've ever started," Dot answered.

"It looks like that stuff you gave us is . . . a . . . a radio station."

"Those German radios were powerful," John said. "When it's put together, you might be able to talk to New York, or even Europe!"

"It won't work without some parts we don't have. We think they might be in the other trunk. Do you have your buddy's phone number so we can call him?"

"A few years ago, he told me he still had the trunk. I'll look for his num-ber in my unit's newsletters and bring it over later."

"Thanks, John."

An hour later the doorbell rang and Dot ran to answer it, not wanting Mom talking to John. "Here's the last address and phone number I have for Bertie," John said, handing Dot a slip of paper. "His name is really Bertram, but all the guys in the squadron called him Bertie. His wife's name is Lydia." John looked at his shoes and his voice sounded sad. "She takes care of him. He can't do anything for himself. It's a shame, best wingman I ever had. When you talk to her, tell her I'm your grandpa. That may help."

"Thanks so much, John."

Back in their garage, Dot picked up the phone and dialed the number. After several rings a woman's faint voice answered, "Hello?"

"Hello. I'm Dot Tyrrel," Dot said quickly, and continued without tak-ing a breath. "Our grandpa, John Kelly, flew with your husband in World War II. Is he available?"

"I'm sorry dear," the woman said in a pleasant voice. "Bertram passed on two years ago." Dot grimaced, which Katy knew was not a good sign. "How is John doing?"

"He's doing great, which is why I called." Dot slowed down. "He gave us a trunk that he brought home from World War II. It's full of German radio components, but some parts are missing. Grandpa Kelly said the parts we need might be in the trunk your husband brought home. I know it's asking a lot, but I was wondering if you still have the trunk and if could you send us those parts?"

"I know the trunk you're talking about, dear. I have no use for it, but I don't have the money to send it. Are you close enough to drive here?"

Dot's frown turned into a smile. "You could send it UPS, COD," she said.

"Yes, I suppose I could do that."

"We have some wiring diagrams in . . ." she almost said "John," but caught herself, "Grandpa Kelly's trunk. Do you remember seeing what was in the trunk you have?"

"I don't remember, dear. I was so thankful that he came home. Many of my friends lost their husbands. We opened the trunk once and I looked at the . . . pardon me but I still remember it as junk. Afterwards, he put it in the corner of the garage. Every time we'd clean the garage, I'd ask him why he kept it. I don't know why men keep things that don't work. Dear, when you marry a man, look at his father's garage. That will tell you what kind of man you're marrying."

Dot rolled her eyes. *Good grief! Who thinks about getting married when you're thirteen? Anyway, boys are icky!*

"Oh, thank you," Dot said, without giving her thoughts away. "How soon can you send the trunk?"

"As soon as I get off the phone with you, I'll call UPS," she replied. "What is your address?"

"Yippee!" Dot shouted, and gave her address, then hung up. Turning to Katy she said, "Let's finish translating the diagram."

It was Thursday, which meant they might receive the trunk Monday or Tuesday. They rode to town and bought a ten-dollar computer program that translated German to English.

With the help of the program, they quickly discovered that the mirrors were for sending and receiving. The more they translated, the more it seemed what they had was not a research paper or prototype, but an actual working machine.

On Sunday, they brought the lab journal with them to church. They were antsy and couldn't wait for the service to end. After the service, they found Russ by the coffee bar in the courtyard and asked him to look at a few pages from the journal.

Russ ran his finger over the drawing, then stopped. His finger back-tracked, then went forward again and stopped at the same place. He looked up from the drawing and asked, "Where did you get this?"

"A neighbor gave us some neat junk when he cleaned out his garage," Dot said.

Russ pointed. "This triple cloverleaf device is a phased transducer designed to amplify signals, then accelerate it at a certain pulse. I don't understand why it's in the wrong place, but it's interesting. It appears as if some type of delay triggers the signal. Is there more?"

"One other page," Dot said with Katy behind her standing guard to ensure Mom or Dad didn't come by and hear something.

Dot flipped to a page filled with mathematical equations. "Does this tell you anything?"

"This is more interesting," Russ replied. "It starts with Max Planck's radiation theory. It appears to deal with exceeding the speed of light. It's beyond my comprehension, but I know some theoretical physicists that might be able to explain it."

Russ waited for a response. Greeted by silence, he continued. "Modern computers are based upon knowledge that goes back to 1930s technology, Dot. Computers only miniaturized that technology, they never revolutionized it. These two diagrams indicate a radical shift that might speed up computers by a thousand times."

"What happens when you go faster than light? Do you burn up?" Dot asked.

"Well, maybe. Some people think it might open the door to time travel. Now that you mention it, the first schematic might have to do with time travel." With that Russ started saying "Doo Doo Doo Doo," mimicking the *Twilight Zone* theme song.

Oh brother, adults, Dot thought.

Suddenly, Katy said their new code word, "Bandits."

Dot acknowledged her by saying, "Intercept."

Leaving Dot, Katy met Mom. "Mom," she said, "can you go with me to get a Danish and some orange juice."

"Is this your first one?"

Katy maneuvered in front of her mom, turning her away from Dot. Then she replied, "Yes, this will be my first."

Katy grabbed Mom's hand and led her to the other end of the courtyard. She didn't care if someone saw her holding her mom's hand. She had to take the risk in order to protect the mission.

"Who's Max Planck?" Dot asked.

"A brilliant man who worked for the Nazis. His research department reported to Hermann Goering. I've seen declassified information that

Planck helped the Nazis develop a crude atom bomb. Goering had ten jet bombers equipped to drop the bombs on New York City during the Battle of the Bulge. America came close to losing the war."

Dot started to worry. She didn't want the government coming to their house and taking their machine. She might get a "thank you" from them, but no horses, that's for sure. She decided to close the journal.

"I have to return the book, so no one knows I brought it here."

Russ nodded. "I won't mention it."

When they got home, Dot reviewed what she'd learned. They were convinced they had a time machine. After lunch, they returned to their garage laboratory and continued translating German.

Sunday night was family game night. So far, Dad hadn't won a Battleship game from either girl. Tonight was no exception, even though he received many clues. Afterwards they fell asleep quickly. Even with the computer program, translating German was tiring.

The next morning a UPS truck pulled into their driveway. Katy opened the garage door, while Dot met the driver as he stepped down from his truck.

"COD for Dot," he said, looking at a clipboard.

"That's me," she said. "How much is the COD?"

"Twenty-five dollars and fifty-five cents."

"Eeeeh, that's a lot. I'll get the money; my sister will show you where to put the trunk."

The UPS driver wheeled the trunk into the garage. Katy pulled back the curtain allowing him to bring it into their laboratory. She had covered the worktable, so nothing was revealed. Dot paid him from her saved up allowance money and signed the delivery receipt. She closed and latched the garage door, and then they opened the trunk. In addition to more switches, gauges, and boxes, they found a packet of pictures wrapped in heavy brown paper. They looked at each item carefully before placing it in its proper position according to the diagram.

When the last part was in place, Katy declared, "Looks like we have everything."

They spent the rest of the day connecting the components. By supper-time they were finished, except that the big switch had to be plugged into a 220-volt circuit. Tomorrow they would unplug the clothes dryer and power up their machine.

After dinner they went to their bedroom and logged into the Web. They hadn't logged in for the past three weeks and immediately noticed that Dieter had sent several e-mails; each with a Word document attachment. Katy knew better than to open the attachments, so she saved all the messages on a zip drive and logged off.

Both girls had taken computer classes, but Katy had become the family's whiz. She opened the first document under the .Net IDE, and discovered a Trojan horse program attempting to place a cookie and a rogue program on their PC. She stepped through the program's actions. It scanned their address book, and downloaded the various registry items that identified their system. She watched it construct a file of their names, addresses, and phone numbers in preparation for sending it back to Dieter.

"All of a sudden I don't like this Dieter guy at all," Katy fumed. "I'm going to send him a message that he won't forget."

She deleted their personal information and placed two obsolete worms inside the file. The first worm would activate when Dieter opened his mail. On his screen it would paste the message:

```
It's our clock! Your tricks aren't very nice! Now watch!
```

The second worm would disable the executive's hard drives. "Normally any virus detection software would catch these old worms," Katy informed her sister, "but I think Deiter will ignore the warning messages since he thinks his Trojan horse sent the mail."

Katy then opened a test link on the Web and transferred the document to his address and closed the link.

Dot watched over her shoulder. "I suppose this means he won't buy our clock," she said. "Remember, we want horses."

"I could have made it worse," Katy replied smugly, "but he'll get the message."

After that she turned off the computer and she opened the packet they found in Bertie's trunk. Inside were several pictures of dials and switches. On a table in front of the dials were the two copper tubes and a full-length mirror.

Dot looked at the picture with their magnifying glass. "You know, it looks like the mirror is the exact distance from the copper tubes as shown in our diagram," she said. "But I can't see what's on the left side of the copper tubes."

"Well this confirms the machine was in operation," Katy stated, looking carefully at the picture. "We need to find out what's on the left side. Let's look at the other pictures."

They went through the rest of the pictures but none showed the left side. They went back to the second picture and studied it some more.

"Look, the copper tubes are placed on the edge of the table," Katy said.
"So?"
"Well maybe it's nothing, but the left side may be the place to stand.

Maybe the waves coming through the copper tubes spread out like this."
She held her arms wide open to illustrate.

"My sister's a genius!" Dot shouted.

"Get ready for bed girls!" Mom hollered.

"Okay!" Dot shouted back, then turned to Katy. "Tomorrow we'll show this picture to John and ask him what was over here. Everything needs to be put together correctly."

The next morning they quickly dressed and ate. Afterwards they got on their razor scooters and started doing figure-eights, waiting for John to come outside. At nine, his garage door opened and they scootered over and found him working under the hood of his car.

"We got Bertie's trunk, John, and have a question we need some help on," Dot stated.

"I'll do my best. What is it?"

Dot handed John the picture of him and Bertie standing beside the dismantled German planes. "We got this from Lydia. Do you remember it?"

"How is Bertie?"

The girls just shook their heads, not knowing how to say it.

John looked skyward before replying. "I think we took that picture in June of '45. Several weeks later Bertie shipped home while I stayed another five months, two weeks, and four days."

"Would you like that picture?" Dot asked.

"Yes, thanks Dot."

"We have another picture that shows the switches and dials you and Bertie gave us," Dot said handing him the picture. "This looks like the control room of a radio station. Can you tell us what was on the other side of this table?"

John held the picture in both hands and gazed at it. Then he pointed to the left edge. "Over here was the darndest thing you've ever seen. On the basement floor there was a large X and two feet behind that was a full-length dressing mirror. Those Germans always looked good. Bertie and I thought it was funny that the mirror was so close to the radio station, but we guessed they wanted to look good before they spoke over the radio."

Dot winked at Katy. With the diagram's measurements and what John just told them they knew where to place the mirror. The last piece of the puzzle fell into place.

"Thanks, John."

They left his garage and went upstairs into their bedroom. They lifted the sliding closet mirror out of its track, carried it down to their laboratory, and placed it at the exact spot the big diagram indicated.

Everything looked right. The garage door was closed and latched.

Mom was rollerblading and wouldn't return until the afternoon so if anything went wrong, they would have time to correct it. They positioned the fire extinguisher—and a baseball bat for emergency shut-down—next to the control panel, just in case.

Though both were thinking it, Dot said it first. "Are we sure we want to do this? We can stop and wait 'til we're older."

Katy had a twinkle in her eye. "Dot, I already thought of that. Last night I left an envelope and a blank sheet of paper underneath the clock. I figured one of us in the future would travel back to this morning and leave a note in the envelope. Are you ready to look?"

Wide-eyed, Dot nodded her head. Katy took the envelope out from under the clock and opened it. Out fell two business cards. Dot picked them up, while Katy opened the folded paper. The note said, "Do it!"

"Katy, look at these business cards!" Dot shrieked.

The cards were embossed with "K & D Enterprises, Dot President". The other had "Katy, Chief Scientist", with a note on the back.

> Study your math harder.
> Katy

"Why didn't we have our last names on the cards?" Dot asked.

"Do you really want to know who you're going to marry, Dot? I'll get Chocolate!"

Chocolate, their pet rabbit, had been a gift from a neighbor who had moved into an apartment and couldn't have pets.

Katy returned and placed the rabbit on the black X they'd made with electrical tape in front of the mirror. She stood up and looked through the tubes into the mirror. Seeing the rabbit in the concave mirror she realized something. "Dot, when the equipment's on, we can't walk in front of these tubes or have our image in the mirror. Let's not get zapped somewhere."

"Good idea." Dot's voice wavered and sounded less sure. Three weeks ago it seemed so safe. Now too many things could go wrong!

Dot stood by the fire extinguisher and held a wooden baseball bat. If she needed to dismantle the equipment quickly, she knew the bat would keep the electricity from burning her.

Katy unplugged the dryer and looked at Dot who nodded her head. Katy plugged in the machine, then looked at all the switches and dials.

A hum filled the garage. The needles moved off zero, pointing straight up. Green lights lit all the switches. They heard movement inside the clock, though its hands remained still.

"Green lights, Dot. Yeah!" Katy shouted.

"Let's wait a few minutes before we do anything."

Katy was careful to walk around the table. She looked at both mirrors to ensure her image wasn't being reflected in either of them. She was ready and didn't like waiting. Dad said her motto was, Do it, then fix it later. "I'm pushing it now," she said.

As the stopwatch hand wound past the 30-second position, the dials gradually moved from twelve o'clock to three o'clock. The hum increased. At the 50-second mark, sparks started jumping from the inner tube to the outer tube. At the 60-second mark, the stopwatch ceased moving and the other clocks began. The sparks of the outer tube moved in rotating waves. Chocolate looked up curiously and wiggled her nose.

The lights remained green. The needles held their three o'clock position. After staring at the tubes for a few minutes Katy looked at Dot and grinned, then her eyes grew wide as she screamed, "Dot! Chocolate's missing!"

Katy quickly pressed the button. The hum died down and the needles returned to twelve o'clock. She knelt on the floor looking for the rabbit. Though she looked everywhere in the garage, she knew Chocolate wasn't there.

Dot held the fire extinguisher in her right hand and the baseball bat in her left. She watched the dials for smoke. After a few minutes Katy came to stand next to her. "I can safely say that Chocolate is traveling somewhere outside this garage," she said. "We've made history, Dot. Let's bring her back. Then we should dismantle the machine and translate all the manuals. After we understand everything, we can try the experiment again . . . in ten years or so."

"I agree," Dot said, as she watched for smoke, nervous at the pulsating hum.

Katy reversed the mirror so it was now convex. Looking at Dot, she said, "Now!" and pressed the stopwatch button.

The second hand moved, and just like before, the needles started moving to the three o'clock position. When the second hand made one full swing, the clocks started moving just as before. This time nothing happened.

The left clock moved one minute while the other raced backwards. Two minutes elapsed, still nothing.

"How long did it take last time?" Dot asked.

"How should I know? Is it important?"

Dot had to shout over the hum which continued to increase in volume. "Katy, dial number sixteen is moving to the five o'clock. Now dial two's green light is blinking and its dial is moving towards the five o'clock as well. Something different is happening. Watch for Chocolate."

Dot shifted her gaze so out of the corner of her eye she could watch the black X. Dial sixteen started oscillating as the sparks started waving between the copper tubes.

Katy's shriek pierced the air. "Dot! Chocolate's back!"

The once sedate rabbit quickly hopped away. Dot and Katy giggled.

"She sure is scared," Dot said.

Katy went to retrieve the rabbit while the clocks kept ticking. Dot watched Katy trying to capture the bewildered bunny. Hearing the hum increase in pitch, Dot looked back at the dials. She noticed that dial number two was blinking again and dial sixteen was wavering as before.

"Katy! I think we got incoming!"

Katy had cornered Chocolate, who bit her. While focused on her wound, Katy didn't notice the figure of a man beginning to form on the black X.

Dot stared at the X, thinking it might be another animal coming through. She first noticed the highly polished brown leather boots with light brown pants tucked into them. Her eyes moved up until she was faced by a man in a brown shirt and dark tie with a shoulder strap and a gun holster hanging under his right arm. His left sleeve bore a red swastika. Then she stared at his face and mustache. The man began shouting German at her as he reached for his pistol. Instinctively, Dot ran forward and swung the bat, smashing it into the side of his head.

Not her usual home run swing—she had to swing lefty—but it did the job. The man crashed to the floor.

Katy dropped the rabbit and looked at the sprawled figure. She could ask questions later, but right now she thought of only one thing. "Dot! Press 'Stop!' Or else our garage might get too full!"

Dot, being careful to stay out of the mirrors' reflection, pressed, "Stop". She looked at dials two and sixteen as they reset themselves to the twelve o'clock position.

Katy came up to the body. Her left toe gently kicked the man's leg, moving it slightly. "Well, he's not dead. Why did you hit him?"

"Katy, don't you know who that is?" Dot shrilled.

"Now, how would I know? I've never met him," she said sarcastically. "He came from our machine. Just tell me who he is!"

"Adolf Hitler!"

"Now we're in trouble! Send him back, NOW! I don't want to be grounded the rest of my life."

Dot shook her head. "We can't. He might tell someone the machine works, maybe change history, and maybe win the war. We have to keep him. He's our problem now."

"Oh, great!" Katy moaned.

Dot, maintaining her composure better than her sister, kneeled down and removed Hitler's wallet.

"Leave that alone Dot," Katy pleaded. "We might get in trouble."

"Like, we're not already in trouble? Duh!"

Dot put the wallet on the table and then removed the white pearl-handled pistol from its holster. A red swastika and the serial number AH00001 were etched into the handle. The initials A.H. were embossed on the holster.

"Take the holster and strap off as well," Katy ordered.

She placed them on the table. Dot removed several documents from the wallet: a Nazi identification card, a German driver's license, and an SS identification card, all with Adolf's picture.

"Wow! Dot, do you realize we did it? We made time travel work! But what do we do with him? We can't call the police or FBI, they'll take our machine. What are we going to do?"

Holding the baseball bat firmly in her hand, Dot glared at Adolf. She turned to Katy. "First, we need proof. Go get our Polaroid camera."

When Katy returned with the camera she helped Dot lift Adolf into a folding chair. She snapped a picture of him by himself then another, posed with Dot. She handed the camera to her sister. "Take one with me."

Dot reviewed each picture with the magnifying glass. Satisfied, she took her scissors and badly cut his thin, black hair. She placed the hair in a baggie then put the baggie in an envelope with the Polaroids.

"Now this will be the icky part, Katy," Dot said with a grimace. "Get Dad's stinky gardening clothes. We have to undress him, then . . ."

They didn't like removing his clothes. When they had his shirt off they noticed several tattoos on his left underarm. So they lifted his arm and took more pictures, adding them to the others. He started coming around so Dot tapped him with the bat again. Dad's pants were a few sizes too big, so Katy cut some nylon twine and pulled it through the belt loops. Ragged sneakers replaced the polished riding boots.

They stood back, looking at the once feared man. "He looks too clean," Dot noted. So she took sandpaper and scratched his face. She took an old sombrero from last year's Halloween costume and placed it on his head. She stepped back. "Perfect. Go get that old wheelchair. We'll take him to County Hospital."

Dot placed Hitler's clothes in a large plastic bag with a handful of mothballs. She unplugged their machine and plugged the dryer back in. After whacking the time traveler one more time for good measure, they heaved him into the wheelchair.

Dot's Dad had let her fire his gun at the range and schooled her well in firearm safety. She picked up the pistol, pointing it at the wall. She released the clip and it fell to the floor. After working the slide, ensuring the pistol was empty, she put the clip and the gun into the clothes bag and they hid everything under their trundle bed.

They pushed the wheelchair to the bus stop and waited. The bus came and lowered the door so the girls could push the wheelchair inside.

"What bus do we transfer onto to go to Natividad County Hospital?" Katy asked.

"Number three," the driver said, looking straight ahead, ignoring the smelly old guy in the rusty wheelchair.

They arrived at the county hospital and pushed Adolf into the emergency waiting room. They left him beside a potted plant and began asking other people in wheelchairs if they wanted to be pushed anywhere. After a few minutes, acting as if they were hospital volunteers, they left and arrived home again before Mom returned from her rollerblading.

They dismantled the machine and placed the items back into the trunks. They stacked the trunks in the corner and covered them with a painter's canvas. Lastly, they pulled down and folded the picnic sheets and put them away, too.

They surveyed the garage. "No one would suspect we made history today," Katy said. Dot smiled.

In the morning newspaper, they read about an indigent man found wandering the halls of the county hospital. After claiming to be Adolf Hitler, the man had been subdued by security and locked in the psychiatric ward.

The rest of the summer they continued translating the lab manual and became quite proficient reading German. Though they wanted to brag about their adventure, their secret stayed a secret, until they were older!

Time Pieces

Love Potion

by Shaheen Schmidt

*T*he last bright red maple leaf finally gave up the branch. It danced in the breeze for a few moments before joining the mix of other leaves spread out across the ground in Donya's back yard.

She stopped raking for a moment and, under the bare branches of an apple tree that reached up and over her brick patio, pulled the hand-knit shawl tighter around her shoulders. Her dark wavy hair felt cold against the olive skin of her round cheeks. The day had been peaceful, but now Al's Chevy pickup, "Old Blue", rolled out of his driveway next door, crunching dry twigs and leaves under its tires. Donya couldn't help but overhear the screechy voice of Betty, Al's wife, as she stood in her doorway calling after him.

"You better eat dinner somewhere else!" Donya's neighbor said, shaking her head disparagingly. "I'm not gonna cook tonight."

"Fine, fine!" Al called back, flicking his cigarette butt out onto the driveway. He stepped on the gas and disappeared down the windy street. Betty disappeared, too, inside, just as a few dark clouds rolled by to block out the sun.

Donya put her hands under her arms to keep them warm in the sudden chill. It bothered her that Betty and Al appeared to have fallen back into their daily routine of bickering. The crows on the redwood fence shared by Donya's cottage and Betty's house seemed disturbed, too. They shrieked and lightly shook the fence before scattering off into the canyon.

"This cold is getting into people's hearts," Donya said to herself, and deciding it was time to go indoors, placed her broom in the small woodshed next to her raised-bed herb garden. She stepped into the living room, pleased to see the logs in the river rock fireplace burning vigorously. Her cottage had warmed up nicely, so she removed her shawl and walked into the kitchen. On her left was a ceramic teapot. She poured boiling water over the Darjeeling tea leaves inside, then added a few dry orange blossoms for more flavor. The flowery aroma was one of the heartwarming memories she had of growing up in Iran. She placed the pot on top of her electric samovar and had begun adjusting the bowl under its spout when the phone rang.

"Hello dear, it's me, Betty." She said it with a deep sigh.

"Good morning, Betty."

"It's pretty cold this morning, huh?"

"Yeah, this is the season for a fireplace."

"Al hasn't chopped the wood small enough, so my fire's not burning too well. I'm wearing lots of layers." Betty sighed again.

"Oh honey, you need to keep warm, otherwise your arthritis will get worse. Or you'll catch a cold."

"Our heater is broke, too. It's like a refrigerator in here."

"Why don't you come over for a cup of Cha'i?"

"Oh, are you sure? That sounds great."

"See you in a minute." By the time Donya had finished saying it, Betty had hung up. Exactly three minutes later she arrived at the door with a shiny brown mug in her hands.

Donya knew her neighbor would be easy to cheer up because of the "good company and good munchies" Betty said she always found in the cottage. The comfortable heat, the crackling wood, and the smell of freshly toasted bread brought a wide smile to her face. Donya smiled back and took the mug from her visitor, but then something caught her eye. She looked down and saw that Betty was wearing a dark brown wool sock on her left foot and a dark blue sock on the right.

"I see you're getting a little color blind!" Donya laughed.

"I can't seem to find anything in that cluttered house. Well, they're close enough. At least they're both wool."

Donya took out a clear glass with a gold ring around the rim and a matching saucer from the wood cabinet. After she poured some tea in the glass, she held it up to her eyes and checked the color of the brew. Its appearance met with her satisfaction, so she filled the glass up the rest of the way. Then Donya put some shelled walnuts next to feta cheese on a plate and poured hot tea into Betty's mug.

Betty wrapped her long fingers around it and deeply inhaled the steaming aroma. Her fine but matted blond-gray hair framed her pale face and stuck out like spider legs from her knitted cap. The loose dry skin on her lips looked sore; her puffy eyes clouded with a dull greenish-brown. The mild smell of Al's cigarettes mixed with firewood smoke clung to her sweater, and though she grinned as she exhaled, the look of joy faded quickly and she drooped her head.

"You heard us today, didn't you?" Betty said, staring at her cup.

"Well, I *was* in the yard admiring the Carmel Valley autumn." Donya pushed the plate with the toasted bread toward Betty.

"He seems so grumpy lately, and he's always working. Driving his trash truck seems more important to him than I am."

"Is he feeling okay? Health-wise I mean?"

"I don't know," Betty replied. "He's always tired, though." She took a piece of bread and after taking a few bites, continued talking. "He dumped the coffee I made into the sink this morning. He said it tasted like dirty water."

Betty blew on her tea and took a sip, examining a small plate of dates and raisins on the table. "I don't know," she sighed, looking at Donya. "We've been married for twenty-five years now and I'm beginning to think he's just not interested anymore." She squashed a piece of cheese on the bread and topped it with walnuts.

"Oh, Betty, don't jump to conclusions," Donya said, taking a small bite of sweet date and following it with a sip of tea. "Here, have some quince jam," she added, savoring the unique flavor in her mouth.

"I spend more time with you than with him." Betty coughed out a laugh. "Look, I'm even eating an Iranian breakfast, like you!" She held up her bread in front of Donya before taking another bite.

Donya leaned forward. "Well, don't tell him that, otherwise he might come after me with his chain saw!" The laughter of the two women broke through the chilly mood and drowned out the sound of pine cones popping in the fireplace.

"Hey, Donya?" Betty's eyes widened. "When are you gonna teach that class?"

"Which one are you talking about?" Donya asked with surprise as she pushed her bangs back from her long black eyelashes.

Betty leaned over as if she were about to share a secret. "You know. The one for lovers! I remember it from one of your brochures. What was it?" She frowned and gazed into space, trying to focus her thoughts.

Donya stopped chewing on a piece of crunchy quince. "Do you mean the love potion one?"

"Yeah, yeah. That one."

"Not until February. I usually teach it around Valentine's Day . . . before spring sets in."

"I don't think I can wait that long!" She looked straight into Donya's almond-colored eyes. "Do you think you could give me a private lesson?"

"You think you're ready for that one, huh?"

"Whatever you think. But you've got to give me some kinda magical elixir to bring my prince back and get rid of that old frog I'm living with now. Make him fall in love with me all over again, make him—"

Donya raised her hand up to stop her friend. "Wait a minute. Are you sure this is what you want? Are you sure you're ready to make the necessary preparations?"

Betty got quiet for a minute. "I don't understand. Do you mean I've got to do stuff for it to work? Isn't it like . . . just drinking the stuff?"

"Nope. It involves you and your house, as well."

"Well, how much work is it then?"

"If your nest isn't ready, your love bird can't come home to roost."

"Donya, don't go trying to get poetic on me. Just tell me the steps and I'll do them. The situation has gotten out of hand."

Donya raised her roundish body off of her chair and walked toward a stand-alone bookshelf pushed up against the wall. It was made from polished slabs of natural wood with curved, rough edges, and held a selection of colorful notes and books neatly arranged by size. Donya pulled out a purple calendar book from one of its shelves. The cover showed a collage of pictures—cooking students working in her kitchen. She opened it and thumbed through the pages.

"This week we're making menstrual tea and learning how to bake sweets with herbs to ease the cycle," Donya explained. "Next week is chicken soup with special vegetables for colds. And—oh!—next week is also a full moon." She looked up at Betty. "It certainly would be a powerful time to make the love potion."

"You mean with the chicken soup?"

"No, silly. The day after the chicken soup. Friday."

"Ooh-la-la. That's perfect! So you're gonna make it for me?"

"That's not quite how it works. I'll show you how to put it together, but you are the one who has to make it." Donya wrote something in the book, closed it, and put it back on the shelf.

"What if I mess it up?"

"Your potion needs *your* touch. *You* have to fill it with *your* energy and intentions, not mine."

"This is getting more complicated than I thought." Betty pulled her cap off and scratched her head.

"Nonsense. It's going to be fun. Let's start with a list of things to do." Donya pulled out a blank sheet of paper and started writing while Betty sat next to the fireplace sipping her tea.

Donya finally finished scribbling. "When you're done with these," she said, handing Betty the note, "come back here Friday afternoon and we'll complete the last step of making the drink, together. Then you'll be ready before Al gets home for a nice supper."

"Donya, you know I'm not much of a cook. Maybe you could just add some especially powerful magic ingredients so he won't be hungry for food, maybe just hungry for me?"

"You don't really want him to see you as a roasted chicken dressed in lingerie, do you? No, I don't think so."

Betty frowned like she'd been told a riddle she couldn't solve.

"Don't worry," Donya assured her, "you have several days to work on that one as well."

When Betty stepped out of Donya's door into the yard, she turned around, put her thumbs under her armpits and waved her elbows up and down, clucking like a chicken.

"Go home, woman!" Donya laughed. Before she closed the door to her comfy little home, she noticed the sky had cleared of clouds.

Betty stumbled over Al's muddy sneakers by the front door. That was right after she'd passed the large firewood stumps that needed splitting at the corner of the driveway.

She took a look around the house and didn't know where to start. Every year their country house seemed to get smaller and smaller. Al's ashtrays and stacks of newspaper were by the old raggedy couch. The stink of Parrot's unclean birdcage hung in the air, bird seed and feathers scattered under it, some caught in the crack of the sliding glass door. Spider webs in the corner of the bookshelf fluttered in the breeze from the open door. A mound of piled mail and *Sports Illustrated* magazines lay loosely on the table, covering the entire surface.

Betty fell into the couch. The warmth from Donya's cottage faded and the chill of her own home sank into her bones. Frustrated and restless, she got up after a minute or two and decided to look for something to keep her warm. She went into the kitchen and turned on the oven, leaving its door wide open. It was the best use she had ever made of the appliance. She pulled up a stool and sat a few feet away from it. In moments she felt the heat spreading out and caressing her. It took fifteen minutes before the icicles in her blood started to melt. The muscles in her face relaxed and her shoulders dropped slightly. She pulled Donya's crumpled list out of her pocket and began to read:

1. *Get rid of unnecessary clutter, and put anything with a musty smell in the sun to air out, especially the things in the bedroom.*

"What on earth was she thinking?" Betty mumbled. "Everything around here is right where Al wants it. He'll be upset if I get it out of order." Then she laughed at herself for referring to the mess as though it were in any kind of describable order.

2. *Put some pictures of the two of you together, on a shelf or in a visible area.*

"Well?" she pondered, "I might be able to find some in the boxes down in the basement. But I'll need my wool cap before I try going into that frosty room. I can't even remember the last time we took photos together."

3. *Place red candles and fresh flowers in the bedroom, bath-room—anywhere you can see and admire them.*

"Damn! Candles would set the house on fire with all the books and papers sitting around. Not to mention what they would do to Al's allergies!" She shook her head, rapidly becoming disenchanted by the whole idea.

4. *Groom yourself from the inside out. Bring loving thoughts to your heart, and maybe tweeze the hairs out of your mole, too.*

"Okay, let's practice the mantra, grumpy man to . . . great man, grumpy man to . . . great man . . ." She touched the hairs of the mole on her chin. "I thought this was about changing Al!"

5. *Wear something warm to his eyes and soft to his touch.*

Her lanky figure in the oversized, puffy yellow down coat she always wore flashed before her eyes. "I'll need that, too, when I go looking for those photos."

6. *Prepare his favorite meal. Make the house smell like delicious food instead of a bird!*

"How did she know?" Betty turned around and looked at Parrot hanging upside-down in the cage (come to think of it, he'd been acting strangely, too). "Well, Donya *did* bring me that home-baked Lavash bread a few weeks ago. And God knows, our house hasn't changed much since her last visit!"

> 7. *Come back over to my place with your teapot to make the potion.*

"A teapot? Shouldn't a potion come in a narrow, long necked jar? Where am I going to get a teapot?" She looked at her coffee maker. "Maybe that will do."

That was the end of the list.

"Humph," Betty said, folding it up and putting it back in her pocket before she turned around to warm her hands.

As days passed and Friday got closer, Donya received more and more calls from Betty asking all sorts of questions:

"Could you give me the recipe for lamb shank?"

"Can I use some of your spices in the stew?"

"How do you keep your lipstick from fading or coming off while eating?"

On Friday morning, long after Al had left for work, Donya heard all kinds of commotion coming from behind the fence. She looked over, and saw Betty cleaning up her house and hauling things around. Donya's neighbor tossed stuff into cardboard boxes, sometimes groaning mildly when she shoved a stack of magazines into the recycling bin. Al's dirty stained sweat pants went to the basement with his tool box and a collection of dusty baseball caps. These she piled up in an old refrigerator lying sideways on the floor, one of Al's creative ideas for appliance reuse.

Betty vacuumed and dusted the cobwebs from the corners of the house, put the birdcage outside (to the horror of Parrot) and opened all the windows. "Thank God it's a sunny day," she thought, and then remembered that it had been a year since she had cleaned the house this well, back when her in-laws had come for a potluck Thanksgiving.

Next she managed to find some green beeswax candles in the back of her bedroom closet, a Christmas gift from Donya three years before. "These will do," she nodded with satisfaction.

At two in the afternoon she walked through Donya's door, one hand holding the empty coffee pot and the other rubbing her aching back.

"This potion had better work fast. I sure ain't gonna work this hard every week!" She placed the glass pot down on the kitchen table.

"I said a teapot!" Donya gently scolded. "But I guess this will do."

Some of the necessary ingredients were already arranged in five saucers on her table. Next to them sat a small jar of honey and an eyedropper full of an orange liquid. A new red candle burned slowly next to them.

Donya noticed a few rollers in Betty's hair, and saw that she had put some finger curls around her face, securing them with bobby pins. A glow of excitement shone in her friend's tired eyes, and when she saw Al's truck drive up, she hoped he would appreciate all the hard work his wife had done.

Donya rubbed her hands together and smiled. "C'mon, let's get to it," she said. "I've already blessed these ingredients. Here, put a pinch from each dish into your pot—slowly now—and think of the two of you together as you do it." She showed Betty the motion without touching the herbs.

Betty looked closely at the arrangement on the counter. Some of the elements were dry leaves and flower petals, others appeared to be different-colored powders. The dry pink rose petals in the first saucer smelled sweet. She closed her eyes, took a deep breath and allowed her mind to go blank. When she opened them, she shook her head, and acted as if she had seen the prescribed images of her and Al. Then she took a pinch of the rose petals, mimicking Donya's demonstration, and dropped them into the coffee pot. She repeated the same actions with the other ingredients and then, with Donya's guidance, added one teaspoon of honey and seven drops of orange liquid.

"This isn't diluted blood or some dead animal's juices, is it?" she said, staring at the orange serum.

"What do you care?" Donya said with a serious face. "You wanted a potion didn't ya? I can't give away all my secrets." She watched the blood drain out of Betty's cheeks before laughing out loud. "Silly woman, after all the food of mine you've eaten, you couldn't recognize the smell of diluted saffron?"

"Oh yeah, of course." Betty nodded as if she had known all along.

"This should make you both laugh and feel merry. Now, you take this pot home and pour some boiling water into it up to here." She pointed at the mid-line. "Let it simmer slowly over low heat for twenty minutes, and then turn it off and let it cool. Finally, pour it through a tea strainer into two clear crystal glasses and drink it, I mean both of you, before dinner."

Betty looked concerned. "Will it taste good? I mean, do you think I can get Al to drink it?"

"Honey, this is the cream of the crop! An exotic taste of the Far East!

Better than any coffee mocha or full-blast cappuccino! And if worst comes to worst, tell him it has caffeine in it. Which of course it does not, but if that will help . . ."

Betty's eyes went round as saucers. Yes, she had the power in her hands now, in the old coffee pot. A secret wisdom. The code to the high security file hidden in her husband's heart.

"What would I do without you, Donya?" Betty said and gave her neighbor a hug. Out of the corner of her eye, she noticed Al driving away again wearing a funny shiny jacket she'd never seen before, and Betty knew she would have time to make a nice dinner.

At a quarter past seven that evening, Old Blue pulled into the driveway. Betty's house was darker than usual. Only a faint glow showed through the kitchen and living room windows. The full moon cast its soft light over the porch, just enough to reveal that the clutter outside the front door was gone. Al noticed that his shoes were neatly placed in one corner, and it brought a smile to his face as he reached to open the door.

The house seemed awfully quiet except for the soft music that caressed his ears as he stepped gingerly through the living room, shocked that there was nothing to stumble over.

Then he saw Betty on the couch. Her head was crooked to one side and she was snoring mildly. Her face looked relaxed and the lines around her eyes were invisible in the dim light of two fat, green candles on the coffee table. Logs blazed in the fireplace.

Over time, Al had come to expect to hear Betty's nagging voice at the door, followed by the litany of chores she intended him to do over the weekend. He would brace himself during the drive from work, and once home, do his best to ignore her while he made a tuna sandwich or some other easy "dinner". But he never expected this. He smiled and watched her sleep for a few more seconds, grinning. She looked like a younger version of herself.

The aroma of stew awakened his nose buds. He took a deep breath and tiptoed into the kitchen where he spotted a large steaming pot. He lifted the lid to inhale the delicious fragrance. His stomach gurgled. "I hope it tastes as good as it smells!" he whispered.

Al looked around in the gentle radiance of another half-melted candle. "Everything seems different in this light. Like looking through the soft lens of a camera."

He further scanned the room and his eyes came to a stop at the coffee pot.

"I'll bet Betty would love to wake to some yummy hazelnut coffee.

Nice and rich." He stared at the light, weak-looking liquid inside the coffee maker. "She's never been able to figure this coffee thing out!"

He took the pot and walked toward the sink to pour it out. As he watched the liquid slowly disappear down the drain, the perfumed aroma of rose petals—he saw now that they littered the sink basin—combined with unknown spices rose up and filled the air in front of his face.

"Must have been some sort of leftover headache tea or something. The fancy coffee'll cheer her right up."

Al rinsed the sink and continued on his mission. He poured the water into the coffee maker and pushed the button. Then he walked back to his room, changed his clothes, put on his clean pajamas and returned to the kitchen. He made up two plates of food, poured two cups of coffee, and put them on a tray. He was bringing it to the living room when Betty opened her eyes.

"Look at the dinner I made for you while you took your nap, honey!" He laughed and placed the tray on the table in front of her.

"Oh gosh, I must have fallen asleep!" Betty looked at his face in the dim light. Then she looked at the food. "Wow! You must have worked all day!" She sat up straight and fingered her curls so they wouldn't look quite so squashed. Her neck hurt.

"Everything around the house looks so good," Al beamed. "Are we expecting company?" He sat next to her and pulled the table closer to the couch.

"No. I just had a craving for a nice hot meal and I remembered what you always asked me to cook. This time I really put some time into it. I hope you like it."

"I already do." That's when he noticed her blue silk dress. She had wrapped a thick beige sweater over her shoulders, which had only now fallen off.

"Where did you get that?" He stroked the dress and slid his hand on her leg to feel the softness. Betty's flesh burned hot beneath. His gaze washed all over her.

"Oh, it's from years ago. You bought it for my birthday, remember?"

Wow! He must have drunk the whole potion already while I was asleep.

She reached over and kissed him on the cheek and added a quick peck on the lips. She felt shy and didn't know what to do. She looked toward the kitchen.

"Al, did you—"

He stopped her comment by kissing her on the lips. "Let's eat, I'm starving."

Parrot sat quietly in the cage and watched them dip their breads in the juice, oohing and aahing as they chewed the tender lamb.

"What's for dessert?" Al asked.

"Just me," Betty replied. She didn't even worry that she hadn't tried Donya's love potion.

Al smiled and said, "You'll go good with the fancy coffee I brewed up."

She took a sip of the coffee and felt its warmth inside of her, before leaning over to kiss him again. "You know how to make this so well and I can't ever get the hang of it."

He rubbed her neck gently. "I know, but that's okay. You continue creating magical nights like this and I'll continue making that great coffee."

They laughed together. Betty moved close to Al so they could cuddle up again.

Wait until I tell Donya the potion was so powerful I didn't even have to drink it for it to work!

The next chilly Carmel Valley morning, Donya, curious, made sure she was out early enough to gather wood from the woodpile. Al backed Old Blue into the street. "Have a nice day, Donya!" he yelled from the car window, waving. She turned to see him drive away, a satisfied smile pasted on his face. Donya waved back and nodded her head knowingly. She saw that her neighbor was out, too.

"Well, honey," Betty said to Donya over the fence, "your potion was stronger than I thought. That's all I have to say. Now I've got to go back to bed and get some rest." She quickly turned to go back inside her house.

"I'm glad that my recipes worked again!" Donya yelled back.

Somewhere over Carmel Valley, cheerful thoughts from Al, Betty and Donya took flight and soared past the crows and over the oak trees, each one thinking: *I did it.*

Love Potion

Canned Hunt

by Ken Jones

"They're natural killers, large and small."
— Clarence Woodall

*T*he thunder of tennis shoes rumbled across the basement ceiling, punctuated by the ice-pick clang of the ship's bell being smacked with gusto by a miniature scholar at the top of the stairs. Clarence Woodall straightened his faded 49ers cap and struggled again to explain to the precocious fourth grader that ships in the mid-1800s didn't have GPS receivers, and that their captains had to rely on lighthouses—like the one they were standing in—to tell them where they were.

But the whiz kid wasn't getting it.

He'd nearly given up and told the little know-it-all to go find his classmates when a stocky, red-faced woman peered down the basement steps and shouted, "Bus!" The boy bolted up the stairs and soon the echo of footsteps faded. Even though the bell still rang in his ears, Woody savored the silence. He checked his watch, surprised that the incursion had only lasted thirty minutes.

Another docent, dressed as the first woman keeper of the Point Pinos Light, Charlotte Layton, came down the stairs rubbing the back of her neck. "That was exciting."

"That's one way to put it," Woody said, starting for the stairs. "I need some air, Evelyn. I'll be outside if you need me."

Woody had an hour left of his first day as docent for the Point Pinos

Canned Hunt

Lighthouse in Pacific Grove, a time-frozen town perched at the tip of the Monterey Peninsula, its Victorian quaintness wedged between the recreated grit of Cannery Row and the lavish dream world of Pebble Beach. He'd volunteered partly out of curiosity about the history of the lighthouse, but mainly because he'd needed a distraction. A friend of many years, Sergeant Tony Scaperelli, had retired from the local police department a year ago to work for a private investigator in the Bay Area. Before leaving, Tony had hinted that he might call on Woody to help him with cases in the Monterey area. No call had come, however, and Woody decided to get his mind on other things.

He slouched onto a bench beside a twisted cypress and gazed at the ocean that formed a hazy blue backdrop to the Pacific Grove Golf Course—a ribbon of green, splitting the dunes between the lighthouse and the rocky shore—and let the pine-scented sea air recharge him.

The golf course generally had little use after five in the afternoon, so it surprised him when a twosome in a cart drove to the tee-box, separated from where he sat by a chain link fence and twenty feet of scruffy iceplant. One of the players, a heavyset redheaded man with a cigar in his mouth, wore bright yellow pants, a maroon windbreaker, and a plaid beret. The other golfer, taller by half and rail thin by comparison, wore khaki pants and a dark wind-shirt. The stiffening on-shore gusts tangled his thick silver hair.

The same breeze carried their conversation, too, so Woody assumed a dozing position, peeked out below the bill of his cap, and tuned in.

"Yeah, well, that's not my problem is it?" the redhead said as he strode onto the teeing ground. "I got scruples, you know."

The silver-haired man teed up his ball and took a graceful practice swing. "Don't give me scruples. Not after everything you've handled."

"None of that was alive, for crissake!"

"Just do it."

"Bullshit! You lied to me. Luggage, you said. Easy market. Jee-sus!"

"Look, Teddy, just make the connection! Get the merchandise on shore. Just do it."

"You should see the mess I've got out there," the redhead continued, stalking back and forth across the tee-box, pounding the head of his driver on the ground. "Do you have any idea how much crap they generate? I'll tell you. Enough to make my crew threaten to throw the whole lot overboard just to get rid of the smell, that's how much."

"You can fix the problem, Teddy. And you'd better start."

"I can fix it all right," the redhead snapped back. "This is hot cargo. I'm telling you Vic, I'm not going to jail over this. They're going over the side."

"Nothing better go over the side, Teddy. Calm down." He addressed his ball and drove it smoothly down the left center of the fairway.

The redhead jabbed a tee into the ground, put his ball on top, and flailed, taking a ragged divot a foot behind the ball but leaving the ball securely on the tee. He turned and pointed his sod-draped driver at the other golfer as if it were a sword.

"This was a stupid place to meet, Vic. What the hell were you thinking?"

"Are you kidding, this is perfect," the tall man said. "Look around you. We got the place to ourselves."

"Oh yeah, what about him?" The redhead swung his club in the direction of the cypress tree. Woody didn't move.

"Don't worry about the geezer, the place is full of 'em. They're harmless as the deer. Now hit the damn ball."

Woody bristled at the geezer comment, but remained still.

Cigar firmly clamped in his jaw, the redhead reared back and launched a high shot that soared out of sight beyond the lighthouse and onto the adjacent driving range.

"Nice shot," the tall one said with a snorting laugh.

"Aw shut up," the redhead grumbled.

The two returned to their cart and drove off.

"Relaxing game," Woody said to himself, walking back to the lighthouse to finish his noon-to-six shift. The geezer comment bugged him, but he'd heard it before. He would even classify some of his friends as geezers, but because of their attitudes, not their ages.

Woody's attitude was okay, he thought. He had more energy than most guys his age, and while his joints often complained, friends he'd pass while walking between Monterey and Spanish Bay along the coastal recreation trail couldn't believe he was 70. His lanky six-two figure with its mop of gray hair blowing around the ever-present red 49ers cap had become a landmark on the winding pathway.

Driving home from the lighthouse that evening, Woody couldn't get the conversation he'd overheard out of his head. He pulled up in front of the little yellow Victorian on Fountain Avenue in Pacific Grove—P.G. as the locals called it—where he lived with Helen, his wife of 40 years. He and Helen had bought the house after he'd retired from the Army. The town's size, friendliness, and pace suited them. They shared the house with Ralph, their overweight orange cat, with whom Woody maintained a healthy love-hate relationship. The cat had been named after Helen's cousin, who'd also moved in without being invited. The two-legged Ralph had departed after a month. The Ralph with four legs, by all evidence, had come to stay.

Canned Hunt

As he hung his cap on the peg by the front door, questions filled his mind. It was clear the golfers had been discussing something out in a boat that the tall man wanted to get on shore and the redhead didn't. Where was "out there"? The bay? And what was generating the "crap" the redhead had complained about?

"What's gotten into you?" Helen asked, walking past him as he stood, lost in thought, in the middle of the living room.

"Huh?"

"Do you feel all right? You look a little peaked."

"I'm fine."

"What, then?"

"Most likely nothing." Woody shooed Ralph off his recliner and took the cat's place. "I overheard a couple of guys arguing today and I'm trying to figure out what it was about."

"At the lighthouse?"

"On the golf course."

"People argue all the time," Helen said. "It's probably nothing."

"It was about a boatload of something messy that could get them in a lot of trouble. I wonder if they could've been talking about people."

Helen stared at Woody. "People?"

"You know, people being smuggled into the country. Like from China or someplace."

Helen chuckled. "Oh, Woody."

"Well, it fits. I'll bet they've got a boatload of illegals in the bay that they don't know what to do with."

The kitchen timer began to chime and Helen went to quiet it. "If you're really that concerned, call the authorities and tell them what you heard. Now go wash up. Dinner's ready."

When the dishes had been done, Woody joined Helen in the living room. He poked at the lazy fire in the fireplace, stretched out in his chair, and pulled a magazine from the pile on the floor nearby. Helen had curled up on the couch and was lost in her latest mystery novel while Ralph dozed peacefully on the back of the couch behind her.

Woody suddenly snapped his chair upright and slapped the magazine he'd been reading. "That's him!" he shouted.

"My lord!" Helen said, dropping her book. Ralph darted into the kitchen.

"That's the guy. I knew I'd seen him somewhere." Woody held up a copy of *Newsweek* open to an article about a San Francisco developer. The picture accompanying the article showed a group of men standing next to an enormous yellow bulldozer. They wore shiny hard-hats and the tallest of the group, with one oxblood Gucci loafer gently resting on a chromed shovel blade, smiled at the camera. "Victor Marcellus," Woody said. "One of the guys at the golf course today." He sat back and grinned at Helen.

As he stared at the picture, he knew he'd seen this Victor Marcellus in person before today, too, but he just couldn't pull the memory up.

Woody sat up in bed at three o'clock the next morning. Though the room was dark, he could see Ralph's lumpy silhouette at the foot of the bed. The cat looked at him for a moment before sighing and dropping his head back onto his paws. Helen's "sleep breathing"—he'd learned *never* to call it snoring—told him he hadn't awakened her.

Victor Marcellus. Woody remembered where he'd seen him before: The Inn at Spanish Bay, a couple of years ago, during a Taste of Monterey event Helen had dragged him to. He remembered also that a friend and fellow walker, Hector Ramirez, had been tending bar that day at the Inn.

Later, after confirming that Hector would be there today, Woody drove out to the Inn to talk with him. He parked in one of the upper lots. It meant a longer walk, but it avoided the stares and wisecracks of the valet boys and other staff. While Woody liked to think of his old Valiant as classic, the impression it invariably gave was tow-away.

Woody ordered a beer and sat at a corner table. He had about 30 minutes to kill before Hector was scheduled to come on and, being a card carrying people watcher, he sat and sipped contentedly, watching the constant flux of staff and guests. A young couple on the terrace outside caught his attention. Woody chuckled. They appeared to be having the kind of inexperienced argument typical of newlyweds: Groom says something stupid. Bride takes offense, wondering if she's made the biggest mistake of her life. Groom apologizes extravagantly, even though he has no idea why. Bride forgives him, and they rush back to their room looking like Siamese Twins.

Engrossed in the exchange outside, Woody didn't notice Hector sit down at the table. "They'll get better at it, man," Hector said, pointing to the retreating lovers. "Pretty soon they'll be pros."

"Hey, Hector! Good to see you." Woody put down his beer and extended his hand.

"Yeah, likewise. What brings you out with the beautiful people, man?"

"What, I couldn't just be missing you?"

"Sure, sure. But I know you. What are you into this time?"

Woody pulled the *Newsweek* article from his pocket and pushed it toward Hector. "Recognize this guy?"

Hector twisted the corner of his mustache absently and inspected the picture. He pinned the image to the table with a forefinger and looked up with a frown. "I know him." His expression darkened as he tapped his finger on the page. "Bad one, I think."

"What can you tell me about him?"

Hector sat back and frowned. He fiddled with his moustache again, looking sideways at the picture on the table. "He's one powerful hombre, man. Not one to mess with."

"He was the center of attention here a year or so ago at that Taste thing, you remember?"

"Sure, I remember." Hector tapped the picture again. "A couple of days after that, he hires me and a couple of the waiters to work a private party at his house in Pebble."

"He lives here?"

"Just a weekend house, I think. But we go out there and, man, does he have a *party*. I don't know who all was there but there must have been a million dollars parked in the driveway. It was something." He nodded toward the opulent Spanish Bay Inn bar. "Enough booze to keep this place going for a month."

"Did you get close to him?"

"Yeah, pretty close. I was cleaning up a little when a guy comes up to me and says to bring a tray with five glasses into the library at the end of the hall. I say okay and follow him. We go in and, man, I've never seen anything like it."

"Lotta books?"

"Lotta heads, man."

"Heads?"

"You know, animal heads. But not deer or those rabbits with antlers you see everywhere. These were big cats. Must have been a dozen of 'em. They were hanging on the walls everywhere." A strangely satisfying image of Ralph's head mounted over the fireplace flashed through Woody's mind.

"What do you mean, 'big cats'?"

"Tigers, man. Big heads, big eyes . . . big *teeth*."

"You can't shoot those things."

"Right. Listen, I'm setting up and pouring drinks like I'm part of the furniture, right? The other guys in there are going ape-shit over the animals, and this guy?" he tapped the picture again, "he's loving it.

"Then one of them points to this really big tiger head and says, 'When were you in Africa, Vic?' Well, Vic laughs and says, 'I shot that bad boy ten years ago in Santa Cruz.' Then he said it was the sweetest canned hunt he'd ever seen."

"Canned hunt?"

"That's what he called it. Well, I'm like invisible, you know, so he goes on to tell how about ten years ago there was this club up in the hills where you could hunt these things, for a price. He points to this one head and says it cost him eight grand to plug it. Can you imagine that, man? Anyway, he says the place was busted in a Fish and Game sting."

"Then what happened?"

"Well, some of the others started talking about how they'd pay to bag one, too. They started bugging this Vic guy to start a club of his own so they could get a shot."

"Amazing," Woody said. He thought back to the argument on the golf course and things started making sense.

Hector looked at his watch and stood up. "Time to go to work. Hope this helps you, but listen man, don't mess with this guy, okay? You stay out of trouble."

The following Thursday when Woody arrived at the lighthouse, Tom, the other docent scheduled that day, stood in the parking lot talking to a group of regulars waiting for their turn on the nearby tenth tee. They all greeted Woody as he joined them.

"Tell Woody what you saw, Tom," one of the golfers said. Tom seemed happy to retell his story.

"Well, like I said, I was drivin' in from Moss Landing when I seen all these police cars and fire trucks down by the docks, all their lights flashing, so I drove down to take a look. It was pretty gruesome, I'll tell ya."

"What happened?" Woody asked.

Tom's face curled into a frown. He shook his head, leaned toward Woody, and continued in a near whisper. "There was a body in the harbor this morning. Fishermen found it around six-thirty. It was still kinda dark so I got closer and saw 'em zip the guy up in the bag. Gave me the creeps, I'll tell ya." Tom looked at the others to make sure they were paying attention. "Hardly looked like a person at all, just all lumpy." He stood back and tucked his thumbs under his belt. "What struck me was how round the body was. Awful!"

Woody thought Tom seemed a little too pleased with his gruesome celebrity. When Woody didn't react, Tom finally couldn't stand it.

"So, Woody, what'd *you* do exciting last week?"

"Nothing much. Same ol' routine," Woody answered.

Canned Hunt

At home that evening Woody poured a glass of wine and flipped on the TV. He stretched out in his recliner and Ralph joined him to watch the news. After a few moments, the cheerful anchorman affected a sincere expression, lowered his voice, and began: "In local news, fishermen in the Moss Landing harbor discovered a body in the water early this morning. While police are not releasing details, they have identified the body as that of San Jose businessman, Theodore McLeod, owner of Universal Imports." A picture of a smiling McLeod filled half the screen and Woody nearly dropped his wine glass.

The newsman droned on: "According to sources, Mr. McLeod had been reported missing by his wife on Friday last. Police gave no details on the condition of the body or the probable cause of death, but did say they have not ruled out foul play. And on a possibly related note, *Action News Eight* has discovered that Mr. McLeod's import operations have in the past been the subject of police, customs, and IRS investigations."

Woody picked up the remote and switched off the set. "So the man with the scruples had an accident, huh Ralph?" He stroked the cat slowly and Ralph blinked at him. "Don't let your imagination run away with you," he cautioned the cat. "People have accidents." Ralph looked convinced. Woody wasn't.

In bed that night, Helen could no longer ignore Woody's pensive mood. "Are you sure you feel all right?"

He felt fine. He actually felt better than fine; his juices were pumping again. "I'm okay, hon. I was mistaken about the boatload of illegal aliens. I'm pretty sure now that it's wild animals instead of people out there somewhere."

"Why would anybody smuggle animals into the country?"

"To hunt 'em," he said, holding up an imaginary rifle and plugging an oblivious Ralph at the foot of the bed.

"Darn, you missed," Helen said.

"Do we know any hunters?"

She thought a moment. "Doesn't George hunt?" George Baldwin worked at the Pacific Grove hardware store downtown and had helped Woody with various home projects over the years.

"*That's* right!" Woody said, and decided to talk with George in the morning.

"Why do they need to smuggle animals in?" Helen asked. "Aren't there plenty already here?"

"These are illegal to hunt anywhere. Tigers and such. They're protected. Big money in it."

"And you think that's what the two men you overheard were arguing about?"

"I'm pretty sure. By the way, one of them turned up dead this morning, floating in Moss Landing harbor."

Helen put her book down and pulled herself up on her pillow. "Oh, my!"

"I don't know exactly what to do about it."

Helen stared openmouthed at him for a moment. "Nothing! Nothing at all, that's what." She put a hand on Woody's arm. "I know you think you're a detective, dear, but something like this is far too serious. Let the people who know what they're doing handle it."

"Don't worry, Helen. I won't get involved."

After another incredulous stare, Helen turned off her light and pulled the covers up. "I suppose there's a first time for everything."

The next morning Woody walked up the hill to the hardware store on Forest Avenue. Brown paper sleeves of fresh flowers crowded the sidewalk in front of the florist, and warm, sweet smells wafting from the bakery next door made him sorry he'd already had breakfast. A refrigerated truck making deliveries to Grove Market across the narrow street had double-parked, causing even the light morning traffic on Forest to come to an amicable standstill. The scene made Woody glad he lived in a town small enough to walk across—and happy that he still could.

An electronic ding announced his arrival as he walked through the door of the hardware store. George came out from between crowded shelves and greeted him. "Hi, Woody. Project day?"

"Morning, George. Yeah, you could say I'm working on something. You're a hunter, right?"

George may have weighed 100 pounds and could make five-four if he stood up straight. He had to tilt his head back to look Woody in the eye, a position that confused his bifocals and caused his head to bob while he talked. "I hunt some. Usually make it out for dove and quail season, why?"

"Ever hunt bigger things?"

"When I visit my son in Arizona we sometimes buy a deer tag and go out." He adjusted his glasses. "Thinking of taking up the sport?"

"No, but I have a question for you. You ever hear of a thing called a 'canned hunt'?"

George stopped bobbing and looked at the ground. His face twisted into a mask of disgust. "Yeah, I've heard the term. But that's *not* hunting!"

"What do you mean?"

George worked Woody back into focus. "It's not hunting! It's glorified target practice."

"Against the law, right?"

"Depends on what you're shooting at. Sometimes the authorities will have one for wild boar."

"What about protected animals, like tigers?"

"Way illegal. Tell me you're not thinking about anything like that, please."

"Oh, hell no, George, but have you ever heard about one around here?"

"I think there was one once, but seems it was a long time ago."

"Do you remember where it was?

"Up north a ways, maybe the Santa Cruz Mountains. What's this all about, anyway?"

As Woody laid it out, George made short whistling sounds. When Woody got to the part about the floating redhead, George held up his hands and took a step back. "Hold it right there, Woody! You're in way over your head. Take it to the cops."

"I can't prove anything. It's just a feeling."

"Let the cops worry about it." George glanced around uneasily for a customer to help. "Don't you have a buddy in the department?"

"Not since Tony retired. They all think I'm a nut case. Anyway, none of this is in Pacific Grove."

"Then take it to Fish and Game."

"Know anybody?" Woody asked expectantly.

George nodded and pulled out his wallet. After shuffling through a stack of business cards, he handed one to Woody. "Here. I met her a couple of months ago when she spoke to the Rotary."

Woody read the name on the card: *Sandra Baker-Harris, Community Relations Officer, California Fish & Game.*

George's face showed genuine relief when the ding announced another early shopper. "Got customers, Woody," he said. "You stay out of trouble, okay?"

"Sure. Thanks, George."

Woody stopped at the bakery for a sweet roll then hurried home to make the call.

Woody felt a twinge of guilt for tricking her, but once he'd convinced the fish and game officer that he was simply doing research, Officer Baker-Harris had proved very helpful. He learned that a big canned hunt had been shut down in the late eighties in Santa Cruz County. Set up on a 500-acre piece of land in the hills known as the Appleby Ranch, the hunt had used ill or excess animals from zoos and circuses across the country. Since many of the animals had been transported across state lines, the feds got involved and the club was brought down by a combination of state and federal agencies.

He hung up the phone and paced through the house. Finally, after perplexing Ralph but failing to dissipate his nervous energy, he left a note for Helen and drove to the Santa Cruz hall of records.

After two hours spent slogging through dusty records, he'd learned that the Appleby Ranch had been sold off in sections beginning in 1995. But he also ran across an old surveyor's map that noted the name of the original owners: Boznell Enterprises. It was a start. Boznell turned out to be a subsidiary of APTCO Properties, which was in turn a subsidiary of Horizon International . . . a company owned by Victor Marcellus. A little more digging revealed that Horizon International currently owned a considerable amount of land in Monterey County.

Nearly giddy over his discovery, he paid for a copy of the map section and headed back around the bay to Salinas, to see what Monterey County's records had to say about Horizon International.

It didn't take long.

He forced himself to stay calm. He had to be sure the dots he'd connected were really there. From the information on the Monterey County plat maps, he learned that only one 90-acre section of Horizon's holdings—near the south end of Carmel Valley, over the hill from the town of Gonzales—was undeveloped and remote enough to serve the purpose. He bought copies of the maps, added them to his pile, and headed for home.

Woody'd lost all track of time and it was well past seven when he closed his front door and hung up his cap. Helen didn't try to conceal her worry. "You're going to put me in an early grave, Clarence Woodall!" she scolded. "I thought . . . I don't know what I thought. If you're going to traipse around all over the place, at least take the cell phone with you. And use it!"

He looked at her and a slow pout spread across his face. Helen finally had to laugh.

"Oh, stop it." She swatted him with the dishtowel. "You worried me, that's all. Take the phone next time. Your dinner's in the oven."

He called Officer Baker-Harris again the next morning and arranged to meet with her. She'd agreed to meet him at twelve-fifteen at P.G. Juice 'n Java near the center of town. Woody arrived early and sat impatiently in the paneled semi-darkness beside a towering potted plant. At exactly a quarter past twelve, a short, trim woman, with chin-length auburn hair that bounced when she walked, came through the doors. Her tailored uniform fit perfectly and Woody thought she came across official enough, except that she looked like a high school student. He rose as she approached the table.

"Mr. Woodall?" She extended her hand.

"Officer Baker-Harris." Woody noted her firm but cool grip. "Please, call me Woody."

"Sandra," she said as they took their seats.

Woody'd decided to come clean about deceiving her the first time they'd spoken, and she accepted his confession gracefully. When the whole story—from the argument on the golf course to the revelations of the Santa Cruz and Monterey County records—had been told, Sandra closed her notebook and sat back in her chair. Her face wore a decidedly uneasy expression.

"An interesting chain of events, Woody, certainly worth looking into. I'm going to brief my boss on all of this." She exhaled and shook her head. "I'd hate to see this sort of thing get started again."

"What can I do to help?" After sharing everything, he didn't like the idea of not staying involved.

"Nothing, really," she said, handing Woody one of her cards. "You can call me if you like, but we'll take it from here. I'll let you know if anything comes of it." She thanked him and left.

Woody felt good about airing his concerns, but somehow the feeling of satisfaction he'd anticipated eluded him. Full of nervous energy, he bought a house decaf and took it out to a table on the sidewalk in front of the coffeehouse. He sipped his coffee and tried in vain to lose himself in the strolling shoppers, the slowly passing cars, and the butterfly banners flapping from the light posts.

After two weeks without word, Woody could no longer bear the suspense and dialed Sandra's number. She was out of the office so he left a message on her machine. Helen had made sandwiches and taken them out to eat on the tiny patio outside their kitchen. He hung up the phone and joined her.

"I'm glad you finally called," Helen said. "You've been in a funk ever since you talked to her. I'd considered looking up psychiatrists in the phone book."

"I guess I have been preoccupied," he said.

"That's an understatement," she said. "So what's up?"

"I still don't know. She was out. I left a message, maybe she'll call back."

He picked up his sandwich and took a bite. The phone rang.

"I'll get it," Helen said, getting up. She went into the kitchen and returned with the cordless. "It's her," she said, and handed him the phone.

"Sandra! I'm going crazy here, what's happening?"

"Well, my boss was very interested. We put together a little team and did some checking. There's been some new fencing and a pretty substantial gate installed at the property where it meets Carmel Valley Road. We observed some traffic in and out, but nothing unduly suspicious. There haven't been any complaints . . . and with our current budget and manpower situation, it just doesn't warrant a sustained investigation. I'm sorry, I've been meaning to call you."

"What if you had proof? Would that make a difference?" Helen put down her sandwich and glared at him.

Woody thought Sandra's voice sounded as if she might be glaring at him as well. "Now Mr. Woodall, I know what you're thinking, and I have to caution you not to do anything on your own. There may be something out there, but there may not be. For now, we'll all have to just wait and see."

"It seems pretty clear to me! Marcellus is gearing up to run a canned hunt. I'll bet he's already got some animals up there. We have to do *something!*"

"There's simply no hard evidence, Mr. Woodall. And we simply don't have the resources. My advice is to let it go for now."

Woody noticed she'd dropped the familiar "Woody". She was playing it by the book and he knew it was pointless to argue. "Well perhaps some evidence will turn up," he said. "Thanks anyway." As he pushed the "Off" button he heard her voice in the tiny speaker imploring him not to do anything foolish.

"What are you planning?" Helen asked, seeing an all too familiar look on her husband's face.

"Nothing, Helen. Just thinking. They need proof of what's going on up there before they can do anything about it. I may try to stir some up."

"Oh, Woody. Please don't do anything foolish."

That was the second time he'd been warned against doing something foolish. Well, he thought, *somebody* has to do something. Tomorrow was Thursday and he'd be at the lighthouse all afternoon. He decided he'd make a trip to Carmel Valley on Friday.

A cold, misty rain blew across the Monterey Peninsula on Thursday and Woody hoped it would mean a slow day at the lighthouse. He brought his maps with him and planned to get some reconnoitering done. When he arrived at the lighthouse, he found Tom standing in the small covered porch, holding a thermos lid of coffee and watching the squalls. Woody didn't wait for Tom's usual query. "Same ol' routine," he said as he passed.

The weather stayed lousy. By the end of his shift he'd located the point at which the Marcellus property paralleled Agua Mala Creek on the south side of Carmel Valley Road. If he got an early start, he thought, he could get situated up there and maybe get the kind of proof Sandra's boss needed to stop Victor's little enterprise.

After washing up that evening, Woody sat in the front room wondering how to approach Helen with his plans.

"You're going to *what*?" Helen gaped at Woody, who lounged in his recliner, trying to look relaxed. "Did I just hear you say you were going to 'root this thing out' yourself?"

"Well, I meant I'm going to take a look around. I know what they're up to and it needs to be stopped. I'm just going to look."

"You're not going up there. That's that."

"Helen, I'm going. And I'll take the phone."

"Oh, Woody! The phone won't help if those bad men catch you snooping around."

"Helen . . . they shoot animals, not people!"

"What about that redheaded man, the one they found floating in the bay?"

Woody knew he couldn't win. Even Ralph looked at him like he had a screw loose. "I'm going up there in the morning, Helen. I'll have the phone and I'll be home before it gets dark."

Helen squinted at him for a long minute, then went back to the kitchen to slam cupboard doors and bang pots. Ralph slunk down the hall to the safety of the bedroom.

So be it, he thought. Sure, he could simply wait and see, but if his suspicions were right, by then it'd be too late. Sometimes you can't wait for the other guy.

He was on the road the next morning at four o'clock. He'd filled a thermos with hot coffee and put on heavy corduroy pants and two pairs of socks. Under his sweatshirt, he wore two extra T-shirts and a knit vest. He decided to leave his 49ers cap at home and took instead a tan crush hat, which he stuffed into his sweatshirt pocket with the cell phone and

Helen's little instamatic camera.

He turned left off Highway 1 onto an empty Carmel Valley Road and wound his way through the rolling hills. When he passed the lush Rancho Cañada Golf Course, his thoughts returned to the sixteenth tee-box at Pacific Grove Municipal where he'd overheard Victor and the red-head arguing. Tom's description of the bloated corpse being zipped into a body bag came to him in vivid detail and he felt a chill. He bumped the heater knob up a notch. The heater was one of the few things on the old Valiant that still worked. That, he thought, or all the firewall seals were gone and engine heat blew in through the rusting penetrations.

The dirt turn-off from Carmel Valley Road at Aqua Mala Creek showed signs of recent traffic. The vegetation on either side of the entry had been crushed and muddy tire tracks fanned onto the asphalt. He eased the Valiant up the gradual slope. The roadway widened somewhat and the overhanging trees opened up, letting the starry night sky show above. After stopping twice to check his maps, he found the newly installed chain link fence and gate. Large "No Trespassing" signs flanked the heavily padlocked entrance. He drove past the gate to a wide spot on the opposite side of the road. As he made a U-turn, he could see that it provided a perfect position from which to keep an eye on the entrance. Even through the hazy pre-dawn light, he could see several hundred yards up the rutted dirt road beyond the gate. He pulled in under the overhanging trees and turned off the engine. When he cut the headlights, a cave-like darkness enveloped him. His ears buzzed in the sudden silence, interrupted only by the tiny ticks and pops from the cooling Valiant.

"Perfect," he said, and, in the light of the flashlight on the seat beside him, filled his mug with coffee from the thermos. Steam fogged the wind-shield as he took a careful sip. He switched off the flashlight and settled in to wait for something to happen.

He awoke with a start. A dazzling blue sky shown beyond the limbs that extended over his parking place. The gate stood open and a faint haze of dust over the road told him something was going on. The dust settled, but no vehicle came into view. They must be going in, he thought.

It struck him suddenly that it was time to pay the rent on the coffee he'd had before dozing off. He got out and grimaced as his knees pro-tested the long sit in the damp car. Using the Valiant as a prop, he man-aged to work the kinks out and hobble into the underbrush for a piss. While concealed, he heard a large vehicle downshift as it passed. Woody moved a branch to see a stake bed truck turning at the gate. Three wooden crates were tied onto the back. Woody felt a rush of excitement.

Though she'd pretended not to be, Helen was awake when Woody'd slipped out of bed that morning. He'd gotten himself into sticky situations over the years by not being able to leave well enough alone. But this present situation really troubled her. This time, things were dangerous. This time, those involved were powerful people with big money. Woody was out of his element. And even though she loved him for standing up for the right thing, she worried.

She couldn't get back to sleep and finally got up and made herself some breakfast. When the paper eventually came, even though she knew it was impossible, she feared reading about something terrible happening to Woody. At a little past nine the phone rang. She froze at the first ring and stared at the handset. She picked it up and pressed the "Talk" button. "Hello?"

A young woman's voice: "Hello. Mrs. Woodall?"

Helen ran down the possibilities: Emergency room nurse? Highway Patrol? SWAT Captain? Grief Counselor? "Yes," she answered, tentatively.

"This is Sandra Baker-Harris with California Fish and Game. May I speak with your husband?"

"He's not here. Can I help?"

"I was hoping to talk with him." The woman's voice faded in and out amidst bursts of static.

"I can barely hear you!" Helen said. "He left early this morning and I don't know when he'll be back."

"Do you . . . where . . . he might have . . ."

"What!" Helen yelled into the phone.

"Do you know where he went?" An edge had come into the young woman's voice.

"He went to Carmel Valley early this morning. To look for proof, he said."

There was an uncomfortable pause. "Can you contact him? Does he have a cell phone?"

"Yes, but . . . please tell me what's happened. Should I call the police? Is he in any real danger?"

"Time is of the essence, Mrs. Woodall. Call him and have him come home. Make the call now."

"What's happening?" Helen asked frantically, but the answer came only as static, then a dial tone. "Oh dear . . ." She took two deep breaths and dialed their cell phone number. Ralph rubbed against her leg and looked up at her from the floor.

Woody crossed the road and stepped gingerly through the under-brush until he came to the fence. He stopped at the entrance and listened for approaching trucks, either on the graded road to his right or the rut-ted dirt track that curled up the hill to his left. Only the whisper of the wind in the treetops and the occasional jay's squawk interrupted the silence. He slipped through the open gate and hurried back into the cover of the trees and brush. He kept to the protective cover of the trees as he followed the twisty road up the hill.

The day had warmed and before long he'd begun to perspire. He stopped to rest on a fallen pine, shrugged out of his sweatshirt, and hung it over a branch. As he wiped his face with his handkerchief, the high-pitched whine of an approaching car made him get up and step farther into the bushes. A silver Jaguar convertible roared past, throwing dirt and small rocks into the trees around him, and slid to a stop just beyond Woody's sight. Carefully, he made his way forward until a clearing came into view.

A low log building flanked an open expanse of cleared ground. Two flatbed trucks were parked nearby, empty of their cargo. Several large wooden crates sat on the ground near the building, one, still on a forklift, rested precariously above the bed of one of the trucks. Dust swirled around the Jaguar and the driver's door stood open.

Victor Marcellus, voice raised and arms waving wildly, berated the two drivers. Woody moved slowly through the brush to a low, ivy-cov-ered rock wall only 50 feet from where the men were arguing.

"I don't know how they found out!" he heard Victor yell. "But we don't have much time. Get these crates back on the trucks and clear out!"

One of the men walked to an empty truck and climbed into the cab. "You're on your own, pal," the man said, starting the truck's engine. Its dual rear wheels created a shower of dust and gravel as the truck fish-tailed down the dirt road.

The second man started toward the other truck but Victor grabbed his arm. The man jerked free and spun to face Victor. "And then what?" the man asked angrily. "We just drive around with 'em 'til things cool off? No way! Somebody screwed up, but it wasn't me."

Victor pulled a small automatic pistol from his waist and pointed it at the man. "What, you going to shoot me?" the man asked, mockingly. "I don't think so." He grabbed the truck's door and swung into the cab.

"I'm warning you," Victor said, raising the gun to shoulder level. The truck's engine roared and its gears gnashed. Victor fired twice into the cab. The first round passed through the open driver's window and shattered the windshield; the second thudded loudly into the doorframe. Snarling roars from inside the containers rose with the sound of the truck's engine. The rear of the truck swung in a slow arc as its spinning tires gained traction, the end of the bed clipping the forklift. The raised container teetered, and then crashed onto the ground, splitting one of its sides at the corner. A piercing howl exploded from the carton as it hit, and the volume of the chorus from the other containers increased. Victor fired wildly as the truck sped away.

Woody hunched lower behind the wall, ignoring the pain in his knees and the pounding heartbeat in his ears. From his vantage point he could see the damaged crate clearly, though the parked forklift concealed it from Victor. Powerful claws systematically pulled the container apart from the inside. With each pull, more of the wooden container splintered away.

Victor swore loudly and walked in circles, swinging the gun and kicking the dirt. In the middle of a particularly forceful oath, "Jingle Bells" began playing from somewhere in the brush beyond the clearing. Victor wheeled and fired three quick rounds toward the sound, then scanned the shadowed underbrush.

Woody cringed. He hated that phone! For as long as he and Helen had owned the infernal thing, he'd been unable to change its ring.

Victor released the automatic's spent clip. Slapping a new one into place, he moved slowly toward the edge of the clearing and the lilting melody, straining to see into the shadows.

Woody could see that as Victor kept walking he would gain a clear view of his hiding place, and so he decided to find better cover. The snarling cats had quieted and Woody wished he'd made his move earlier. As he strained to move quietly, a brief but robust flatulence escaped him. *"Damn!"* he muttered. Victor spun and his eyes met Woody's.

"Who the hell are you?" Victor asked in a raspy voice.

"Nobody," Woody said.

"What are you . . ." Victor seemed at a loss for words.

"Maybe you oughta worry more about geezers," Woody offered, immediately regretting it.

Victor smiled and raised the pistol while "Jingle Bells" continued to play. As he slowly squeezed the trigger, an orange shape streaked across the clearing.

The size and speed of the animal astonished Woody. In no more than three bounding strides, the tiger covered the 50 feet from the now open container to where Victor stood. Victor tried to bring the gun around but the tiger flattened him like a blind-sided quarterback, coming to ground with Victor's right shoulder and neck clamped tightly in its huge jaws. The gun discharged harmlessly in the air before falling from Victor's limp hand. The big cat whipped Victor's doll-like form against the dirt and rolled over it, holding it in a tight embrace. While the attacking cat made no sound, the howls from the other containers grew to a riotous din. Woody swallowed back a sudden wave of nausea at the unexpected gore before him. He fought the urge to simply stare as parts of Victor were strewn about the clearing, and quickly moved to stop the phone's cheery ringing.

"Hello," he whispered.

"Woody, is that you?" The sound of Helen's voice was comforting, though its tone wasn't. "Why didn't you answer?"

The smell of blood had stimulated the still-boxed animals to produce even more aggravated roars. "What's that horrible noise?"

Woody didn't want to attract the attention of the tiger. Victor's blood matted the fur on the cat's massive head and forelegs as it slowly circled Victor's scattered remains, huffing and sniffing the air, occasionally adding its own chilling voice to the others.

"I've got to hang up now," he whispered.

"Oh no you don't!" Helen demanded. "You have to come home right now! Do you hear me?" He pushed the "End" button and tried not to move.

Woody had the tiger's full attention now. The cat had stopped pacing and stood statue-still, deep rumblings accompanying each puffing breath, staring into the brush where Woody hid. Methodically, the tiger began to walk toward him.

He could smell the animal and almost feel its breath. Their eyes met and Woody thought of Helen. She had been a loving wife, he thought, but she'd never forgive him for what was about to happen. He wished he'd said good-bye. The cat's mouth hung open and it muscles tensed. It lifted its head and sniffed the air, and then it crouched, eyes burning through the branches.

Woody heard a pop and the big cat spun around and growled, a brightly-colored bouquet of feathers sprouting from its rump. The animal took a few steps into the clearing before its hindquarters became tangled and it fell. It gave one last roar before dropping its head to the dirt. Puffs of dust blew up around flared nostrils and the big cat began to snore.

People were running into the clearing from the opposite side, among them Sandra Baker-Harris. It took a moment for Woody's mind to comprehend what had just happened. He straightened up with some difficulty; his knees had lost all their strength and shook almost uncontrollably. As he walked unsteadily into the bright sunshine, Woody could see men and women in green Fish and Game outfits, some in civilian clothes, and still others in sheriff's uniforms.

Two young men ran to the sleeping tiger and knelt beside it. One put a stethoscope to the cat's ribcage, frowned with concentration, then nodded to the other with a smile. Woody noticed that nobody needed to assess Mr. Marcellus' condition.

Again, "Jingle Bells" rang out, this time from Woody's hand, where he still clutched the small phone.

"Hi, Honey," he said cheerily. "Everything's fine now."

"My lord, Clarence Woodall, you will *surely* be the death of me. What's happening? Are you all right?"

"I'm fine, it's all over now."

"What's all over?"

"Well . . . ah, everything's fine, really."

"Woody!" Helen's voice shrieked from the tiny speaker.

"Here," he said, handing the phone to Sandra, who'd walked over to him and now gave him a puzzled look.

"It's my wife, Helen. Tell her I'm okay, will you?"

Sandra took the phone. "Mrs. Woodall, this is Sandra Baker-Harris again. Yes. Yes. Yes, he's fine. No. No, he's not hurt. He'll tell you all about it when he gets home, I'm sure. Yes, I promise." She handed the phone back to Woody.

"See, I told you everything was okay," he gloated, but to a dead line.

"I told her you were okay," Sandra said. "Are you?"

"I think so. Sure glad you came along." His legs were beginning to regain their strength. "That was pretty close."

"You're a very lucky man, Mr. Woodall," she said. "Based on your information, I talked with a friend of mine in the Monterey County Sheriff's Department. I told him there might be a connection between McLeod's death, Victor Marcellus, and a possible animal smuggling operation. My friend went back and talked with McLeod's widow. She'd found paperwork, after she'd been questioned, that proved her husband's involvement with Victor Marcellus in the shipment of several animals from Europe and Africa. Specimens in their prime."

"So, I was right all along?"

"When the police went to Victor's home in San Francisco yesterday to arrest him, he was gone. And his gun case had been emptied.

"We put this operation together a week ago, but I couldn't tell you about it. On the way out here this morning, I had the feeling you might have decided to . . . let's say, get involved."

"And you called Helen," Woody said, pocketing the cell phone.

Sandra nodded. "When she told me you'd come looking for proof, I . . . well, I hoped we'd get here in time."

The young fellow with the stethoscope walked up to them and looked at Woody carefully.

"This is Terry Grant," Sandra said. "He's a state vet."

"How are you feeling?" the man asked.

"A little shaky, but okay."

Dr. Grant listened to Woody's heart for a minute, then took his pulse. "You're a little revved up, but you sound okay. Take it easy for a few days and if you start feeling funny, see your doctor, okay?"

"Sure," Woody answered. He felt fine. What did this animal doctor know, anyway?

"Can you get a lift from someone?" Dr. Grant went on. "I'd rather you didn't drive yourself home."

"I can drive myself home, for pity sakes."

Sandra spoke firmly. "Give me your car keys, Woody, I'll take you home. We'll have one of the guys take your car back for you."

Woody studied her for a moment, then reluctantly handed over his keys.

He sat on a log in the shade while the Fish and Game people finished securing the scene and the sheriff's people, who'd used several yellow sheets to cover Victor, waited impatiently for the coroner. It wasn't long before Sandra came and sat beside him.

"There're ten cats here, all in surprisingly good shape. There's no evidence that any hunting actually got started. They were just setting it up."

"So we stopped it in time."

Sandra chuckled. "Yes *we* did. It might have gone on for a good while before we got wind of it. No telling how many of these beautiful animals would have been slaughtered."

"You're welcome," he said with a grin.

Sandra laughed and patted him on the knee. "Stay here, I'll go get my truck."

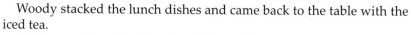

Woody stacked the lunch dishes and came back to the table with the iced tea.

"It'll be good to get back to the lighthouse," he said as he poured Helen's refill. "Been kind of dull around here this week."

"Are you sure you feel well enough to go back so soon?"

"Nonsense, Helen, I feel fine. Don't worry."

"Promise me you'll take it easy." Helen figured it couldn't hurt to ask.

"Sure, I'll take it easy." Woody figured it couldn't hurt to humor her.

As Woody sipped his tea, he noticed Ralph on the patio, prancing on his hind legs, batting at a moth that flitted just out of reach. "Look at that, will you," Woody said, pointing at the cat.

Helen smiled. "Behold the great hunter."

Woody had told Helen about everything except his close encounter with the tiger—and how the tiger had left Victor. No sense going in to that much detail. It seemed enough that he'd almost been shot. Helen had recoiled at the bullet holes in his sweatshirt. The fact that it was slung over a tree branch when it had been ventilated hadn't lessened her jitters. Besides, he figured, telling her about the tiger would only sound like boasting.

"Instinct," said Woody, as they watched the cat stalk the moth. "They're natural killers, large and small."

"It's a shame it has to be that way," Helen mused.

Woody thought about that for a moment. "Not always."

He finished his tea and said, "Well, I'm off to the lighthouse. You be careful while I'm gone."

"You stole my line." She smiled and gave him a peck on the cheek.

When he approached the lighthouse, Woody saw Tom raising the American flag on the pole next to the building.

"Any excitement this week, Woody?" Tom asked with a grin.

"Nothing much," he said, a noticeable spring in his step. "Dodging bullets and staring down killer tigers."

"Yeah, right," Tom laughed, tying off the ropes. "Same old routine."

Dead in Time
by Linda Price

Alate October storm added hours to Darlene Franklin's drive from Corte Madera to the Monterey Peninsula. The Friday afternoon traffic guaranteed rock hard muscles—not the weightlifting kind—and her nerves were on edge. Dennis and Fanny McFarland, friends of her late husband, Brent, had pressured her to get out of the house and spend the weekend with them at their Carmel Valley ranch. She knew the impending weather would make the trip hard, but had agreed in spite of her reservations. *I have the spine of a jellyfish.*

Gusty coastal winds coaxed the clouds apart as she turned up the long moonlit driveway off Carmel Valley Road, ten miles east of Carmel Valley Village. The old three-story Victorian that Dennis McFarland had inherited from his parents sat at the end of the drive, looking just the way she remembered. Still woefully in need of fresh paint, weathered outbuildings, including a large barn topped by a wrought-iron Labrador retriever weather vane, added to the atmosphere of neglect. A few new boards had been added to help prop up the rickety fence that surrounded the house. Overgrown rose bushes, begonias, and Mexican sage grew amongst the rusting wheelbarrow and other abandoned tools scattered throughout the yard.

The sound of dogs barking from the barn replaced the "Anger and Intimacy" call-in radio program she had listened to during the drive when she turned off the ignition. Years of psychotherapy had convinced her that she, too, could stop showing up as a doormat. She had practiced "I" statements, "No" is a complete sentence, and "appropriate" boundaries in her mind over and over, with the goal of putting these "tools" to work in her life. She'd begun to believe she'd put down a foundation for rebuilding herself after her husband's death. The spooky drive made her realize she was nowhere near her goal.

Darlene sighed and glanced at her watch. Almost eight. *Oh, for a hot shower and a home cooked dinner.* Instead, a message pinned on the peeling green screen door greeted her, explaining that her hosts had suddenly been called away on urgent business. The message, "Make yourself at home and please feed the animals and keep an eye on things and we'll be back in a few and we're sorry and we love you," added an uneasy tone to an already unsettling day. *Why hadn't they called her?*

She decided to see to the animals before going inside. The two old Yellow Labs, Jack and Morpheus, leaped around her as she replenished their food and water. She patted their heads and rubbed their ears. They nosed her sweatshirt pocket for treats and wiggled and circled as she fed them a couple of cookies. The horses were in their stalls with plenty of feed and water. She closed the barn door, gathered her things out of the car, and climbed to the third story guest room. Emmy Lou, the McFarland's longhaired Persian, lounged on the bed.

"I'm tired, sweaty, and hungry," Darlene complained to the disinterested cat as she peeled off her clothes.

The hot water pounded on her achy neck and shoulder muscles. *Heaven!* She'd just arched her back to rinse her hair, when the lights went out and the shower slowed to a dribble, then stopped.

Blinded by soap and with her heart pounding way past aerobic, she climbed out of the claw foot bathtub onto the slippery linoleum. Struggling to escape the clingy plastic liner, she fell, banging her forehead on the edge of the wooden toilet seat.

"Damn it!" she shook her fist at the moon that provided scanty light through the paned bathroom window. She dabbed at the bump on her head with a towel, and gathered up itinerant strands of her graying red hair, storing them behind her ears. She wondered if the storm had blown a transformer or if a fuse in the basement had failed, *again.*

The basement! A memorable room indeed. The place where, during the many parties the old house had hosted in her youth, laughing, loaded guys would charge down the stairs to the fuse box whenever the electrical system gave out, silencing the disco music, *and turning off the well pump.* She remembered how their laughter had roared up the stairs as they screwed the new fuse in, and then out several times. The 30-year-old memory made her smile, but a grumble of thunder interrupted her reminiscing. *Or, was that her stomach?* She found her discarded clothes on the bathroom floor, wet from the rain. *Great!* Her robe and slippers were inside her suitcase somewhere in the dark bedroom so she wrapped herself in towels from the bath.

"Towels will have to do," she exclaimed, patting the sleeping cat on her way to the nightstand phone to call the power company. However, twinkling lights through the bedroom window from homes on the surrounding hills provided the answer to the cause of the power outage. She would have go to the basement.

Feeling her way along the wainscoting, Darlene threaded a painstaking path through the house to the basement door in the kitchen, bumping and scratching her bare arms and legs along the way.

A rubber dog toy squeaked in unison with her outcry when her foot squished it. "Ouch!" She stopped to take in a few deep breaths as she assessed her latest injury before starting down the basement stairs. Cautiously, she stepped onto the top platform and eased her way down the stairway to the second landing where the steps turned along a sidewall. Systematically, exploring each step with her foot before taking the next step, she eased her way downward. Grateful to be near the basement floor, she searched down the front side of the last step with the tip of her big toe, finding the sharp end of a protruding nail. "Damn it!" It had become her mantra.

She repeated it, louder this time, as a splinter from the rough unpainted railing pierced the soft skin between her thumb and first finger. Muttering under her breath, she adjusted the towel on her head, then rearranged its larger twin over her sagging 55-year-old breasts and pulled it securely around her bony butt. She stepped forward until her foot found the edge of the worn rug covering the cement floor. She soothed her hand for a few moments as her eyes adjusted to the dark.

The half-open bathroom door revealed a pull chain toilet with a wall-mounted tank and small pedestal sink. Intermittent moonlight through the small window over the tank illuminated the messy rectangular basement revealing old wicker lawn furniture, art supplies, tools, and a washer and dryer covered with unfolded laundry. Four wooden support posts were spaced evenly across the center of the room. The smell of cleaning supplies, potatoes, and fruit stored in wooden boxes mingled with the musty odors of forgotten items packed away in neatly stacked cardboard boxes. Dennis McFarland was a high school biology teacher near retirement, and he saved everything. An ancient desk dominated one corner; a dusty red phone rested on top next to a triple beam scale.

She wiped her soapy forehead with the back of her hand and listened to the rain drip from the eaves of the house onto the metal roof of the potting shed. Her thoughts began to wander.

Her husband, Brent, had gone missing nearly two years earlier while boating just north of San Francisco. Since then, she frequently found herself drawn to the coast, hypnotized by the neatly timed ebb and flow of the surf, like the questions that came rhythmically in and out of her mind since his disappearance. One of their neighbors, Sheila Tyler, had been the only person to see Brent on his 30-foot sailboat floundering in the surf just before it went down with him on board. Based on Sheila's statement, Sacramento had issued a death certificate.

How was it that Sheila just happened to be on the shore that day? That nagging question had charged existing fears in Darlene about a relationship between the two. They'd spent a lot of time together. "Just chitchat," Brent had assured her. Brent's dark looks warned Darlene not to pursue the subject. Shortly after the memorial, Sheila had sold her home and moved to Mexico.

An old furnace and ancient hot water heater sat on a platform in the corner under the stairs. Their fluttering pilot lights caught her attention. The frustrated guest-turned-house-and-pet-sitter sighed and rolled her shoulders as she watched the hearty little yellow blurs endure the drafts of wind from the partially open window. They wavered like the hopes she had during her marriage, she thought. After a round of abrasive, often cruel comments, Brent would bring home flowers, or take her to her favorite restaurant. A trip to Hawaii was her reward for the time he shoved her on her knees in front of him, and . . . Darlene decided not to relive that episode. Stopping the memory with a boundary wasn't easy outside of therapy. She looked around the basement and shuddered as she thought about the way he'd treated her. *The way I let him treat me.* She wanted to go home. But even if she didn't have the animals to look after, she was too tired to drive in this weather. She'd just have to make the best of it.

The dogs began to bark just as she reached for the box of fuses. She froze, listening intently. The sound of footsteps on the gravel driveway filtered through the partially open bathroom window. *Had her disgruntled thoughts and the din of the intermittent rain caused her to miss the arrival of a car?* I'll bet the storm caused Dennis and Fanny to return early, she thought. She would go home in the morning. At least there, the transformation to her new self seemed well underway. Here, her thoughts continued to wander.

In spite of the challenging relationship and unexpected financial difficulties she and Brent faced, Darlene had always deferred to his wishes in order to keep the peace, a role she unwittingly repeated with men she'd dated since. She had decided to temporarily stop dating and practice assertive techniques in other areas of her life. After all, developing healthy relationships would raise her self-esteem, she'd been told. *Insisting on good service from the people at the car wash and the snotty clerks at Whole Foods counted. Didn't it?*

Nonetheless, her life was unsettled. Fragmented. She had bought a small condominium at Lake Tahoe for a getaway. It provided a break from everything that was supposed to be familiar and comforting, but wasn't anymore. Adding to her consternation, questions about Brent constantly scratched around the edge of her mind, haunting every aspect of her life.

Darlene focused her thoughts on the present and readjusted her towels once again. She would stay put until Dennis and Fanny came down to the fuse box. They would realize the electricity was off shortly. She strained to hear through another brief earsplitting downpour. Was the kitchen door opening? The wood plank floor above her answered with tired creaks. The footsteps stopped right above her, then walked toward the basement door. The door opened and someone stepped onto the top landing. Before Darlene could call out, a teenage voice whispered, "Can't see shit."

Darlene squatted behind cardboard boxes. She pulled the hand towel partially over her face, and secured the bath towel, pulling the ends between her legs protectively. A dim figure groped its way down the staircase but hadn't reached the landing yet. She decided she had time to move behind a higher stack of boxes. Encumbered by the towels, she made her move.

"Ow, fuck!" A tumbling human windmill of arms and legs spilled down the stairs. A flailing arm caught the edge of her bath towel before she could escape its path and tossed it away.

"This is just great," the wounded teen chastised himself. Darlene didn't move as the boy continued, "Where are my glasses? This isn't worth it!"

She saw him try to stand up and fall back down. He moaned as he patted the floor for the glasses.

Darlene stepped back toward her hiding place. The sound of crunching metal and plastic filled the air.

"Fuck! Who's there?"

Darlene stood still, peeking from behind the stack of boxes. She saw the boy pull himself up and lean against the washer. Muttering to himself, he limped over to the fuse box. The scratch of a new fuse rolling in, followed by the sound of the refrigerator humming from the kitchen above, signaled Darlene to duck lower behind the boxes before he pulled the light cord for the basement lights.

Too late. The naked bulb played on her like a stage light. The goose bumps melted as her skin turned bright pink. She guessed her gaping audience was about seventeen years old.

Darlene kept an eye on the boy as she picked her towel off the floor. The teen was a heavy-set strawberry blonde. His hair was the color of hers when she was young, except his looked like it had been electrically shocked as it wired out from under his San Francisco Giants baseball cap. He wore a Giants T-shirt and baggy green hiking shorts. His feet sported old Teva hiking sandals. His blue eyes were traveling from her bare feet up to her half shampooed hair.

Darlene cleared her throat. "Are you okay, and who *are* you?"

"Who are *you*?" he asked,

"I'm an invited guest of the McFarlands, and I think I'd have remembered if they had mentioned they were expecting someone else. So, why are you here?" He did look somewhat familiar, she thought.

He rubbed his fingers gingerly up and down his leg. "My leg hurts like hell. You broke my shades, and your foot is bleeding."

She bent her knee to look back at the bottom of her foot. "Considering what I've just been through, what's a little more blood? Sorry about your glasses."

"That's okay. You look kind of familiar."

"So do you. How bad is your leg?"

"Humph," the teen snorted. "My knee is swelling, and look how red it's turning!" Darlene moved closer to examine the back of his leg. He continued, "You used to come here a lot."

She swallowed and took a deep breath. "My late husband went to school with the McFarlands. I'm Darlene Franklin. My husband was Brent Franklin."

"The dude that drowned?" He twisted toward her, temporarily forgetting his leg. "Ow, ow, ow! You're her?" he cradled his knee.

"Yes," Darlene said quietly.

The boy's jaw dropped. "That dude was Dennis' real good bud, wasn't he? I remember you. But, you look different. Thinner. Not that you were fat. You know about the money."

She laughed. "I know about the supposed buried treasure, those stories are terribly exaggerated."

He smiled. "I came to borrow some of it."

Darlene thought about the story of Dennis' father losing his job when the Salinas Firestone Company folded, and how they had started growing pot to make ends meet. After his dad found another job, they continued farming small crops, having acquired a high-quality strain that fetched top dollar. Plastic containers buried on the property and canning jars hidden in the basement stored millions around the property, or so the rumors went.

"Borrow? How can it be borrowing if you sneak in and take it while they are away? Weren't you really after the . . . pot?"

He shook his head. "No! No! My parents are having money problems, my mom's got cancer, and my dad's spending a lot of time taking care of her. He's a realtor and not selling many houses right now." His shoulders sagged and he shook his head.

Darlene watched him fight back tears. "What's your name, honey?"

"Seth Ritchie."

"Pleasure to meet you, Seth." Darlene extended her hand, carefully holding her towel tightly around her with her elbow.

He reached out to shake her hand. "I'm sorry to be such a pain. I don't think I can make it up the stairs."

"First things first, Seth. I'm going to run upstairs to rinse this shampoo out of my hair and get dressed. I'll be a few minutes, but you'll be okay down here." She settled him in a wicker chair and walked up the stairs to the first landing, then four more stairs up the back wall to the platform outside the kitchen door. She gripped the small round doorknob, turned it, and pushed. It didn't budge. She pushed again. "The door is locked!"

"What?" Seth looked up toward the landing.

She leaned over the railing. "The door is locked. Was anyone with you?"

Before he could answer, she sneezed and climbed back down the stairs. "Hold on," she said, "I'm going to see if any of this laundry will fit me before I get sick. Dennis is about my height, heavier, something of his will do. I'm in no position to be picky." She sorted through the pile of clean, unfolded laundry on top of the dryer.

"Towels!" she said. She examined the contents of the dryer.

"More towels!" She opened the washer and searched its unwashed contents.

"Sheets, dirty sheets. Yuk." She slammed the lid.

Examining the towels on top of the dryer as if she were shopping at Nordstrom's, she selected a large orange beach towel to replace her cold wet one. She found a smaller one to cover her wet hair. She smiled and modeled them for Seth's approval. Seth returned her smile and had started to say something when the basement door squeaked open. The voices of a man and a woman whispered secretively to one another from the top platform.

Darlene called out, "Dennis! Fanny! I'm down here! This, uh, uh, boy . . ." Darlene stopped talking abruptly. Her knuckles turned white as she gripped the towels. Her face, flushed from running up and down the stairs, dulled to gray-white. She slid down to the floor and sat, leaning against the washing machine.

Seth looked up the stairs and whispered under his breath, "Dude, you're supposed to be dead."

Brent Franklin's six-foot-four, 225-pound frame filled the staircase. Sheila Tyler stood behind him with her hand on his shoulder.

Sheila stood on her tiptoes and put her lips close to Brent's ear. "What in the hell are we supposed to do with the kid?"

"Shut up, let me think," Darlene's suddenly not-so-dead husband snarled. "No one is going to screw things up for me now. Move your ass, get that rope off the wall, and help me tie them up."

Sheila scurried to the basement wall and pulled a spool of clothesline from the array of arts and crafts tools hanging from various sized hooks. As she rejoined Brent, she said, "Honey, you mean *us*. Nothing is going to screw this up for *us*."

"Get that damned rope over here!" he bellowed, ignoring her comment.

Sheila's face turned as red as the basement phone. "Right, honey, I'm coming."

Brent grabbed Seth under his arms and dragged him to Darlene's side. Seth screamed and clutched his knee. Darlene tried to form words to speak to the frightened boy but her pale lips wouldn't move. Their eyes locked in shared fear.

They tied Darlene and Seth's hands together, and then bound them back to back to one of the four support posts. In the process, Darlene's towel had fallen to her waist. Brent and Sheila were halfway up the stairs when Darlene called out, "For God's sake, please cover me . . . I'm freezing. And, this boy is hurt." Brent just laughed as he reached the kitchen door. Sheila frowned, and then walked back down the stairs. Avoiding eye contact with Darlene, she picked up one of the large towels and wrapped it around Darlene's shoulders. She also put a towel across Seth's legs. Without a word, she climbed the stairs, turned off the basement light, and closed the kitchen door.

The rain had stopped. The room filled with broken shadows from the thin shaft of moonlight peeping through the moving clouds.

Darlene could hear Seth gulping and coughing. He whispered, "You okay?" When she didn't answer, he repeated the question. "Are you okay?"

She was trembling. *Why not divorce? The money? Does he want all of the money? Are they going to rob me? Kill me? And what about Seth? And, are Dennis and Fanny involved in this?* The realization that Brent and Sheila had somehow faked his death to be together overwhelmed her. Yet she began to realize that, deep down, she already knew he was capable of the unimaginable. She shook off numbness and shock as she accepted the reality of her present situation.

"I'm, I'm okay, Seth."

She thought about the days before and after the accident, remembering Sheila testifying convincingly that she saw him go down with the boat.

"What are they doing? Why?" Darlene voiced her thoughts.

Seth shifted his shoulders to try to get some blood flow to his hands. "There was money, right? Life insurance. We all heard it was a lot."

"Three million. I used most of it to help get the business out of trouble." She squinted up the stairs. "Two months ago, Stan, our partner, bought me out for four million." As she said the words, knots formed in her stomach and perspiration dampened her face. Brent's plan suddenly became clear to her.

"Shit. What're we gonna do?" Seth's voice quivered.

"Do? Tied up like a couple of jailbirds, me in towels and you with one good leg?"

His back stiffened. "Listen. Is that a car?" Darlene leaned in the direction of the bathroom window. "Sounds like Dennis' old Dodge truck," he said.

The two captives looked up at the ceiling as the sound of footsteps and voices filled the room above them. Brent and another man were yelling. Chairs and the kitchen table scraped the floor above them, a heavy cooking pot or metal vase hit the floor, and the basement door opened. Dennis and Fanny McFarland descended into the dungeon with their hands in the air. Brent towered over Dennis, pushing the balding, pony-tailed hippy along with a shotgun pressed between his broad shoulders. Dennis' nose was bleeding profusely down the front of his T-shirt. A few steps behind, Fanny stumbled along looking over her shoulder at the pistol Sheila pointed at her. After tying Dennis and Fanny together against another post, they started back up the stairs.

Darlene called out, "Wait. What do you want? Talk to us. The boy is hurt."

The pair, who had reached the first landing, stopped and looked down. Sheila tugged at Brent's shirtsleeve.

"Brent?"

"Fuck the little bastard," Brent said rubbing his left shoulder. "Fanny's a pot-head," he hissed. "Maybe she'll share some of her stash to ease his pain. Come on, we need to get the computer hooked up."

The kitchen light shining down the stairs reflected off Brent's pasty, scowling face. Darlene remembered how vain Brent used to be about his appearance. He was always tan from sailing, and fit from working out. He and Sheila whispered angrily as they disappeared into the kitchen.

Finally, Dennis broke the silence. "Darlene, I don't know where to start . . ." Sounding relieved to finally be letting it out, he went on about how Brent knew about the pot farming operation, and used it to black-mail them into keeping his faked death a secret. Then, when Sheila's money ran out, he'd started extorting money from them. Dennis explained that when Brent learned Darlene had sold her share of the business, he'd decided he was entitled to some of the proceeds. Finally, his voice breaking into sobs, Dennis admitted that he and Fanny had invited Darlene to the ranch at Brent's demand, and then disappeared, leaving her alone for him.

"I swear, Darlene, we knew he'd planned to get money out of you, but we never imagined he'd hurt you, until . . . just a few minutes ago."

So, that was the deal. Brent plans to kill me, and live happily ever after with his bimbo and the money from the business the life insurance saved. Son of a bitch!

Dennis went on, "We knew he'd faked his death to get out of the bad situation with the business and, well, you had the life insurance that put it back on top financially." Dennis tried to wipe his nose on his shoulder but the ropes were too tight. "Brent told us he just wanted to be with Sheila. I'm so damned stupid."

Fanny's bloodshot eyes peeked out from behind shoulder length slate-gray hair. Her thick voice echoed her husband's sentiments dramatically. "Darlene, we are so sorry." The tie dyed V-necked T-shirt heaved as she breathed. Her loose breasts, braless for decades, floated over folds of stomach fat. An ankle length black tiered skirt hung from her narrow hips over skinny legs and huaraches-clad feet. Her serious mood left her and she giggled, "Where are your clothes?"

Before Darlene could respond, Brent and Sheila opened the kitchen door. They heard Sheila whisper, "We can't just burn four people. Let's just transfer the money like we planned and get the hell out of here."

"Shut up," Brent snarled.

Sheila tapped him gently on the top of his shoulder with the barrel of her pistol.

"You shut up, smart ass. You promised me this couldn't fail. A fire is going to attract a little attention," she added sarcastically.

Brent grabbed Sheila's throat and pushed her to her knees glaring into her eyes. She looked away and he released her. She dropped to the floor. Sweating and breathing heavily, Brent wobbled into the kitchen. Looking back over his shoulder, he said, "Get up, bitch. Get that god damned computer going." Waves of memories washed over Darlene. Her eyes were riveted to Sheila's face and she felt sick to her stomach.

The light from the kitchen emphasized Sheila's washed-out complexion and the shadows surrounding her hazel eyes. Her dark hair was pulled into a tight bun at the back of her neck revealing creases and lines on her face. Her thin neck extended out from tired, rounded shoulders. Darlene thought how beautiful and healthy the 46-year-old woman had been just a few years ago. She felt a tinge of sympathy for Sheila, except . . .

Sheila slammed the door and locked it. The small group sat quietly. Shadows of the room's contents seemed to move around them. Cold wind blew leaves through the bathroom window, decorating the floor and fixtures. After about ten minutes, the light spilled down the steps again when Brent stepped onto the landing from the kitchen.

"Okay, assholes, listen up," he shouted as he descended the stairs to the second landing where he stopped, sweating and out of breath.

"Sounds like dialogue from a bad movie," Seth murmured.

"What's that, you little shit?"

The three adults clucked protectively. Dennis said, "Nothing. Nothing, Brent. The kid's a little scared, that's all."

Brent rubbed his left arm with his right hand as he pointed the shotgun from person to person with his left. "I want all of you to sit still and be very, very quiet while Darlene and I conduct a little overdue business."

He walked over to Darlene, bent down, and breathed, "You're going to give Sheila all the info she needs to transfer the money you got from my business. Comprendo, Señora?"

His breath repulsed her. She closed her eyes and fought off the urge to beg him. *Beg him for what?* She felt his fingers pinching her chin and opened her eyes. His bloodshot brown eyes stared at her.

She held her voice steady. "Fuck you." *Not an appropriate response,* her therapist's voice rang in her head, *but better than the usual.* She felt amazingly clear-headed.

He laughed, "Whoa, little woman learn to talk nasty words after husband goes away. Codes, passwords, pin numbers are the only words I want from the hole in your face. I'm claiming my money, sweetheart."

"Humph."

"I'm not impressed," he snorted. "Maybe you'd even die to fuck me out of the money, but what about one of these?" He turned the shotgun toward the group, pointing directly at Dennis, then Fanny, and finally Seth.

"This one's already wounded. I'll take him out first."

He looked at Sheila.

"What do ya think, baby? How about the kid first?"

Darlene and Dennis began speaking at the same time. Fanny nodded in agreement with all the deals proposed to save their lives. Dennis promised to give Brent all the money he could find on the property, sell the ranch, if necessary. Darlene argued for a divorce and agreed to give up all the money in exchange for their lives. Seth kept his eye on the shotgun and said nothing.

A knocking sound from upstairs interrupted the negotiations. Brent hushed the group and looked at his watch.

"Ten-thirty, who could that be? Sheila, keep everyone quiet. Cut Fanny loose. She's going upstairs with me. Get that laptop set up. Hurry up, baby." He watched her untie Fanny, but didn't notice she forgot to tie Dennis' bound hands back to the post.

"Good, baby." He attempted to pat Sheila's butt, but she stepped away from him.

He pushed Fanny up the stairs with the shotgun. She put her shaking hands in the air and tried to stay ahead of the barrel.

"Put your hands down, stupid," Brent instructed her. They disappeared into the kitchen and the lock snapped shut. Sheila seemed deep in thought as she studied the stacks of cardboard boxes, then the ceiling, the walls, and finally she just stared out the small bathroom window. She drummed her fingers slowly on top of the computer.

"Thanks for putting the towel over me, Sheila," Darlene said.

"You're, uh, welcome. It's cold down here." Sheila pointed the gun barrel toward the kitchen door then across her lips to remind everyone to be quiet.

"Right. Yes, keep quiet. Well, I just wanted you to know how much I appreciated the gesture. You were very kind." Darlene smiled.

"He's not very nice to you," Seth piped in.

"Seth, stop," Darlene warned.

"Well, he's not," he said with disgust.

Dennis joined Seth's chorus. "He's a monster. Sheila, can't you see that? Look at yourself . . . at what you're becoming. He's planning to burn this house with us in it, isn't he?"

"Of course not." She wound the telephone cord around her hand.

"We heard you whispering about it," they all chimed.

Sheila mumbled, "Just talk. He wants . . . He's been tired . . . all the time. He hasn't been dealing with the stress of living in hiding, the food, and weather. When he has the money, things will be better. We'll tie you up and be out of the country before you're rescued. Everyone just shut up about Brent. I have to set this computer up before they return or he'll kick someone's ass. I'd prefer it not be mine."

Darlene snorted.

"What do you mean by that?"

"I've known the man for thirty years, Sheila. He has two moods. Nice when he wants something, nasty when he gets it. He knocked you to the ground, called you names. He doesn't care about anyone but himself. He's a pig. Don't you have any self-respect?" Darlene felt good as she expressed her feelings toward him for the first time outside of therapy.

The kitchen door opened and Brent came down with Fanny.

"No one was there, the wind knocked a window screen loose," he said angrily. "Is that computer set up?"

Darlene squared her shoulders and held her head up.

"Fuck you."

Brent pointed the shotgun at Seth. Without hesitating, he fired as he swung it above the boy's head hitting the wall and ceiling. A rain of silt, wood chips and padding, and the acrid smell of cordite filled the air. They all screamed and turned their faces toward the floor.

"For Christ's sake, Brent," Dennis yelled. "You could've killed the kid."

Sheila had dropped the cord she had taken out of the phone to put in the computer. She fell to her knees searching for it behind the desk.

"I'm almost there, Brent," she said holding up the cord in her shaking hand.

Brent glared at Dennis. "What the hell do you care about that brat? The little prick probably came here to steal from you. Sheila, get off the floor." His eyes were bugging out of sagging, ring-lined sockets.

He pointed the shotgun toward Fanny at the foot of the stairs.

"Quiet down, you assholes. Fanny, tell Darlene how fast that old barn would burn."

"Please, don't hurt my animals," Fanny begged.

Darlene caught a glimpse of the dogs as they darted past the bathroom window. She wondered if their doggy door was unlocked. She noticed that Dennis had seen them, too, and saw in his eyes that the loose dogs could open an opportunity to escape. Dennis leaned toward Brent. "Jesus Christ, Brent, are you going to kill all of us?"

"That depends on Darlene."

"I'll give you the passwords and pin numbers, everything you need. Just let them go . . ." Darlene practiced her most assertive tone.

"No deals, Darlene," Brent said.

"You'll kill me anyway. Let them go."

"If you don't cooperate, I'll kill them one at a time right in front of your fucking ridiculous face."

She could feel Seth loosening the line binding their wrists. She wondered if he had seen the dogs, too.

"I don't have them memorized. They're upstairs in my purse."

Running, whinnying horses caught everyone by surprise as they ran by the window.

"What the hell?" Brent was beyond furious. "Fanny's god damned horses are loose? Sheila, get your ass up there. Fanny, go with her and you'd better catch those animals before they reach the road."

Sheila shot Brent a tired look. She picked up the pistol. Reluctantly, she pointed it at Fanny and motioned for her to go upstairs.

The rest watched wide-eyed as Brent paced back and forth cursing and swearing under his breath. He kicked at the dust bunnies and laundry lint that cluttered the basement floor. The veins on his flushed face and neck looked like red and blue lines on a road map. He grimaced and seemed to fight to breathe.

Something began bumping and scratching at the kitchen door.

"Now what?" Brent snarled.

He crept up the stairs, stopping a couple of times, coughing. Suddenly, he assaulted the stairs, awkwardly ascending them two at a time.

He reached the top landing out of breath and wet with sweat. Gasping, he turned the doorknob. Jack and Morpheus pushed the door open and bolted past him. He tried to lift the shotgun to fire at them but lost his balance. He hit the cement stairs hard and rolled down to rest on the landing in the corner. The shotgun clattered to the floor next to Dennis. The dogs stopped to sniff Brent's motionless body, then jumped over him, running to sit quietly by Dennis.

Sheila and Fanny appeared on the platform. Sheila screamed, dropped the pistol on the landing, and ran down to Brent. She examined his face and eyes with her hands.

"Help," she cried.

Dennis ran up to the landing and turned his back to her.

"Untie me, Sheila."

"Untie us, we'll all help," Darlene called out.

"I'll do it," Fanny said and ran down the stairs. While Sheila untied Dennis, Fanny untied Darlene and Seth. Dennis checked Brent's neck for a pulse.

Darlene rubbed her wrists. "Is, is he . . . dead?"

Dennis nodded.

Sheila frowned. "Yes, Darlene, this time he's really dead. And, the son of a bitch left me holding the bag. I should've known."

Dennis picked up the pistol and retrieved the shotgun from the floor. "Come back down here, Sheila," he said.

She was shaking and crying, but Darlene wasn't moved.

"You would have let him kill us!"

"Do you really believe I had any control over him? Ever? He made everything—*everything* uncomplicated. Faking, lying, stealing sounded like going Christmas shopping coming from him." She pounded on her chest with clenched fists. "I was hooked on his promises. During the past few hours, I was as scared as any of you. I didn't know that he planned to push you down the stairs, Darlene. Then Seth showed up so he was going for a deep-sea swim. Then when Fanny and Dennis returned . . . yes, yes, he talked about burning the lot of you. I didn't want to kill anyone. Believe me." She thumped her forehead with the heel of her hand. "At least I'm not going to prison for murder," she laughed. "I'm going because I'm a fool."

"Sounds like a line from a bad western song," Seth moaned.

"I don't think anyone here wants to call the cops," Darlene said. "Do you care what happens to Brent's body? I sure don't."

"Neither do I," Sheila spit out the words. She walked over to the desk, packed up her computer, and headed up the stairs without looking back. They heard her running through the kitchen and out of the house. A few moments later they heard her van speed down the driveway.

Dennis started up the stairs, but Darlene stopped him. "I say we let her go. She's alone and broke. Why let her end up in some country club prison?"

They all nodded in agreement.

Dennis addressed the group. "We'll give Brent a proper good-bye. But, I want all of you to remember, he drowned two years ago. Deal?"

"Deal," they chorused.

With some effort, Dennis dragged Brent's body into the kitchen while Fanny pulled some sheets out of the laundry to wrap it.

"Darlene, if we're not calling the cops, what happens now?" Seth asked.

"Very little," Darlene yawned, rubbing her empty stomach.

"What do you mean?"

Darlene stroked the dogs' heads and ears as she spoke. "I mean, you'll still be a student at Carmel High trying to figure out a way to help out your parents." *Maybe Dennis will discover some buried treasure while he's digging Brent's grave.* "Dennis and Fanny will continue as before." *I may suggest they look into some of those twelve-step programs.* "Sheila, well, she's probably half way to Mexico by now." *Broke and alone.* "As for me, I will still be Brent's widow." *Free at last.*

She felt Seth's hand on her elbow.

"What are we going to tell my folks?"

"Your parents will be thrilled that you're in one piece. Now, if you've completed your interrogation, I am going to change. Jack, Morpheus.

Stay."

He pulled the dogs close and winked at her as she walked toward the stairs. "Everyone's going to miss your toweled look."

Divine

by Lele Dahle

In the night I still whisper,
Can you feel my breath to your ear?
I tell you you're mine forever,
And that I'll always be near.

He awoke surrounded by the ghost musk of Chantal's scent. It mingled with the dank breath of the ocean, and swirled through sounds of howling wind and pounding surf. Still awash in the mire of dreaming, Moran found himself tottering over a high rocky cliff, gazing down into an eddy of angry sea foam. Corbusier stood beside him, also watching, then leaned over the cliff's edge and spat into transparent space now separating living from newly departed.

A deep involuntary sob escaped Moran's throat before he managed to wrench himself loose from demon memories to face a streaky red dawn.

Moran finished measuring and filling five and ten pound bags of chicken mash. He'd done the scratch, some pellets, and was starting in on wild-birdseed, dipping the measuring scoop into a 100 pound bag when his granddaughter Laura walked in. She'd take over at the feed store for the remainder of the day. Will, Laura's father, would be outside backing the truck to the warehouse and pulling up heavy aluminum doors, commencing afternoon feed deliveries.

Laura dropped her school books on the counter, shot a quick hello in

Moran's direction, then went over to where the guinea hens and rabbits were housed and pretended to busy herself with cleaning. He knew she only fussed this way in his presence, because mornings after, the cages still lay in their mucked up state. But hell, she was only fifteen.

"Take it easy there sis, don't work y'self too hard." He hunkered the Stetson securely down on his head and walked out, chuckling under his breath. She wouldn't be working too hard. But her Pa out there wrestling with hay bales and sacks of barley was a good one. Strong as a goddamn Clydesdale, like he himself had been once upon a blue Kentucky moon.

Moran hefted himself into the truck and drove westward, leaving the sprawling city of Salinas behind. He passed orderly green fields of lettuce, and then the road began to ribbon through country dappled with oak and low lying brush. He made a left at Corral de Tierra Road.

It was still early spring, but the last few days were unusually hot, soaring into the high 80s. Rain had fallen steadily for weeks prior, and now, contained within the clear blue swelter was lung-smothering humidity. Once freely growing plump grass was laying flat. Moran drove into gently swelling hills that would be golden too soon if this weather prevailed. Oaks grew thicker, the road narrower. He veered suddenly off the pavement and braked in front of an orange cattle gate, pressed the remote to open, and then moved carefully through to the road there; dirt soft, choked with weeds. His 90 acres. Up, up, driving, topping a hill-crest, and before him, broken and weathered, lay the skeleton of the house he'd set out to build for Chantal nearly four decades before.

Moran parks his truck; picks up the slim, rectangular box lying on the seat next to him. The wood is cherry, deep-grained and recently oiled. He steps down, walks over to the half-constructed house that was fresh smelling raw timber in 1966, turns briefly to admire the vista, then sets the box down on what was once the promise of a porch.

Carefully, he raises the lid and takes out one of the divining rods; there are two of them in there. The one he chooses is made of whalebone. It looks like an oversized turkey wishbone. Walking to the back of the dilapidated house, he scans the hills until his eyes rest upon a shed. The pump house. Moran carefully positions his fingers upon the rod-ends, tip pointing forward, and makes for the well. This can be only ritual now. He already knows how the rod will quiver and dip, for he divined this water himself those many years ago, with his dark haired wife Chantal watching, and her daddy, Nathan Corbusier, mentor and teacher, looking on.

A vast sea is within the dominion of every human. Housed in the brain, it is called the unconscious, and has possession of about 90 percent of our thought processes. The measly remainder, which comprises our conscious mind, swoops and dips into this measureless imponderable during waking time, much as a bird might wing down for a drink. It is believed by some who have studied the nether-land of the brain, that contained within is every particle of knowledge ever collected, including the physical laws of the universe.

The student of divining learns that each cell in their body knows how to find water, and has always known. There is but one discipline: to achieve a state whereby one's conscious mind can gain passage to their inner sanctum of fathomless wealth.

Moran's consciousness isn't perceiving in any ordinary manner. He has surrendered to a diviner's reality. He has given an order. The answer comes. The rod begins to vibrate, and then it dips full down; a rich vein of water has been identified deep within earth.

The California coastal mountains are home to the western rattlesnake, a pit viper, member of the family Crotalidae, one of the most dangerous snakes in the world. If winter had held, this female viper would've still been hibernating underground. But unusual warmth has drawn her out, and she is basking in the tall grass near the pump house, her winter-cold blood molten.

Moran isn't thinking about snakes. His mind is floating; he's as unencumbered as air. What was it Corbusier told him? "Matter is in no way solid, but merely a manifestation of energy in its most dense form." Then he'd asked, "Okay . . . what do you think water is?"

He has gotten a positive reaction from the rod and located the main stream. Now Moran must go sideways to identify stream band and parallels. Inner parallels are points on either side perpendicular to the main stream, where the rod will have slightly less pull than the main stream. Using graduated parallels, he will be able to make an estimation of water depth. Moran swivels lightly away from the reaction point and blindly tramples on the reposing viper. She shatters the quiet with a frantic rattle warning and bolts upward. Her body wraps around Moran's leg as she sinks fangs deep into flesh. He shrieks, tries to shake her off, stumbles and falls.

With lightning speed she strikes again, and again. Moran scrambles to rise, and then runs. Safely away, he rips his shirt open to see if all of this has really happened, for it is too unreal and horrible to have actually happened. On the side of his chest are visible fang marks, more on his forearm, already throbbing with pain.

He goes to the porch, sits, and pulls his jeans down to his knees. Skin is already beginning to discolor and swell around the punctures on his thigh. Moran realizes that he most likely will die. He wouldn't survive a strike to the torso, even if help came this moment. His eyes search longingly down the weedy road; they can't focus far enough now to see the cow gate.

Pain intensifies and is excruciating. But as a merciful cocktail of endorphins and shock-inducing adrenalin begins to flow into his bloodstream, a hazy cast of mind takes over. Moran leans his back up against the house and waits. He wonders; if a whole lifetime does indeed flash before one's eyes in those minutes preceding death, why is it now he can only think of *her?*

It was long before things went down with Chantal. In those days, Moran possessed a brightness and optimism that infected everyone around him. He'd been a quiet, luminous child with curious gray eyes, sandy hair and a muscular build. In 1965, at the age of 24, he was already half owner of Ranch Hay and Feed, and engaged to marry Patsy Rainer, his childhood sweetheart. He'd put a thousand dollar down-payment on the 90 acres out in the hills that lay between Salinas and Monterey, and was making plans to build a home there.

Old-timer Pete Satterfield was at the feed store one morning listening to Moran talk about sinking a well on his 90 acres. Pete told him the best thing would be to hire a water-witch. There was a diviner he knew down in Big Sur. Called Nathan Corbusier. Somewhat clannish, this Cajun, had two grown sons and a daughter. "Finest there is, kid. He'd be your man. Hell, I'll look him up for you."

A week later Pete told Moran that Corbusier was going to divine a water site out in Carmel Valley. He'd wrangled them an invitation by explaining that Moran was a potential client. The occasion would be at the Jenkins ranch, some fifteen miles out beyond Carmel Valley's village. The well that had been going strong there for twenty years dried up suddenly, leaving the rancher desperate for water, with limited financial resources. There would only be enough money for one sink, so this diviner needed to be as good as all get out.

Moran waits in the shadow of the flagging day. He's sweating, feels heavy as a boulder, and is straining to breathe. The sticky mess of erupted vomit all down his chest is beginning to attract flies. There are two parallels of thought going on: monitoring his poison racked body, and framing the day he met Nathan Corbusier.

Though of average stature, Corbusier seemed larger than life. He had broad shoulders, thick silver hair tied back into a ponytail, a narrow, tanned face and the most intense blue eyes Moran had ever seen. One of his grown sons accompanied him that morning; Jacques, a spitting image of the old man in a younger time. The two were already out scouting the 160 acres when Pete and Moran showed up, coming down only to have a hurried lunch. Corbusier apologized for not allowing spectators; he said they were working too great an area and needed to concentrate without distractions, but when water was located, they'd give a demonstration of the rod's ability.

By late afternoon, father and son could be seen ambling toward the house, Corbusier swinging his rod in one hand. An underground stream had been divined, wide and plentiful. Corbusier led them all back to where the new well would be sunk, which he'd marked with an oak branch. Unlike the brooding, uncommunicative man Moran had witnessed earlier, Corbusier was now in a festive mood. His walk was a strut. He practically danced around the stake in the ground. Moran got caught up in the swirling vortex that seemed to be radiating from the man, and began to feel lightheaded.

Corbusier was still brandishing the rod when he came up to Moran. He held it out. "Have you ever tried the rod?" Moran was speechless. "Give her a whirl, man. This is the way to hold it, just so, put your fingers on the edge, then pull it taut." He placed his own to demonstrate, then took Moran's hands and positioned them upon the rod.

"Okay. Now we're gonna find water." He raised one arm with a flourish. "Water!" His words were punctuated around a Cajun-French dialect. Corbusier instructed Moran to close his eyes, then gently led him away from the site and turned him around a couple of times. "Okay, man. Now. Where's the water? And keep your eyes closed. Don't move yet. Feel the rod. Sense the water." Moran held himself still. "You know where it is. You don't know how, but you know." The sun slid behind the mountain, birthing a sudden chill. The small group watching was silent; mesmerized.

As Moran concentrated, he had the growing sensation of his body pulling downward into the bowels of the earth. The rod began to lightly vibrate through his fingers like a captive insect. He moved cautiously forward, then swiveled to the left, didn't know why, just felt compelled to do so, and soon the rod was trembling to the rhythm of some song in his body. Suddenly, it jerked downward. He opened his eyes, surprised.

"Bingo." Corbusier's voice was muted, his expression serious. Jacques scowled.

Moran murmured, "I don't know how that happened . . ."

Corbusier clasped his hand around Moran's shoulder and spoke furtively into his ear. "You'll do it, man. Divine your own well site. All you need is a little guidance. Come down to my house next week and we'll have a lesson. Brother, you've got the gift."

Moran is reclining now, his swelling body racked with pain; breath coming in short rasps. His eyes can only see blurs of color, yet his mind is still thinking clearly, rabidly clear, which seems a miracle. He is reliving the day he first met Corbusier's daughter, Chantal. Her hair was dark and shiny like Jacques', but she had a face that was broader, fuller lips, and hazel eyes shaded by dark eyelashes. With a lithe build, beautiful posture, and a way of moving through space that seemed like gliding, she reminded Moran of a swan. Chantal, the dark swan.

The Carmel area possesses inimitable magic; a unique blend of heady scents begot of union between mountain and sea. Southbound, the coastline is unrivaled upon earth for its beauty. The ocean bottom falls abruptly offshore into a mile-deep ravine called Monterey Canyon. From sandy, rockbound beaches, gently molded hills give way to steep cliffs that ascend skyward into the chaparral tangled Santa Lucia cordilleras. Two-lane Highway 1 meanders the edge of this, with only occasional protective stone barriers between road and a spectacular freefall hundreds of feet down to the Pacific Ocean. The going has no choice but to be slow as the highway ascends and dips, curving; always curving.

As he navigated the coast road, Moran felt like he was entering an enchanted world. From childhood he'd made a pilgrimage every spring to go Steelhead fishing at the mouths of the Big and Little Sur rivers. Succulent trout that didn't get cooked over a smoky beach fire were wrapped and stored in the freezer for summer barbecues. Pan fried in winter with butter and herbs, the aroma conjured up memories of himself in waders knee deep in rushing water, silently acknowledging that life didn't get much better than this.

The late summer morning was suspended in drifting fog. Corbusier was to meet Moran at Fernwood, a cluster of tiny rental cottages perched alongside the road near Big Sur's village. His place was south of Big Sur, and, according to Corbusier, difficult to find. Moran pulled off the highway in front of Fernwood and waited. No cars came from the south for a good ten minutes. Then a rusted Studebaker coupe drove through, slowing in front of the cabins. Moran watched the female inside make a visual sweep. She spotted his Ford truck, crept over and rolled the window down. "Are you Moran?"

He choked a reply. "Yep, I'm he."

"My father wanted me to show you down to our place. Follow me." She gave him the hint of a smile, as if she approved of this man with the wholesomely boyish demeanor and cowboy shirt, well-favored in the looks department. He made a quick assessment of her; a few years older than he and starkly attractive, her pale complexion set off by dark hair pulled loosely into a ponytail. The French accent edged her into a category of exotic.

A few miles south of Big Sur they turned onto a narrow switchback dirt road that roamed up through lanky redwoods until finally straightening upon a knoll with breathtaking ocean views. In front of the house stood a tall, roughly sculpted wooden sculpture of some kind of bird; a Phoenix, Moran would later learn. The home was an unimpressive shack that looked to be 1930's vintage, with two more recently constructed wings, like afterthoughts.

As Moran's eyes scanned the grounds, he couldn't help but think of his mother's crocheted doilies that were displayed upon tabletops, and hand knit afghans draped over couch and chairs. Her quaint china cabinet with an odd assortment of County Fair won trinkets and delicate bone-china teacups. The Isthmus of Corbusier was a universe apart from the faded, dusty-rose wallpaper on bedroom walls of the modest South Salinas childhood home where he yet lived and slept.

Inside the house were concrete floors imbedded with pebbles and pieces of sparkling abalone shell. Adorning them were well worn, richly patterned oriental rugs. Discordant Picasso-esque paintings hung upon unpainted redwood paneled walls. The furniture was crudely carved like the Phoenix outside. Ferns and other potted plants sat in corners and upon tables. Classical music streamed out from one of the wings.

Moran is lying down, his body curling into itself. Strange how it could be chilly now, when earlier the sun had labored down such infernal heat. The day has degenerated to inky black. He feels cold, tries to pull the jeans up beyond his thighs, manages somehow, then swings his mind back to the scene unfolding before him.

Chantal wordlessly left him in the living room and disappeared down the hall. Corbusier emerged. "Good! You've come. We have work to do." He swept an arm up, gesturing Moran toward the kitchen. Upon the table were various wood branches and a tangle of metal wire. "We're gonna make you some instruments."

He poured two cups of thick black coffee from a pot on the stove; Moran could see broken eggshell amongst grounds in the bottom. "Hobo coffee! The way I like it. With chicory."

They spent the next hour constructing rods, one of metal, and one of wood. Then Corbusier took him outside and led him to the well. "This is where we start. Water is here, we know it is, so we'll begin by walking away from the well, then returning to it, so that you can get accustomed to the reaction of the rod. I want you to concentrate on nothing but the earth down underground. You need to learn to see, not with your eyes, but with your whole body.

"The rod there you're holding is only incidental. The instrument is you. Remember this always. There are diviners out there who don't even need a rod. Ever heard of Einstein? Einstein told the world, he *proved* this: matter isn't solid, but energy manifesting itself in its most dense form. So, we are pure energy. What do you think water is?"

Moran thought hard so he could respond, but Corbusier continued. "Water is energy we are very, very attracted to. Wild animals, they know how to find the water. Okay, now, what is thought? Thought is energy, just like our bodies are. Thoughts themselves can be tracked, because scientists have figured out how the brain sends out signals and all of that . . . what you'd call a measurable function. So . . . what about the content of the thought? What's that?"

He started to feel the same way he had at Jenkins ranch, like some kind of current emanating from Corbusier was affecting his perception. The sensation was fervent and confusing.

"When your brain gives a command to your body, say to make it sit down, or walk, you are performing another kind of thought, or measurable function. You are giving your body an instruction. Right? I'm going to show you how to take this concept one step further. You will instruct your body to find the water. The process of divining is just like you telling it to sit down, or walk. However, you will be accessing a different state of consciousness, one that is immeasurable; without bounds. Don't worry about understanding this now. In time you will come to feel and know what I'm talking about.

"I want you to give a command to your body. Okay? That day at Jenkins ranch you did it."

"I found the water."

"Yes, you found the water."

⟍

Moran had stumbled into an enchanted world that held him spellbound. Corbusier was an apt teacher, leading Moran through time-layers of sediment, into his antediluvian sea. He learned to swim in Corbusier's described "consciousness of immeasurability". In that cast of mind he discovered Chantal. She was seeing a married man. Their secret meeting place was a cabin her lover had rented south of Big Sur, near the tiny settlement of Lucia. In the unfolding months under Corbusier's tutelage, he studied her when he happened upon her, divined her longing for the man who wouldn't or couldn't leave his wife, and came to bask in the luminary glow of ardor and torment that radiated from her. He didn't realize he was falling in love.

Corbusier and daughter fought often over her relationship with the wedded man. After their worst fights she'd leave and be gone for days, but always came back, would be subdued for a time, then the cycle began again. On one occasion when Moran arrived at the house he was shocked to find her nursing a swollen face and black eye. An unanticipated fury ignited as he pondered which had struck the blows, father or lover.

His new life was causing complications at home, and with his fiancée Patsy. Nathan Corbusier hadn't merely taken him under his wing; he'd made Moran a disciple and demanded full-out commitment. The job description was dubious; often he'd call Moran to his house and they'd do nothing but sit on a knoll and wordlessly gaze out to the ocean.

Patsy, who'd known Moran since childhood, grew bewildered and angry as he increasingly disregarded her. Childish threats to leave failed to get any kind of reaction. She'd been helping out at the feed store, and felt short-changed by his absences as she covered for him more and more. His parents regarded the relationship with Corbusier with guarded suspicion, and were rebuffed whenever the subject came up.

⟍

Moran is no longer conscious. He has lapsed into a tormented sleep. Still, the story goes on. He dreams of Garrapata Beach.

⟍

One morning while he was waiting for Corbusier in the living room, she came to him. Later he would wonder if Corbusier had been a party to it all, and became convinced; not only was he party to it, but must have been master designer.

"Moran. I need to talk to you." She'd never needed to talk to him before. As was usual for him, he remained silent for longer than seemed acceptable, so she continued, flustered. She put her hand on his arm. "Moran." He looked searchingly upon her face. It was a troubled face, and one distorted by desire. What kind of desire, he couldn't discern. He wasn't fool enough to entertain, even casually, any manner of expectation, yet the current of excitement caused by her touch rendered him breathless with its suggestion.

"My father wanted me to tell you he had to leave. Won't be back until tonight." She paused, hunting for the right effect. "Moran. Let's go to the beach! I can pack a picnic."

They got into her car and headed north to Garrapata. It was a perfect Indian summer day, warm, with a fragrant whisper of breeze. The long stretch of beach was deserted. They set towels and picnic basket down upon pebbly sand in a tiny cove sheltered by high rock outcroppings. The tide was low, the smell of exposed seaweed pungent. Flies buzzed around piles of kelp tossed up by the now receding high tide.

Chantal pulled a bottle of wine from the basket.

To Moran's touch, Chantal's skin felt smooth like the surface of a water polished river rock that still had all the heat of the day in it. She pressed her body hard against his chest and forced her tongue into his mouth. His body responded to her fervor, but there was something unsettling about it that momentarily disturbed him. He dismissed the sensation, buried his face in her ocean spray scented hair and succumbed. The bottom fell out of the world.

It was around midnight when Moran pulled up in the driveway of his parent's house. His was physically drained, skin parched, but felt buoyant. Curiously, all inside lights were on. As he walked hesitantly toward the front door, his father abruptly opened it. His eyes were gleaming with dark emotion, and Moran felt instant panic. "What's wrong?"

"Your mother." He put a hand up over his eyes. "Your mother has passed on. A very bad heart attack."

Moran's legs threatened to collapse. The perfect enchantment of that afternoon, lying naked on the beach making love to Chantal became, in one instant, a punishable offence. He pulled his father into an embrace and began to weep.

Moran was finished at the feed store and locking up when Corbusier emerged from the darkness, wearing an angry scowl. "Chantal is pregnant." Moran's breath sucked in and wouldn't come out. Corbusier grabbed the front of Moran's shirt and thrust him against the building. "You gotta marry her, man." Moran heard the words, but grappled clumsily with their meaning.

He mentally counted the weeks—it had been about five since the occurrence at Garrapata Beach. Those weeks had been all about burying his mother, consoling his father, and wrestling with guilt.

There hadn't been any contact with Corbusier or Chantal since the night he'd telephoned with bad news. Moran reconciled with Patsy, they'd even set a wedding date.

"Is it mine?" At this, Corbusier made a fist and socked him in the gut. Moran was too shocked to react.

"You bastard! Listen. You're gonna go to her. Tonight. Now. You're gonna propose to her."

Moran had never seen Corbusier in such an agitated state. His voice held an edge of fear when he responded, "I can't. I'm marrying Patsy."

"Tonight. You go to the house and talk to her. She needs to see you. Talk to her, you owe her that much." Corbusier abruptly turned and strode away.

In his dreaming, while lying on rough planks of the unfinished porch, Moran wonders what would've become of his life if he hadn't gone to her that night. He puzzles about this; comes to the same conclusion as always; he *had* to go. A weak man will barter his lot in life for a few moments of soaring rapture, even knowing the consequence; that torturous anguish must follow in its wake forever.

The night was mourning cloak black, with a myriad of glittering stars flung across the sky. Moran drove solemnly down the coast highway wondering at the night's beauty, and emotions that filled him to overflowing.

She answered the door. Her eyes were swollen from crying, hair matted. She stood, not offering a word, so he ventured, "Can I come in?"

"Suit yourself." Moran followed her down the hall. She went into her room and sat on the bed.

Moran framed the doorway. "Should I go?"

She looked up and their eyes met. "No. I want you to stay. Turn off the light and come to bed."

He shed his clothing in darkness and went to her like it was all preordained. She smelled like seaweed and mountain sage, and Moran found himself holding her with ancient desperation, moaning that he loved her and would always love her. She gave herself back silently; urgently.

He awoke to sunlight streaming through filmy curtains. Chantal was already up, and Corbusier stood over the bed holding out a steaming mug of coffee.

Corbusier had already found them a place to live. Practical, he said, for all parties involved. A small guest cottage perched over a rugged promontory of coastline called Rocky Point, some dozen miles down the coast towards Big Sur, a short distance from Al and Jack's Rocky Point Restaurant.

Sitting at the dining table in fluid morning light, an uneasy sense that something was off-kilter pulsated alarmingly within him. Corbusier was going off like Fourth of July, pacing, gesticulating, planning the wedding, his eyes sparkling like a child's. Then Chantal came in and sat down. She wore a stormy, brooding expression, and her father abruptly fell to silence.

Within his dreaming, Moran's imagery shifts. He has stumbled upon a new train of thought. It is cryptic and requires examining. He's not sure what connection this has to anything, but the issue appears immediate and potent, so he allows himself to be carried further backward in time to an early divining session.

He'd been dowsing at the Corbusier well for a couple of weeks by this time, learning to recognize precisely how his rod reacted on the main stream band, and the slightly weaker reaction to the inner parallels lying alongside. He already knew the perils of mistaking parallels for the main stream bed, and how to counteract that problem by measuring their distances from the main stream, and watching for graduated reductions in rod force. Corbusier had made him do this repeatedly at a known water source—the well—so the process would become second nature; the object being to eventually apply the same discipline at a site where the water source wasn't known.

Corbusier had been watching Moran all morning. "Good. You're finally learning how to think through your whole body."

As usual, Moran didn't reply, but waited for Corbusier to continue. "We've already talked about accessing the immeasurable state of consciousness. And, we know that thought is pure energy. Einstein said so. For the time being, lets just call 'thought', 'energy'. What is consciousness? A state of awareness . . . we know to be immeasurable. What happens when we marry the two? What if we substitute the word, 'spirit' for 'energy'? We have a new concept. 'Spirit aware-

ness'. I want you to conduct an experiment. Put the rod down."
Corbusier continued. "You are an instrument. You are spirit, and you are awareness. You know this to be true. Okay? Now give a command to that body you're inhabiting. This is what you will tell it. Tell it to stop sending blood to your left arm. Tell it to stop." Moran focused his energy inward and found himself perceiving through an awareness that didn't seem to relate to or require cognitive thought. He and the universe were bleeding together into a timeless and mystical entity.

Moran wordlessly gave the command. Corbusier walked slowly over, picked up his arm, and pressed two fingers upon the pulse-point at his wrist. *"No pulse."*

Moran has figured it out. He's given himself a parable; a symbolic message. *No pulse.* He is astounded to realize that his spirit-awareness is now hovering somewhere out in space; it looks down and sees its mottled, snake-bitten, dying body; heartbeat faint to fading. But . . . he is already halfway to the stars. Could go, could stay and try to divine life back into the body and scare out the poison. He ponders only momentarily, then sees what he must do. It's what he has always done. Always had to stay and do hard time . . . *what was that* . . . a weak man will barter his lot in life for a few moments of soaring rapture, even knowing the consequence . . .

Carmel in the sixties was a summer haven for tourists. After foggy summers spent themselves and the best weather arrived to welcome autumn, the parade of tourists went home. Restaurants that survived long winter months needed to be patronized by the local populace. One such eatery was Rocky Point Restaurant.

Moran settled uneasily into their new life at the Rocky Point cottage. Most mornings he left before sunrise to open the feed store. His elderly and ailing partner worked afternoons, enabling Moran to head home after first stopping to visit his depressed and despondent father. More often than not, Chantal would be absent upon his return. She'd arrive back at odd hours, never offering an explanation as to where she'd been.

During the day she treated him with stony indifference, but when they slipped into bed at night she hungrily sought pleasure in his arms. Long after she succumbed to sleep, while sea-wracked winds lamented through eaves and rattled window panes, he would lay awake. In awe he'd gaze upon her sleeping body. With each night's passing, he was swept deeper into ruinous desire.

Chantal took a part-time hostess job at Rocky Point Restaurant. She was beginning to "show", and Moran protested her working, but only mildly, for at least he knew where he could find her, even for those few hours.

One stormy mid-week evening, Moran arrived to an empty house. He drove the short distance to the restaurant and saw her car parked out front. Sheets of rain assailed him as he half-ran through a nearly empty parking lot. He strode dripping wet into the foyer, and looked across to the bar. There were several people perched on barstools. One was Chantal. She was leaning against the man next to her, his head bent to hers. They were smiling; his arm stretched casually across her lap.

The scene held an intimacy impossible to misread. The sting of rage was so fierce and unexpected that he stood momentarily dumbstruck. Chantal sensed his presence and looked up. She casually crossed one leg over the other causing the man's arm to shift. He saw Moran, slid his hand off her and assumed a hunched position over his drink. She waved.

"Moran!" Her voice resonated through the restaurant. "Guess what? Everybody's coming to dinner! Dad, Marques and Jacques. Marques drove down, even in this storm! I made reservations for seven o'clock." Before Moran could react to this, she looked into the space behind him and waved. "Here comes Jacques!" The man who'd had his hand on Chantal brushed quickly by Moran and slipped out the door just as Jacques entered.

Moran got drunk. It would mark the beginning of many inebriated nights.

Six months and two weeks after their wedding day, Chantal went into labor. Moran guiltily did some figuring that left a month missing from the supposed date of conception. He mentioned this to Corbusier, trying to sound casual, but Corbusier assured him their clan regularly had eight-month babies, not to be concerned. She had a healthy boy, born June 12, 1966, at Community Hospital, weighing eight pounds. He was given the name Christopher William.

The day following her delivery, Moran was on his way to Chantal's hospital room carrying flowers when he saw a man depart, then walk quickly in the opposite direction. It was the same man who'd been at the bar with his hand on her stomach. Even within rising anger, Moran marveled that he seemed so ordinary — coming into middle age, brown eyes; square jaw; wiry body. This observation inflamed him. He burst through the door. Chantal was sitting in bed with tears streaming down her cheeks. "Was that him? Is that your married man?" He was shaking.

Moran had never raised his voice to her before. He could see fear

showing through watery, surprised eyes, and a charge of excitement con-
vulsed through him. He was yelling now. "Who was that man?" He ele-
vated the hand holding flowers in a gesture to strike.

Chantal found a shaky voice. "Moran. Please calm down." As she
spoke, she gained composure. "That man, he was . . ." She paused for too
long. "George is a family friend. That's all. Moran, what nice flowers!"

Moran inhaled deeply, struggling to rein-in the beast that was laboring
to liberate itself.

It's just that he so desperately desires her; needs everything wrong to
be right. He wants forever to watch slippery moonlight cast its light in
infinite shades of beauty upon her sleeping face. He'll do anything not to
lose her; including believing any lie she chooses to tell.

But the repressed anger and shame of it all . . . has had to go somewhere. It lies in his muscles, so they ache, and he feels hot-wired most of
the time. His head swells with tension pain. He drinks, and somehow
drinking doesn't pacify, it unleashes terrible, suspicious thoughts. He
drinks more so that he can at least lose himself in a stupor of delirium. He
doesn't dare to examine those inconsistencies surrounding the baby,
because they conjure up wrathful emotions that swarm upon him like
locusts.

Moran's body shifts fretfully on the porch as he dream-remembers all
of this. It's almost morning and the air is heavy with dew. Swelling has
already subsided in those areas where snake fangs injected their poison,
and his heart beats strong and sure.

Christopher William's arrival brought on the merest whispers of har-
mony that would materialize, swirl about like vapor, then disappear into
thin air. Chantal bustled around the small house and fussed happily over
baby Will. Moran awoke from his troubled dreams each morning to
renewed optimism until his eyes fell upon the boy, then tumultuous
emotions associated with his mother would cast their mocking shadows.

Since the birth, Chantal had not allowed Moran to touch her in bed,
and the rift of space between them was now a trackless wilderness.
Moran struggled daily with growing adoration for the baby, and the
alarming impression that his whole existence rested upon an eroding
sandbank.

It was Corbusier who provided the inspiration that would pull him to
high ground. "When are you gonna build up there on your property?"
Simple as that. Moran became suddenly excited. It could be an offering of

a real home for Chantal and the baby. He went to his father for a loan, and his dad gave him ten thousand dollars of his mother's life insurance money as a wedding gift.

The first order of business would be to divine the well site. Wasn't that where it had begun? One Saturday in mid-September, they all got up early. Moran drove his truck with Chantal and baby in tow. He'd been surprised at her willingness to go, and viewed it as an unquestionable omen of better times ahead.

Corbusier met them at the property, and they spent hours scouting up and down the hills. A deep, good stream was found. Moran wanted to pick absolutely the most perfect and abundant site upon the breadth of it, so they went back and forth repeatedly, checking and double-checking the stream band and parallels. Chantal had packed a picnic for the occasion that was reminiscent of Garrapata Beach. He felt reborn under the ashen sky. That night, watching her as she slept, he made a pact with himself to be patient, and then went out to gaze at the stars.

After the well had been sunk, framing the house went quickly. Every day after work Moran was at the property, making sure that each and every nail had been pounded correctly. It was coming on to Christmas. He brought home a tree and adorned it lavishly with gifts.

Every New Year's, Corbusier gave a bang-up party. On New Years Eve day, Chantal packed up baby Will and went over to help set things up. Moran made his entrance after the party was in bright regale; Corbusier whirling and swirling, the throbbing din of music vibrating walls, and champagne being swilled by the bottle. Moran found Chantal gliding from room to room sipping on a glass of wine. She ignored him, so he took to drink. Hours before the new year was ordained, he stared unfocusedly into the colorful scene playing itself out like a tragic movie.

Corbusier's house was dark and silent, all the partygoers gone. Moran realized he'd dozed off in his chair. He pulled himself unsteadily up and headed for home. Upon arriving to an empty house, he grew quickly sober, and telephoned Corbusier, choking back panic. Chantal and baby had gone home before midnight, Corbusier explained. She'd left because she was tired. Then he told Moran, "Wait there. I'm coming over." After Corbusier arrived, the two men drove slowly down the highway in case there had been a breakdown. Back at the cottage empty-handed, Corbusier restrained Moran from calling the sheriff, and spent the remainder of the night purposely focusing him away from the obvious, inevitable conclusion.

Inside a rosy dawn, the phone rang. "Hi."

Moran, more furious than relieved to hear Chantal's voice bellowed, "Where are you!"

There was a long pause before she replied. "Moran, I'm moving out. With Will. I'll come later for my things. It would be better if you weren't around when I get there." Moran stared blankly.

Corbusier snatched the phone away. "Where are you?" His voice was venomous. He listened to her, and then responded in a low, threatening voice. "You will come home. Today. Now. Come first to my place. We'll have a talk about it." Then he slammed down the phone.

"I can handle her." Corbusier was already to the door. "I'll call you later. Don't worry, she'll be back."

Moran wasn't as upset as he imagined he might have become after having his absolute worst nightmare realized. The scene had been mentally too well rehearsed. It was what transpired after she was gone that he could never see the other side of. For now, the only thing he knew with certainty was, he wouldn't just sit back and allow his family to slip away.

Around mid-morning, the phone rang. "Moran. Come on over. I know where she is." Neither man spoke as they drove south down Highway 1. Just north of Lucia, Corbusier pulled into a weed-tangled driveway. A small cabin stood against cliffs, obscured by tall cypress trees. Chantal's old Studebaker was parked outside.

The two men went into the house. A few hours later, Moran and Corbusier left; Moran cradling the crying child in his arms. Neither man looked back as they drove away.

Will picked Laura up at school, and then drove to the feed store. The "Closed" sign was still in the window. He looked over to his daughter. "What's up with your grandpa? I know he oversleeps sometimes, but this is ridiculous!" He gave her a smile and rolled his eyes. Laura didn't find it funny; she'd begged him in vain to let her spend the afternoon at a girlfriend's house, so punished him now with a non-response.

The store hadn't been open all day; no invoices were generated, the answering machine was filled with requests and inquiries as to when somebody would be answering or showing up. Will asked Laura, "Did he say anything to you about where he was headed yesterday afternoon?"

She pondered a few moments. "He told me he was off to 'the wild blue yonder', whatever that means."

Will called his father's house and got no answer.

It's going to be another scorcher. Moran realizes this even before the sun has arisen. He tries to sit up, and manages only to raise his head a few inches. His body is dehydrated, and the poison has rendered his muscles nearly useless. At first he thinks he should try to make it to the well, but remembers that electricity was shut off there more than 30 years ago. *Water is in the truck. So is my cell phone.* Five hours later, Moran, on his belly, is halfway to the truck. By dusk he's unconscious, with one hand resting upon a truck tire.

Will drove up Corral de Tierra Road and saw his father's truck parked near the old house. He couldn't remember the gate combination, so instructed Laura to wait, then climbed over the fence and hiked up the hill.

Moran regains consciousness in the ambulance, while life-sustaining fluids drip from an IV into his veins. He sees Chantal's child looking down at him. Christopher William. Will. All grown up now. He has his mother's beautiful eyes, but cast there is an expression of love and concern, something he'd never divined in *hers*.

A vision comes to him, of Chantal standing helplessly on the cliff's edge. *On New Years Day.* Upon her face is defiance mixed with fear as she focuses her gaze first on her husband, and then her father. The wind is blowing fierce and cold, and somewhere lost inside are dismembered sounds of a baby's frantic cries; who had just been wrenched out of his mother's arms and put down in dirt behind where the two men stood, side by side.

"Oh my God, no!" A sudden panic grips him and he tries to rise.

Will leans over his father to hold him down, and tears begin to well in his eyes. "Dad. It's okay. You're going to be fine. Don't try to talk now. Just rest."

> *In darkness she lays down beside me,*
> *As waves reach for the shore.*
> *I can feel her warm arms around me,*
> *And she holds me and loves me once more.*

Framed

by Frances J. Rossi

*T*he November wind whistling up Ocean Avenue in downtown Carmel lifted the large painting Rosalie clutched and threatened to pull her into the street. Wrestling to keep her balance, she turned onto a side street where she found a welcome relief from the wind. The damp air chilled her. *So this is winter on California's Central Coast!* A string of sleigh bells tinkled outside a gift shop, and while most of the gaily-decorated boutiques hadn't yet opened, the merchants were inside busily preparing for the day. Rosalie spotted Figueroa Frames across the street, two doors down. She could see Pete working in the window, wrestling with a large Christmas elf with an infectious grin. Her stomach clenched. *What's he going to say when he sees me again after four months? He obviously didn't want to start a relationship with me or he'd have kept in touch.*

To her right, a narrow white-walled passageway led between two buildings, reaching back to a courtyard. Rosalie edged into it far enough to be out of Pete's possible view and eased back against the wall. She'd psyched herself up for this reunion over breakfast, and getting her unwieldy canvas in and out of the car and through the windy streets of Carmel had kept her mind off her apprehension. But now, standing against the cold wall, her chest tightened and she began to feel light-headed. She'd made herself a big bowl of granola this morning, but stress always made her ravenous. Lifting the picture in trembling hands, she followed the passage back to the courtyard. Umbrella-covered café tables, still dripping from an overnight rain, waited outside the back door of a coffee shop. Through French doors she could see customers at the counter and at tables, all bathed in a warm glow of a corner fireplace. She could go in and sit down, have some coffee, maybe forget this whole scheme. She'd seen another frame shop, around the bay in Seaside somewhere. Was this attack of shyness a sign that she should let go of the Pete thing?

Shivering, she glanced around the courtyard. Under this leaden sky, bright pink and snowy white cyclamen blooming in earthenware pots glowed all the more brilliant, reflecting in the puddles that still glistened in the paving stone hollows. *Plucky little things!* she thought. Unwilling to bow to Dame Winter. Ivy covered the wall across from the coffee shop, and a sturdy vine with glossy oval leaves stood guard at the corner, framing the passageway that led out to the main street.

She dried a chair with a piece of tissue and sat down, catching her reflection in the window. She noticed her golden curls, corralled by a maroon beret, and wondered if vanity made her cover the growing sprinkling of silver strands with a blond rinse. The gold came from the German-Russian Kansas side of her family—her dad's—and the curls from her mom's Annapolis Italian side. She'd been born Rosalia Marie Galliardt, with her mother's olive skin, still smooth at her age. "Oily skin holds up better," Mom had promised back in her acne days.

She relaxed her grip on the heavy painting resting against her boots. *But I'm here. And I can do this.* She thought again of what she'd planned to say to the man who, four months ago, she'd thought she'd fallen in love with.

Pete, nice to see you again! I don't know if you'd heard . . . I've moved here. Did I tell you about my Blue Nude? No, she should focus on him. *How are you, Pete? What's happening . . .?* Could she say that without betraying her wounded feelings over the news blackout from him?

The French doors opened, releasing a warm cloud of kitchen fragrance, and a middle-aged man dressed in khakis and a dark blue windbreaker came out carrying a steaming coffee cup. She tried to continue her self-psyching up process, but the smell of muffins overpowered her consciousness. *A minute more without a latte and she would collapse.*

She entered into the warm atmosphere of coffee and mouth-watering baked goods, set the painting against a free table, and went to the counter where fresh muffins and scones riveted her attention. At the espresso machine, a dark-haired young man with a two-day stubble shot foamy milk noisily into a mug. Yes, she'd have some of that.

"A café latte and one of those muffins with the sunflower seeds, please." Her hands shook as she pulled out a five-dollar bill, and when the young man handed her the change, it dropped through her fingers onto the worn tile floor.

Rosalie sat at the table with the large white china cup of foamy coffee and milk and the muffin. She took a few comforting sips and bit off a hunk of muffin. As she stared at the large brown-paper-wrapped canvas next to her, she forced herself to deal with her day's mission.

As Peter Mahlberg shifted the wooden elf to make room for the latest gift frames in the window display, the vase of fresh holly tipped over, spilling water onto the green velour underneath. "Shit!" His back hurt from wrenching over at this awkward angle into the display area, and he straightened up to rest it. *Damn the feng shui police in Carmel!* The elf had been set just outside the door, next to a potted chrysanthemum, where there was plenty of room, but the city had threatened to cite him for having something on the sidewalk.

He looked across the street. Earlier, he'd caught sight of a woman with golden blond curls that reminded him of Rose—Rosalie—a ray of East Coast sunshine that he'd met at an art conference at Asilomar last summer. But now all he saw were the usual shops—the Oriental carpet dealer from Afghanistan; the Pacific Tides Gallery, its window boxes bursting with pink and white impatiens; and Domani, the new Italian trattoria. Hussein, the Afghani, was out sweeping the sidewalk, dressed in his usual dark pants and crisp white shirt with the sleeves rolled up. Pete went to the back room for a towel to mop up the spilled water. Even though the dark green material didn't show the moisture, it still irritated him.

He'd *imagined* seeing Rose this morning, must have. Maybe because he'd dreamed about her the night before, of all things. In the dream, she stood in the middle of a dancing crowd in the parish hall at St. Joseph's Church in Liebenthal, Kansas, waving to him. He'd tried to make his way through the couples twirling by, doing a high-stepping polka, but somehow he could not get to her. She was always just beyond the dancers. Suddenly she was gone, and he was on the playground at school in Willow Creek, California. The dancers changed now to kids on the playground, laughing at him. He was wearing the corduroy pants his grandmother had sent from Kansas, the ones the kids used to feel between thumb and finger before jeering: "Quality!"

Trying to clear his mind, Pete switched on the tape player with practice music from the upcoming Christmas concert, and then dried his hands with a rag hanging from the pegboard where his tools were organized just as his stepfather had taught him when they'd worked together, back during his high school years. The sight of his framing tools still gave him a rush of excitement—symbols of his new life here on the Central Coast.

Framed

He kept his regular carpentry tools in the basement of his Carmel home, which he'd been remodeling over the past couple of years.

Making a final adjustment to the holly, he glanced once more across the street and thought of Rosalie. He'd brought her to the shop this past summer during a break in the art workshop at Asilomar. He'd wanted to make love to her right then, but they'd been pressed for time. Had he loved her? Could you tell after just a week? It didn't matter anyway. She belonged back on the East Coast, and he had his new life here now. No use thinking about what might have been.

Warmed by the frothy beverage, Rosalie settled back into her chair and her thoughts jumped back to the last time she'd been in Pete's shop. He had been one of the vendors at the Asilomar art workshop last summer where he'd taken frame orders from the artists attending. He'd sat next to her at dinner.

She tried now to picture the look on his face when he'd taken his first bite of the noodles that night. He'd rolled his eyes just like her favorite uncle back in Kansas. "If you knew noodles, like I know noodles . . ." he'd sung, making rhythmic motions with his hands.

She'd laughed and sampled a bite herself to see what he meant. Not like Aunt Ann's. When your family was either German-Russian or Italian, noodles were not "just noodles". She'd given him a sympathetic nod. "So, how do you know noodles so well?"

By dessert time they had discovered they each had German-Russian relatives in the same Kansas county. Over the strawberry shortcake he'd told her a little of his life history—how his mom and stepfather had left Kansas during the Dust Bowl years and raised him in California's Central Valley; how he'd been in construction most of his life, but recently moved to Carmel.

After dinner they'd strolled along the beach toward Pacific Grove. She told him about her life growing up in Annapolis with her mother's Italian side of the family—getting her degree at a small Catholic college, working as an accountant, raising her kids in a suburb of Baltimore, and then the premature death of her husband ten years ago. She'd mentioned the upcoming art show in New York and her excitement in being accepted to this first important exhibit.

"What's the painting like?" he'd asked.

"It's a human figure—a nude," she'd said, hesitating to explain that she painted male nudes.

He'd been candid about his life. Interesting that men talked a lot about their work and activities, but not much about their emotional life. She'd learned very little about his relationship status, except that by reading between the lines she'd figured he must be more or less unattached.

Of course, she'd avoided telling him about Rick, her boyfriend in New York—the one she'd started seeing two years after her husband's death. The feelings had never kicked in with that relationship and, figuring you didn't fall in love after 50, she'd resigned herself to enjoying the companionship.

That was . . . until that evening at Asilomar. She and Pete had walked arm in arm all the way to the Point Pinos Lighthouse and back, talking all the way. By the time they got back to the conference center, Rosalie knew she wasn't too old to fall in love.

"Chemistry," her best friend back home in Greenbelt, Maryland, had called it. Something about Pete had attracted her on an elemental level—was it the cultural aspect or something more physical, she wondered? Hard to put your finger on it. She'd loved the way his blue elfin eyes twinkled, crinkling at the corners, brimming with laughter. His voice was tuned like a violin's "A" string—mellow, but with a tautness that belied his bass tones. His hair was golden brown, still thick, disciplined to the comb but begging to be disturbed. His smile was infectious, like that of her favorite troll when troll figures had been popular back in college. There was an edginess about him, with his quick, decisive movements, his readiness to spring into action. During the few short days of the seminar, he'd made himself her tour guide to the Peninsula and quickly found his way into her heart.

She'd painted a few small ocean scenes at the workshop, which Pete had framed for her. On the day they'd come to the shop to pick them up, she was amazed to see how his expertly chosen frames brought out the blues and greens in her seascapes. She'd bought lots of frames, but had never found a craftsman who knew his métier like Pete did.

She'd let her fingers caress the grain of the wood. "You make framing an art in itself!"

"I see it as a kind of marriage," he'd said. "You know, in the wrong frame, the painting isn't complete. But in the right one, it appears in its full glory." He gestured appreciatively at her ocean scene.

It was after six that Saturday evening when Pete had taken her in his arms and kissed her there in the shop. There wasn't time to linger over it, because he had to return to the conference. Later that evening—their last one together—they'd walked on the beach again, where the waves broke silver in the moonlight, and again he'd pulled her against him and kissed her, their bare feet pressing into the sand. They lay down on the sand, beginning to relax into each other in the privacy of the surf's roar, only to have their wall of sound pierced by youthful cries. A group of teens arrived with frisbees and flashlights and took up their play just yards away.

Rosalie remembered the packing she needed to do, and struggled to her feet, brushing sand from her clothes.

"Are you doing anything before your flight leaves tomorrow?" Pete shook sand from his shirt and picked up his shoes.

"I kind of wanted to go to mass at the Carmel Mission."

"Mind if I come along? We could have breakfast afterwards."

Drawing the warm, sweet froth into her mouth, Rosalie felt her tight, cold muscles relaxing. She leaned her elbows on the table and glanced around her. An elderly couple sat comfortably nearby reading the paper, their tawny-furred cocker spaniel curled up under the table. The man to her right, his hair still beaded with moisture, fiddled with his PDA with one hand between gulps of coffee. Rosalie gazed beyond the tables, toward the far side of the shop, where gunnysacks of coffee beans were stacked against one wall, near a coffee-roasting oven. But the memory of that last day with Pete at the mission crowded into her mind. He'd taken her hand . . .

Holding hands during the Sunday liturgy at the mission, the hallowed walls had seemed to give a silent blessing to her feelings for Pete. How many other couples over the centuries had stood in this very place, anticipating the life they would one day share? It had seemed so right. So real. A new memory jolted her—he'd let go of her hand, patted her shoulder as if in reassurance, and gripped the dark wood of the pew in front of him until they sat down again. After that, he'd seemed cooler toward her—she saw that now and wanted to blot out the memory. Why would his feelings have changed so abruptly?

They had gone to From Scratch restaurant for breakfast before going to the airport early Sunday afternoon. He'd made no mention of staying in touch, although he did give her his business card with his e-mail address on it. Embracing her before she boarded the plane, Pete released her with seeming reluctance.

"Take care," he'd said, his voice soft.

"I'll e-mail you," she'd promised.

"Sure, me too!" he'd assured her.

But he didn't really keep in touch. Not like someone considering a relationship. She drained the last of the latte, and stretched her tongue into the cup to lick out the remaining foam. Oh, he'd written a time or two over the summer, mentioning a few of the activities he was involved in—his little theater group, the Symphony Board, ushering at the Bach Festival, kayaking on nice weekends, and—he slipped it in, but for her it might as well have been written bold in red letters—the Sugar Pine weekend. From what she could gather, it was a kind of Club Med singles experience in the Sierras. He didn't say so, but she did the math—where there was one single guy, there were bound to be single women, and that usually added up to a couple. She felt that in the bottom of her stomach, but refused to accept it. He couldn't have faked his feelings that well last summer. It must be something else.

I feel like such an adolescent! She pulled her jacket back on reluctantly, in no hurry to leave this warm oasis. *One minute I think we might still have a chance, and the next I see no hope. But I didn't come here just for him.* She had a life, after all. She got up resolutely, grasped the painting, eased it through the door, and started down the passageway toward the street.

How would Pete take this painting? She'd been reluctant to show it to him last summer, but surely he'd seen his share of nudes in his business. And here on the Central Coast of California, where attitudes were more liberal, maybe the Blue Nude would get the recognition it truly deserved.

She would not be here on the Peninsula today at all if the Nude had done well in Manhattan last summer, or if she'd gotten any encouragement from her family or her boyfriend Rick. The opening in New York had made the decision for her.

"I think it's the frame, dear," her teacher Helena Kobell had whispered over her champagne flute. "You really must have it redone. That painting is absolutely outstanding and deserves better. It should have gotten Best of Show."

"Oh, I don't know about that. Best in the nude category would have been nice, though." Rosalie scrutinized the Blue Nude—the high point of her art efforts over the past two years. With her instructor Helena, known for her method of "Painting the Inner Person", she'd worked at bringing out the true essence of the subject through her skilled use of color and line.

"No, really, dear, I can't tell you how proud I am of what you've done here. This is a truly spiritual work—exactly what I've been trying to get my students to do." Helena shifted, allowing a new group of spectators to view the painting. "I guess it's a bit selfish on my part to want it to have the recognition it deserves."

To their left, Rick worked his way though the crowd to join them. "Hi, ladies! Just got off work."

Helena excused herself, moving over to another group of students. Rick stood staring at the painting, arms crossed, champagne cup squeezed in tight fingers.

"So, what do you think of the finished product?"

"Uh . . ."

"I'm just bummed that it didn't get some kind of recognition." She waited for him to agree.

"Y'know, hon, I can kind of see why. I mean, if you want this to be accepted as serious art rather than porn . . ." He said it almost jokingly, but she heard derisiveness in his tone.

"Porn! What are you talking about? This *is* serious art!" Her right hand went up in an unconscious Italian gesture of disgust, tossing the contents of her glass of champagne onto the flowered crepe gown of the guest standing next to her. The woman pulled away in irritation as Rosalie dabbed at the sleeve with a piece of Kleenex.

Rick pulled her aside. "Calm down, my dear," he whispered hoarsely. "It's just that, look at the size of that . . . uh . . . organ. Did you have to make it so prominent?"

"It's not *prominent*! It's just *articulated. That's* what you don't like."

"Can we please not have a scene here?" *Now he was Mr. Reasonable.* "Look, there's nothing wrong with porn. I was just offering a suggestion as to why you didn't get first place, that's all." Keeping her mouth shut, Rosalie led the way over to the Best of Nudes winner, and Rick studied it, taking another sip of champagne. "Look at this one!" he said. "It's not so . . . so exposed. The parts aren't all that clear. You just get the suggestion."

"And it's a woman! Am I right? Men like female nudes, but not male. And men spend the money—is that it?"

"Could you please calm down? It's just that certain kinds of nudes fall more into the category of erotic art. If you don't believe me, check the Web." He could always come across sounding infuriatingly pat.

They had drifted to a point directly across the room from Rosalie's painting, and looked at it across the room of the assembled artists, judges, and guests. "Frankly, I think the Blue Nude would do fine in an erotica exhibit," he said in his most patronizing voice. "It just depends on what direction you want your art to go." He drained his champagne glass and glanced around for the steward with the bottle. "The thing is," he went on, deliberately lowering his voice to a point that was barely audible—his way of indicating that she was being too loud in public, "I'm kind of amazed that you, a good Catholic college graduate, can still produce sm . . . er, stuff like this. But I suppose there were a lot of Catholics in *The Godfather*, too, and look . . ."

She'd slammed her empty glass down on a nearby table and headed for the door. Outside, she fought back tears, furious. Scratch him, and Mr. Patron of the Arts showed his thinly veneered contempt for her work and her family. This was the last time he'd play the mafia card on her.

He was taking his time to follow her, and her thoughts, like fall leaves, began to swirl less chaotically and to settle in neat piles. *I'm so tired of being hemmed in by this East Coast mentality,* she thought. First there'd been the old-worldly Italian community she'd grown up in, with all its restrictions. She wouldn't even show them her nudes. Then there was the tight competition of the art community. And now, besides that, she couldn't keep up the pretense with Rick. Standing in front of the gallery in Chelsea, hugging herself with shivering arms in the first hints of fall, she knew she'd been wrong. She'd found love and acceptance on the Monterey Peninsula, and that was where she needed to be

It was late September when she managed to drive away from her Greenbelt home. With her possessions all packed into a Ryder truck, she took the onramp to Interstate 70, westbound. She'd stopped to visit the aunts and cousins in Kansas, listening more closely now to the stories they were still eager to retell—the history of their century of farming in Russia, the mass migration to America, the settlement in Kansas, where farmland was plentiful and rich, the Dust Bowl years when many lost everything they'd worked for.

Arriving in Monterey, she idealized letting her life sprout anew from her true roots, and Pete sharing it with her. She'd clung to that hope for a while, but by the early October day when she turned off Highway 1 onto Aguajito Street to her new apartment, she had no illusions. She had to accept that Pete might be just a friend. She hadn't even told him she was coming.

With the help of an agent, she'd found an "affordable" (on the Monterey Peninsula, that was a relative term) one-bedroom apartment on 4th Street, not far from El Estero, where she discovered a walking path along a quiet lagoon with its geese, ducks, and other wild birds. She'd buy a bird book, she decided, and start learning their names.

Painting alone would not pay the rent, but Rosalie had worked as an accountant in Maryland after the death of her husband, so she applied for work at several accounting firms on the Peninsula. The first week in November the H&R Block office on Forest Hill in nearby Pacific Grove called her for an interview, and hired her, starting on a part-time basis.

She kept busy, but couldn't stop thinking about Pete. She wanted to let him know she'd moved, but felt frustrated to have her e-mails falling off into empty cyberspace. Still, if he knew she were here . . . what excuse could she find to see him once more? There was still the Blue Nude, which she hadn't even unpacked after the move. She'd decided to take it in to be framed.

Now, looking across the street at the frame shop, Rosalie found herself humming under her breath, "If I loved you . . . longing to tell you, but afraid and shy . . ."

Pete walked to the shop door and opened for business. Music from his choral practice the night before played in his head, crowding out the thoughts that had troubled his morning so far. However, as he turned the sign in the door to read "Open," the sight of that familiar face hit him like a tsunami. He *had* seen her! There she was, struggling with what must be a painting packaged in cardboard, angling across the street toward the shop. He pulled open the door and went out with a curious lilt in his step, singing, "Touro-louro-louro cocks are crowing—hey!" He took the painting from her with one hand and with the other reached to pull her to him in a tight embrace. He couldn't think of what to say. She looked even better than she had at the workshop—possibly slimmer, her face brighter.

"So, what's with this 'cocks are crowing'?" she said, screwing up her face in that cute little teasing look she had.

Was that a Freudian slip or what? "Oh, a carol we're practicing for our Cantadores Christmas concert—a group I sing with. It's like, chickens—cocks, ya know?" *Maybe she didn't notice.* "What are you doing here?"

"I've moved here." Her hair shone like spun gold—just as he remembered it.

"You didn't tell me." He leaned the painting against the checkout counter.

"Well, you weren't answering my e-mails." Her probing blue eyes unnerved him.

"I got pretty busy. Did I tell you I was ushering for the Bach Festival? And then, there was that Sugar Pine week. What a blast!" Her eyes darkened in the way he'd become accustomed to in that short week they'd known each other. He blundered on. "And I sing with Cantadores, and with some other groups. Seems like I'm out about every night."

He eyed the dark brown leather of her neat jacket, the slim hips under her blue denim skirt, the jaunty plaid wool scarf at her neck, the maroon beret. Very Back East. Just as in her speech. Not just the accent, *crisp* was the word that came to mind, in contrast with the soft and flowing feel he'd gotten used to in people he knew now.

All the feelings from last summer had surged back when he saw her, like an extension of his disturbing dream the night before. For some reason, on that June morning at the Carmel Mission, as they stood holding hands, he'd been back at St. Joe's in Kansas. He was standing there in front of the altar with Nancy in the blur of Father Meinrad's Latin nuptial mass. He could still see Nancy's waxen face, beaded with little droplets of perspiration, and the bulge under her wedding dress. When Aunt Marie finally began playing her reedy organ rendition of the wedding march, he began the long walk down the aisle into what felt like captivity.

He'd managed to stick it out with Nancy through two pregnancies and the war in Vietnam, but after they'd moved to Sacramento, Nancy had taken the kids and split back to Kansas.

So that was what came of falling in love!

Rosalie said something that brought him back to the present. "Excuse me, I was distracted," he said, quickly straightening the counter.

"I said, I thought you might have mentioned the Sugar Pine weekend in an e-mail."

Did he really want to go there? "Well, it was fun. Fun! I mean . . . you should have seen the food! And they had more activities than you could ever take part in—something for everybody."

She nodded, smiling too broadly. "How nice for you!"

"Well, let's see what you have here!" He untied the cord that held the heavy brown paper wrapping on it, pulled out the painting and turned it to face them. The painting depicted a well-built male nude painted in intense shades of blue oil, so lifelike that he appeared ready to step forward out of the picture. His skin glistened from the hot tub he had just left, with water droplets, like tiny translucent teardrops, still poised on his stomach and groin. He wore a crimson towel around his neck, which heightened the blue radiance of the skin. His eyes were large, dark, and intense, effectively riveting the observer's gaze. The genitalia were fully exposed, prominent between his spread legs, painted in shades of red and purple. Behind him, steam rose from the hot tub, fogging the background into a misty scene of bathers.

"My God!" he said, stepping back involuntarily—he'd expected another seascape. "Uh, cool! Yes, this is . . . nice," he managed to say, a smile frozen all the way to his ears. "So, you wanted me to see this?" he squeaked, and cleared his throat. *Why was it bothering him so much?*

"It needs a better frame." Her voice was calm, mellow, like warm honey.

"A frame, yes! Well! I guess we should try to bring out the color of that pe—uh, pectoral muscle. My, how that glows!"

Pete felt his cheeks burning and abruptly turned away. "I think I've got something appropriate in the back room." *Appropriate?*

Taking a few deep breaths in the back room, he managed to calm down. What had gotten into him? He'd seen his share of nudes, after all.

Framed

What was it about his one? *Think of the girl, Pete! She's done you the honor of trusting you to frame her masterpiece.* He sorted through his samples and emerged with several possibilities.

"First of all, with a painting this large, you need a substantial frame. The one you've got on there is too small." *And looks cheap, he wanted to add.* "I mean, you've got an imposing work of art here." *You could say that again!* "Look how this one, with its gray-blue tone and the off-white inner frame, sets it off."

Her face lit up, her blue eyes widening. "Hmm. Yes, that makes a big difference. You're an artist with frames, Pete! I'll take that one." There was an awkward silence.

"I'm busy today, or I'd ask you to lunch," he said. "How about next week when you come to pick this up?"

"Sure! That would be great! Well," she slid her hand across his back affectionately, "see ya then."

Involuntarily he found himself responding with another hug. He wanted to kiss her, but knew he had to restrain himself. She left, and he watched through the window as she walked away.

He should have told her about Andrea.

How could he explain it? Love had led him into his first big mistake, with Nancy. He'd blundered into a second marriage as well; a rebound situation, and that hadn't worked out either. He'd had a lot of dates—mostly just for sex—but few serious relationships. Maturity had finally clicked in—he'd thought—and he'd decided to take charge of his life. Last May he'd joined the Redwood Singles Club, and had arranged to go on the singles' week at Sugar Pine—only $675 for the entire week—where he planned to meet a compatible woman. He'd already figured out what qualities he was looking for: a California girl, mature, bright, with mutual interests, age somewhere in the forties or fifties, physical attractiveness. Not too extroverted. A good conversationalist. And this was important: one who wanted to live on the Central Coast.

He'd met Andrea during a hike on the second day at Sugar Pine. She had heavy dark hair streaked with gray, cut in a long pageboy style; heavy-lidded eyes, a straight nose and thin lips. At 52, she was a bit thicker at the middle than he would have preferred—but then so was he—and her bust was full. Her skin was still smooth, although frown lines between her neatly plucked brows added character. He'd learned a little about her from some of his friends in the group. She'd gotten a degree at UCLA, lived in San Luis Obispo.

They'd sat together by the pool before dinner for a glass of Pinot Blanc. "What did you think of the hike?" he'd said to get the conversation going.

"It was very nice. A bit strenuous, but I liked the views."

"You do much hiking?"

"It depends. Lately, I've been pretty busy getting my shop moved."

"What business are you in?"

The frown lines deepened as she stared cross-eyed into the glass of wine she tipped to drink from. "I guess I'm still not used to calling what I do business. I'm an art historian." Her chin tipped up slightly as she said it. "I've had a gallery in San Luis Obispo for a couple of years now, but I'm planning to move it to Carmel."

"Oh? When would you be doing that?"

She drained the last of the pale vintage from her glass. "I've got a place rented already, so it's just a matter of moving on up."

Pete put down his half-full glass, feeling slightly ill. "I guess I told you I'm from Carmel."

"Yes, at some point you must have. And what do you do there?"

"Frame shop. I own Figueroa Frames."

"Wonderful! So, I'm sure we'll have some business dealings—and maybe get to know each other better." She purred now, and held up her glass for the wine steward who passed by with the bottle.

"You've found a house?" He pushed his chair back slightly to give himself some stretch room. *Maybe it was the heat . . .*

"Yes, a really neat little place up on Santa Rita, under the pines. I'm just going to rent for now, but if things go well, I might try to buy something." She leaned forward, resting her arms on the table. "And where do you live?"

"Off lower Junipero, almost to Rio Road. About a five-minute walk to the mission." He didn't know why he'd thrown in that bit of information.

"Are you Catholic?"

"No, I'm a Lutheran—when I go to church." *Although I've had a couple of serious brushes with Catholicism, he didn't add.* He thought he should determine her religious leanings. "And you?"

"I guess I'm more spiritual than religious, but maybe it depends on the church."

So far she met all his requirements, more or less. He gulped the rest of his wine. "What do you say we head off for dinner?"

Later in the evening they'd danced. Twirling Andrea around the floor, he remembered the last time he'd been on a dance floor—that evening in June—with Rosalie. Rosalie . . . but at that point she'd have been on the East Coast, with her family and friends.

Nothing had actually *happened* between them during the Sugar Pine week. They'd agreed to get back in touch when Andrea moved. Pete offered to help her move into the shop. She'd gotten established in her house and opened her De La Guerra gallery for business in mid-

September, and Pete had made sure they spent time together. It was just a matter of time before things progressed to the next romantic level.

He felt he'd gotten his money's worth from the singles' week. Andrea was musical—that is, she liked concerts. That was one reason she was moving to Carmel. Liked dogs. Well, she'd have to if she wanted to date him, since his old black lab, Truman, was an integral part of his life. She had a dog of her own—a miniature poodle, which she kept immaculately groomed and coiffed. Truman would have to get used to that.

And there it was, Pete thought. If he'd had any inkling that Rosalie might be moving to the Central Coast, things might have been different.

Pete had the Blue Nude boxed and ready to go, and when Rosalie came to pick it up, they went across the street to the little trattoria for lunch.

They talked in generalities—her move, what he'd been doing since last May. He carefully stayed off the subject of Sugar Pine, and she didn't ask. Then she brought up her art show.

"Yes, I was going to ask you about that," he said, working a piece of lettuce onto his fork.

"Can you imagine? After I'd been accepted to this prestigious show, right there at the opening, Rick says, 'So, what next? Are you the next Mapplethorpe?'"

Pete leaned back, allowing the waitress to set down his hot, crusty calzone. "Hard to figure, huh?" He pushed his fork into the calzone, releasing fragrant steam. "You wanted him to be a little more supportive."

So far, so good. He was showing sensitivity.

"What did *you* think of the Blue Nude, Pete? I mean, for *real*."

"Ya know, I'm fine with that sort of thing," he said, gulping some water to relieve his tight throat. "It is a beautiful painting."

"You didn't see it as too erotic?"

"No, of course not. It's just that . . ." He paused to finish chewing the bite of ham and tender crust. "Just that, I'm surprised that a Catholic woman like you would create such a . . . such an overt nude." He'd said more than he meant to. When he'd gone to mass at the mission with her, old images, words, rituals had worked their magic on him, leaving him more agitated than comforted. An unsettled feeling, plumbing the deep undercurrents of his life not quite resolved. "What I mean is, it seems as if you had to focus pretty closely on that body." The more he said, the worse things got. He wanted to drop the subject, but she wasn't going to let that happen.

"Actually, the Vatican is full of nudes. The Catholic Church has always reverenced both body and soul. In fact, most people don't know that

Mapplethorpe himself is a Catholic."

Body and soul. Like the dancing and partying of Pete's Mahlburg family. "Ya don't say. Didn't I hear somewhere that some pope went around the Vatican chopping genitals off the statues and substituting fig leaves?"

"That would be Pius the Ninth." She chuckled. "Not one of my favorites."

"So, obviously you find it natural to sketch nudes."

"Surprisingly, it's kind of impersonal when you sketch from a model. These guys just pose for you in class, and you concentrate on the lines of their bodies. Later on I put in the skin tones and some of the details."

Details! Well, there were some pretty vivid details in that picture. "I don't know how they can just sit there naked in front of a whole class." *Be careful what you say . . .*

"Oh, they get used to it. I've talked to some of them after our sessions, and it's really no big deal for them." Rosalie lifted a forkful of the calzone to her mouth, trailing a strand of mozzarella that refused to break off. "You should try it sometime."

"Maybe I will." His voice trailed off leaving a feeling of possibility. *What had he just said?*

"You know, I'm living on a shoestring right now, since the move, and I need to produce some paintings, to get some money coming in." Her tone was confidential, and he nodded encouragingly. He was in a position to give her some leads, introduce her to people.

"Would you ever consider posing for me—because I desperately need a model, and I can't afford to hire one or take classes right now?" She looked pleadingly into his eyes.

"With *my* body? Look at this gut! I'm working out, of course, but it's not where I want it to be yet."

"That wouldn't matter. I could enhance it, if you like. But really, I like to draw people as they are. I don't need a perfect specimen."

"And you say it's impersonal?" His shoulders were tightening up, and he stretched them to ease the tension. *How had he gotten himself into this?*

"We would do it in a private place where nobody would see you, of course."

If he posed for her, maybe he could get her to do a regular portrait of him, to send to Aunt Marie or to his daughter. "How about Saturday?" he said. "Could you come over to my place?" He chuckled inwardly at the look of gratitude she flashed at him. "Just one thing, though . . ."

"Sure, anything."

"That you'd also include a painting of my face."

Her eyes widened. "No problem."

Rosalie followed the detailed directions Pete had e-mailed to her and managed to find his house, tucked down on an oak-shaded lane off lower Junipero Street in Carmel. She came up the neat walk of brick outlined in green moss, and stood at the carved oak door holding a portfolio stocked with sketching pencils, charcoal, and a new pad of paper. Pete opened the door to her, and his smile reminded her of her favorite troll doll—the one whose infectious beaming had cheered her through the down days of her college years. She saw him glance appreciatively at her long blue denim shirtdress that hung softly against her figure. It was also comfortable on these cool days.

He was wearing a navy velour robe and slippers. If he felt awkward, he didn't show it. "C'mon in," he said. "I'll show you through my house."

The house was one of his works of art, she saw, as he showed her the remodeling he'd done—the tile work, oak floors, new closets, windows. The tour progressed to the kitchen. "How about a glass of mineral water?"

He filled her glass and showed her to the study. "Want to set up in here?"

The room was about fifteen feet square, with one wall painted deep red, and the rest in tan. On one side was a plush couch. There was also a straight chair next to a desk, as well as an office chair. "Let's start you out on the straight chair," Rosalie said.

As she set up her easel and prepared paper and pencils for drawing, Pete perched on the chair, still wrapped in his robe. "You never did tell me how you came to choose nudes."

She had to think about what to say. "I guess I believe there's truth in beauty. Seems like that's in the Bible somewhere. And in the beauty of the human body, you see the reality of the person showing through." She settled back onto the chair Pete had given her and took a sip of her mineral water. "The body tells the truth about the inner person—especially when you see it undisguised by clothing."

She put down her water. "Ready?"

"Ready as I'll ever be," Pete answered, sounding surprisingly comfortable with the idea. He slipped off the robe, which fell behind him on the chair. "How shall I pose?"

"Try just leaning back, kind of natural."

He sat back stiffly, his back rigid, feet flat on the floor.

"Umm, no, you have to relax a little more than that." She felt her fingers beginning to perspire under the pencil, as her heart fluttered in her chest. "Relax your legs. Can't you, like, spread your knees a little?"

"Spread my knees?" he asked incredulously. "You'd better demonstrate for me. I'm a novice at this, you know."

Her own knees shook slightly as she got up from her chair, and went over to him. She'd drawn from nude models for several years now, but had never reacted physically like this. "Lean back like so." She pushed him gently back against the chair, and lifted one arm to rest behind him. Taking his knees in her hands, she pushed them apart to what seemed like a natural distance, exposing his genitals. She felt her face burning, the flush extending to her neck, and she couldn't look him in the face. "This okay?" she managed to whisper.

He cleared his throat. "Let's try it."

She moved quickly back to her easel and began to sketch, waiting for the moment when she would become unconscious of everything except the flow of the penciled lines on the paper. Awkwardly she traced the arm, resting casually on the chair, the torso on that side, the legs. Her hand began to shake and she couldn't get it to stop. Glancing up at his face, her eyes met his. Embarrassed, she looked back at the stiff, unnatural drawing she'd done so far.

Pete straightened his back and, trying to forget about feeling so exposed, he focused on the quick sketching movements she made. Her pencil moved deftly—was it shaking or did he just imagine it? This was no big deal for her, so why would she be nervous? He spread his knees, which had begun to press inward. He could adjust to this, just as he'd adjusted to so many other things in his life since moving here. He managed to keep his mind calm, but a throbbing began between his legs that signaled an erection he could not ignore. He had to try to regain control of this involuntary reaction, but it was a little like avoiding a sneeze or stopping the hiccups.

He looked at the wall and studied each irregularity in the surface, but found himself looking at her again. Her hair reminded him of the night on the beach, when she'd had to shake it to get the sand out. What would it be like to draw her body? His eyes began to trace her curves, but that didn't help his situation. Instinctively he moved his knees back together, hoping she wouldn't notice.

"Rosalie," he said, "I have an idea."

"What?"

"Come over here." She got up uncertainly and went to him, eyeing him as if planning to change his position. "If what you said is true—about the truth of the person coming through the unclothed body, maybe we should *both* be undressed." He took her hand and pulled her closer. "Can you crouch down a little more?"

He began to unbutton her dress, starting at the top, and she let him. He eased the dress from her shoulders, allowing it to fall behind her. She stood, slipped off her sandals, and removed her underwear.

"Mind if I break my pose for a minute?" he asked, and not waiting for her response, he stood up, put his arms around her, and gently kissed her on the lips. He felt her body relax, as she slipped her hands up around his shoulders. They stood embracing for a moment that seemed timeless. Finally, he said, "How does this feel?"

"Isn't this where we left off last summer?" she whispered.

"It could have made all the difference." He didn't want to let go of Rosalie, but was too aware of their purpose in being there. Besides, Andrea was coming over later that evening, and he had to be ready for her.

Andrea. The thought broke the mood. He found himself irritated, now, at the thought that she had intruded into this moment. No, he corrected himself; I invited Andrea in, but for the wrong reasons. Somehow it helped to admit it. He held Rosalie close, feeling the warmth of her body melting into his, her embrace tightening. "We've got to get back to work, honey, 'cause I've got to go out tonight." He squeezed her, not wanting her to get the wrong idea—because it was the wrong idea, he realized. But how would he tell Andrea?

Still basking in his newly awakened feelings, Pete released Rosalie from his embrace and sat back down, while she returned to her easel.

He's taking her *out tonight.* She knew it without his telling her, but somehow it didn't matter, because for the rest of this hour they were present to each other. "I'm starting over again on this," she announced, tore off the first page, and began drawing on a clean sheet of paper. This time the lines flowed as she'd hoped they would. In a short time she'd captured this pose, and arranged him in new ones.

Finally, she began the hardest part—his face. "Don't smile!" she ordered, as his face wrinkled into a grin. He pulled it back into a semblance of sobriety, but his cheeks kept twitching. She managed a couple of drafts from this angle, then went over to move his face for a different view. Playfully he bit her finger as she tried to manipulate it. "Stop grinning!" she told him fiercely, struggling not to laugh.

He tickled her. She couldn't hold it back anymore. Laughter began like a wave rising up off the beach, mounted, began to froth, spilled over onto itself, then crashed onto the rocks of their nakedness. Her eyes began to gush tears, as she rocked with laughter that infected Pete as well. He groped for the sleeve of his robe to dab at his streaming eyes. Standing up, he stamped his foot as he chortled on. Finally, he pulled her into a hug, as they both panted, exhausted by the hilarity of the moment.

After Rosalie left, Pete showered and dressed for dinner with Andrea. They were invited to the Valley to dine with a photographer and his wife who lived out past the Village. His tan turtleneck under the new tweedy brown sweater he'd splurged on at Khaki's would be just right, he thought. For some reason, his arms and legs seemed lighter, and he found himself singing that "Touro-louro . . ." again. Couldn't get that tune out of his head.

As he pulled on his khaki pants, a thought invaded his consciousness. *Did I stress that she was not to use that nude sketch with my face on it? I told her I wanted a* portrait, *right?* All he needed was his naked body hanging around in Carmel. Well, if it was on one of those calendars, sure, but that was done tastefully, not with everything hanging out. Next time he saw Rose he'd have to clarify that with her. She could use the body sketch any way she wanted to, as long as it was somebody else's face. He'd have to call her after a week or so and see when the portrait would be ready. He could send it to Aunt Marie for Christmas.

H&R Block was giving her more hours each week, as December came, but Rosalie used every spare minute for painting. She'd nearly finished the full portrait of Pete, which had come out even better, she thought, than the Blue Nude. She'd tried to capture all his dimensions, including the German-Russian history, using a muted scene of Kansas wheat in the background. *What was it he'd said about his face? Well, she'd ask him about that later.*

I've got to get the Blue Nude into a gallery somewhere, she kept telling herself. She'd asked Pete to suggest some, and he hastily scribbled out a few names for her to try. Her best tip, however, came from an artist she met at the art supply store, who suggested the De La Guerra Gallery, owned by a newcomer from down south. "She's open to new artists — especially women," the artist had told her.

The next morning Rosalie took the still-wrapped Blue Nude to the De La Guerra Gallery in Paseo Viscaíno, an inner courtyard filled with small shops and boutiques extending in off Lincoln Street in Carmel. Next door was a small coffee shop, where she got a café latte to sip as she waited at the fir-garland festooned windows of the De La Guerra Gallery and studied the paintings in the windows. There were several done in a Cubistic style with characteristically heavy dark lines and bright colors. Peering through the window, she saw a female nude on one wall, done in a similar style. This might indeed be the right place for her Blue Nude.

The click of a key in the lock drew her attention to a woman dressed in a flowing burgundy skirt and top, about to push open the door. "Sorry you had to wait. Would you like to come in?"

Rosalie maneuvered her painting through the door and put it down. "I'm Rosalie Smith. I heard you were considering paintings for display."

"Glad to meet you! I'm Andrea Manchester. Yes, well, I'm still looking at paintings. As you can see . . ." She swept her hand out to indicate the already-filled wall space, ". . . I don't have a lot of room, but I do still have a few empty spots, so I can definitely *look* at some new works." She asked Rosalie about her background. The mention of New York and the Manhattan show got her attention, and her voice grew softer and warmer at that point. "And you say you do nudes?"

"Yes, mostly. I brought my Blue Nude for you to look at. This is the one I'd like to be showing at this point."

"Well, let's see it." The tone was still condescending. Gallery owners could afford to be selective.

Rosalie stripped off the paper and turned the painting to face Andrea, whose face froze momentarily. She said nothing for a few moments, then spoke. "This is very good! A powerful work, Rosalie." She squatted down and bent over to study the detail. "Really, a marvelous painting! Who did you study with?"

Rosalie told her about Helena Kobell and about the workshop.

"I should have known. Of course, you've got a phenomenal background. And of course, the frame sets it off so perfectly. An excellent choice; you have a good eye."

"Oh, I can't take credit for that. My framer chose it."

"Ah yes! Those New York frame shops do such a good job."

"Well, actually . . ."

Just then the UPS man opened the door and backed in pulling his cart loaded with boxes. Andrea flew over to hold the door. "I'll write up the contract in just a minute, Rosalie." After signing for the UPS order, she came back to make arrangements for the consignment. "You know, I'd prefer to have two paintings minimum from a single artist. Often if people like your style, they'd like to choose from a selection of pictures. Do you have anything else we could show?"

The picture of Pete was nearly finished. Anything else would take her a week or so at the rate she was finding time to paint. "I could bring you a nude I'm completing now, just for the time being, and then I'll have something else ready in a couple of weeks. Otherwise, I've got a couple of seascapes."

"Oh, the nude would be much better! I don't get many male nudes.

And now is the time to get it up, because it's getting close to Christmas."

That night Rosalie worked until after midnight applying the coating that gave the skin its sheen, creating the sense of inner glow. Pete appeared in the work as the whole person she had known, with all the reservoir of feeling developed during the workshop, and deepened during the drawing session together. Finally, she left the painting to dry. In the morning she would take it over to De La Guerra Gallery.

Rosalie woke at six with a nagging worry. Would Pete mind having his painting up in a gallery? He'd have to understand, of course, that she needed to do this, and she'd explain to him that it was just until she could get the nude surfer done. Better not even to bring it up to him, she decided. What was the chance of his actually seeing it there before she made the switch?

Her first appointment at work was at eight-thirty, and she had another at nine-thirty, so she'd be delayed getting the painting over to the gallery. The nine-thirty appointment went on and on, with all kinds of complications, and it was almost eleven-fifteen when Rosalie finally called Andrea to let her know she was bringing in the picture.

"That's fine! I'm not going to lunch until noon," Andrea said.

Rosalie careened up Highway 68 through Del Monte Forest, past the Seventeen Mile Drive gate and onto Highway 1, turning at Carpenter Street to take the shortcut into Carmel. Down on Junipero, she was amazed to find a parking space and eased into it. She took the painting, which she'd placed in the old frame from the Blue Nude, and headed over to Lincoln Street, her step lightened by the Christmas music that floated out of many of the shops.

De La Guerra Gallery was empty of patrons when Rosalie entered at 11:45. She took the painting, draped in an old sheet, to the counter. Andrea joined her there. "I can't wait," she said. "If this is anything like the first one, I'm going to love it." She waited in respectful anticipation for the unveiling.

Rosalie pulled back the sheet and looked at Andrea, who stood with her mouth open, saying nothing. Her face had paled, but Rosalie told herself it must be awe that left her speechless.

"It's . . . it's . . ." She began to cough, her face turning red. Finally regaining her aplomb, Andrea said, "Did you do this from a live model?"

"Yes, of course," Rosalie said. "I think I like it even better than the Blue Nude."

"Uh, yes . . . yes, I suppose . . . a New York model, of course. He just looks like someone I . . ."

The door jingled and both women looked up abruptly. Pete paused in the doorway looking as if he'd just remembered something important he had to do—elsewhere. He looked back into the street, and then came in, letting the door close. "Well, if it isn't . . ." He hop-skipped up with a nervous flourish. "And what do we have here?"

"Yes," Andrea said in a brittle tone, "I was just telling my new artist that her model looked a little—actually, *a lot*—like you." She stepped back to scrutinize it more carefully. "Oh, uh, I guess I should introduce you two. Rosalie—"

"We've met," Pete and Rosalie uttered together.

Rosalie froze in horror as Pete stared at the painting, the twinkle in his blue eyes hardening momentarily. "Huh!" He looked at Andrea and then at Rosalie. "I thought I said *portrait!*"

"This *is* a portrait." *Had he meant head and shoulders? Oh, man.* "Pete, I need to explain," Rosalie said. "Andrea wanted more of my work, and I had only this one. I was hoping you wouldn't mind. And the frame . . . it's the old one, I hope that's okay. I just threw it into that old frame because Andrea said . . ."

"No, I guess I need to explain," Pete said. "Last summer I thought you were going back to New York. I didn't know you'd be moving here or I wouldn't have been looking to meet someone else, or, well, whatever . . ."

"Well, believe me, I'd like to hear the rest of this explanation," Andrea said, "but I don't think I have time." She threw her chin forward, and went on through clenched jaws. "I've got a million things to do this afternoon, so I don't think I can make lunch with you two. Maybe you can tell me this story another time." She spun around and started toward the back of the gallery, then stopped abruptly, as if in afterthought. "Oh, Angelina—no, what's your name? Rosalie, yes? I've decided I don't have room in the gallery for any nudes right now, so I guess you'll have to try elsewhere. Sorry!" She retrieved the Blue Nude and clunked it down in front of Rosalie. It still had its wrap on.

Her brass gong of a voice reverberated in Rosalie's ears, as this potential venue closed its doors to her. Leaning to grasp both sides of the large painting, she saw Pete picking up the new nude.

"C'mon Rose, let's go to lunch, okay? And afterwards we might bring the picture to the shop so I can dress it in something more appropriate." He kissed her on the forehead. "Believe me, I know lots more galleries you can show your Blue Nude in . . . but, I think I'll just hang the one of me in my bedroom, if you don't mind."

Moving Day

by Mike Tyrrel

Jn slow quarter-time, the Monterey Bay waves lapped the shore, tempting bathers with cool relief from the afternoon sun. Sand castles, built during low tide, crumbled with each successive wave. Newly tossed seaweed marked the ocean's encroaching domain.

At Del Monte Beach, some played volleyball; others played catch with either frisbees or softballs. Marines from the Defense Language Institute played an aggressive game of football in the soft sand. All the fire pits located near the bicycle trail were in use, so beachgoers either waited in line or labored to bring their grills to the ocean's edge.

With Friday forecasted to be unusually warm, Fred Schleck had called in sick to enjoy a day at the beach with his family. Throughout the day, several families set up near the Schleck's area, only to soon move away. For one thing, their boom box was annoyingly loud. Secondly, the music sounded like a troop of Boy Scouts being forced to walk across shards of glass. During some tunes, Fred played an imaginary set of drums. For others, an empty Coke bottle became his microphone and his awful wailing blended with the song.

Fred and Beth Schleck both had short bleached white hair, midriff rolls of fat, and tattoos of question marks and exclamation points prominently displayed on their biceps. Their two daughters, Cary and Tonya, used Mehendi Henna tubes for their temporary artwork, and dyed their hair to match the color of their clothes, which this week was aqua blue.

Fred threw chips laced with high octane Tabasco sauce and crackled with laughter as the seagulls gagged on the "treat". Other birds flew off in sympathy with the yelping gulls, leaving the Schleck's area empty of begging paupers.

As the latest victim flew away shrieking, Beth said, "That was a good one, Hon, but this is getting boring. Let's go home."

The Schlecks gathered their belongings and made their way to the car, leaving behind Coke bottles, half-eaten sandwiches, and several empty chip bags. They didn't care about tidiness; someone else had to clean up after them. When caught, Fred usually told the Park Rangers that the mess was there when they arrived.

Driving home on Route 68, Cary, age fourteen, threw a banana peel that landed on a passing bicyclist. "Five points!" she shouted out the window as the cyclist shook his fist at the Chrysler, as it motored away belching blue smoke. Tonya, two years younger, complimented her sister's throw. Just before the Salinas River, Fred turned east on River Road, ran two red lights, ignored a stop sign, then entered the long access road to the Pine Springs subdivision. Luckily for Fred the security gate was open since his clicker needed a new battery. As they drove up Pine Canyon Drive their neighbors didn't wave at the decrepit car. No concern to him, he never waved either.

Fred automatically pulled into the driveway. Then he noticed it was lined with flowers, the lawn was fairway green, and the house a light brown with dark trim. He put the car in reverse and said as he backed out, "Looks like I pulled into the wrong drive."

Back on the street, the car lurched as he slammed on the brakes. "What the hell is going on here? Over there is Sam's house. There's Chris', and below us is Washburn's. So this should be our house! But it's not. I don't get it."

"Dad, where's our house?" Cary screamed. "Something ain't right."

He parked the car on the street and got out. With his hands on his hips, he surveyed the driveway as Beth walked up beside him. "Maybe this is a new reality television show and they've fixed up our house. Let's put on a smile for the hidden cameras," she said as she tried to straighten her T-shirt.

"Can't be, this isn't our house," Fred answered. "You kids coming with us?"

"No, we're staying here," they said in unison and quickly locked the door.

"No, matter. I need a shower; the sand is starting to bother me," Fred said.

Sam, their neighbor up the hill, was watering his plants. He moved toward them when he saw them standing in the street. "Hello. I didn't think I'd see you again. Are you here for the barbecue or just getting one last look before you leave?"

"Sam!" Fred shouted, "What happened?"

"Darnedest thing I ever saw," Sam said pointing to the sky. "Moments after you left this morning, three cranes and a series of big trucks arrived. They lifted your house and helicopters replaced it with that one." He pointed toward the new house with his water hose. "Never would've guessed they coulda done it that fast. The new place looks nice. The yard's landscaped, new driveway, and they even removed the oil spots right where you're standing."

Fred and Beth looked down. They realized the road was clean and the scraggly ice plants bordering the curb had been replanted. Not a weed could be seen anywhere.

Fred's face turned red. "They can't do this to me! I live here!"

Sam returned to the sanctuary of his garage. Fred looked at Beth. Hearing his daughters crying and not knowing what to do, he balled up his fist and said, "I'm going to find out what's going on!"

Beth quietly whispered in his ear, "Sam may be part of the reality show, so calm down, Brutus. Let's not look stupid on TV."

Fred blew out the air he had built up in his lungs and undid his balled fist as he draped his arm over his wife's shoulder. He walked to the front door, expecting microphones to pick up his voice, and he said, "This herringbone brick sidewalk is much better than the cracking concrete that used to be here. Look at those fruit trees; the apples look ready to pick. This is certainly a nice change."

He stepped up and pressed the doorbell. Beethoven's *Fifth* had replaced their Adams Family screech. Their doormat, which said, "GO AWAY," had been replaced by a "HOME SWEET HOME." Over the intercom they heard a pleasant, "Be there in a minute."

The door opened and a smiling woman in a blue apron stood in the doorway. She put down a feather duster, reached behind the door, and handed a yellow rose to Beth. "Hello, I'm Kathy. My husband Bob is out buying tri-tip for tonight's barbecue. Will you be joining us?"

Playing the part of the unexpected winner and hoping for the surprise answer, Fred asked, "What's the reason for the party?"

"We want to meet our new neighbors. Where do you folks live?" Kathy asked.

Fred never stuttered before, but he couldn't say the obvious. All Kathy could see was his right foot plopping up and down, along with his forefinger in the same rhythm pointing to the stoop. Finally words came. "Here! Right here! We live right here!" he said defiantly.

"Oh, Bob and I weren't expecting you, but come on in."

Fred and Beth entered the rose-scented hallway. They followed Kathy into the dining room. Centered on the table were more roses in a crystal vase. A fat brown envelope lay in one corner. Fred looked out the picture window and saw the familiar horse pasture and houses. He looked at the knick-knacks on the windowsill, then down at the plush white carpet. White wouldn't work in his house, for their once brown carpet, now a faded gray-green, hid food spills well.

Kathy opened the brown envelope and pulled out several documents. "This is the registered title for 4896 Pine Canyon Drive. Here's the court order allowing residency to take place today. The Monterey County tax assessor appraised and accepted our check for the first year's taxes. The Monterey Coastal Commission accepted the structural changes to the property. We've paid the full year's homeowner's associations dues, plus your arrears, and penalties."

"I'm confused," Fred said. His eyes wandered on the ceiling, then to the floor before he continued. "This is *your* house, not ours?"

Before replying, Kathy picked up a cell phone and punched in 23. "They're here," she said.

Flipping the phone closed, she said, "Would you like some fresh squeezed lemonade?"

"With some vodka, sure!" Fred said.

They followed her out onto the polished redwood deck—not the half rotten fir that had been their deck—then up the step that led to the back of the house where the same oak tree now shaded the rear of the deck. But instead of the Schlecks' haphazardly nailed plywood and two-by-four tree house, a miniature version of *this* house rested snugly in the tree. The tree house windows had blue curtains and a cedar shingle roof. Fred's mouth dropped as Kathy stepped off the deck and walked to a ten-foot lemon tree—which was not there this morning—and pulled off five large lemons.

"Bob is planning to put a gas cooker next to the outdoor wet bar. We haven't experienced the evening sky yet, but we expect the stars to be spectacular; so we might get a hot tub first."

Fred listened to her droning. Typically, his one ear heard while the other one ignored. Sometimes his boss had to explain a task several times before he understood and completed it, but having a government job meant he couldn't be fired for practicing ignorance.

As Kathy talked, she rolled the lemons on the granite counter, sliced, and then squeezed them. She opened a cabinet, pulled out five glasses, making fresh lemonade when the doorbell rang. She pushed the intercom and said, "We're out back on the deck, just come around behind the garage."

Fred had already taken a big swig and said, "This is better than the canned stuff." He watched Kathy place the rinds in a bag for disposal. He would've tossed them down the canyon . . . that is if he had a lemon tree. Which made him wonder if his mess in the canyon had been cleaned up.

On his next sip, he noticed two Monterey County Deputy Sheriffs approaching the deck. When they stepped up, Kathy handed each a glass of lemonade. Fred wondered how she knew, then realized that's who she called five minutes ago. *Now that's even stranger, since the county takes an hour to respond to any emergency.* Taking the initiative, so things would go his way, he said, "I'm glad you fellows showed up. I was about to call you to help me straighten out this problem."

The officers looked at Fred, then turned to Kathy. "Ma'am this is terrific lemonade. What variety is your tree?"

"Double Bearing Meyer. It retains last year's fruit while growing this year's, so we have fresh lemons year 'round."

Officer Stevens, polished brass nametag above his left pocket, and a polite smile that said, "I caught your hand in the cookie jar," told Fred, "Am I correct in assuming that you're the previous owner?"

Fred slammed his glass down, spilling some. Through clenched teeth he said, "What's this *previous* stuff? When I left this morning my house was here. When I came back, my house was missing, maybe stolen, and I think this lady knows where it is."

"Sir, she doesn't know. However, my partner Officer Franklin and I do. We're county process servers, and you've been served," he said as he handed papers to Fred.

Frowning and shaking his head, Fred asked, "You're going too fast for me. Served for what?"

Officer Stevens took out a laminated card from his left shirt pocket and read from it. "Under the Financial Security Act, Title Twenty, banks are required to preserve their loan's equity." Reciting from memory he continued, "Property loans are structured in two parts: land and building. Should the tenant not maintain the building in good condition, the bank is at risk. Tax rolls are diminished for a devalued home. Schools suffer, infrastructures deteriorate, and fellows like Bert and I do not receive fair wages for our work. Hence the county's enforcement of the Financial Security Act."

He returned the card to his pocket. "Sir, there is a benefit to you. When the bank moved your house, you received a clear title. Your outstanding loan was transferred to this property, of which this couple is now considered the legal tenant. In the papers I handed you are directions to your home's new location, title, county registration, post office change of address, and a greatly reduced tax rate of which the bank paid the first year."

Moving Day

The two officers finished their lemonade and commented to Kathy that she had a remarkable view. Fred and Beth silently sipped their drinks. As the officers were leaving, Stevens said to the Schlecks, "Sir, Ma'am, we have to ask you to leave with us. And we give you a gentle warning: don't come back, don't harass these people, don't call or send letters. Should these folks feel that you are bothering them, your first punishment will be three days of community service. Recently the judge has been assigning the community service to the cleaning of the town's sludge ponds." Both officers snickered. "Which seems to have greatly reduced grime. So if you'll follow us out, we'll be leaving."

Fred, with years of practice stonewalling his boss, stood his ground. "I've never heard of this. This can't possibly be legal!"

Officer Stevens said, "It's your right to review the packet of documents with your lawyer. But let me save you some cash, because some lawyers will collect the money up front then take eight hours to review the documents. Others, after one quick look at the county registrar's embossed stamp, will confirm what I've said. I know it's a shock, but look on the bright side, you have no house payments, a lower tax rate, and neighbors just like you."

The silent officer snickered again.

"Now follow us, please," Officer Stevens said.

The officers guided Fred and Beth to their car. As Fred started grinding the starter motor, Stevens stuck his hand into the open window. "Sir, why not hand me your gate clicker? No one enjoys working the sludge ponds."

Fred gave it to him and started toward the gate. When he reached River Road, he stopped, not knowing which way to turn. He looked in the packet of papers, and found the directions. Right on River Road, left on Chualar Bridge, south on Route 101, right on Stage Coach, take the first right.

He followed the instructions, and after driving an hour he entered the Lazy Springs subdivision. The horse pasture on the right had seen better days; the termite-eaten fence was falling down. The horses all looked overweight and sway-backed. The large pond had a thick coating of algae and trash lined the shore. The ballpark's grass had not been cut for months; its backstop leaned over home plate. The nearby park's swings had broken chains and overflowing trash bins.

Cary and Tonya, silent during the journey, finally spoke in unison: "This place isn't going to be much fun."

Following the last directions, Fred saw his house and entered the driveway. He noticed the peeling paint was not as bad as the other houses. He surveyed his new neighborhood and wondered if a paid up house was going to be worth it.

The neighbor across the street was setting up a barbecue on his front lawn. They watched him pour gasoline on the charcoal, then throw a match. The flame whooshed up eight feet for a few seconds before adjusting to a two-foot height.

"Howdy neighbor," was the shout from across the street, as the man waddled penguin-like toward them. The heavily spotted, once white T-shirt tightly covered his shoulders and chest, but only hid the top half of his hairy, watermelon-sized stomach.

"So, you're the new guy. At first this place'll take some getting used to, but you'll be able to figure out what to do with all your extra money. Me, I have a collection of foreign beers that probably rivals any sports bar. Frank, that's his house on your right, is a burned-out disk jockey. He has every album from the late sixties to the early eighties. On Saturday he takes requests and the whole neighborhood enjoys his stereo system. We don't like party poopers around here, pal."

The friendly neighbor took out a crumbled packet of Camel cigarettes, lit one, then threw the match into Fred's dying bushes. He looked into the packet and realized it was empty, so he threw it into the bushes too. "Where was I? Oh yeah, your other neighbor, we think, is from the government witness protection program. He and his wife keep peeking out from behind the curtains. Nobody has ever seen them outside. The TV reception is lousy out here, so order cable now because it'll take them six to nine weeks to install it. Let me know when they come so I can have them fix something at my house."

While the neighbor just sucked on his cigarette, Fred realized it was his turn to speak. "I'm Fred Schleck. We used to live over there," Fred said, pointing toward Black Mountain peak.

"I'm Tom. Yeah, yeah, yeah, we all used to live somewhere else. Nobody cares where you're from, okay! We stay here because it's easier to live here than anywhere. I've been here two cars, some folks have been here four."

"Two cars?"

"Well, when your car dies, you leave it on your lawn. Much cheaper than taking it to the dump. Plus an old car is great for kids to play in and the neighborhood dogs have a place to sleep. Mine's nicknamed Ford Apache. The neighbor kids shoot paint balls at it, which helps protect my house."

Fred looked closely and realized the house's lower portion was indeed paint ball stained, then noticed that the two cars, jacked up on blocks, were arranged as a side border hedge. "Any kids?" Fred asked.

"Yeah, your two girls are about my kids' age. My oldest girl doesn't come out too much, she's pregnant again. If I catch the boy, I'll beat his father or mother, whichever is easier, to a pulp."

"My oldest daughter's fourteen," Fred said.

"I think they'll get along. I gotta get back to my grilling. If you need anything for your house, I can save ya a trip to Orchard Supply. I keep all my old stuff in back of the house. Sinks, fridges, toilets, et cetera. It's a lot easier than taking anything to the dump. Never know when someone might need a part for a '68 Frigidaire. Nice meeting you, neighbor."

As the Schlecks walked toward their house, Cary said, "Did you see his belly button sticking out like a thumb? And it's tattooed, is that gross or what?"

Their keys worked, the door chime screeched as usual, and their ratty doormat looked clean. Inside, the house was just as they'd left it that morning—in disarray. Dishes from the past four days were stacked in the sink. In the living room were piles of newspapers and magazines. Beth opened the fridge and pulled out hamburger for Sloppy Joes, and Doritos and Cokes to go with them. She prepared their meal as if nothing unusual had happened. After the meal, she wedged the dishes into the sink.

The TV couldn't receive anything so Cary popped in a DVD.

"Anyone want to walk around our new neighborhood?" Fred asked. Beth nodded, while the girls ignored him, glued to the TV.

Fred and Beth walked outside and saw Tom brushing off a steak that had fallen on the ground before he placed it back on the grill. "Remind me to never eat anything our friendly neighbor cooks," Fred said.

Every house they passed was nearly in identical shape. Peeling paint, dried grass, weeds amongst the bushes, dead trees, and soiled driveways with piles of sludge from dripped oil. A few homes had broken windows taped up with weathered cardboard. Some had no stripped cars on the front lawn, while others made up for those missing artifacts. At one house a man was planting flowers as his wife watered the shrubs.

Surprised by this activity, Fred stopped to talk. "Howdy," he said.

"Don't try and stop us," the man said defensively, "'cause we have a plan."

"Stop what?" Fred asked.

"You must be the new people," he said, less on guard, and received a nod in return. "Well in that case, the only way out of this pigsty is work. That's right, work! Work will set you free! I'm tired of being tired, so is my wife. You may become like the others and feel comfortable here . . . your choice, neighbor."

Fred smiled and said good-bye. House after house was the same story, a mess. Yet here and there a few people were making attempts at keeping their place up. After talking to six couples, they had made a complete loop of the subdivision. Though everyone seemed friendly, no one asked about them or offered any refreshments.

That night, instead of watching TV in bed, Fred and Beth talked. Fred asked, "Is this what you want?"

Beth replied, "There's a lot we can do with more money; better vacations, go out to dinner, and buy a better TV. Doesn't seem so bad living here. Think about it, we won't have to worry about the neighbors complaining over every little thing."

"That's the point. I get the feeling that instead of outdoing each other, this neighborhood tries to outgross themselves." Fred thought before he continued, "I used to be the star gross-out, but here I'm an amateur. There's no reason for the complete trashiness of this subdivision. First thing tomorrow morning, I'm going to visit a realtor and sell this house. We'll start over."

"If that's the way you feel, okay, but as long as we're here, why not order cable?"

The Beatles woke the Schlecks at six-thirty the next morning. Fred hated his dad's music. He closed the bedroom windows, yet the music still penetrated the glass. Other than the loud music, everything seemed normal. The shower water was hot, *The Monterey Herald* was delivered; yet it landed in goopy dog turds, and mail overflowed their mailbox because he hadn't bothered to check it last night.

Fred fished a frying pan out of the sink and gave it a quick once over with a paper towel. The dishes wouldn't be washed until their two-week supply of plates and silverware had been used.

After breakfast Cary asked, "Dad, since we don't have to make any house payments, why not get a new dishwasher to replace the busted one?"

"I'm going to check that out. Anyone want to come with me?"

Greeted with silence, Fred slipped on his flip-flops and left. Outside he saw the neighbor on the left peering through their curtains, which quickly closed when Fred waved.

At the house on the right, the DJ sat on the deck behind a soundboard and three turntables. He interrupted a song and announced that the new neighbor had stepped outside, and would everyone give him a round of applause for his first day of freedom. He then played the Pink Floyd song "Money", very loud.

Tom was outside pouring more gas on the grill. He waved and shouted, "My stove's broke and I need help dragging it behind the house. Got some time to help a neighbor? Beer's on me!"

"Sure, I'll help when I return," Fred said automatically, climbing into his car. He heard an explosion as Tom lit his barbecue.

A belch of blue smoke and loud rattles sounded as the Chrysler rolled out onto the street, causing Tom to shout, "Looks like you'll have a lawn ornament soon enough, neighbor."

He drove away thinking to himself, *I hope not.*

Fred pulled into the ReMax Realtor parking lot. As he stepped inside the office, the receptionist greeted him saying, "Good morning. First time here?" Seeing a nod, she handed him a form. "Please fill this out."

When finished, he handed it back. The receptionist looked it over then announced, "Tilly you're up!"

An older, blue-gray haired woman shuffled toward Fred. "Good morning, I'm Tilly, and you are?"

"Fred Schleck."

Tilly quickly reviewed the form. "Let's go to my desk. I see you're selling. You couldn't have picked a better time. Today's real estate market is exploding with more buyers than sellers. Do you have another home you're buying, because yours will sell in a week?"

"No, I don't. Could you do both?" Fred asked with a half smile.

Tilly's eyes brightened. She was ready for a double-play. Her office manager always said, "You can't have a triple without first getting the double." She entered numbers on her calculator and looked pleased, for she figured this double-play might be worth ten grand.

"Mortgage?" Tilly asked.

"I have a clear title," Fred said proudly.

"You might want to consider offering a loan to any buyer." Then she said softly under her breath, "You wouldn't have to report that income to the government. Just something you should think about."

Fred nodded his head in understanding.

"3597 Dodo Lane, I'm not familiar with that address. What subdivision is that in?"

"Lazy Springs."

"Lazy Springs Ranch?"

Fred nodded. Tilly pushed her chair back. "You *did* say Lazy Springs Ranch?"

Fred again nodded yes, but this time with no smile.

Tilly stood up, and announced to everyone in the office, "This fellow wants to sell his house in Lazy Springs Ranch."

The other eleven sales personnel, including the receptionist, started laughing. Tilly joined in the laughter, but only after Fred asked, "What's so funny?"

Tilly looked him in the eye and said, "No one has ever sold a home in Lazy Springs. No one, means no one! Even if your house is the best looking one in Grunge City, it'll never sell once the buyer sees the other homes!"

In a pleading voice Fred asked, "What can I do?"

"Just walk away. I understand a few homes have been abandoned." With that Tilly stood up, leading a perplexed Fred to the door. She held out her hand, "My pen, please."

Frustrated after hearing the same thing at every real estate office he stopped at that morning, Fred drove home and parked in the driveway just as the mail was being delivered. He waited at the mailbox. When the carrier stopped his truck, he held out a bundle of mail. Fred asked, "How many homes are abandoned here?"

"Right now eleven, but they all come back after a few months. This place has a strange allure."

"How did you get so lucky in getting this route?"

"Yeah, tell me about it. This route has no Christmas tips. Originally the route was for beginners, but to tell you the truth, I was a goof-up. I never took my job seriously and I got stuck here. The fact is, I've changed. I do my job over and above what's expected. If you need stamps, I have them in the truck and I'll gladly make change. If you're missing postage, I pay for it and leave you a note. I deliver packages to your door instead of leaving them at the curb. My supervisor and inspector say I've changed, and thankfully, today's my last day. Monday I have a new route."

"Congratulations," Fred said as walked to his house.

The letter carrier stuck his head out the window. "Good luck with the new guy; I sorta know what he'll be like."

When Fred closed the front door behind him, the kids yelled from the living room. "Dad the TV reception is bad. The neighbors' kids don't want to play; they have to watch their babies. I swear, Dad, every girl has a baby. When I asked who the dad was, they all shrugged their shoulders. Dad, this place is the bottom of the food chain, get us out of here!" Cary ran crying upstairs to her room. Her door slammed.

Beth came in the house and plopped onto the sofa. Lifting her feet up on the ottoman, she said, "You're not going to believe this. I went door to door trying to sell my *Natural Look* cosmetic line, and every woman swears they get their makeup at 7-11. Every house I entered, I gagged from cigarette smoke. Maybe I can make money selling Pampers door to door! So, did you get the house listed at a realtor?"

"Let me tell you *my* bad news. I visited five realtors; none of them would list the house and each wanted their packet of materials back. We seem to be in a tar pit that no one escapes." Fred looked into the bag of doughnuts he'd bought for lunch. "You know, maybe this place ain't so bad. Let's give it some time before we decide."

"Cary and I have already decided," Tonya said. "Three boys tried to get me to go into their bedrooms. I'm only twelve, Dad! These boys are creepy! No one wants to catch lizards or climb trees. This is not the place I want to grow up."

Beth looked at her daughter. "Fred, our children deserve better. I deserve better! You have to do whatever it takes to give it to us!" She jumped to her feet, went upstairs and slammed the bedroom door.

Fred looked at Tonya. "Aren't you going to run upstairs and slam your door?"

"Can't, Dad. The hinge is broken."

For lunch, Fred grabbed a doughnut and reviewed everything in his mind. He hadn't painted the house because he often said, "trees are wood and they don't need paint." He hadn't repaired the driveway because the car leaked. He never fixed the Chrysler, because he never cared about mechanical things. He didn't wash the windows since the dirt protected them from UV rays. As he gazed out through the filmy dining room window, he remembered how clear the view had been out of the windows in the house that replaced his.

Never easily motivated, Fred told himself he would wash one window, the large dining room picture window, then he'd watch a movie. He finished off his fourth doughnut then went into the garage looking for a bucket.

It took five scrubbings to remove the accumulated grime on the outside. Walking back inside, he sighed as he realized the inside was layered with grease smudges that would drive a crime scene investigator crazy.

It took a Windex bottle and a whole roll of paper towels to spotlessly clean the inside. As he wiped, he saw the neighbors peering from behind their curtains. He waved; they only stared. With the window perfectly clean, he went into the living room and popped in a DVD. As he watched the movie credits, he noticed a column of light, the color of melted butter, streaming into the dining room through the window he'd just cleaned.

Fred looked at the dirty windows; no light penetrated them. He walked to the clean window and looked outside. He felt the sun's warmth and had to squint in the bright light. He walked to a dirty window. Nothing. No warmth nor brightness. He moved back to the clean window and remembered how the sun had warmed him lying on the floor as a kid doing his schoolwork.

He saw millions of dust particles dancing in the sun's rays. Then he had his second flashback as some of the rays penetrated the cobwebs in his mind. Some poem, read in some dingy coffee house at an open microphone, "The eyes are the windows to the soul." At that moment his rebellion had found its rally cry, for he had closed his eyes, so as not to see, and not to judge others or himself.

Fred looked around and shuddered. He picked up a stack of newspapers and with them started to clean the windows. With the inside windows cleaned, he tackled the outside. He had to empty the bucket after each window because the water was completely dirty. During their seventeen years in Pine Springs, he had only sprayed the hose on the windows, which he considered good enough.

When he'd finished, Fred turned to the peering neighbors who continued to stare at him. "I only did what was good enough!" he shouted. "Well, that's going to change!"

That night at the dinner table Fred announced his great plan: "Work will set us free. Today I cleaned all the windows."

Tonya said, "I thought the glass was missing. I bumped my head trying to look out."

Fred strained to look where she was pointing. Sure enough, he saw a forehead smudge along with three smeared hand prints. He said, "Honey, after you're through with dinner, I'll give you the materials to clean the window."

As Tonya was about to complain, Beth stepped in to defend her hubby. "Your Dad's right. We need to take responsibility for our inactions. We've had it too soft. There is a reason why we're here at Lazy Springs Ranch."

On Sunday, the family went to Orchard Supply and purchased shrubs, fruit trees, vines, fertilizers, shovels, and rakes. When they got home, Cary and Tonya worked for an hour before going inside to rest. Fred and Beth kept at it. Tom came by with two cans of beer.

"Howdy, neighbor. I hate seeing a man work up a sweat, so I brought some of my favorite Latvian beer."

"Thanks," Fred replied, "but I want to get these in before the sun sets."

"Uh, huh," Tom said as he popped, then gurgled down the contents of the can. "You and I know it won't work. I tried, we all tried. Just relax and enjoy life." When he received no reply, he said, "Suit yourself neighbor. All you're going to do is give the dogs a nice place to aim." He waddled home to start his grill.

Fred stood in the twilight watering the new plants. The neighbors who continually peered from behind their curtains came out to talk to him. "You think this will work?"

Fred noticed the man's eyes were wide open, seeking an answer. "Think real hard, fellow," Fred said. "Was there a house here before mine?"

The neighbor nodded. "I never talked to them. They're gone, you're here, so I'm curious."

"Why not come on over next Sunday for a barbecue?"

Moving Day

Not replying, the neighbor retreated home in silence.

With no TV, Fred noticed the downstairs was dark as he climbed the stairs. He sighed and leaned over, stretching his back as he undressed for a shower. Waiting for the water to warm up, he continued stretching, trying to remember the last time he did any exercises, let alone work that exhausted him. After the shower he climbed into bed and instantly fell asleep.

Monday morning looked like trash day, so Fred rolled out the green waste container. His car groaned as he started it and drove to work. At a particularly long light, he looked around inside the car. It, too, was dirty. The windows had a filmy build up, the carpets had accumulated dirt, the ashtray overflowed with credit card receipts. The car behind him honked and woke him from his inventory. Pulling into his usual spot, he glanced into the back seat. It, too, was the same mess.

At lunch he ignored his buddies and took his sandwich to the car, and did something that would have been unthinkable last week: he cleaned out his car. He didn't care what it was; everything went into the trash bag. After work he went to the oil and lube center. The mechanic had trouble, since the filter had rusted to the engine. Fred thought, *I may have ruined this engine but no more oil is going to drip on my driveway.*

That night, after the usual Sloppy Joes, Fred announced, "Tomorrow let's have pasta, like we used to. Four cheese sauce, with homemade garlic bread."

Beth, mopping up the lingering sauce on her plate, looked up. "With a little Chianti! Sounds good to me."

After dinner Fred looked out the kitchen window and noticed all the neighbors had full containers on the curb. He stood up and pointed out the window. "What's with these full trashcans here?"

Beth said, "Minor problem: the trash guy never came. According to Tom, everyone leaves the container curbside until he comes. Tom said it helps keep the smell away from the house."

Fred shook his head. "I don't like living here. For some reason, I'd become lazy and addicted to a life of mediocrity. I didn't like my parents' standards, yet I never developed any better ones. I mocked everyone who played the world's game, yet I played my own game." Fred stood up and looked out the window. Gesturing with his hands he continued, "We can stay here and continue to fool ourselves, or we can change and become the family we should be. If you want out of this dump, tonight we open the window and shout, 'We will *work* our way out!'"

His family clapped, then all came and hugged him. Beth said, "Let's go for it, Rocky!"

Fred looked at them with a tear in his eye. "That speech was the easy part. But tomorrow the hard part for me will be calling my Dad and saying I'm sorry for trying to hurt him all these years."

The Schlecks' shrubs, flowers, and trees bloomed, bringing color into an otherwise drab environment. The family painted the house on the weekends and had the driveway resurfaced. The gutter salesman couldn't believe his good fortune. He received an all-expense paid trip to Las Vegas for being the first salesman to sell a gutter in the Lazy Springs subdivision.

Fred came to work early, stayed late, and never again needed multiple instructions from his boss. He continually asked for more work and was promoted to area supervisor for his diligence, with a nice bump in pay.

Over the next year, the Schlecks completely refurbished the house. The Chrysler was towed to the local recycler and replaced with a Prius. That winter they picked bags of persimmons and lemons. For Christmas they bought a potted tree, then planted it in January. His daughters joined the park district softball and lacrosse leagues, and became the top scorers. Beth joined the PTA, brought brownies to every meeting, and somehow became the secretary. During the Schlecks' second year at Lazy Springs, Tom added a third car to the front lawn. The sonic posts Fred had installed kept the dogs out of his property, thus no more littering, and clean morning newspapers. Several times the curtain people came over for barbecues, but continued to peek through the curtains.

On the third anniversary of leaving Pine Springs, Fred visited his old property and knocked on the door. The door opened, assaulting him with rose fragrances.

"You're Kathy, right?"

"Yes. How can I help you?"

"I used to live here."

"Hmmm, I see."

"Three years ago you moved here and we moved somewhere else. In those years my family has changed. We even have two fine lemon trees." With furrowed brows Fred asked, "Can you tell me what I have left to do?"

Kathy paused a moment to reflect. "So, you think your journey is complete. I can't help you except to say, you must have something left to do or undo. For us, we took advantage of the previous owner. Nothing happened until we made restitution. Find what's left for you, do it, and then you're out."

Seeing a perplexed man, Kathy continued. "Search everything you're doing and not doing. You'll see that one something's missing, then go do it."

"I'm missing one thing?" Fred asked.

"Yes, you have to find it on your own. Dig deep. Once you find it, you're free!"

Fred stood there, looked at his feet, then smiled and said, "Thanks."

On his way home he reviewed everything he had done over the past three years and realized where he was still cheating. The next morning he called the Monterey County Assessor and made an appointment to share his problem.

In the official's office Fred asked, "Could you send one of your assessors to my home in Lazy Springs Ranch?"

With a practiced blank stare the official inquired, "What kind of problem do you have?"

"Our house has been remodeled and I believe it should be assessed at a higher rate."

With eyebrows raised and a genuine smile on his face he replied, "I don't get many people asking for higher taxes. Are you sure you want to do this?"

"I'm sure," Fred replied. Filling out the required paperwork took twenty minutes. The usually lethargic county official arrived that same afternoon and was working on his laptop in the driveway when Fred arrived home that evening. Fred walked up and asked, "Would you like to come in for a look?"

"Thanks, but there's no need," came the reply.

"It's hot out here; would you like some fresh lemonade?" Fred offered.

After tapping at the keyboard for a moment, the official replied, "That sounds good."

Once inside, he finished typing and turned off his laptop. "Nice place you have here. Too bad you're in this location." After a moment he went on, "I think this house belongs in a place like Pebble Beach."

"Well to tell you the truth, the family's ready for the move, and we would fit in there," Fred said.

A scribbled notation in his calendar and the official was done. "Your new assessment will be in the mail. You don't have to see me out." He rose and headed for the door.

A few days later, an hour before sunrise, the doorbell rang. Fred, grouchy from being awakened, made his way down the stairs and opened the door. Eight people in blue coveralls crowded on his porch. Confused, Fred asked, "Can I help you?"

"We're here to prepare your house. You have an hour to leave, here's a packet of instructions."

Fred quickly gathered his family, clutched the package given to him, and left for breakfast at the local diner. As they pulled out of their drive-way, the family saw trees and shrubs being wrapped and men on the roof were placing thick ropes. Tom was out front lighting his charcoal grill, but kept his back to them. The curtain people peeked out as Fred tried to wave to them. But they were staring at the men on the roof.

On their drive to the diner, his daughters pointed at the package and peppered their father, "Open it, Dad! Open it." But he just shook his head, No! He was afraid to open it.

Fred asked for a large booth and placed the brown envelope in the center of the table. After they finished their breakfast, they squeezed together on the same side of the booth. Fred opened the brown envelope and pulled out a packet of documents.

He held the top sheet. The first word said, "Congratulations." As they continued to read, the Schlecks started to cry. Sobbing loudly, they held each other. Their sobs were the only sound in the suddenly quiet restaurant. The other diners had stopped eating and looked on, wondering what tragedy had struck this family.

Moving Day

Bloodbank
by Mark C. Angel

Kamil climbed out from under heavy covers. He ran his fingers through his kinky hair and stepped over to the picture window in his room at the Bernardus Lodge, Carmel Valley, where he flung open the blackout curtains to gaze out.

Beneath the moonless night, the soft light of outdoor lamps revealed a manicured courtyard filled with colorful native flora, elegant wood furnishings, and modern California ranch-style architecture. But those trappings didn't interest Kamil much; he was more taken by the vista above. January stars filled the sky, an outstanding view courtesy of the coastal fog's inclination to hang west of the Laureles Grade. "I love winter north of the tropics," Kamil said to himself. "Nice long nights with plenty of time to hunt."

The sky seemed to darken as his preternatural vision adjusted and countless points of light blazed more brightly than any mortal would ever know. A few more moments passed, and Kamil saw what he thought might be a satellite passing across the inky blackness of the azimuth. If it were a satellite, however, it was unlike any he could remember: its light faded in and out at regular intervals.

Kamil contemplated that it might be an asteroid tumbling through space, destined perhaps to miss the blue planet by the narrowest of margins, or . . .

"Wouldn't it be ironic if it hit us?" he mused. "Maybe then the Thirst would set us free."

The Thirst. It drove him to drink human blood again and again, and as such it was the core cause of his powers—heightened senses, enhanced strength, perfected memory, and a psychic link to each victim which permitted perception of the Flash.

But all of these came with a price and his willingness to pay that price had faded. So his thoughts came to rest upon the one for whom he had come.

Where might Lilac *be?*

Kamil's first and only interaction with Lilac had been in the summer of 1859, a profound exchange he still recalled vividly.

He had been following the Italian wars of independence fought against Austria, visiting battlefields after skirmishes to hunt and collect the treasures of the nearly dead, while stealing personal histories from both sides of the trench via the Flash. It was while he grazed on injured combatants after the Battle of Solferino, Italy, that he met the ancient lamia.

Smoke from cannon and musket tainted the warm night air and a downpour at dusk had transformed the earth into a bloody quagmire. Bullet- and bayonet-damaged bodies writhed in the throes of death in the midst of human remains sprinkled about impact craters. The sounds of misery were everywhere. So were putrid smells.

Kamil felt right in his element.

Lilac was squatting near a man with precious little time left. She wore clothing more befitting of an Austrian boy than of an experienced nighttime predator, her amber hair tucked beneath a black fisherman's cap so the back of her neck glowed pale in the moonlight. Her thin build—90 pounds or so had she been flesh-and-blood—was misleading; a vampire's skin and bones were much denser than that of a mortal's, with blood that thickened over time into something akin to liquefied iron.

Lifting the soldier's head slightly, she held a canteen to his lips. "You will be with your god soon, do not fear," she told him. Only after he had gasped his last breath did she help herself to his remains.

Kamil recalled his revulsion at the sight of a fellow vampire feeding on the already dead, sucking at lifeless wounds. He had gone up to her boldly, even though he couldn't tell how strong she was without touching her to gauge the density of her flesh.

Since bodily contact was a risk he hadn't been ready to take, he instead cleared his throat. "Excuse me," he offered. "Don't you find that a bit repulsive?"

"Not as repulsive," she replied without looking up, "as countless sets of memories crammed into my mind. I value my sanity, thank you."

Kamil chuckled at her glib dismissal of the Flash. "Suit yourself," he replied, dabbing a drop of blood off his chin with a handkerchief and flicking the mud off his shoe with a short kick that cracked like a whip. He continued to watch her feed with a grim fascination, until she began to exsanguinate a spleen.

"That truly is disgusting!" he cringed.

Lilac looked up. "And who asked for your opinion?"

Kamil shrugged. A bad taste carpeted his tongue.

She resumed sucking the soldier's stagnant blood into her mouth.

"What's the point?" Kamil straightened his topcoat. "Let their hearts do the work, pumping the blood as the gods intended. You are certainly giving meaning to that distasteful slander, 'blood sucker'."

He slid over to another "moaner". "It is alright, friend," he said in a soothing voice, "you will be just fine soon enough." Then he ripped the man's neck open, enjoyed the natural flow of nectar, and reveled in his final moment, as the victim's life flashed through Kamil's mind.

"I see you have yet to lose your enthusiasm for the Flash," Lilac said, as she moved on to another soldier.

Kamil licked his lips with the faux innocent look of a boy who had pulled the wings off a butterfly. "I see it as preserving their memories for posterity; my duty as a historian, you see." He spoke as if he believed it.

His conviction failed to move Lilac. "I was making that same argument to myself when Alexander took Persepolis," she replied. "But I have grown tired of reliving human suffering over and over again."

Kamil gave her a patronizing smile. "You ought to meet the Swiss businessman I heard talking this evening at a nearby inn. He was completely beside himself with horror at what he saw here. Dunant was his name . . . yes, Henri Dunant." Kamil chuckled. "He had been seeking Napoleon III to discuss a deal of some sort, and passed by this very place: tens of thousands of men, each alone in the dirt, their lives leaking out from all sides. Lacked our innate appreciation for the spectacle, I guess."

Kamil bent down and gathered up another broken man. He drained the gasping soldier of his remaining blood and let the Flash pass into him—the ecstasy of knowing all the victim ever knew in a final frenzied flurry of right brain cell activity.

Lilac continued ignoring him as she administered water to the fallen. Undeterred, he continued to talk to her. "This Dunant said something about following in the footsteps of Florence Nightingale and swore to anyone who would listen he was going to do something about the misery. He was looking for an appropriate symbol . . ."

Lilac got up and brushed her hands against her front, before fixing him with a firm gaze.

"You sneer at me." Her statement was unencumbered by emotion. "Well, maybe your Henri Dunant is right."

Kamil found it difficult not to be unnerved by the grip of resolve in Lilac's glance, and just barley managed to smile. "Please. I did not mean to offend your sensitivities. But it is not only a matter of blood. I just like knowing a little bit about these people. Have the gods not given us pristine recollection of all life memory details? Even languages? It is our nature."

"Who can say what our nature is—certainly not your victims!—not anymore!" Lilac stepped toward Kamil, regarding him closely. "And I, for one, am not presumptuous enough to assume I understand the motivations of the gods. Thousands of lives, all unique, all special to someone, if only to themselves. Then why, after centuries, have they come to seem all the same to me? Perhaps that is the path the gods are asking us to take, to come to a greater, a deeper understanding of the fates. Get past the pleasure of the Flash and discover what lies beyond. I am sorry if these concepts cause you discomfort and disdain."

She was back ministering to another dying man. Unshackled from her gaze, Kamil knelt to help himself to the next closest groaner. The hearts of these dying soldiers failed after only a few pumps, making it harder for him to satisfy his thirst. Fortunately, the Flash remained undiminished.

"Maybe when you have been around as long as I have," Lilac suddenly offered, "you will remember this night with a better understanding of my sentiments."

"Perhaps, perhaps not. I *will* say that it was good to have your company. I rarely run into a battleground companion. Most like us prefer healthy kills. But I do *so* like to vary my diet."

"Well, if you ever *do* tire of this mundane existence, consider looking me up in North America. I am headed there soon. It is a big country with big ideas, and the surroundings may help me find a more dignified way to satisfy the blood Thirst."

With those words she disappeared, too quickly for even Kamil's keen eyes to follow.

Lilac settled on the central coast of California. She gave last rites to Padre Serra before she sipped his serum near the Carmel Mission. Later, while John Steinbeck was writing about dustbowl immigration to the Central Valley, she enjoyed dead Muskogee Bloody Marys. When little Shirley Temple smiled on celluloid, soliciting membership for the American Red Cross Disaster Relief program, Lilac didn't shed a rosy tear. But decades later, when she heard that the Red Cross' Carmel chapter sought volunteers to staff their burgeoning blood program, she remembered the long-ago conversation about Dunant, and her interest peaked; evidently the man had founded his humanitarian organization and chosen a symbol like his native Swiss flag as its banner. She decided to investigate, hoping to find a way to renew her withered body, long deprived of fresh human blood. The advent of modern health care had been rough on her; fresh corpses were hard to come by, meaning far too often she had been forced to feed on road kill.

But Dunant's Red Cross program . . .

The sun had just set when Lilac opened the doors to the detached garage of her modest Carmel Comstock cottage, nestled among twisting back roads in the southeast corner of the city. The heavy hinges protested loudly, stale from age and inactivity. Inside the musty garage, she pulled the cover off her black 1909 Silver Ghost, and slid behind the wheel.

She backed the almost 60-year-old automobile out, wheels crunching on gravel, just as two neighborhood squirrels began to chew out a cat that watched them from its perch on a rickety redwood fence—as exciting an event as took place in this neck of the woods. The rodents launched a chewed pine cone at the feline, but their aim was wanting. The woody missile bounced off the hood of the classic Rolls-Royce.

Angered, Lilac leapt up into the air from the convertible, shooting past the tree's lower branches and, in a single motion, grabbed the furry perpetrators. By the time she dropped back to the earth, more gracefully than any feline could, the gray critters were drained of their blood, their scattered little memories dancing like dragonflies in her mind. She instantly regretted her action, and shook her head in a vain attempt to rid herself of their thoughts. She dropped the twin carcasses on the ground for the benefit of the fat cat that was now caressing her legs. The lazy hunter sauntered off with first one, then the other, and disappeared behind a hedge.

Lilac regarded the small dent on the roadster's hood, and considered how the vehicle—which she had bought new to celebrate her 50th anniversary of swearing off the Flash—was the only thing in her life she preserved with any particular care. In truth, she felt an affinity to her cherished Ghost, as she shared many characteristics with it. Her skin was nearly as hard as metal, her eyes shined like silver trimmed carbide headlamps, and her temperament could run as cold as its midnight steel.

Lilac slid behind the wheel gingerly and backed out—protected from the last rays of the setting sun by the dripping summer fog—and in no time found herself cruising down Ocean Avenue looking at the pedestrians mindlessly enjoying their evening walks. She found a parking space on Eighth Avenue near Dolores Street and got out into the brisk offshore breeze. She turned the corner and walked up to the front door of the Carmel Chapter House, passing the cockling American flag and Red Cross colors. Even though it was after closing time, she saw one person through the brightly-lit windows—a middle-aged woman who sat talking on the phone.

Lilac hid her gaunt face and pallid complexion behind a loosely-tied head scarf, and knocked firmly. The woman hung up, straightened her red blazer and came to greet Lilac, smiling through the glass with plump, rosy lips that were almost too much to resist.

"Hi," the woman called out cheerfully through the panel-glazed split French door. "We're closed now. Is this an emergency?"

Lilac cleared her parched throat. She hadn't spoken in a while and her larynx had become stiff. "I, hchm . . . would like to volunteer."

"Um . . . well . . . ah, yes," the Red Crosser said skeptically as she scrutinized this creature who appeared to be on the very threshold of death. "We are always looking for volunteers."

She cracked the door open and reached through it to take her visitor's hand. "I'm Dee, the chapter manager."

Lilac kept her hands huddled inside her cloak.

"Listen, I don't mean to be rude," Dee began, retracting her hand awkwardly, "but do you think you could come back another time? I was just getting ready to go home."

The gaunt woman stared with a purposefully unreadable look, before she replied, with a well-calculated pinch of desperation. "I . . . ah . . . only have evenings available, and I really feel the, ah . . . craving to volunteer."

"Well, we do need volunteers, but the work is sometimes physically demanding." Lilac knew this last was meant to discourage her, but she also knew that if she persisted, this woman would not be able to turn her away. The neediness flowed off of her; not to mention that Lilac had read it in the newspapers: the chapter was having a hard time filling its volunteer ranks. Lilac focused her concentration on the visage before her.

It didn't take long. "Well, maybe I can stay a little longer," Dee said. "Why don't you come in for a moment and have some coffee and cookies?"

The chapter manager opened the front door fully and stepped aside to let Lilac enter. She led her visitor in and gestured toward a table with a plate of sugar cookies on it, helping her guest take a seat next to it before disappearing into the kitchen. "Cream or sugar?" she called to Lilac.

"Black, thank you."

Dee brought two steaming mugs to the table.

"Now, let's see," Dee sipped her coffee. "What kind of volunteering did you have in mind?"

"I was thinking . . . hchm . . . blood."

"Blood?" Dee repeated meekly. Lilac watched her hostess' stomach muscles twitch and the hairs on her neck stir—a visceral reaction to Lilac's force of will. The vampire took care to ease up. The woman was obviously somewhat agreeable by nature. No need to overdo it.

Dee brightened almost immediately. "Oh . . . right, right. Since we announced our new partnership with the Red Cross Blood Center in San Jose, we *have* been seeking volunteers to help us collect blood."

The look of skepticism crossed Dee's face again.

Lilac snickered quietly enough not to be heard. "I-I don't look so good right now," the vampire stammered, while slightly increasing her command. "But I'll get better. I haven't taken my . . . medication for some time."

Dee looked as if she were deep in thought, then snapped out of it. "I think I have an idea!" she said.

In a month Dee's brainstorm had come to fruition. *The Carmel Pine Cone* ran a hand-painted portrait of Lilac—she had refused a photo shoot, citing religious reasons—along with a full page plea for donors to collect blood for the brave soldiers fighting the good fight in Vietnam.

Using Lilac as a poster girl worked famously. People said that if this little old lady—who looked as though she could barely walk—was willing to offer her best efforts to the program, how could any healthy, vibrant member of the community refuse to donate the gift of life? The nascent campaign soon established what would become a tradition: Saturday evening blood drives.

In the months that followed, Lilac attended special Red Cross training for blood volunteers, and began to register and interview potential blood donors. After the blood was collected, she helped nurses log the units. The post was ideal. Using creative inventory methods, no one noticed the occasional missing bag. The program was such a success that—even after Lilac secretly appropriated her meager rewards—more blood was donated per capita than in most similar programs throughout the country.

Lilac took care not to ingest too much of the pilfered blood at any one time, lest it cause her appearance to change too drastically (each pint she sipped smoothed at least a year off of her). Thrilled to have found a way to ease her thirst without succumbing to the Flash or having to find corpses, she gave unspoken thanks to Henri Dunant.

One evening in December 1973, after an especially successful drive, Lilac decided to undergo a full transformation. People had begun to wonder how she kept on going, year after year, so Lilac arranged for a cooler full of bags to turn up missing. In the small fiasco that ensued, Lilac claimed she had lost track during a senior moment. Soon after, she announced her retirement as a volunteer, and the local legend disappeared forever.

A few weeks after Lilac's "retirement", Jeannie appeared at the doorstep of the Chapter House. She announced her presence by knocking loudly. A woman opened the door, at which time the visitor said, most promptly, "You must be Dee. I'm Jeannie, Lilac's granddaughter."

Jeannie spoke rapidly and with a youthful exuberance. "I've heard so much about you from my grandmother," she smiled, ignoring the woman's outstretched hand, and stepping inside immediately. "Lilac never stopped talking about the good people down here. She felt so badly about misplacing that old batch of blood."

Ignoring the woman's somewhat dubious look, Jeannie took measure of the office, applying great care in lingering over everything as if it were her first time there.

Dee gestured for Jeannie to enter her office and sit down. "Oh, how is Lilac, the poor dear? We miss her. After all, she helped us get our blood services program off the ground."

"She's not well." Jeannie sat and saw a wave of concern wash over Dee's face. "Grandmother's health is failing, I'm afraid. And she was doing so well, too, thanks to the new lease on life this place gave her. She wanted me to come down and let you all know how much she missed the crew."

Something about that satisfied the woman. She smiled, and said, "How sweet. Well, you be sure to tell her not to worry about that blood incident. We all felt so badly for her. Will we be seeing her again soon?"

"I don't think that will be possible, but she'll be thrilled when I tell her how well things are going here at the Chapter House."

They chatted for half an hour and by the time Jeannie left, she had exerted enough influence over Dee that the older woman believed the idea for Jeannie to volunteer was hers. When the next blood drive came—the crew wearing red ribbons in honor of the memory of their dearly departed friend—Jeannie filled Lilac's shoes as though they were made to fit. She suggested that blood donations to the Red Cross in her grandmother's name would be an appropriate condolence.

With the arrival of the 1980s, the Community Hospital of the Monterey Peninsula (CHOMP) started their bloodbank, and soon replaced the San Jose Blood Center as the beneficiary of the Carmel Chapter's Blood

Services donor base and volunteer network. Jeannie wasted no time securing a part-time position at the hospital and became a night shift employee. Most of the job benefits were of no use to her, but she took full advantage of the one resource that kept her looking and feeling as young as she had the night she crossed over into her life of eternal darkness.

It became her responsibility to account for and dispose of any blood that was rejected or had outlived its shelf life—a simple matter of tried-and-true creative inventory and accounting kept more than enough fresh blood in her possession. Since she had so much extra, Jeannie began to share it with other vampires with whom she had become acquainted during her long years of earthbound wandering; those who she knew to be interested in an alternative to killing—as donated blood lacked any psychic link to the donor.

More came, and then more—all unnoticed to the Chapter House admin staff—and eventually, the mortal lives Jeannie preserved by redirecting donated blood to those with the Thirst equaled those saved by the traditional medical use of blood.

Jeannie reduced her own blood intake incrementally over time to simulate the normal course of aging, but still managed to look better than anyone else "her age". She continued to work at the CHOMP Blood Center, and remained a Red Cross volunteer. She served several terms as Chairman of Blood Services for the Carmel Chapter, helping the donor program flourish into the twenty-first century. Over the years a few of her own kind even began to fill the ranks of the dedicated volunteers committed to helping the American people "Give the Gift of Life", while purloining some for themselves.

Kamil turned away from his stargazing, stepped into the tiled shower at Bernardus, and closed the glass door to the sunken basin. He turned the hot water on and stood under it waiting for the warmth of the stream to penetrate his time-hardened skin, taking the edge off the perpetual chill of his cold, undead body.

Barely a month had passed since he had last swallowed blood, but the cravings were back and had grown to almost consume him. He rubbed his elongated upper incisors as he contemplated the purpose of his visit to Carmel. It certainly wasn't recreational—say a round of golf or a tour of scenic vistas. No, it was a matter of life and death for the mortals who would fall victim to him if he didn't find a less lethal way to quench the Thirst.

Shutting off the water, Kamil shook the moisture off himself in the shower stall. He did it with the motion of a dog, but at the speed of a hummingbird, and then stepped out and looked toward the mirror: it revealed nothing—no sign of his olive Mediterranean skin, no sign of his kinky black hair; no sign of his muscular frame; no reflection at all.

That didn't bother him, although it seemed a shame that he couldn't see his own features beneath the finery he had draped over himself, the most attractive items garnered from a myriad of past victims. Tonight he wore a red silk shirt and gabardine slacks from a successful London businessman; a vintage tie from a nineteenth-century Italian noble; patent leather shoes from a Chicago mobster, and fine silk socks from a Burmese banker.

Kamil placed a handsome tip on the mahogany bedside table and left the room, hunger gnawing at him. Summoning his strength, he sped off through the shadows toward the village district of Carmel-by-the-Sea, where the nightlife was underlit, if not subdued.

Where might Lilac be?

By the time he had reached the damp darkness near Eighth Avenue off Lincoln, just a block or two from downtown, Kamil had yet an inkling of how to find the woman who might offer him salvation. He did, however, find another.

At first he tried to ignore her by averting his senses. But it was too late—he had seen it and it was irresistible.

She wore a snakeskin jacket that was to die for.

Kamil's desire for the jacket overwhelmed his willpower to stifle his instincts and he gave in to the Thirst: slip, skip, and slide into the shadows, a hundred paces in mere seconds, no mote of dust disturbed. Now, mere inches behind his oblivious victim, he placed his hands on her shoulders. She flinched, but he soothed her with the power of his mind and hushed her softly as he turned her toward him.

He caressed the snakeskin that she wore. Her eyes met his and she seemed to recognize something in his look.

"You can't resist it, can you?" she asked knowingly.

He leaned toward her and, as if captured by a secondary thought, brushed his cheek against the coat's lapel while fondling the hem with one hand and stroking the back with the other. She heaved a sigh of pleasure at his touch and closed her eyes, fading off into whatever imaginings might be hers. When Kamil sensed her full surrender he pulled back her short black hair, exposing her pulsing artery, and bit down, opening the vessel, drinking in the warm liquid life pumping out of her. He spilled not a precious drop until her heart failed, and the Flash overtook him. In it, he came to know a shy woman from Modesto, who had come to Monterey in a hideous little yellow car to attend University. He experienced the profound influence of the snakeskin jacket upon her. He felt, with intensity, how she had desired it; her satisfaction the first time she wore it; the liberation that swarmed her soon after. It was as if it had transformed this meek woman into a huntress, helping her shed the social conditioning that had once repressed her impulses, setting free her latent urge to kill.

He "watched" as she waded through the murky waters of El Estero in Monterey, dragging along with her, just beneath the surface, a small victim she had abducted near Dennis the Menace Park. Kamil knew it was one of several who had fallen victim to her unshackled appetite.

Kamil also knew that the woman had *welcomed* her death. Guilt from the murder of innocent children raged through her, consuming her, as unrestrained as the murderous instincts that had been set free within her.

She might have made a better vampire than I.

He let go of her body. As she crumpled to the ground, he held onto the jacket, slowly peeling it off of her as if she were molting. He realized then that it was the first kill he had made in a long time that wasn't boring. That he had relished this one final Flash, unlike the mediocre recollections he had amassed over the centuries. It made him think he didn't want salvation. That perhaps it was just a matter of being a little more selective about whom he consumed.

Kamil looked at the scaly coat that hung from his clenched pale fingers. He turned each sleeve right side out before slipping his arms in. The woman's attachment to it lingered in his mind, memories that enriched the experience even more. As he pulled it on over his shoulders and it formed around him, he realized that, indeed, he had been driven to take her by more than the Thirst.

"This garment mus-s-s-t have been made for the likes of me," he hissed, gathering it around his waist. First he thought, *It's found a fitting home.* Then: *How is it affecting me?*

He contemplated the experience and began recollecting feelings and thoughts he had nearly forgotten. He recalled life before his resurrection, and understood that he had not been a natural killer like the woman whose body lay before him.

He found the revelation dizzying and sped off without thinking.

At an undetermined time later, Kamil found himself beyond the village, in the midst of something substantially less charming called the Crossroads Shopping Center. From just beyond a drug store window, he watched a pair of men with his keen black eyes. The sun having now dipped well below the horizon, florescent lights lit the scene brightly. It played out before him as mute—if low-brow—theater.

He could easily read their lips.

"Hey there, Willie," he watched the checkout clerk say as he straightened his green uniform shirt with the "Longs" logo. "How's your rich Uncle Sam treatin' ya this month?"

"He's cheatin' me again, Frank," a rather derelict-looking man replied. With one thinly gnarled hand, he put a U.S. Treasury check on the counter. With the other he scribbled an endorsement on its back.

Kamil stepped back, somewhat overwhelmed by the realization that he had so enjoyed his last Flash that he was immediately contemplating another—even without a strong thirst. He watched the episode inside the store with rising interest.

The clerk took the box of wine from the basket and ran it through the scanner.

"Will that be all for you today?"

"Got some meat and vegetables there, too," the ne'er-do-well pointed at his basket, wiping his nose with his other forefinger. He began to cough, but it didn't stop him from talking. "They're slowly stealing all of what they owed us, Frank! Each month the check comes a day later. I got it all worked out."

The clerk—"Frank"—turned away until the coughing ended. Then he continued to tally the groceries. Willie wiped a line of drool off his lip with his sleeve, and continued. "They put it off a day each month. Then after thirty-one months we lose one check, all of us, Frank, every loyal veteran who fought for this here old country!"

"No way, Willie," Frank asserted, while continuing his bagging. "You come in the first week of every month with that check."

"What day is it, Frankie?"

"Tuesday."

"No it ain't, Frankie. It's the fifth. Last month I came in on the fourth, and the one before, it was the third. I tell you Frankie, the government's filled with blood sucking fiends! I'd bet my life on it!"

Kamil smiled.

"Here's your change, Willie." Frank gently closed the other's dirty fingers around the bills before letting go of his hand. "Now make sure it lasts you the rest of the month."

"Don't you worry about me, Frankie, I'm ready for 'em. But if I'm not back soon, it's because they found out I caught wind of their schemin' and they had to shut me up."

"I won't tell, Willie . . . I promise. Just don't be spreading it around too much yourself."

The old fool made the sign of a zipper across his lips and ducked out into the parking lot, looking over his shoulder with rapidly darting eyes.

Against a background of occasional car noise floating down from Highway 1, Willie headed beyond the shopping mall property, passing through cars dusted with yellow pollen, until he hit the river bed near the Highway 1 bridge that spanned the Carmel River. There his pace slowed as he began to watch his footing.

Kamil tensed in anticipation. He watched the bum from the store stumble haltingly up and over the bank down into Carmel's little publicized, but widely known, riparian ghetto.

Despite his lust after the Flash, Kamil wondered why he had been attracted to this quarry. The man was simply wretched, and appeared to possess nothing that Kamil—who liked to think of himself as an artist—would want to add to his selective composition of mortal mementos.

So, why am I drawn to him? He admitted he hadn't felt a hunger like this before. It was much different from the Thirst that spread from the teeth to every cell in the body. This one burned in his belly and stayed there, a fire of excitement for the hunt itself. It added a fascinating dimension to the experience.

What's this?!

The jacket seemed to tug, snugly at his mind. Kamil thought of the great snake, its owner, and its death at the hands of Amazonian poachers. Those images departed, replaced by a sequence of visions of life and death, but mostly death. One after another they hurtled at him, with enough intensity that anyone but Kamil would have been repulsed. What he felt was *much* different.

He felt the snake's final struggle for life, and he felt it as if he were the snake. Before he knew it, an appreciation of the fragility of life seeped into him in a way it hadn't since he'd resurrected from the life of mortal men. He hesitated; for what he wasn't sure of at first, until he realized he was rapidly losing his enthusiasm for the hunt and lacked the Thirst to overcome it.

Then, something underneath, something centuries old within him, took over and ignored that realization. With nary a thought, he slithered in front of the homeless man and laced the fingers of his left hand through his greasy hair. He pulled slightly, while placing his right palm on the man's chest. A pungent, but intoxicating odor emanated from the bag of filth.

The deliciousness of life!

"Hey! What'ya doin'? You from the Government or somthin'?"

Kamil tilted the man's head back and prepared to sink in his teeth, but first he let his mind touch the victim's. The sensation always greatly enhanced the Flash, and this time proved no exception. Kamil shared Willie's thoughts of how good it was to be alive, to have one's pockets full of cash, to have all one's life's pleasures within the confines of a grocery bag. Stepping into the Flash from here was the ultimate.

Without warning, remorse crashed in, laying waste to previous feelings. It seemed to have entered from the jacket. Kamil gave the creature in his grasp a light shove away from him.

"Sorry, I thought you were someone else."

An instant later Kamil was back in the shadows, trying to figure out what had just happened to him.

An instant after that, something slammed into him from the side, like a cannonball, sending him in the opposite direction of his would-be victim. A hundred paces to the rear he landed, flat on his back. He opened his eyes to see a youthful stranger straddling his chest. At least, the features were those of a stranger. What lay behind them was anything but. Kamil realized it immediately, a clench in his bowels.

"Lilac?"

The very creature he had sought out had, apparently, sought him out. She appeared—now, at least—to be in her mid-twenties, with bobbed yet wavy umber hair and bangs that fell to her eyebrows. Her black eyes looked into the empty place inside once occupied by his soul. Her deceptively delicate fingers dug into his brawny biceps.

They linked, a habit, and it was as if they were back standing in the pile of butchery at Solferino. Kamil felt as if he were lying back in a sea of carnage, his old adversary towering over him.

"'Lilac' is a name not currently mine," she replied, sounding amused, fangs gleaming in the moonlight. "I go by Jeannie now."

"Well, Jeannie, I can see that drinking the blood of the dead hasn't put any lead in your britches." The comment was intended to be glib, but underneath he was struggling, as he had just realized he couldn't break out of the Solferino scene, or pry her from atop him. She controlled everything, had taken it out from under him, and now held him within it—a vampire half his size!

"This is none of your business!" he yelled at her.

"Anyone who feeds in our territory happens to be my business, thank you." Her grip on his arms intensified, as did the pressure on his chest, yet she looked to make little effort doing so. Indeed, she looked to be studying him, and after a few moments she stated in a clear voice, "You don't have to kill to feed."

He felt like gasping, but managed to eke out a chortle. "I certainly didn't expect *this* kind of greeting."

"Was it as good for you as it was for me?" she asked from atop him, looking at first playful, but then her smile changed into a scowl and her eyes began to burn. "I don't expect you to admit you have a problem, but if you remain in the area, don't hunt again. We keep a low profile here. I won't be as nice next time."

She stuck a card in his jacket pocket. "If you want to discuss abstinence further, call me." Her last words faded out as she disappeared.

About a week later, Kamil pulled the card out of his breast pocket and examined it for the hundredth time. It looked the same as ever: blood-red cross embossed in linen paper and the name and number of "Jeannie Vanhoft" printed in black.

In a marked contrast to the first 99 times he'd contemplated it, he flipped out his cell phone and dialed the number on the card. He did it with the slightest hesitation, as one might when calling an old girlfriend after years of separation.

Later that evening, Kamil arrived at the Carmel Chapter House. He looked sharp in his reptilian jacket, mohair trousers and patent leather shoes. His silver belt-buckle, which sported two fang-shaped prongs, lent an intimidating, but elegant accent to his persona.

At the door of the Chapter House he was met by one of Jeannie's high school youth volunteers. "I'm here to see Li—er, Jeannie," he told her, bowing as he entered, taking the young girl's hand gently and kissing it softly. Her skin was warm and soft. He inhaled her succulent fragrances, only slightly contaminated by Victoria's Secret body wash.

The girl backed away slowly, her eyes moving from his face to his belt buckle, lingering on the snakeskin jacket in between. She seemed torn by something.

"Oh, the Blood Queen, she's just through there," the girl said, gesturing indecisively through the doors behind her. Jeannie picked that exact moment to enter the room, and Kamil froze when her eyes met his. Her face imparted an unmistakable message: stay away from the volunteer or suffer the most devastating consequences.

He imagined she wouldn't hesitate to tear him limb from limb and stake his parts on a variety of local mountain tops so he could turn to dust in the sun's burning light. He released the girl's hand and nodded politely before entering the manager's office.

"You may go home now, Samantha," Jeannie told the girl right before she closed the office door behind her and shut the blinds.

She turned to Kamil with a gaze of great interest, but with much less intensity than before. Kamil did his best to avert it. He focused on an outdated blood drive campaign poster on the wall, with the depiction of a decrepit old lady soliciting donors. He might have been able to identify her—something about it made him think that he could—if not for the unsettling presence of Jeannie. She had just slid fluidly behind the desk and exerted an executive air.

"I take it you're interested in Blood Services?"

"I meant no disrespect out there," he nodded toward the reception desk. He placed his palms on his chest and slightly bowed his head. "Not now nor the other night."

"What will you sound like when you need to feed next?" she asked.

"I'd just like to explore alternatives," he said, fast, as if he had to get the message out before it evaporated. "Ones that require less killing. Much less."

A calm rushed over him. His instincts told him it was manipulation, but he didn't care.

Jeannie's look sharpened and she crossed her hands on her lap. "How much do you enjoy the kill?" It was a challenge, but one with an undercurrent of understanding.

"Not as much as I used to. I seem to have remembered the sanctity of life. That miscreant under the bridge, I could not kill him unnecessarily. Maybe it was the jacket . . ."

"The jacket's a crutch, but if that's what you need to give up the kill, then use it."

"No, really, there is something about this jack—"

"My crutch is charity work. It wasn't the killing that bothered me, it was the Flash—it grew so taxing . . ."

Kamil couldn't stop thinking about the jacket. "I sensed its life force," he muttered, while running its lapel through his thumb and forefinger. "It tempered certain . . . inclinations."

"I can offer you additional, long-term assistance," Jeannie continued, "but only if you remain steadfast in your conviction to abstain."

He freed his mind from the jacket long enough to consider Jeannie's proposition. She picked up a pencil with a Red Cross insignia on it and began to twirl it slowly between her fingers. "We have a good thing going here, not just for our kind, but for potential victims. Help is only a phone call away. When the urge comes upon you, we can share our testimonials, the life stories from countless mortals without the kill, like a methadone fix for a heroin addict, if you will. Just take the first step and admit you want to change."

A long, but comfortable silence passed. "I'm interested," Kamil finally said, and he meant it.

"Then see you here Saturday at midnight — and we serve refreshments!"

———

Saturday at midnight, Kamil arrived at the Chapter House. He entered the front door and passed the kitchen, where an elderly-looking, androgynous vampire with gray hair heated what appeared to be plastic bags in a pot of steaming water. In the meeting room, a dozen chairs were placed in a circle. Only the ambient light from outside lit the room, plenty enough for the group that had gathered.

A tall blond man took Kamil by his elbow. "Welcome, brother. I'm Jay." The traditional greeting then followed, as Jay squeezed Kamil's arms to estimate his density and bone structure. Kamil did likewise, estimating his cheerful new acquaintance to be at least twice his own age and strength.

"I'm Kamil."

"Make yourself comfortable, we start in a few minutes."

Kamil nodded as he watched the seats fill around him. He took his own. In no time, Jeannie had taken a place next to him. She leaned into him. "Good to see you, brother."

"Sister," he nodded politely.

Eventually, Jeannie called the meeting to order, and offered a short invocation. "We ask the gods to forgive us as we pursue alternatives to the natural course prescribed."

The others uttered the riposte, "May the gods forgive us."

"I'm Jeannie and I am addicted to the Flash. Now I work in the blood center and the Red Cross as a distraction."

The elderly vampire tossed her a warm bag of blood from the large pot Kamil had seen earlier. "B Positive, dearie. Your favorite."

"My name's Jay and I'm addicted to the Flash. I am a phlebotomist for distraction."

Another bag entered the circle. "'O' for you, Brother Jay, flavored tonight with a little aspirin from the donor's own medicine chest, no doubt."

Finally it was Kamil's turn to speak.

"My name is Kamil and I seem to have regained an aversion to killing."

Silence fell. Dismay flowered all around him, further compelling his honesty. "It's the jacket . . ."

The others nodded their heads, perhaps skeptically.

"Here you go, sonny. A special bag of AB Negative just for you, rare you know. Drinker's blood; smells like a Tequila Sunrise."

Bloodbank

For a distraction, Kamil began to take regular shifts at the CHOMP bloodbank, a white concrete building with walls covered by a relentless 3D square-in-square design, inside and out. Scheduled to cover the blood donation reception room for the evening, he settled into the front desk.

It was a relatively slow night, but a few hours into his shift, a young woman wearing a smart business suit came in to register. Kamil lifted his head and smiled warmly.

"Are you here for a deposit or a withdrawal?"

Night Wounds Time
by Chris Kemp

"Don't look back, something may be gaining on you."
— Satchel Paige

J'm in a gully thoroughfare on abandoned Fort Ord, struggling to keep my balance in the tempest. Carpets of ice plant slope up and away on each side of me, their fingers flickering in the false lightning, a bright contrast to the backdrop of night.

The not-quite tornado bears down on the disused service road, and I see Windy and Sam a few paces down, buffeted rag dolls in a lightning storm. All eyes are on the bizarre display in front of us.

Minutes ago it was the unlit entrance to a tunnel running underneath Highway 1. Now that same opening is crackling and glowing like the scrambled reception of a hundred-square-foot TV. I almost believe what the others have been saying all night: that it's some kind of time portal — a cosmic rabbit hole.

Barefoot Sam, homeless man, almost hero, gyrates like his engine's idling, hands on top of his head, fingers interlocked, keeping his "hair" in place. Windy, the hippie girl, crouches next to him, unfazed, ready to leap into the bands pulsating before her. It looks scary; she doesn't care. She's hell-bent on getting back to the life she left in 1967.

I have my doubts about why I've become so attached to her in such a short time, but seeing the little blonde go will definitely be, as she would say, a "bummer". Another bummer, and one far more troubling, is this: if this shortcut through time is the real deal, *what happens here in the present if she goes back?* Didn't worry about it before 'cause I thought the whole thing was a joke but—

—now what?

Maybe it's only me looking for an excuse to keep Windy around, but I decide we need to think this through before she takes off. She probably won't hear me if I yell for her to stop, so I don't even waste the time. I jump to tackle her, but a checkered blur blindsides me from the right. We tumble to the ground. I smell kitty litter and feel tingling all over my body.

Can't believe I forgot about *him*.

His weight keeps me down, and he tries to cover me completely, but a burst of brilliance breaks through and I know Windy's jumped into the portal.

Objects, big and small, pass above. Over the racket, I hear Sam shout, "It's bad! Ba-a-a-d!"

SNAP

Pacific Grove. Night. Absent yesterdays, rumored tomorrows.

It's a few minutes before ten and I'm picking up smokes in Ron's Liquors on Lighthouse Avenue when a car crashes through the front window, shards and splinters everywhere. *Something's* been following me, but this isn't it.

Behind the counter, the eyes of the crater-faced rehab chick spring wide, back-dropped by a mosaic of bottles that glow as if heated. I'm slow to take it all in, but only because my friendly neighborhood clerk has pulled out a gun. She's a vibrating twig; the piece hangs heavy like an ornament dangling from her multi-ringed hand.

"He . . . he . . . he . . ." she babbles. Don't know what she's aiming at, but I don't wait to find out. I reach for the piece, grab it, and jam it into the pocket of my parka. She's frozen in the headlamp spotlight, I walk squinting toward the car. It's like a monster's poked its head into a pile of rubble, all beaming eyes and chromed-out smile. Looks friendly—if you ignore the hissing, the billowing steam, and the swampy cocktail of lemon-lime drippings and spilled red wine.

I yank my hood over my head and slip on a pair of Unabomber shades. I look so average people immediately forget me, but you can never be too careful.

Stepping out into a pocket of sidewalk light, I see what's left of the chassis. It's a cab, door open, driver spilling out, a young guy with bleached blonde Jeri-curls and a baked-on tan.

"You see that?" he croaks. His arm rises marionette-like, points past my shoulder.

Down a few blocks, in the dimness of downtown, I spot a human form cutting on and off like a failing neon lamp. He?—appears to be wearing a checkered jacket. Reminds me of someone, or something . . .

"All of a sudden he appeared . . . in front of me," the driver continues, breath heavy. "In the middle of the street . . . out of nowhere. I swerved to miss him . . . I heard him laughing, like it was a big joke."

Oh. So *that's* what it is.

The red streaming from under the cabbie's shorts distracts me. In his outrage, he doesn't notice how hurt he is. "You letting him get away with it?" he gasps.

Marbled green eyes lock onto me like they know me. I think he may be one of the few that call me patron saint of PG, caretaker of the quiet, and when he whispers, "I don't think it's human," I know he is.

Here's the thing, though. If he just had a brush with what I think he had a brush with, it's best to keep your distance. Folding a wild card into the deck never pays, even when an unidentifiable force isn't tidal-waving behind you.

Late diners and stragglers trickle in our direction. A woman gasps and I know I gotta get out of there. I backstep in the direction of my car. An old man wearing a 49ers cap approaches from the side, newspaper in hand. I've seen him around; he's got a rep as a busybody and I'll use it.

"Pops! Call 9-1-1!" I shout, and he says something I can't hear but I see him fumble in his pocket as I dash up 16th Street, as close to an alley as you get in downtown PG. Big Iron, my rusted out 1974 Chrysler Imperial with the sweet stock 440, sits behind a line of dumpsters on the sprawling lot between 16th and 17th. But what's this?

Little skater pukes *pissing on my car!*

The aroma of reefer clings to them. A bottle tinkles as it rolls across the blacktop. The little cadavers see me and start to laugh, their second mistake. There's only three of the longhaired miscreants, so I *could* beat the crap out of them, but I don't have time. What I *do* have is a gun, so I pull it out and wave it around in the dim light.

That spooks them and they rip away on their boards, tossing a merry chorus of "Fuck Yous" behind them. Their quick exit gives me a second to think, so I mull over the flickering, checkered thing I saw moving away from the accident. I feel a little guilty for not pursuing it; I'm not following up for the cab driver. But you don't agitate something like that; you stay out of the way and hope it ignores you.

I reach into my pocket for my keys, and there's a stirring behind the dumpster—gravel scraping; paper-bag mashing. A dark blot-of-a-man leaks out. He wears a moth-eaten Navy watch cap pulled down over his head and a frayed peacoat to match. He's smallish; maybe mixed Asian decent.

"I . . . need . . . help." He delivers the softly accented words with the short-circuited cadence of irregular thought.

"Sorry, pal," I tell him as I slide behind the wheel. "Got no money, no food, no booze."

He's at the open door; just appears there.

"*We* . . . need help. And . . . you . . . help people." His eyes blaze with insanity or . . . is it focus? Makes him hard to ignore, especially 'cause he's right. I *do* help little old ladies across the street, I *do* chase down vandals and, sometimes, I *do* deal with problems that would fry the mind of John Q. Citizen—if he ever found out about them.

"Who's the 'we'?" I ask.

"There is . . . a girl."

A damsel in distress? Hmm . . .

"Get in," I say, and start the engine, again sensing the distinct need to get moving.

The little man bows ever so slightly before shuffling back to the dumpsters and dragging out a tormented-looking bicycle. Has he been staking me out? I shrug it off. Guy's been cold cocked by life; probably just needs human contact.

He lugs the bike toward the car and I pop open the trunk. The disenfranchised like to keep their transportation close and Big Iron's got more than enough room to spare. When he's finished, he hops into the passenger seat, the tang of fish soaking his clothes. I grab a chocolate bar from my sugar stash in the back seat and toss it to him. He gobbles it down, eases back in the seat, and closes his eyes for a minute.

"Where to?" I ask.

"Hidden Place," he replies softly. Big Iron screeches across the adjacent lot behind Grove Market, and I rip a left down Forest without much fear; the cops, for sure, are at the liquor store, stoked that they have a real crime to investigate. I turn right on Lighthouse, heading away from the red strobes flashing back at the crash site. We're creeping toward Monterey and . . .

Hidden Place.

You won't find it on any map. It's a simple stretch of sandy soil and greenery tucked between the Monterey Bay and the rec trail that parallels the Plain Jane stretch of Del Monte Avenue that runs from the volleyball courts to the Seaside border. Hidden Place is smack in the middle. Its sandy hills rise above a small parking lot across the street from the Navy School, the heavy bedspread of trees and bushes making it primo real estate for those that choose to stay out of the public eye without straying too far.

We head out of downtown PG, moving past silhouetted one- and two-story buildings with glowing goldenrod windows. Four blocks later the scenery changes, getting more residential, with big high houses on one side and a tree-lined median on the other. As we approach Sixth Street, I see Clark Ashton Smith's ever-vigilant gargoyle, poised atop the stone wall fronting the house where the writer/sculptor once lived. The creature crouches like a panther, ready to pounce.

I find it comforting.

Before long we're cutting through New Monterey via a razor straight stretch of Lighthouse hemmed by flat-faced buildings. "Out here" in the brightness, the atmosphere changes. PG's dark remoteness attracts certain quiet, yet considerable forces most residents can't—or won't—see. In the two Montereys, it's different; night time borderlands culture and arcane practices keep aggressive entities on the down low.

Of course, this has nothing to do with the great unseen crest rolling toward me from behind, driving me forward.

"What's your name?" I ask my new buddy.

"I am . . . Glenn."

"Uh-huh."

"What is . . . yours?"

"Don't have one."

His thin-lipped smile is a thimbleful of serenity. I drink it down just in time to catch a checkered blur out of the corner of my eye. It causes me to ease up on the gas—Big Iron's moving pretty fast now—but when I turn to look, I don't see anything except a used record store with a vintage psychedelic poster hanging in the window. Some band called "H.P. Lovecraft".

I rub my eyes.

"Yes," Glenn says. Might be a question.

"Seeing things," I reply, but then, just as we're about to be swallowed by the tunnel that bores underneath Custom House Plaza, a plaid-shirted figure beckons to me from the lawn sweeping up toward the Presidio. The vision extinguishes, appears again, flicks from spot to spot to spot like a bad film edit, and vanishes one last time, smiling like the Cheshire Cat. I hear a pop and there's a rippling effect, like when you pull something out of water. Except the ripples I see aren't in any water; they're in the air, coming toward me and passing through the car. Gives me a slight buzz, but it's more than that—dèja vu and vertigo rolled into one.

The feeling passes in time for me to straighten out the wheel so I don't crash into the curved wall of the tunnel. Looks like I've got unwelcome company for the night. Tricksters can be as tenacious as tooth decay, but maybe I'll get "lucky" and it'll neutralize what's been dogging me all night. Could make it worse, too, but I won't think about that. Wouldn't change my strategy anyway: keep moving, don't look back, no allowance for fear.

We emerge out the other side of the tunnel, passing Fisherman's Wharf on our left, getting close to the lot across from the Navy School. It butts up against the rec trail, a short walk from Hidden Place. Go early enough, you'll get a sense of the culture. Compact, rusted RVs. Hibachi hot dog breakfasts cooked in the back of dented pickups. Ratty blankets on the dirt. It all plays out under the tranquility of a massive eucalyptus grove, and it's all gone by eight in the morning.

This time of night, though, the place looks nearly deserted—a couple of ancient vans and a pickup/camper shell combo—but I wouldn't bet on it. We pull into a space and I grab my heavy-duty flashlight, stuffing my pockets full of treats from my sweets stash.

I depress the auto lock button and the hollow crunch of solenoids reverberates through the night time air. We close our doors. There's a wash of light from the street lamps on Del Monte Boulevard behind us and those lining the path before us, but it's more ghostly than bright. The eucalyptus grove to our left looks forbidding, larger than in the daytime. It swallows the rec trail and the ambient light. The air is still, but the trees rustle—deeper in, I think, because I don't see them move.

"Glenn, how long is this going to take?"

Brows furrowed in intense concentration, it's as if he's trying to bend something to his will.

"Night . . . wounds . . . time," Glenn says in an almost canny voice, like a detective assessing a crime scene. I ask him what he means but when he doesn't respond, I don't push it.

We cross the rec trail. The slope looming over us looks ominous, but Glenn doesn't hesitate to make his way catlike and silent up the incline, which is essentially a dune clumped with bushes. I struggle to keep up, each step sinking ankle-deep in gritty sand. He's climbing toward a mass of shrubbed treetop domes further up.

We near a particularly expansive tree and I hear voices. Glenn whistles. A similar trill echoes back. Glenn squats and disappears into an umbrella of dense branches. A quick sweep backward with the flashlight and I'm on my knees and under, too.

Inside it's tent-like, high enough for standing, wide enough to accommodate the half-circle of seated figures and their assorted bits of cloth and refuse. Smells pretty bad in here, cigarettes and body odor mostly, but I'll deal.

There's four of them, mute vacant stares until Glenn mumbles something their way, inducing a discharge of untranslatable chatter. One's a white guy crowned with a honey-colored wig. He sports a fungus of a beard. Another's a beefy Latino with a scar running down his cheek and a permanent frown. The third's a lanky, sleepy-eyed brother wearing a bowler hat.

And then there's the girl. In the murkiness she glows, a flower in the dustbin, a beauty out of place. Doesn't fit with the others; cleaner, sure, but that's not it.

I think I may know her.

Shoulder-length blonde hair, wavy where it's not matted, crowned by a belt-wide headband. Beneath the U-Haul blanket draped over her shoulders, she wears a white cotton embroidered top cut to reveal her navel and a dark ankle length skirt spotted with paisley. Amber stones decorate her neck. That she's still in possession of them speaks well of the group.

Her sapphire gaze challenges me. "If this is the future, it's a bummer," she says, like it's my fault; a sharp voice, but refreshing—club soda splashed with bitters.

Wait. Did she just say "the future"?

She grabs a bottle wrapped in a brown paper bag and takes a healthy swig. "So this is the cat that's supposed to help me trip back home?" she asks no one in particular. "Looks like a narc."

There's a rapid thumping in my chest. I don't think it's sexual attraction, but I can't place it, either. It's like I feel protective, like she's my charge, but the details are submerged below memory.

And did she say "the future"?

I know I'm in deep when I turn to Glenn for guidance. He nods affirmatively with the blissful look of a Buddhist monk, but just what is he affirming?

Commotion breaks out next to me. The black guy, eyes brightened by anger, breaks into a semi-coherent stream of angry words, directing them at the Hispanic who wastes no time firing back. Between the fractured syntax and chopped syllables, it sounds like religion's on their mind. I catch a reference to Mohammed, and another to "John the B".

"Hey, Mannix," the blonde chimes over the din, "cat got your tongue?"

"Glenn, what's going on?" I ask.

"*Armageddon time!*" yells the man in the hat. He pronounces it, "Armagideon."

With a string of barely comprehendible syllables, Glenn tells them to take their act outside. They don't move. I pull out a few candy bars and cigarettes. "Please?" I ask.

It works.

"She is . . . from the past," Glenn says quietly after they leave.

"Nineteen sixty-seven," the girl declares, "and babe, do I ever want to get back. This place is some funky shit. Age of Aquarius, my ass."

I just stare. The connection I feel seems . . . enhanced. Artificial. And her wild story! Just the same, when she frowns and wrinkles her nose at me—as if I'm an idiot—it warms my insides.

"Hey, how about turning me on to one of those candy bars?" she suggests. "Are they some groovy kind of future chocolate?"

I hand her one. "You're from the past?" I sound like I'm half asleep.

A torrent of words spills from a voice I haven't heard. "*The slide! The slide! The slide!*" It's the guy with the bad hairpiece, which is creeping down his forehead.

Glenn's mouth tightens and he barks, "Sam!" The man steps back with wide-eyed silence.

"Sam found her," Glenn explains. "Yesterday. Near fort."

"Fort Ord?" I ask.

Glenn nods.

Another refrain breaks out—"*The slide! The slide! She came outta the slide!*"—and this Sam character's waving his hands up and down while sand dandruffs off his wig, which has slipped to cover his eyes. Glenn punches him lightly in the upper arm. It calms him. I think. He adjusts his "hair".

"Freaky, huh?" the blonde says to me. It's admirable that she's treating this as some kind of game, and I can't help but notice that she's really cute with a mouth full of chocolate.

I need to concentrate! Find out what really happened.

So I ask and she huffs as if telling me her story will sap all her energy, but she gets into it right away. "It was like this, man, I'm beginning to kick out on a tab of acid at the concert when—well, who freaking knows? I spaced out. Wandered around. Fell into some far out rabbit hole and Sammy, the white rabbit, got me here all safe and sound." She stops and takes another drink out of the bag. "These guys looked creepy and they're a little gross," she whispers, "but they've been cool. At least they're not into material possessions."

The girl stands up—she's not an inch over five feet or a day over twenty—and walks to Sam, pecking him on the forehead. The noise he makes is close to "whee-whee-whee." Beats his screaming.

She turns to me. "So, when are we leaving?"

"Are you high now?"

Eyes glint green with irritation. "Straight dude! Do I *look* high?"

No, but *so* damned familiar. It's enough to make you lose track of time, which is what I realize I've done when I hear something big thrashing through the trees and brush above us.

"Yeah, well, I gotta get going," I say.

Just keep moving.

"Take her with," instructs Glenn.

"Where?"

"Back, back, back," Sam sings. He's pulling on the sleeves of his tattered leather jacket, one at a time.

"Yeah, c'mon man, let's split," the little hippie chick says.

The ground trembles slightly.

"Sam go with you," Glenn says. "He knows where. He slid once."

Could explain a lot.

I sink to my knees and crawl out. "I'm on a tight schedule!" I call behind me. "If you're coming, make it now!"

I tread carefully down the incline, not disappointed to hear the girl's light footfalls behind me. Can't say I feel the same about the sound of breaking branches and crunching vegetation from inside the eucalyptus trees. Seeing the grove come alive with shakes and shivers rates even lower. Something King Kong-sized looks about to poke its head through. Did it eat those religion ranters? The two of them are nowhere to be found.

Across the lot Big Iron's dome light winks on . . . and that's not all. The car and its immediate area wobble, like I'm viewing them through gelatin. I see a familiar figure in a checkered jacket behind the wheel, but then I blink and everything looks normal again.

Peering cautiously into the driver's window, I see the remnants of a fading smile. When I open the door, a draft of kitty litter escapes.

Trickster's taking this Cheshire Cat thing a little too far.

The girl's next to me. Sam, my semi-coherent would-be guide, trudges across the lot in bare feet. The locks click open and I tell him to get in back. Blondie can ride shotgun. I ask the girl her name as Big Iron rumbles to life and turns left onto Del Monte. She says, "Windy." She looks totally unfazed in the roomy front seat, legs in Lotus position, a sunflowered backpack beside her. "My dad has one of these," she says, tapping the dashboard with a painted fingernail. "No bullet cars with big fins yet? Figures."

"I could be a maniac, you know."

Her sapphire eyes twinkle. "I hitchhike all the time and, anyway, Glenn says you're cool, even if you look like a cop."

"That how you got to Hidden Place?"

"Huh?"

"Is that how you got to the big tree? By hitchhiking?"

"Tried, but we walked." She leans over to me and whispers, "I think the drivers on the road were freaked out when they saw Sam." She looks over her shoulder and spots something in the back seat. "Hey, what's that 'Ding-Dong' thing?"

How do you explain something like that? "They're kinda like Twinkies or Snowballs."

"Never seen 'em. Can I score a pack?"

"Ding-Dong good," Sam says and hands one over. She rips it open and stuffs a chocolate covered disk in her mouth. "Susie-Q, too," Sam adds, placing a pack next to her as if he were handling a baby.

Windy makes little throaty sounds as she gets the first Ding-Dong down. I can't help but find it charming or fetching or something like that. But it doesn't make me any less skeptical about *"The slide! The slide! The slide!"*

See, with the Trickster in play, it's only natural I consider this whole thing to be some drawn out practical joke, especially with the air of familiarity that clings to Windy. Will playing along get me to the heart of the matter? Do I have a choice?

At least I'm moving again.

"So, if we dump you back into this slide," I say, "how do you know where you'll end up?"

"They say it only goes to one place and one time."

"A to B and B to A," Sam explains, sort of. "A to B and B to A."

"Glenn and Sam aren't exactly quantum physicists," I remind her. "You listening to them?"

"Hey, if things get bad you'll be there, won't you?" She smiles flirtatiously before tearing into the second Ding-Dong, flakes of delicious chocolate shell landing on her top. To wash it down she pulls a can of Coke out of her backpack, vintage down to its diamond design and detachable ring tab. She pops it open, takes a big gulp and sighs. "Mind if I smoke?" she asks.

She pulls out a joint.

"That's not what I thought you meant. Put that shit away."

"Okay, Dad." She scrunches up her face.

"Getting busted's not on tonight's agenda."

"Busted? It's *still* not legal?"

Sam boos. It makes her laugh and so do I. She ends up settling for a Marlboro, taking a deep drag, shutting her eyes, expelling the smoke through her nose. She gets deeper into her story. How her and her "old man" were at something called Monterey Pop, "digging the sounds", when the acid kicked in. In her altered state, she wandered away and walked into what she thought was a bathroom only to find it a maintenance shed.

"After that, it gets kind of fuzzy," she adds, "except I felt tugged down, dropped forever, and wound up in the middle of a bunch of trashed out buildings. Bad trip. Got worse, when I grokked it was for real."

"Here! Here!" Sam cries, grabbing my shoulder. We're at the freeway exit for the main entrance to Fort Ord, a name synonymous with rumor and innuendo. The unexplained aversion of the homeless to squat in certain areas. The undisclosed condition of several corpses discovered on the property. The reluctance to turn huge stretches of land over to the public. The supposed aftermath of certain classified Army "experiments". I always thought the insinuations were crap, but tonight they taste more real. And if there *is* a portal . . .

The main entrance to the fort is lit up as bright as daylight, though the night sky ceiling stretched above looks ready to drop.

"Turn," Sam shouts at a flashing red light, and we swerve onto First Avenue. It parallels Highway 1 going north, a direct route to one of the rickety unconverted parts of the post. Behind me Sam rocks back and forth going, "Uh-huh, uh-huh, uh-huh." Windy smacks her lips and starts in on the Susie-Qs. Devil's food crumbs tumble onto my velour upholstery, but I don't care. Outside it's gotten quite dark, and a bank of fog covers us like fleece on a sheep.

"Man, that dropped right down on us," Windy declares. "Did you flick a camouflage switch?" She snickers, a dab of creamy filling on the corner of her mouth. I'd enjoy the sight more if I could spare the concentration, but driving's quite hazardous. The thick white absorbs my high beams. I see enough to crawl as slow as a tourist in downtown PG. Everything or nothing could be outside. The others don't seem to care. Sam's humming sounds like a mantra.

We continue to creep forward when the mist pulls back like a magician's cape. Street signs tell me I'm at the corner of First Avenue and First Street, but Desolation Boulevard would be more appropriate given the condition of the buildings squatting in the background. The whole thing tastes apocalyptic.

Sam points to the left. "Here! Here! Here!"

Another parking lot, this one saturated with blackness. I keep my headlights on when I pull in. Barely visible to our right, the old soldiers' theater squats like a sleeping dragon. In front of us, three flaking cottages glow in the halo of Big Iron's beams. Even though I know Highway 1 is maybe 300 yards behind their roof-lines, I can't see or hear cars. Can fog be that dense?

Windy polishes off the last of her tasty treat and mindlessly drops the cellophane wrapper in the footwell, a rudeness I should take exception to but don't. She hops out the door. Sam does the same.

I sigh. "Here, take this." I hand them my spare flashlight before stepping out myself.

"This place looks familiar," Windy says. It's so quiet her voice sounds amplified.

"This way, this way," Sam hisses, moving forward and to the left, still shoeless.

I start to follow, when I hear a noise near the trio of shacks, the kind of zap you hear when a fly gets nailed by one of those ultraviolet electrocutors. I catch a fluttering image, ponging between the gaps separating the houses, movements too quick for a human. It poofs and fades, a low-wattage firework. Seems the Chancellor of Chance is craving attention. As usual. I turn a blind eye, kind of like the public does with Weapons of Mass Destruction.

"This is it for sure," Windy declares. In a few seconds she and Sam have covered quite a bit of ground. I follow the odd pairing—Windy looks like a fairy princess; Sam, her trollish protector—hoping that they'll get this bogus quest out of their system before I have to cut out again. We're walking off pavement now, slicing toward the highway, ice plant crunching beneath our feet. Their bobbing circle of light crosses First Street.

Princess and troll drop below my line of sight, as they navigate a steep bank. When their heads disappear, I hustle forward to make sure I don't lose them. They're headed down toward a road leading to a large tunnel that runs under the freeway to a more desolate side of the fort. The cracked blacktop is set low enough that a casual driver would never see it. I do my best not to lose my footing on the slick bank leading down to what is essentially the crook of a fat "V".

In the manmade ravine, I feel claustrophobic. Our flashlights reveal no scarcity of rubble on the ground—cans, bottles, rusted iron piping, and pieces of concrete. As the fog hasn't chased us down here, I can clearly see the mouth of the freeway undertunnel. The black square looks somehow absolute, with three concrete cubes arranged in front of it, great gray teeth that might once have served as a blockade. Tendrils of vegetation hang down from the top of the tunnel, waving back and forth in a breeze that's just begun to kick up. Under different circumstances they might remind me of a boy's tousled bangs, but right now they look ready to coil around someone's neck.

"This it!" Sam shouts, and the three of us move toward the opening. The closer we get, the more hemmed in I feel. It's the perfect place to get trapped from behind. My internal alarm clock goes off; I'm torn. I need to get moving, yet I can't deny that I feel invested in this little adventure, or maybe just linked to the girl.

I shine my light past my companions and into the tunnel's interior. It reveals nothing, and I do mean nothing. The black absorbs the light completely, no reflected circle, like the beam's cleanly chopped. In the push of the wind, which I notice is gaining velocity, the tips of overhanging branches disappear and reappear as if they're being dipped into a sideways pool of ink.

"The slide," Sam whispers in awe, before the wind drowns him out. I bend down and toss a rock at the blackness. It disappears soundlessly.

"The way home," Windy shouts. "Awesome!"

A gust from behind forces me a half-step forward.

She laughs. "Beam me up Scotty, the future sucks! Except for the dong-dings!"

"That's Ding-Dongs," I shout over the growing gale, which is when the black square starts to crackle with static electricity, making it look like a big screen TV with scrambled reception.

I'm starting to believe their story.

Sam's jacket flaps in the torrent. He's gyrating like his engine's idling, hands on top of his head, fingers interlocked, keeping his "hair" in place. Next to him, Windy crouches slightly, unfazed, ready to leap forward into the jagged, pulsating bands just ahead of her.

A tangle of thoughts clog my mind, one unraveling into clear view: if this shortcut through time turns out to be the real deal, if Windy does go back, *what happens to the present?* Didn't worry about it before, but—

—now what?

I might be looking for an excuse to keep Windy around, but we need to think this through before she takes off. I decide this, even though I suspect the surrounding windstorm is the herald of what, after a nightlong chase, is soon is to be upon me.

I see Windy move forward in the chaotic light; her white top almost glows. There's no time for talk—it's gotten too loud for that anyway—so I sprint forward, knowing I have to close in fast, but when it's time to leave my feet to tackle her, everything downshifts into slow motion.

Sam watches on my left, head cocked, the shock in his eyes aimed behind me at what has to be the Big Rolling Inevitable.

That's what I get for staying in one place too long.

The realization hits me with an impact that's as good as physical, and I jump a second or two before I want to. A checkered blur with the distinctive bouquet of kitty litter—*how could I have forgotten about him, even for a minute?*—flings itself at me from the right. I think it wanted to grab me, but as if thrown off by my premature leap, it misses and hits the ground in an explosion of sparks.

A particularly powerful gust comes up and knocks him into me. Windy stops to look as I'm driven toward the black patch. The flashlight flies out of my hands. The last image I see is the little hippie girl kneeling down, mouth open, one hand reaching out. Sam stands over her, covering his ears. His hairpiece flies off.

Over the racket, I hear him scream, "It's bad! Ba-a-ad!!"

There's a burst of white heat. I fall backward, spinning head over heels until I stabilize horizontally, face up, speeding head first, blindly.

I'm bathed in yellow light and the temperature's so intense I shut my eyes. I'm leaching sweat like a pig. Trickster might have been knocked out of commission, but *did anything else follow me in?*

Dark spots cluster in my eyes, my head feels like blowing up and I know I'm going to check out soon, I just hope not permanently.

I'm on my side, cheek against a rough surface, legs curled in against my gut, fetal. The light touch of a wall on my shoulder. Concrete filling my limbs. Unseen wasps swarming in my ears. For someone whose priority has been perpetual motion, the current situation is—how did Sam put it?—"Ba-a-ad!" If something wanted to have its way with me, it could help itself. And though I'm not prone to alarm—and maybe just a tad blasé thanks to years of facing down the unthinkable—I like doing what I do and I'd like to do it some more. So . . .

I strain to raise myself. My body doesn't cooperate. Can't flop over, much less get onto my elbows and knees. A few minutes of extraordinarily unsuccessful effort and I'm exhausted. I close my eyes and listen to the buzz.

Can't remember falling asleep, but when I wake up I'm glad I'm not sharing space with a pernicious myth *or* the Big Bad Whatever. Not yet. I stare at a shelf lined with cans of wood stain. Smell's dizzying, or maybe it's not the smell.

I try moving again, and find I can. A little. I start with short rocking movements, back and forth, in order to build enough momentum to roll away from the wall. I manage half a body rotation so I'm looking up at a splintery wood ceiling with exposed beams and a peak. I'd guess my "landing" spot's not much bigger than a toll booth. Windy's words pop into my head: "Maintenance building".

There's a window above me but from where I lay it's a sliver, not enough to see outside. Brightness pours in from it; maybe the result of an outward pointing floodlight. I know it's night; it's chilly.

My head's clearing, the imaginary wasps start to take their leave, but in their place there's another continuous noise. I mistake it for the ocean's roar, but the seconds pass and the sound becomes differentiated, granular. It's collective; hundreds of voices, shot through with squeals, shouts and vocal eruptions—some quite close. There's an undercurrent like a heartbeat, too. Congas? A street party, maybe.

As I'm not quite sure what to do, low-grade panic seeps out—the enclosed space doesn't help—and before I know it, I roll over on my stomach and manage to prop myself up on my elbows. I can move!

The relief is short-lived when an invisible barrier presses against my back and prevents me from rising off my knees.

What the hell is it? I don't smell cat litter, so the possibilities are endless, being I'm a first-time "slider" and all. I crawl toward a door on my hands and knees, serenaded by guitars impersonating screeching cats. A man's amplified voice says, "We tune because we care." It drips with sarcasm.

Reaching out with one hand from my kneeling position, I push against the door. It swings open, and the combined scent of marijuana and incense rushes in, chasing out the glue-like fumes. Refreshed, I stand, but involuntarily corkscrew to face the shack.

Who's in control here?

Feeling vulnerable in the open, I attempt to stride sideways and am happy that I can, even with my nose pressed against the shack's peeling wall. From behind I hear a "Hey, man" and a "Check it out." Shrill harmonies break out in, "I think that maybe I'm dreaming." This has to be Windy's concert.

I'm past the structure, walking sideways, face down. I can't turn. Bodies move all about me, most in the opposite direction toward the too-trebly, out-of-pitch music. Someone says, "Birds. Yeah." The song playing is so loose it might fall apart.

I see suede and fringed footwear, there's lots of that, and enough ugly sandaled feet to last a lifetime. Makes me crazy I can't lift my head; my body seems to have a will of its own. Some kind of space-time continuum crap? After years of successfully dealing with the unnatural, it figures I might be done in by the laws of the universe. Almost makes me wish I was a physicist. Almost.

About the time I think I'm going to pull a neck muscle, I'm allowed to look up and—hey!—I can actually turn, and in the direction from where I came I see a house-like structure with a chimney-shaped extension on the back. Rickety is an understatement. Looks stapled together. Not impressive for a way-station to another time.

The Monterey Fairgrounds—it's obvious that's where I am—are alive in a way I've never seen. In the backdrop of light from many, many candles and about a dozen unidentified sources, I see I'm far from the stage but close to the park-like half of the property tucked under a grove of oak trees. Underneath their twisting branches crouch rows of patio-like structures—roofs without walls—filled with booths and banners and candles and all kinds of young, long-haired men and women, many with headbands and painted faces. There's costumes, too, lots of costumes. I see drum majors, clowns, and white guys trying to look like Native Americans.

A Renaissance fair. They sell food and crafts and clothing. A banner strung above announces "The Monterey International Pop Festival" in melting letters.

I'm walking, almost normally now, to the less populated street side, across from a grassy knoll that swarms with humanity. They sit on blankets, share food and drink, dance. The congas I thought I heard *do* play. Back here they're as loud as the music on stage. A circle of women in long, flowing robes, garlands of blossoms around their heads, and little flowers painted on their cheeks, dance to the undulating rhythm, eyes closed, mouths in dreamy smiles.

I collapse between two shrubs to contemplate whether I'm awaiting my fate or creating a new one. The music stops and the wise-guy on stage rants how much better the world would be if everybody just dropped acid.

Naive times. Would Windy agree? I shut my eyes and let the atmosphere sink in. It *does* feel different. The pangs of tension, the undercurrents of worry flowing out of people—the feeling that something bad is inevitable—don't hang in the air.

Picking up a twig, I inscribe my name in the soft dirt before me. Or try, at least. The ground acts like it's marble or glass. In frustration, I zigzag the twig across the dirt. My random marks show. I try to write my name again. No dice.

I'm about to try writing Windy's name, when the little shack starts to "breathe", slightly expanding and contracting. No one notices but me. The music's started again. Everybody's "grooving".

I can't get up.

The little house stills itself as I watch a small bulge rolling its way under the earth, heading toward me like a burrowing animal.

I can't get up!

It's under me now, and I'm yanked down into an amorphous shape that blots out everything. I'm being torn apart, drawn and quartered, sliced open without anesthesia. I'll never be able to confirm it, but I bet this is what being hurled through the invisible confining wall is like, the rending of the fabric of time. The Big Cosmic Inevitable's caught up with me.

That high-pitched Banshee's scream could be mine.

SNAP

Pacific Grove. Night. Rumored yesterdays, absent tomorrows.

It's a few minutes after ten and I'm on my way to pick up smokes at Ron's Liquors on Lighthouse Avenue. Everything feels right, in the groove.

Just as I'm crossing the large window in front of the store, I hear the squealing of brakes and turn. An old style seventies cab is speeding right at me. I don't have time to move, I can only stand and watch as it climbs the curb like a grimacing chrome clown.

I brace for final impact as I see a figure in a checkered coat standing in the middle of the street. It laughs at me before running away.

Time's up.

SNAP

Author's Note:
The space and time portal near the intersection of First Avenue and First Street on Ford Ord lies dormant most of the time during which it looks like an ordinary—albeit, somewhat forbidding—freeway under-walk. Readers should be advised that inquiries submitted to the authorities administering Fort Ord will result in brusque, at times threatening, denials of the phenomenon. Inquiries forwarded to this author will likewise result in denials, albeit somewhat less threatening.

Author's Second Note:
Though their performance at the Monterey Pop Festival was not their finest moment, it should in no way diminish the fact that the Byrds, to this day, remain the most influential American band in rock and roll history.

Night Wounds Time

About the Authors

Mark Angel was born and raised on the Monterey Peninsula and currently resides in Carmel Valley. He will soon publish a science-fiction novel entitled *Rexriders,* about a civilization that coexists with dinosaurs.

Mark has a Bachelor's Degree in Psychobiology with a minor in music from the University of California at Santa Cruz and an Associate of Science in fire protection technology from Monterey Peninsula College. He is currently employed as an Emergency Medical Technician with American Medical Response, and he has been a volunteer with the American Red Cross, Carmel Area Chapter, for over twenty years.

Lele Dahle is a founding member of FWOMP. She is currently working on two novels, one of which she hopes to have completed in 2005.

Walter E. Gourlay, a native New Yorker, and a World War II veteran, has had a varied career. He's been a labor union activist, a writer and copy editor of pulp fiction, house manager of a noted concert hall in Manhattan, and public relations director for an international firm.

He earned a Doctorate in Chinese History at Harvard and taught graduate and undergraduates at Michigan State University for twenty years before moving to California. His monograph, "The Chinese Communist Cadre", was published by MIT, and another of his papers, "Yellow Unionism in Shanghai", was distributed by the Harvard Program in East Asian Studies.

Walter is a founding member of the Fiction Writers of the Monterey Peninsula (FWOMP), is a member of The Monterey Writers' Workshop, is on the steering committee of the local chapter of the National Writers Union, and is program chairman of Central Coast Writers. He writes a monthly page for the newsletter of the Carmel Residents Association.

Two of his short stories—"Marriage Makes Strange Bedfellows" and "The Night We Killed Music" —were included in the anthology *Pebbles* (Thunderbird Writers Group, 1999) and *The Barmaid, the Bean Counter and the Bungee Jumper* (Pebbles Group, 2003) contains five short stories by him. One of these, "Laundry", is excerpted from his wartime memoirs, a work in progress. His story, "Reunion" appears in *Monterey Shorts*, published in 2002.

He is now researching a monograph on "Chiang Kai-shek and Mussolini", and doing research for a historical novel set in New York City, Java, and Japan during the Wars of the French Revolution and Napoleon, based on Dutch and Japanese sources and New York City archives.

Walter lives in Carmel, California.

Ken Jones moved to the Monterey Peninsula after retiring from the Boeing Company in March of 2001. Southern California natives, he and his wife felt a growing attraction to the Central Coast that finally became too powerful to resist.

Ken holds a Bachelors of Science in Personnel Management and Industrial Relations from Northern Arizona University and his working career involved technical and business writing. He began writing for pleasure in the mid-80s, focusing primarily on short fiction. The past four years, Ken's short-short stories have received Honorable Mention in the *Coast Weekly's Annual 101 Word Short Story Contests*. In '03, in addition to one HM, his "Holiday Dinners" was awarded first prize.

He is also working on a novel-length mystery that builds on the primary characters from his story "Borscht in The Bay" published in *Monterey Shorts* in 2002. Five of Ken's stories are contained in *The Barmaid, The Bean Counter and the Bungee Jumper*, a collection of short stories and poetry produced in November '03 by the Pebbles Writing Group of Carmel.

Ken and his wife Anne have one daughter, Nora, and one grandson. Ken and Anne live in Pacific Grove with their deaf, one-eyed (or in the more sensitive words of her loving veterinarian, "sound challenged and monocular") cat, Lucky.

Chris Kemp has no recollection of his past and is in no particular hurry to comprehend his future. For now he is content to dwell in his quiet, mist-shrouded apartment complex in Pacific Grove — of which he suspects he and his wife, Linda, may be the only tenants — transcribing half-recollected dreams and revealed fragments of someone's life, perhaps his own.

Byron Merritt lives in Pacific Grove, California and works as a full time emergency room nurse and part time writer. He has a set of beautiful twins (a boy and a girl) who have grown into teenage aliens, but they still think their dad is cool. His fiancé, the Polish princess, Stasia, has put up with his writing life for so long that she's beginning to understand the mountainous life-choice—that of the author—he has chosen.

Byron has taken first and third places in local writing competitions and posted numerous science-fiction stories and articles on the Internet for various webzines. A short story he wrote, "Father Figure", was published in Australia in July 2003. It placed first in an Internet poll of favorite stories for *Andromeda Spaceways Inflight Magazine*. In addition, Byron has interviewed such famous authors as Janet Evanovich, Thomas Steinbeck, and Greg Bear, among others.

Byron says that he derives much of his writing abilities via his genes; his grandfather was the internationally best-selling author Frank Herbert of *Dune* fame. His uncle, Brian Herbert, has appeared on the top ten *New York Times* best-seller list every year for the past six years with the newly released Dune prequels.

Byron, a workaholic author, is currently writing multiple science fiction and fantasy short stories, novels, and novelettes.

Linda Price is a founding member of FWOMP. She took a year off following the death of her husband in a boating accident in 2001. "Fiction draws from the real life drama that puts people's lives on 'pause', she claims. "Whether a personal tragedy, or shared, such as the trauma of 9/11 or the 2004 tsunami, sharing stories is healing and helps build bridges of empathy and compassion."

A licensed Marriage and Family Therapist, Linda has devoted most of her professional life to counseling in private practice and on staff at CHOMP. She has taught high school for fourteen years in local schools and worked as a flight attendant for United Airlines. When asked what she does now, she says, "I write mysteries."

Frances Rossi's love of writing has evolved naturally out of her interest in language and its speakers. She has earned university degrees in English and French, and has learned other languages as well over the years. Her career has spanned several continents, from Peace Corps experience in Iran to teaching at Tougaloo College in Mississippi to directing the religious education programs in Delta, Colorado and Pacific Grove, California. At present she works on web sites for a toy store in Carmel and for FWOMP. Her other language is music. When she isn't writing, Frances is singing with I Cantori di Carmel or the Carmel Mission choir. She sang in the Carmel Bach Festival chorus in Summer 2004.

She lives with her father, Robert Paquette, in Pebble Beach. Her three children live with their families in Denver and Brooklyn.

About the Authors

Shaheen Schmidt, a native of Iran, has lived in the United States since 1985, and currently resides in Carmel Valley. Although she works in Carmel as a hair designer, she has an insatiable curiosity and interest in visual arts, dance, music and writing and is one of the founding members of FWOMP. Since childhood, she has kept a journal and special notebook to write her stories, fully illustrated in her own hand. Shaheen's writing is often inspired by music she hears, or spending time in nature.

Mike Tyrrel and his fine wife Sue are refugees from Chicago's brief summers and long, cold winters. They now reside in the hills overlooking the Salinas Valley, where the days are long and warm, and the turkeys and deer munch on their garden. Mike has been in data processing since high school, and over the years has built and managed several large-scale IBM data centers. He designed the software that controls the automobile assembly line at the New United Motors Manufacturing, Inc. (NUMMI) plant. After eight years at NUMMI, Mike still gets a kick out of watching rolls of steel turn into shiny finished products that are driven off the assembly line in a mere twenty hours.

With no television in their home, Mike told stories to his two daughters, Dot and Katy, every night. The girls picked the two stories included in *Monterey Shorts 2*. The daughters have also written their own stories, and have invented numerous board games. They have been fortunate to be home schooled by their mom. Dot, the older sister, is second on the list of most active public library users with over 4,000 withdrawals! Katy is catching up.

Ages ago, while working at a bank and managing 35 people, Mike wrote an interoffice memo that his boss, Senior Vice President Tom Kimble, gave a grade of "F". But the memo truly *was* bad, and his boss' honesty started Mike on a journey to improve his writing skills. Through FWOMP's critique process, by enduring seemingly endless rewrites, and by pouring through how-to-do-it-correctly books, Mike has grown as a writer and his work continues to improve. He's put his novel on hold for the moment, and is currently working on an anthology of children's short stories. Mike thanks Tom Kimble for caring enough to give him that "F", and FWOMP for their thoughtful criticism.

Praise for Monterey Shorts

"The stories in *Monterey Shorts* capture the mythical flavor and real details of the Monterey Peninsula—through ten sets of eyes. Some stories use the landscape as just a jumping-off point, others for the heart of the story. It's the next best thing to being there."

— *Kevin J. Anderson, author of* Dune: The Butlerian Jihad

"Well-written with a nice eye for local detail, the stories of *Monterey Shorts* are a pleasure to read and showcase some talented area writers."

— *The Monterey County Herald*

"For those who enjoy stories with lots of local color and recognizable settings, *Monterey Shorts* is a delight. . . . Another major plus is the overall quality of all the narratives in this anthology. . . ."

— *The Salinas Californian*

"An entertaining and eclectic clothesline of writer's shorts hanging in the breeze and offering engrossing stories set in an enchanted land."

— *RebeccasReads.com*

"These stories are like moments of time plucked from Monterey life. This book is a delightful and diverse read."

— *BookReview.com*

Order Your Copy Today
Available at finer bookstores and Amazon.com